I0691198

# DISGUSTA

## Faith DaBrooke

*Disgusta*© 2022 Faith DaBrooke

This is a work of fiction. Names, characters, places, and incidents are products of the author's imagination or are used factiously and are not to be construed as real. Any resemblance to actual events, locations, organizations, or person, living or dead, is entirely coincidental.

All rights reserved. No part of this book may be used or reproduced in any manner whatsoever without written permission, except in the case of brief quotations embodied in articles and reviews.
.

For more information contact:
Riverdale Avenue Books/Magnus Lit Imprint
5676 Riverdale Avenue
Riverdale, NY 10471

www.riverdaleavebooks.com

Design by www.formatting4U.com
Cover design by Scott Carpenter

Digital ISBN: 9781626016262
Trade ISBN: 9781626016279

First edition, June 2022

"We're never done with killing time
Can I kill it with you?"

--Ella Yelich—O'Connor

# Chapter One

## "Not My Idea of a Good Time"
## August 20, 1995

Seriously, I don't understand why church has to start so early. God is omnipotent, omnipresent, and exists outside of time and space. Surely He'd be okay with us sleeping on a Sunday. Yet, here I am, sitting in one of the rows of folded chairs on cheap hotel carpet in a room that looks like someone spared quite a few expenses trying to make a gym look nice. Even the two sugar loaded coffees I had this morning are barely keeping me awake. The preacher calling for 'every head bowed, every eye closed' during the end of the service's praise and worship section didn't help. That is a clear napping posture.

I open my eyes. That's probably a sin. One more thing to feel guilty about. Craning my neck, I look around the sanctuary to see if she's here today. Every last day of my four years at American Christian Academy— seventh through 10th grades—was spent thinking about her, watching her, occasionally even speaking with her. Finally I spotted her at the back of the congregation, sitting with her parents.

Hillary Barton was wearing her green dress with the empire waist, scoop neck, and tight long sleeves. Her long, ashy blonde hair was pulled up into a tight, high ponytail and she had her head dutifully bowed and her eyes closed. My gosh she was beautiful.

Tomorrow I would be starting at a new school, one that Hillary Barton did not attend, in downtown Augusta. On the one hand it made me sad that I wouldn't see her every day, wouldn't get to see her look especially dressed up and pretty on Tuesday chapel day, wouldn't get to try and talk to her in biology, world history, or Bible class. On the other hand, it also provided me with an opportunity to ask her to hang out with me outside school. It was a good excuse. I vowed to myself that I would find her in the parking lot after the service.

1

The preacher was going on and on about salvation, sins being washed away by the blood of Jesus, and eternal life, as though people at church had never heard the Gospel before. Thankfully it was starting to wind down. Some preachers did 10 or 15 minute altar calls. At Agape Christian Fellowship they kept it short. The band started back into the chorus of "Light of Your Mercy."

All the adults—my own dad especially—liked to pretend that Agape was a cool, hip church because they had a band instead of the traditional organist or a choir. It was not a cool band. Sure there was a drum kit and a bass. But there was also an acoustic guitar instead of a real electric one. Nirvana it was not. Heck it made John Denver look edgy and dangerous.

As the band played on in their folksy inoffensive impression of rock music, my fellow church members read along with the lyrics that had been projected up on the wall behind the band. While most people were only singing, a few had gone full-blown "praise and worship." The Holy Spirit had come upon them. They shook in place, fell to the floor in ecstatic heaps, or started muttering prayers or nonsense gibberish.

Though I'd first gotten saved at age five, I had never felt the spirit descend upon me to launch me into ecstasy, to make me roll around on the floor, or to let me speak in tongues. There were times over the past couple of years when I really tried. I stood there in church, my eyes closed, my hands out, and I prayed as hard as a person could. I begged God to send the spirit to me. Philippians 4:7 rattled through my brain and I longed to feel that peace that passes all understanding. But it never came. The Holy Spirit never descended upon me or filled me up. It left me feeling a little cheated. Had I not tried hard enough? Apparently not.

I looked up with my eyes wide open. The preacher was wrapping up his altar call. As the band started up a simple instrumental song, the preacher set us free to go have the traditional Southern post-church lunch out.

Outside, it was oppressively hot and humid. Though the Georgia heat would probably assault us until at least October, summer vacation would end in a few short hours. This summer had been an odd one. It was hard to put my finger on it exactly, but my parents were acting differently in a way that was hard to quite nail down. It was probably, almost certainly, my fault. First, I had managed to utterly fail them in every way by getting expelled from my Christian high school and then on top of that

I had rebounded by managing to get into the top magnet high school in the state.

Excited as I was about the prospect of finally attending public school for the first time ever, I was slightly more excited that it gave me a reason to ask Hillary Barton to hang out with me outside of a school or a church situation. Stopping to the side, I separated myself from the stream of people who were slowly moving from the sanctuary to the parking lot. Scanning the parking lot, I spotted her and my stomach sank.

I had rehearsed this conversation a hundred times in my head. At night, lying in bed unable to sleep I had rehearsed what I would say. Sitting bored in church, I had rehearsed exactly the right words. And as I walked over to her, I rehearsed it one more time.

"Hey, Hillary," I said. She looked up at me with a genuine smile, her brown eyes contorted into a squint thanks to the bright noontime sun. I loved her smile. It beamed light and joy straight into my soul. Seeing it made me think about all the smiles she had ever thrown my way. They weren't many. But they were each meaningful to me. And there was one that I remembered best. It was from two years earlier.

* * *

There had always been this particular smell to the locker room. It was the aroma of dampness, stale sweat, of jocks. We had to change there for P.E. and I always dreaded it. Changing meant spending at least a few minutes in the locker room. The problem was that the locker room, and in fact the entire hour of P.E., was something of a free-for-all where the bullies could get away with anything they wanted to.

It was a Friday and P.E. was our final class of the day. All I had to do was change out of my school-mandated khaki pants and golf shirt, into my also school-mandated shorts and T-shirt. Then it would be an hour of trying to stay out of the way during soccer, kickball, or warball, which was an extra brutal form of the already brutal dodgeball. Then I would change again and be free for the entire weekend. It was never that easy, though.

As soon as I had walked into the foul-smelling pit lined with rows of metal lockers, Jason Evans gleefully stepped up and shoved me hard into a locker. While it didn't hurt in any real way, it would make the entire row of lockers rattle in a loud and metallically dramatic way.

"Hey, faggot," he called out with wicked laughter. "You like dicks better or balls?" Calling Jason Evans a Neanderthal would really be an insult to Neanderthals. Especially considering that they survived for 100,000 years, hunting large game using only stone tools. That takes a certain kind of craftiness. Jason, on the other hand, was lucky that football was prized in the South. Otherwise natural selection would have killed him off years ago.

A few of Jason's cohorts came around and formed a tight circle around me. Though I wasn't short by any means, I was fairly skinny and lanky. Jason and half of his friends seemed to tower over me. Though they might have only been an inch or two taller they were built like dump trucks. Josh Calvert, the only 19 year-old in 10th grade, was a particular bruiser. It was he who grabbed me and threw me to the ground.

Pulling down his shorts, Josh sat on top of me and pulled out his penis. While he and his buddies laughed at my desperate and futile struggling, he pushed his penis right into my face.

"You gonna suck it, faggot?" he said, his mirthful tone suddenly becoming much more threatening. A beating I could take. I had taken plenty. But the more sadistic of the bullies liked to add an additional element of humiliation to the whole process. Though I tried to get up, Jason and another of the football players held me down while managing to continually pummel my shoulders with punch after punch. "I bet you just love sucking on cocks all day long. I bet you go home at night and just dream of sucking a big ol' dick all night."

Above me the entire class stood to watch. Some of the smaller kids—worried they would be next—stood back and tried to look as invisible as they could. Others merely laughed at my humiliation. Then the door opened and the coach, a paunchy, balding, former high school baseball player of no renown, came in.

"What are ya'll doin?" he laughed as he looked down at the scene. He chuckled. After a good minute of watching Josh wave his genitals in my face, the coach shook his head and finally stopped it. "Ya'll girls wanna go have class or you wanna stay in here and play grab ass all day long?"

"Faggot!" Jason added just to punctuate the assault. He gave me one last hard punch, knuckle heavy, in the side of my arm. If I had to venture a guess, I would say that the shoulder punch was most popular because it was the least obviously damaging. The high school thugs of American Christian Academy wanted to have fun whaling on the weak, but not so much fun that the weak were left with visible bruises. That might actually get someone in trouble. Not that the coaches ever seemed to care. I was lucky that Coach Edwards didn't join in as well.

Jocks always got away with everything. In the South sports and jocks seemed to be everywhere. Augusta, Georgia was a small-to-medium-size town in not exactly the buckle of the Bible Belt, but maybe in one of the holes. It was that extra hole that had been awled in when the Bible put on weight over the holidays.

Life in town seemed to revolve around golf, high school football, college basketball, NASCAR, and religion, with religion only narrowly beating out sports for importance. Just barely. If Jesus ever appeared one morning to declare that Atlanta Braves baseball was a waste of time, the principal of American Christian Academy would have held an assembly to explain that Jesus didn't really mean that.

Once we had gone out to the football field, I felt a little better. The P.E. soccer game would keep the other guys focused on competitiveness instead of me. As the class ran around in the bleaching sun of a bright Georgia afternoon, I hung back by myself. My attention was drawn not to the game that I was in theory participating in, but rather to the girls' P.E. class down at the far end of the field.

The girls, dressed in their own shorter shorts and tighter T-shirts were being led in aerobics by their short, stout, mulleted female coach. Everyone called her a lesbian, but then again calling someone gay was the only insult most kids bothered to use. For a little bit I watched the girls bop about, but my eyes were mostly drawn to the cheerleaders.

The squad had, for whatever reason, been exempted from the class' activities. They were instead sitting nearby on the away bleachers. There was a football game later tonight and so they were in their uniforms. They always wore them on game days.

I loved them, I loved them all, but Hillary in particular. There was just something about them, there was everything about them. Their long hair pulled back into tight ponytails, their animated skirts and tight shell tops, the way they flaunted their femininity with bright, bold make-up. It was almost as if they were a different species altogether, a group of glamorous aliens who had best friends to laugh and gossip with, who could sit and lotion their legs, and practice their cheers, dance and move, flash their skin and be desired by everyone.

I wanted to be one of them. I wanted to be a cheerleader. I wanted to wear their uniform and feel my ponytail bounce around. I wanted to move like they moved, and have best friends, and smell of strawberry shampoo and lotion. I wanted to be important and noticed and free. This, of course, bothered the hell out of me. It really freaked me out.

Half pretending to be interested in the goings on of the soccer practice, I jogged my way down to the end of the field. I longed to be a part of their world. But failing that, I wanted to at least be closer to them. I didn't want to have anything to do with the guys. I wanted to be with girls. I wanted to be a girl.

When the other guys would push me or hit me, shove my head into the locker doors, pour sodas on me at lunch, steal my backpack, trip me, punch my shoulder, or put me in a headlock they never called me a loser. They never called me weak, or spineless or a reprobate or an imbecile or a moron. No, they always called me a faggot. Just like Jason had done earlier when he ran up behind me, grabbed my backpack, threw my stuff everywhere and then started pounding me. Because he thought I was a faggot. That's all I ever heard. That I was a fag.

Not only did I not have any real friends, I feared that the idea of being gay meant that I would never have friends. Worse than that, it meant I was going to go to hell and would be tortured for eternity. Plus my family would probably disown me and I'd be a pariah for life, never fit to be a part of normal society. But was I a faggot? Sports and hunting didn't interest me at all and I was certainly drawn to femininity. I was always jealous of the girls, even those who weren't cheerleaders. Plus, I enjoyed dressing up in girls' clothes, which definitely didn't help the non-faggot argument. Of course, I was definitely attracted to women, in what I was beginning to understand was a sexual way, so in the end I was just confused about my potential faggot-ness.

"Think fast, numb nuts!" someone yelled out across the field. Before I could even turn to see what was going on, I caught a soccer ball right in the side of my head. Jason, my ever-present tormenter, was still running toward me, a vile and hideous laughter coming from his maw. Josh and a couple others were coming toward me as well.

"Matt came up to me in the locker room and said he wanted to suck my dick," Josh said as he shoved me. I stumbled back but managed to retain my balance. At least until I got a second shove from Peter Hicks. That one sent me tumbling onto the itchy grass and packed hard dirt.

"What a faggot!" Jason said as he came up. Having retrieved the ball, he threw it as hard as he could right into my face. It rattled my teeth and bounced off, leaving me with a stinging red mark from my mouth to my ear. Cackling, they grabbed the ball and ran back over to their game.

I picked myself up and tried to maintain my dignity. It hadn't helped that my beating had occurred right near the bleachers where the popular girls, the cheerleaders, were all sitting. Of course, they may have been the intended audience for Jason's display of adolescent macho violence and it didn't really matter who they were beating up, provided someone of a lesser social stature was humiliated in front of the pretty girls. There were many days, entire days, that were spent in abject embarrassment. Entire days embarrassed, and that is not a good way to live life by any means.

Not that I really, actually, had anything to be ashamed of, but that's how I felt. Well, I certainly never thought of my family as poor, though we were working class and I would overhear my parents talk about how we couldn't afford some things or how we had to be frugal to make ends meet. When I was younger my mom would insist on patching my jeans with big ugly iron on dark blue rectangular patches when they got a hole in the knee. And even though I was only maybe eight at the time, I still felt kind of stupid wearing them to school. Then when I was older in junior high, it was even worse because I would have to show up at school with a stupid haircut, dorky clothes my mom would buy for me without even consulting me, and cheap white athletic shoes that were probably purchased at the grocery store.

I had hoped high school would be a little better than junior high, but as the red mark on my face could attest, high school was not showing much promise. I felt like I stuck out like a sore thumb, that I was the weirdest, strangest, most poorly dressed person on God's green earth, or at least in God's green football field. I stood covered in dirt, my face stinging, my shoulder still aching, completely emasculated in front of all the cheerleaders. And worst of all, in front of Hillary Barton.

After P.E., I ran back to my locker in the main school building. The school was quite small, consisting of one main hallway with classrooms on either side. At the end of the day, it was full of students and a sort of electric, pre-weekend buzz. As I grabbed the books I needed for weekend homework—algebra and biology—I saw her walking up through the crowd of students.

"Hey Matt!" Hillary came up and smiled. In red and white cheerleader uniform she looked beautiful. She looked perfect.

"Sorry about the guys. They can act really un-Christian sometimes." It was nice of her to comfort me and I was appreciative, but I also noticed that neither she, nor anyone, really bothered to ever say anything to the jocks who liked to beat me and the other weird kids up for sport.

"It's fine." I lied. "They don't even bother me."

"Did you do your bio lab-sheet yet?" she asked. She smiled a bright red lipstick smile and looked up at me with her big brown eyes surrounded by clumpy mascara and a line of thick black eyeliner. While I still wasn't entirely sold on everything they were always saying about Jesus Christ, I was definitely thankful for the Alphabet Gods placing me—Matt Bailey—right next to the lovely and amazing Hillary Barton. That not only made us lab partners, but it also meant that I had many great chances to talk to Hillary.

"Yeah, I turned it in in fourth period," I said. "I guess you were out planning the prep-rally."

"Yeah," she said. Then she looked up at me and smiled this wonderful, beaming smile that seemed to brighten away every last punch or kick or genital in my face. None of it mattered. All that mattered was that a beautiful girl was smiling at me. "Thanks for doing all the work. You're the best!"

"No," I said awkwardly. "You're the best."

"Okay, I gotta run, talk to you later!" she said as she bopped along down the hall, leaving me, my locker. It wasn't much. It had been a smile, a smile that showed she genuinely appreciated me. Maybe all she appreciated was me doing all the lab work. But even that was enough to elevate me. Because as much of a loser as I was, at least I meant something to Hillary Barton. It wasn't much but it would get me through another day of this. That was the only thing I needed, something to get me through one more day of this hell.

* * *

Now the hell that was American Christian Academy was over. Tomorrow I will start at a new school. It was art school and so that meant—in theory—no jocks. There wouldn't even be P.E. as the state didn't require it for juniors and seniors. It was done. And yet, out in the church parking lot I found myself unwilling to let go of my past.

"Hey, Matt," Hillary greeted me. With learned instinct I tried to analyze the tone of her voice. Was she happy to see me? Annoyed? Ambivalent? "Are you going to school tomorrow? At ACA? I heard you got kicked out."

"Yeah," I said with feigned nonchalance as though I got expelled from high schools every day. "It was a whole thing. But I got into Davidson. You have to audition to get in. And I got in."

"That's great!" Hillary said, seemingly happy for me.

"Yeah, it's a really good school," I said. My stomach was churned up into tight knots. There was a reason I had come over to her. Sure, I always loved to see her with her perfect blonde hair and those big brown beautiful eyes. Hillary and I had talked so many times. In my 10th grade yearbook she had even written a personalized note referencing an inside joke we had. She hadn't just wished me a nice summer or something lame. I wanted to keep seeing her every day. I wanted more. I wanted everything. I wanted her. That meant saying something. So I nervously coughed it out. "So, um, that means yeah I won't be seeing you every day in class."

"Yeah, that sucks I guess," she replied, an ever so slightly forlorn look on her face.

"So, since we won't have bio and stuff, I thought maybe we should probably hang out. Like, outside of school. Like you know, other places. The mall or there's that coffee shop downtown everyone goes to." In my mind I wished and prayed to the good lord Jesus to make Hillary say yes. I wanted her to love me as much as I loved her.

"Oh, yeah. Sure, Matt," she said. Then she smiled and touched my arm. My gosh, she touched my arm. "We'll hang out outside school. Are you going to the September lock-in?"

"Absolutely," I said. I hadn't been planning on going to it. Lock-ins were lame, like going to church all night. But now that I knew Hillary was going to be there and that she potentially wanted me there, I was going. Come hell, highwater, or the Second Coming of Christ in all His glory, I was going to that lock-in.

"Great, well I'll see you there. Oh, there's my mom. I gotta go though, but I'll see you, Matt." Then she hurried over to her family's minivan and climbed in.

As I made my way over to my parent's own mini-van, I mulled it all over. While she hadn't done something like offer to go to the mall or to the movies with me, Hillary had still made a sort of plan with me. Sure, it wasn't the sort of plan I would have wanted. It was more church. I didn't really want more church but it would mean seeing more of her. Then I realized that I was in fact using church—and by extension God—as a means to further my own lustful, sinful intentions.

I am not a good Christian. Besides lusting after Hillary and other girls, I also I think I might be gay. But not actually gay. I mean, I'm definitely attracted to girls. But I also really want to be one. I'm not sure if that makes me gay or not, but it's definitely a sin and probably my number one sin. It makes me do stupid things. Hopefully God would forgive me. That was His job, right?

# Chapter Two

### "Falling Into Night"
### August 20, 1995

After church we would always drive out to Fort Gordon, the nearby military base that had been my dad's final post. He had retired from the Army three years prior and for some reason—as yet unfathomable to me—my parents had decided that the family would stay in Augusta, Georgia. While I had to admit that it was better than the barren wasteland of Aniston, Alabama or the frozen winters of West Point, it was nowhere near as good as D.C. Our nation's capital felt like a real city. I love urban environments and longed to return to them. Augusta felt like a giant parking lot. Really, I'm not sure how Augusta stacked up against Germany or Fort Ord, California. I didn't really remember those.

Up in the front of our minivan, my dad drove while my mom sat silently in the passenger seat. Christian talk radio droned on. That and conservative talk radio were all my dad ever listened to. Today our listening consisted of some old man, presumably a preacher, telling us all about the killing of unborn babies across the nation and how God was going to eventually get around to destroying the United States for allowing abortion to be legal. Abortion was the main evil they railed against, though sometimes they would change it up and talk about how liberals, ACLU members, and the homosexuals would burn in the everlasting flames of hell.

"Can we listen to something else?" I whined. My dad's radio choice was particularly frustrating as he had also banned my listening to my CD player in the car. Not only was it rude, he had said, to block out the family, but it also irreparably damaged one's ears. Personally I would have been fine going deaf, if it had meant not having to listen to Christian talk radio every time we got in the car.

"When you're driving," my dad retorted from rote. "You can choose what you listen to. But I am driving and we'll listen to something edifying." This was a particularly obnoxious stance of his considering that he had banned me from listening to the radio whenever I did get to drive. It was, he said, a distraction.

"Matt," my mom scolded. "Don't complain." Looking over at my sister, I saw her look up briefly from an outdoors magazine. We shared an eye roll. But she didn't complain. In two weeks, she would be off to Athens to start her freshman year of college. I'd be off in two years. It felt like it would be forever.

"You take the name of Christ, Matt," my dad said accusingly. "And you're always griping and talking back." That was my dad's favorite way of trying to really guilt me. Taking the name of Christ meant being a Christian. It bugged me whenever he said it because I felt like it was never really my decision to be a Christian. I had to go to church. I had to go to a Christian school. I didn't know what he would do if I ever told him I wasn't a Christian. It definitely wouldn't be good.

My dad even had a sign on our door that said, "As for me and my house, we will follow the Lord. —Joshua 24:15." It bothered me in the same way. I was in that house and no one ever asked me if I wanted that sign up. It had always been assumed that I was a Christian. Of course, I absolutely was a Christian. I had gotten saved and been baptized too. But quite frankly, a lot of believers—my dad included—tended to tee me off most of the time. That was another one of the things that made me a bad Christian.

Doing my best to ignore the radio preacher's new topic of how Jesus would have opposed Planned Parenthood, I looked out the window at the endless pine trees, parking lots, and power lines blurring past. Then we drove past a strip mall where the stores were all closed. What had once been the large anchor store had been turned into a church. A cheap looking sign that had once said Magic Mart or Hills Discount now proclaimed that it was the Hallelujah Church of Christ. A church in a strip mall summed up Augusta perfectly.

"Sorry," I half, or possibly quarter, heartily apologized. Slinking down in my seat, I thought about tomorrow and the day after that and the day after that. There were 104 more Sundays until college, give or take. One hundred and four more church services until I could leave this town and this family. It felt like forever. Today was just another one to get through. At least the food at the Officers Club brunch was pretty good, mostly the Belgian waffle station.

\* \* \*

Back in my room, I tore off my itchy church clothes and tossed them on the floor with the rest of the clothes that covered the floor. Fishing about, I found a pair of shorts and a T-shirt that were mostly clean. Back in comfy clothes, I collapsed onto my bed. On my ceiling above me were tiny pale green glow-in-the dark stars, waiting to come alive when the night came.

On the far wall were hundreds of photos that I had cut out and taped or sticky-tacked to the wall. Kurt Cobain, Courtney Love, Gavin Rossdale, Layne Staley, and Eddie Vedder looked out at me from the covers of various music magazines. A few choice *Calvin and Hobbes* comics intermingled with smaller photos, mostly of musicians. There were also a number of post cards I had gotten back from bands and record companies after a project of writing to every single address listed in the liner notes of my CDs.

Getting up, I went over to the CDs I had on my shelf. Though every penny that fell through my fingers ended up being spent on music, there were only 25 or so CDs in my collection, plus a handful of tapes and a few classic rock records that I had chanced upon at thrift shops. Even with so few CDs, I kept them in alphabetical order.

Rock music was considered one of the worst of all sins. At American Christian we were literally told that rock music derived from ancient African tribal music that was intended to summon demons. If you listened to rock music you would become possessed. And certainly you'd go to hell. Music could also lead to dancing, which somehow also led to pregnancy. Rock music was Satanic. Even so-called "Christian-rock" was looked upon with a wary eye.

It never mattered to me. Music was the one thing that I had. My awkward gangliness and poor coordination were never going to earn me a letter jacket. While I could mostly get straight A's, I didn't care enough about school to join the Honors Society or try for valedictorian. But I could get into music. And so I had something that was just mine. It wasn't forced on me by my parents. It wasn't something I was dragged to. It was something that only I understood.

Today called for something angry. Going to near the end I selected Stabbing Westward's *Ungod*. It was an industrial album full of emotion: anger, sorrow, loss, pain, fury. Perhaps it was the blasphemy of the title that had first drawn me in, but it was the music and lyrics that made listening to it over and over again worth it.

Laying back on my bed, I stared up at the ceiling and closed my eyes. When I listened to music, there were always shapes and colors that I could see with my mind's eye. Closing my eyes, I could see them more vividly. Bright white circles formed with every pound of the heavy bass drum, while jagged light blue and red lines marked the shredding of the distorted guitar and synth notes. I shouldn't have been listening to secular music. I wasn't being Christlike.

My mom opened the door and walked in without knocking. Locked doors and knocking on his children's doors were two other things my dad didn't believe in. It was his house, he would say, and as long as we were under his roof we would be expected to obey his rules. Among those rules was the idea that I had zero privacy.

"Hey Matt." My mom came in and sat down on the edge of my bed. Sitting up, I looked up at her skeptically. "It's a big day tomorrow, huh?"

"Yeah," I said, though by my count this would be my sixth time starting at a new school. You could get used to being the new kid, but it was never easy. There were always established friend groups with histories, people whose whole extended families lived in town, people with roots.

"The family's counting on you to be on your best behavior," my mom said in a familiar voice that always left me feeling slightly insulted. It wasn't enough that I should be on my best behavior because it's the right thing to do or so I don't get in trouble. No, she had to drag the whole family into it to try and guilt me into behaving. "What you do reflects on the family."

"Mom," I said, verbally putting my foot down. "I told you all about the expulsion thing, alright. It wasn't fair. It wasn't right. I'm not sorry about it. I did the right thing and I would do it again. Someone had to."

"I don't disagree with you," she said with a sigh. "But you have to choose your battles sometimes. Some things in this life aren't fair, but you put up with them anyway because you only have so much energy to fight. You have to pick the important battles. You have to use good judgment, Matt. That's part of being an adult."

"Fine," I said coldly.

"I just care about you is all," she replied. "You have so much potential and I don't want to see you waste it."

"I'll do my best, Mom," I said frustrated. "Jeez, you act like I'm this terrible burn-out slacker of a bad kid. I got straight A's at American Christian. And I only got detention one time in four years."

"I know," my mom said as she patted my knee. "I just want you to be smart, like I know you can be. Causing problems is only gonna make your way harder."

"Fine," I said. Instead of responding, she simply gave my leg another pat. Her expression threatened to turn to tears, but instead she simply got up and walked toward the door.

"Be sure and be in bed early, Matt. It's a school night. No more late nights," she reminded me as she left. I shook my head, got up, and closed my door again. Turning my music up, I grabbed a paperback from my stack of library books. It was Carl Sagan's *Cosmos*. If my dad saw it, there would be yelling as the book mentioned the universe being billions of years old and talked about evolution. Sundays were good days for satanic books and blasphemous music.

* * *

Though it was nighttime, it was still hot and muggy outside. Shuffling through the leaves I found my sister Ellen standing on the side of the house. All I could see of her at first was the glowing orange tip of a cigarette.

"What's up?" she whispered. Two years older than me, Ellen was everything I wasn't. She was valedictorian and by sophomore year had earned her letter jacket. Her room was always clean and well organized and she was always helpful and polite. During summers she would happily participate in my grandma's Children of the American Revolution events, while I was forced to go and spent most of my time there talking about how the Founding Fathers all had slaves. Whereas I had no interest in the military or West Point, she had gone to the trouble of attending afternoon ROTC classes at the public school.

"Can I bum one?" I asked. Dutifully she handed me the pack, then tucked her shoulder length ashy blonde hair behind her ear. With the same greyish green eyes and the same hair color, people often said we looked alike. Sometimes I'd look at her and try to imagine how I would have looked had I been born a girl.

"Thanks," I said softly. She held her light and I took a puff. It was scratchy but I managed not to cough. Though I was hardly a smoker, it was not my first cigarette. Ellen had given me a few here or there but I was being careful not to get addicted. It was another of my many sins. Later I would pray to God to forgive me. But there was time for that later. "You all packed up?"

"Mostly, yeah," she said wistfully. "It'll be good to be out, you know."

"Totally," I agreed.

"They're fighting," she said as she glanced over toward the back of the house. Straining my ears, I could hear the all-too-familiar sound of my parents having an argument. Growing up, it was as constant a nighttime song as the chirping of crickets or the sound of trains passing in the distance. When I was really little, it would frighten me, but as I grew older it became more of an annoyance. "You're the only one who knows how fucked up our childhood actually was."

"I guess so," I said as I continued to sort of smoke my cigarette without really inhaling the smoke. Mostly I held it and let it burn. "You think they'll ever get a divorce?"

"I've started to suspect," Ellen responded with a bit of a desperate laugh. "That they've stayed together 'for the sake of the kids.' I bet the moment you get your college acceptance letter they'll make it official."

"Yeah, and in the meantime, more of this," I said hopelessly.

"Try not to go insane," she said. "You know, with just you and them."

"I'll do my best," I tossed out.

"And stay out of my room."

"Why would I ever go in your room?" I asked, doing my best impression of proper sarcasm. Instead of responding, she gave me a curt but knowing look.

While Ellen was many things, she was not a girly girl. Sometimes, when I was alone in the house, I would sneak into her room and try on her dresses. Sadly she only had three or four in total, all of them for church and chapel day at school. Not only that, but she never wore make-up either. Still, she left the church dresses behind, and she almost certainly would, then of course I was going to go in and borrow them.

* * *

Carefully, I slid my blank tape into the VCR. With a mechanical whirr and a *cachunk* the machine queued it up. The living room, lit only by the bluish glow of the TV, was quiet. Everyone had stopped fighting and was hopefully sleeping soundly. Making sure that the TV was set to the right channel and that the VCR settings were correct, I pressed the record button.

A moment later the commercial ended and the familiar intro of MTV's *120 Minutes* appeared on the screen. Keeping the volume fairly low, I settled myself onto the carpet only a couple feet from the screen. They started with some lame bands that I didn't really care for. But then they played Presidents of the United States of America, who were fun. Then there was a new video I had never seen before.

It sounded different. While it was kind of industrial, the lyrics were polished, melodic, sultry. The band was playing in a set full of old vintage TVs and the video was fuzzy and distorted in parts. But, it was the singer that really caught my eye. She was a redhead and was wearing a cool looking fuzzy red coat. Despite the melodic nature of her voice, the words she sang into a vintage microphone were angry. The song rocked but in a way that was different from what I normally listened to. And she was beautiful. But also she was powerful and angry and sexy and cool. I sat watching, utterly enchanted.

When it ended, I was sure to watch for the band's name. Garbage. That was, I thought, a pretty cool name for a band. Though it sounded more like a punk band. Garbage definitely weren't punk. If anything, they were sort of techno and maybe even a little girly. For the most part I only listened to male singers, with the exception of Hole and L7. Would listening to a less angry and shouty girl singer make me kind of gay?

I hit the stop button halfway through a song from Hole's *Unplugged* show and rewound the tape. After setting it to play, I fast-forwarded to Garbage. The song was called "Vow" and that was all I knew about them. This weekend I would have to go see if I could find their CD. As I re-watched the video, I couldn't take my eyes off the singer. Not only was she totally hot, she was also super cool. I thought about how much I wanted a coat like that, how much I wished I could look like her and be cool and sexy and feminine and tough.

If I wanted to be like a girl, maybe I was gay? After the song played a second time, I shut off the TV and hit eject on the VCR. The tape popped out and I grabbed it. I had already screwed up my taping anyway. But at least I had this new band Garbage on there. And I could always watch *Alternative Nation* tomorrow.

Alone in my bed with pale green stars above me, I imagined that there were a secret pill that the government had. Somehow I would get my hands on it and turn into a girl overnight. It was super top-secret science. Maybe I would even dye my hair red—it was starting to get long—and get my own clothes and wardrobe. And I could go out and be a real girl and know what it felt like. It was all I had ever wanted.

\* \* \*

Sleep would not come. As the red numbers on my bedside digital clock continued to advance into the early hours of the morning, I did my best to rearrange pillows, to reposition myself, and to try various blanket configurations. Nothing worked. I could never sleep when there was something important waiting for me in the morning. It was a little after two in the morning. Four hours till I had to get up for school.

Getting out of bed, I pulled on a pair of jeans and a T-shirt as silently as I could. Then I managed to be even quieter as I snuck into my sister's room, found her bag, and helped myself to a cigarette and her lighter. The sliding glass door in the back was the quietest so I snuck out there and made my way down to the street.

The neighborhood was in hibernation. The only sound I could hear was from the chorus of crickets hidden in the bushes. Lights dotted a few houses though most of them were obscured by trees. Streetlights illuminated small portions of the street. The air was heavy and wet, ready to cover the grass and plants with condensation. Standing at the curb there was a little click of the lighter as I lit up my pilfered cigarette.

Tomorrow—later today really—I would be starting a new school. I let myself imagine that I lived in a world where I could start at a new school and really start over. I could wear girls' clothes and make-up and introduce myself as Mathilda or Melanie and no one would ever know that I had ever been a boy. I would dye my hair red and wear heavy black eyeliner and hang out with the girls and be one of them.

I sighed a cloud of smoke. The world didn't work that way. God was all-powerful and had, for whatever divine reason suited Him, made me a boy. Even thinking about wanting to be a girl was a sin. So was smoking. I really was letting myself backslide. Then again, it would be amazing to be a real girl.

I took another drag on my smoke and looked up. Two large black eyes met my gaze. A ghostly white owl was perched on a street sign that was only a few steps away from me. It was enormous, almost as tall as the stop sign itself. Perched there, it looked right at me as though it were studying me. The owl was entirely white except for its big black eyes. It almost reminded me of a grey alien.

But I couldn't look away. I was entranced. Our house was suburban but there were still plenty of wild animals about. Little bright green anole lizards and box turtles had made our yard home. I'd even seen possums on a few occasions. But I had never seen an owl. Looking it in the eyes, I felt like it was saying something to me, beaming something to my head, but if there was a message I couldn't interpret it.

And then suddenly it was gone. Its giant wings unfurled and it flew away without making a single sound. Not a flap or a hoot or a single decibel. It was as silent as a ghost. Was it a ghost? Or a demon or an angel? I shook my head. It was just an owl. It was cool but it was just a bird. Looking around above me I tried to see if I could see it in the trees or flying about but it had disappeared. I tried to remind myself that it was a bird and nothing more.

Stubbing out my cigarette, I let out another sigh as though to shake something off. The owl was a predator. It was ghostly and alien but I didn't feel scared at all. It felt peaceful. Maybe it was a good omen for the first day of school. And hopefully it wasn't God sending me a warning about my smoking, my secular music, or my perverted thoughts about wanting to be a girl. Hopefully not.

# Chapter Three

## "Things'll Be Great When You're Downtown"
### August 21, 1995

Being 16 and starting a new school can be difficult, though it was something I'd gotten quite used to being an Army brat. It was almost refreshing to know that starting my junior year at a new high school would quite literally be my last time at a new school. Assuming, of course that I could manage to not get kicked out in the next two years. Despite my recent history, I was quite hopeful.

John S. Davidson Fine Arts School was a dilapidated husk of a magnet school located in what arguably was one of the most run-down areas of a long-neglected Southern downtown. White Flight's great exodus had managed to strip the once-thriving business district of most of its residents, leaving just a handful of businesses, a greasy spoon diner, endless cracking pavement, abandoned buildings, and weed-filled vacant lots. Across from the school stood one of America's seediest bus stations and next door was a beat up mom-and-pop funeral home. The latter was, by happenstance, located right next to the cafeteria which I could only assume allowed for an endless series of morbid jokes concerning both the provenance and quality of the school's hot lunch program.

It was the start of 11th grade and, for me, my first time at a non-Christian school. Public schools were something that, as mundane as they were for the rest of the country, were something fascinating to me. Would the science teachers actually teach evolution as a fact? Would we start each day with just the Pledge of Allegiance to the American flag without bothering to pledge allegiance to the Bible or the Christian flag? At Christian schools, one heard stories and rumors of kids getting expelled for bringing Bibles to class, witchcraft was taught by teachers along with masturbation and homosexuality, the godless masses of misled students

20

did drugs, had premarital sex and got in fights while sinful teachers stood by and handed out free condoms. It was a scholastic Sodom and Gomorrah.

As I walked cautiously up to the front doors, I started to notice that most of my classmates looked less satanic and more poindexter. Not only were many kids already loaded down with books on the first day, many more were dragging along bulky black instrument cases that dwarfed them completely. My fellow Davidson students were an altogether unimpressive collection of gangly, nerdy outcasts. Though, to be fair there seemed to be small cadres of cool kids here or there; blue haired girls, punk kids with skateboards, alternative kids in hacky-sack circles, pretty ballerinas finishing their last morning cigarettes before homeroom. Chances are, I wouldn't be the coolest kid, but I definitely wouldn't be the geekiest. Not by far. That was mildly reassuring.

Over the summer, my parents had given up on forcing me into the barber's chair, so my dirty blond hair fell over my ears and past my chin, and it was just beginning to show some slight waves and curls. I wore it in a suitably 90s fashion, long but unkempt and probably in need of a wash. I thought it was cool to wear oversized clothes, including extra-large T-shirts, hiking boots and baggy jeans. Though the decade's grunge fashion had originated in the chilly climes of Seattle, I insisted on wearing a giant black and white unbuttoned flannel shirt as a jacket despite the 98 degree August heat.

"You're new," I heard a young female voice behind me. Turning around, I met my first Davidson student. She was short and cute, with glasses, dark red Manic Panic dyed hair and a wicked smile. One strap of her light blue denim overalls hung down to her knee and there were little plastic kids' barrettes in her hair and black Doc Martin boots on her feet. Her ever-so-slightly pimpled face beamed with a bright smile. "Hey, I'm Lindsey."

"I'm Matt," I said sheepishly as a few of Lindsay's friends began to coalesce around us.

"You're the new junior," added a small, thin blonde girl with watery blue eyes and her blonde hair held tightly in a ballerina's bun. Apparently, word got around quickly at this new school. Later I'd know this girl as Tara who had only recently fired the first shots in the war with her parents, the ultimate victory being liberation from the rigors of far too regular dance practice.

Then she looked up, eyes wide and shouted. "Michelle!" They all looked up and greeted Michelle in high-pitched, exciting voices. Clearly, this was the ringleader. Michelle strolled up, her straight dark hair bouncing over her shoulders, a sly smile on her dark purple painted lips, her clothes black, sleek and long. If not for the colorful tin Wonder Woman lunch box she carried, she would have looked more than a little bit like a witch.

"Who's the new guy?" Michelle asked, giving me the slightest of glances. Michelle looked at people like she was sizing them up. She wore a half smile on her face as though she were secretly amused by something that she kept entirely to herself.

"This is Matt," Tara explained. "He's the new junior."

"Are you cool, Matt?" Michelle asked.

"Yep," I affirmed, though after I'd said it, I started to wonder if perhaps I had just agreed that I did drugs. While I didn't have anything in particular against drugs for other people, I hadn't been known to partake of them myself, other than at Thanksgiving when my parents would let me and my sister have a glass of wine with our turkey. "Totally cool."

"Excellent," she purred like a snake. "Then we'll see you around." Already I could feel the pin pricks as dozens of students looked me over, checking me out. The anomaly. The new fish. Despite being generally anxious over the new start, I felt like I had a reason to be optimistic. The day had barely even begun and already girls were talking to me.

* * *

After first period, I found my locker. It was a block away from the main school building, in a converted warehouse that everyone called The Annex. Cinder block walls divided the space into classrooms. My locker was far in the back, past the dance studio, opposite the bio lab. The thin nauseating smell of formaldehyde hung in the air but I tried to ignore it.

Second period was starting soon. Walking back out though, I had to pass the dance studio. It was open air and the ballerinas were hanging out before class. They were all dressed in their practice outfits: tight tops and equally tight leggings. Some wore delicate, gossamer skirts of pink and others wore loose shorts. Some were stretching, others were standing around in small groups talking, laughing. They all had their hair pulled tightly into buns.

My pace was brisk as I walked by. I didn't want any of the dancers to think I was perving on them or anything. No, that's not why I was here. I glanced over, and a feeling of deep longing shook me. All I wanted was to be one of them; to be pretty, to be feminine, to be accepted into their groups, to hear their stories, to share in their inside jokes, to be their friend, to be one of them. It was an old jealousy, one that I had carried with me for a long time.

Even back before I knew how to tie my shoes, I understood that something wasn't exactly right. Maybe it was genetics, though I could also blame my sister. She was three years older than me and spent much of my preschool days treating me a bit like a living doll. When she wanted to play, she'd dress me up in her old hand-me-downs and then parade me in front of my mom or take me out in the yard to play. But you see, that's where maybe genetics comes into play. Whereas most boys would have tolerated it for a few minutes before angrily tossing the frilly things aside to go run and play in the mud, I was perfectly happy to wear the frilly things while playing in the mud.

It became so common that my mom actually bought me my own dress to wear (and this in the 80s, so she must have been ahead of her time). Honestly, I can't remember if I asked for my very own dress or if it was a gift. I must have asked for it and probably repeatedly. Sadly, I don't remember what it looked like, but I can imagine something light blue, because if you're going to get a little boy a dress you should at least make it blue. I imagine it was light cotton cloth, with a satin ribbon around the waist and a little bit of white lace at the edges of the hem and the sleeves. It was A-line and you could run in it on a nice spring day, playing outside.

Not to self-psychoanalyze, but at this point, I should also mention that I didn't get my first haircut until the week before kindergarten. My dad had insisted it not be cut until his great uncle, a barber, could give me my first haircut. Apparently it was something of a family tradition, but as we rarely visited him, it left me with long blonde, slightly curly hair that hung about my shoulders and elicited a lot of compliments from grown-ups about what a pretty little girl I was. Each time, I would adamantly insist, perhaps stomping my tiny feet in an ultra-cute fashion, that I was a boy. Yes, I was a boy, but I was also a boy with beautiful long blonde hair running around in a pretty blue dress.

That first week of kindergarten was not a good one for me. From what I remember it involved quite a few tears. For one thing, no one bothered to explain to me that getting your hair cut doesn't hurt. I mean they're cutting off part of you. How could that not hurt? So they had to drag me up to the chair, tears streaming down my blubbering face and long strips of blonde curls fell to the floor, a dead pile of my flaxen locks piling up as I sat there bawling my eyes out.

Maybe a week, maybe a month later, I naively asked my mom the difference between boys and girls. My mom, perhaps with a bit of a shaky voice, ad-libbed that girls wore dresses and had long hair and that made them different. At that tender young age, I believed her. That conversation may have been the direct reason why I remember being five years old, standing on the bathroom counter, wearing one of my sister's dresses and attempting to brush out my short hair (believing that one need only brush it to make it long). That would make me a girl, right? That would turn me right back into a girl, right? I brushed so hard and willed myself to turn into a girl. I wished upon every falling star that ever fell. Of course, nature doesn't answer wishes so casually.

People talk about someone getting a sex change and that was my first real experience with that, because against my will, I had a sex change thrust on me. Before kindergarten my gender was something nebulous, somewhere between male and female, but in a few short weeks my parents had forcibly picked me up, put me in the boy camp and locked the gate behind me. There were new rules, set behaviors, new social norms to follow. Sure I could still play with my big yellow metal Tonka dump trucks but Barbie couldn't drive them. Yes, I could still play in the mud, but I certainly couldn't wear a dress while doing that.

\* \* \*

Other kids ate lunch with their friends. Michelle held court. Though only a junior, she had a table for her and her friends, who were generally the freaks, punks, goths and ravers with a handful of regular alternative kids. Besides Lindsay and Tara, there was Alicia who was really into theatre, Michael Vig whose brother was in the local punk bands, Simon who wrote a zine, Mary who wore rainbow nail polish and always won the annual student art awards, Chad who was always getting detention, and Mary's brother Tall Preston who skateboarded and played trombone in a ska band. Michelle was in the art program and fancied herself a rock & roll photographer. Her goal in life was to be a Warhol superstar, but she was tragically a few decades late to that party. Then there was me, Matt, the new kid. The whole table smelled like Teen Spirit and Sunflowers perfume.

Michelle was quiet as she ate, quiet yet observant. She let everyone around her speak and gossip as she took it all in and filed it all away for future use. For the most part I just observed as well, though as the new guy I was also hit with a fair number of questions. Most were basic enough, and throughout the meal, I felt Michelle and I catch eye contact with each other a handful of times, just sizing each other up. Michelle never asked me any direct questions, instead letting those around me probe me for any information I might give. Being new, and generally nervous, I refrained from asking too many questions of my own and answered the barrage as best I could.

"Are you going to Orwell's on Saturday?" Lindsay asked me. Orwell's was a huge, dimly lit, coffee shop downtown frequented by the punks, grunge-heads and riot girls of Augusta. Its decor may have been the first example of industrial chic but that was just because it really was in an old converted auto shop. It was next door to a head shop, a hole-in-the-wall punk venue and a tiny record shop that also sold skateboard parts. All of it was surrounded by the endless dilapidated blocks of an all but abandoned Southern downtown. For a 16 year-old marooned in suburbia, it was close enough to heaven.

Luckily Orwell's was owned by a former Hell's Angel biker who had found Jesus. As he and my dad went to the same church, my parents had no issue with me hanging out at Orwell's and would happily let me spend my afternoons at the downtown library after school and pick me up at Orwell's later in the evening. It made social Friday and Saturday nights quite easy without a car and I could hang out with my friends while blowing my meager allowance on ridiculously caffeinated coffees. My favorite was the Red Eye and featured six shots of espresso, to which I would add about a cup and a half of sugar.

"Totally," I answered. One year below me, Courtney had natural red hair, bright green eyes, dark eyeliner, and bright blue mascara, and a ring on her thumb. She wore a white tank top and baggy jeans with Doc Marten boots and she was fascinating. "Courtney, haven't I seen you there?"

"Oh sure," she responded. "I was there, like, last week with Rachel R. and Tucker. Do you know Tucker?"

"Yeah," I said. I had no idea who Rachel R and Tucker were. But I figured that an in was an in. If I was ever called on it in the future, I could just claim that I knew a different Rachel R and Tucker. You know, those other ones from across town. Downtown was a regular enough hangout and the crowd wasn't that large, so chances are I at least knew their faces. "Are you going Saturday?"

"Yeah," Courtney lit up a little "Ill Skunks are playing at the Catalina Club." Despite its name, Catalina Club was not the least bit breezy or idyllic. Mostly it was just an unpainted windowless cinder block box with a plywood stage and old speakers that were way too loud and gave off so much high pitched feedback that the bands could barely be heard anyway. Ill Skunks were a band I knew well as their bass player had done a short stint at American Christian before getting kicked out for some reason or another. Most of the bands that played the Catalina were punk, generally assembled from the dozen or so punk musicians who hung around Downtown, often with rotating names, logos and lineups. Ill Skunks regularly performed, though its members were often in a couple side projects too. Tad the Drummer was in constant demand and must have played in 20 or so different punk outfits.

"Cool. I'll probably see you there."

* * *

I had been intently watching the door of Orwell's for the past hour. Like any Saturday night the place was busy, but large enough that it wasn't uncomfortably packed. Though the usual crowd included a handful of severely dressed punks, some Rude Boys and Skinheads with their Chelsea-haired girlfriends and a black velvet clad Goth or two, most of the kids were fairly normal though with looks that leaned toward the Alternative side of things. There were lots of torn jeans, flannel shirts, yellow-laced Doc Marten combat boots and colorfully dyed hair. In anticipation of a good night I had worn my best vintage corduroy pants, black Chuck Taylors and my black Therapy? T-shirt. My thought was that sporting a shirt with the Irish hard rock band would let Courtney know that I had good musical taste and was friendly with the whole punk and hardcore scene. For a good minute I just sat there watching the door, watching them all come and go. Watching Courtney not come in.

"Who are you waiting for?" Michelle asked in a way that indicated she already knew the answer.

"No one," I lied. "Just wondering where Lindsay and Tara had gone off to." I knew precisely where they were. Lindsay and Tara had gone outside to find their friend Mary, who had gotten a separate ride downtown. I couldn't have cared less where they had gone off to. Quite frankly I was happy that they had found something else to do other than hang around me. Michelle was probably right. Their liking me would definitely explain their far too keen interest in everything I had to say, everything about my life, or how I looked like Gavin Rossdale even though I didn't look like Gavin Rossdale at all, other than the hair. When Tara and Lindsay had finally bounded off, I breathed a sigh of relief and Michelle decided to stay with me to no doubt study me like a scientist would study an insect.

"You don't like either, do you?" Michelle said quietly, sipping coffee from her gigantic mug. As I had seen her do on the past five days, she had worn all black, sleek lacy clothes and knee high boots with lots of laces. Pale foundation hid her acne as best it could and dark, slightly smudged eyeliner had been enthusiastically applied, along with deep purple lipstick. "Like-like, I mean."

"Dunno," I muttered.

"Really?" Michelle asked incredulously as she set her giant coffee down on the beat up old coffee table in front of our nasty old yard sale couch. "What's your deal, Matt?"

"What do you mean?" I asked, giving up on the door and finally turning back to Michelle. No one good was bothering to come through the door anyway. While I had a good idea what she meant, I wasn't about to own up to anything. After all, admitting to liking a girl was embarrassing if she didn't like you back. And in my experience, especially at American Christian, no one ever liked me back. Now all the sudden it seemed like it might be a possibility. "I don't have a deal."

"Sure you do. Everyone's got a deal, right?

"What's your deal?"

"I'm gonna be rich and famous. Obviously. Not sure for what though. Art, photography."

"Think I want to be a film director," I mused. Recently I had viewed such films as *Goodfellas*, *Pulp Fiction* and *Natural Born Killers* and had begun to daydream a future for myself as some sort of brilliant, edgy auteur of loud, flashy and incredibly violent films. Luckily the local video store didn't stock French New Wave movies or else I would have become insufferably pretentious.

"That's cool. We should team up. You know Andy Warhol's Studio?"

"No, I never heard of it."

"It was in New York," her eyes went wide and she gave herself goosebumps as she leaned in to tell me more. "And it was awesome." Michelle spun a yarn of silver covered walls, drag queens, rock stars, screen printing, Super-8 cameras, heroin, wigs and experimental sex. Warhol's Factory was a creative, free and dynamic space where all the brilliant, cool people would come together to change the face of art, redefine fashion, turn film on its head, take Rock & Roll to strange new places, and wear sunglasses inside at night. It was heaven on earth and I was apt to believe her. As teens growing up in the suburban South we believed that when good people died they'd go to New York.

"You just gave me a great idea, Matt," Michelle said, wild fire in her eyes. Though, I was certain the idea had been fermenting in her head for quite some time. "We are gonna restart the Factory."

\* \* \*

Outside the air was hot and hung heavy with humidity. The angry noise of music from the Catalina Club was all you could hear, the helicopter beating of the drums and grinding out of tune guitars mixed with the shouts of the tiny packed in crowd, all the noise muffled only by a single layer of concrete blocks. A few kids were outside, huddled in little groups either playing hacky-sack or smoking, talking, laughing. It was dark Downtown and at night it was nearly deserted except for the punk kids and the homeless people. A block away from Orwell's was an abandoned hotel we called the "Homeless Hilton." It still had beds in all the rooms so it was a popular spot for people who didn't have anywhere else to go. Freight trains still slowly rolled through in the early pre-dawn hours for those who figured the rails might give them somewhere to go. A while back the homeless people had all realized the punks didn't have much money so they kept to themselves and remained in the shadows, leaving only a broken liquor bottle here or there as a calling card.

For a while I stood there, watching the life there on 8th Street, enjoying the scene, just taking it all in. Then I saw her. Bathed in the sodium yellow glow of the street light, she stood there, eyes down, smoking a cigarette, her cherry red hair blowing gently in whatever breeze a Southern summer night could send. And she was perfect. In her torn and safety pinned black T-shirt, short plaid punk schoolgirl skirt, torn thigh-high fishnets, and black Doc Marten boots she was perfect. With her thick black eyeliner and blood red lips she was perfect. With her colorful little plastic kids' hair barrettes she was perfect.

My stomach immediately decided to flutter me as I sat there thinking about what to do, wondering if I should dare disturb the universe. It was just a few steps to take, just a simple hello and all I had to do was overcome a lifetime of rejection, uncertainty, fear, nervousness and self-doubt. A part of me was also completely jealous of her clothes and longed to be able to be out in my own skirt and fishnets and boots. In my heart I was a punk girl too, but I pushed that down deep. I'd just made friends. Girls liked me. Now was not the time to let the freak flag fly, especially with a girl as perfect as Courtney. With a few deep breaths, I was able to work up the courage to take a few steps toward her.

"Hey, Courtney," I shuffled up, trying my best to look as cool as possible.

"Hey, Matt," she said slowly and looked with a little bit of a smile, her eyes half closed, a little unfocused. Despite the cigarette she was smoking, she gave off a heavy scent of pot, a smell I only recently began to recognize. "D'jya go to the show?"

"Yeah," I half-lied. I had paid my two dollars and gone into the Catalina Club but ducked right back out. Sure, I fancied myself an excellent mosher who could jump in the pit with the best of them, but the noise was ungodly, the crowd far too large and wild for the tiny space and the smell of sweat and body odor ungodly. I'd gotten out of there as quickly as possible and spent my night in Orwell's, where, oddly enough I could still hear the bands through the walls. "It was okay."

"It was just, okay, yeah," she agreed and added. "Punk's okay, I guess, but I like more mellow stuff. That's more my scene."

"Sure, yeah. It gets pretty crazy in there."

"You know, I'd rather just listen to good music, just do an X and like chill, you know," Courtney explained in serious tones. "That's just like the connection right there. You feel it with everyone in the room, like it's so positive you know. Punk just can be good right, but it sucks the positivity out of the room. That's why people mosh."

"Yeah, totally," I said, though I had no idea quite what she was talking about. Was she a raver? I'd never met a raver before. Word had it that they did drugs and partied for like 40 hours straight. But I thought raves were something that only happened in big cities like Atlanta or DC or New York. "That sounds great."

"You should come some time. Mikey Magic P rents out that old abandoned bowling alley out past Gordon Highway like whenever. You have to be like, within the grape vine to know about it. But I know you now so you're all like inner grapevine." While I had no idea who Mikey Magic P was, Gordon Highway was the most run down part of town, full of abandoned strip malls, a handful of pawnshops, possibly the world's seediest looking strip joints, a creepy looking military surplus store, and a couple of the less fashionable mobile home parks. Anything that could be described as "out past Gordon Highway" was almost certain to be sketchier than a Da Vinci notebook.

"Wow, awesome. Thanks," I genuinely smiled, my head swimming with visions of meeting Courtney one Saturday night down over at the abandoned bowling alley for trippy music, flashing lights, pacifiers, glow sticks, ecstasy tablets and hours of wonderful, wonderful making out. Maybe if she was all hopped up on X, she'd let me touch her boobs.

"Crap, I gotta go, Jordan is here. Wait here," She spat out quickly then instantly started walking away. Looking over, I saw him. An older guy, with a motorbike. He walked up, wearing a cool jacket, goggles pushed up on his head. He hadn't shaved in a couple days, but he wore it well. He was tall, with sharp eyes, spiky dyed black hair, torn up jeans and must have been in his late 20s or early 30s. There were definitely shining flecks of grey in his stubble. He walked right up and she lit up immediately, tossed her cigarette aside and jumped into his arms, kissed his stubble covered face and kept going on about how great it was to see him.

The butterflies in my stomach all condensed into one giant knot that sunk down inside me. Slinking back a few steps I tried my best to avert my eyes as they publicly displayed their affection. Instead of running away, I just stood there like a dorky boy scout standing next to a war hero, watching the love of my life, at least the love of my life for that week, making out with the guy who was either her boyfriend, or at least ahead of me in line in the boyfriend department. Thankfully, after not too long they broke it off and Courtney looked up to sort of acknowledge me, then looked right back to Jordan.

"C'mon, Courtney, let's go. I don't have all day," he snapped.

"Sorry," she said quietly as he led her away down 8th, toward the coffee shop. She just walked away with him, leaving me there on the sidewalk. For a second I thought about kicking his motorbike over or engaging in some other wanton form of destruction, but didn't have the energy. Instead I just slunk off in the opposite direction, walking by myself into the shadows. While you'd think I was used to rejection at this point, it stung just as much as every other time. So, I kept going, past Broad Street, up to the river.

* * *

Sometime before I had arrived in Augusta, the city had invested tens of millions of dollars trying to revitalize what was left of downtown. They had built a high-end shopping mall and a promenade on the old levee that protected the town from the river floods. There were public art pieces, an amphitheater and a fountain. But, the mall closed its doors after six or seven months and no one ever bothered to stroll along the poorly maintained promenade atop the levee. No one that is except for the kids who found the steps of the stone seats of the amphitheater to be a good spot to smoke pot or make out.

Luckily no one was making out at the amphitheater when I walked up and sat myself down. I wasn't sure I could bear to be near that. In fact, I was the only person I could see along the entire length of the river. There weren't even any homeless people wandering around. Sitting down, I just enjoyed the stillness of a hot late summer evening. A flat filthy looking barge slowly floated down the placid brown waters of the Savannah River, under a rusted old cantilevered railroad bridge. That's all there seemed to be in this town; brown water, pine trees and rust. Augusta was a tired, old town, worn out and rusted. The cotton money had evaporated, the people had moved to the suburbs and all that was left were abandoned buildings and desolation. I'm not sure why we kids flocked to this downtown, but whatever the reason, we were the only ones. Maybe misery loves company, maybe we wanted to pretend we were living in a real, gritty city, or maybe we just didn't have anywhere else to go.

But, I didn't want to be downtown anymore. Not tonight. Courtney had seen to that with her stupid motorcycle boyfriend who was far too old for her. Plenty of girls had rejected me, Courtney hadn't even bothered to reject me and it had been the same with everyone. As I sat there, the only human being around for what felt like miles, I watched the barge slowly float down along the way to Savannah, a couple hundred miles down the river. And I wondered if this would always be my life. Always alone, ever surrounded by rust and decay on the boring fringes out while in other places glamorous people led glamorous rock star lives of sex, drugs and rock & roll. I could see why Michelle longed to make the Factory alive again. It was hope. It was all we had really, but as I thought about Courtney, I felt my hope sinking away to black.

# Chapter Four

## "Just a Rat in a Cage"
## September 23, 1995

"Dear God," I started. There was plenty that I wanted to say but I could never be sure how to put the words together in quite the right way. Lying in my bed staring up at the glow in the dark sticker stars on my ceiling, I tried to gather my thoughts. Then I closed my eyes and started up my prayer again, silently beseeching God.

"You're the all-powerful creator of the entire universe. And I know You know that there's one thing I want. It's only one thing. And really I don't even think it's that bad, but you're God, so you would know that better. I wish you could use your infinite power to just magically make me into a girl. If you did that one thing I would always pay attention in church and in Bible class too. And I'll stop listening to secular music. And I'll try to stop having bad, sinful thoughts about girls. I'll stop having bad, sinful thoughts about Courtney and Hillary. Just make me a girl. Please. Please, God. In Jesus name, amen."

Outside, a car drove past. Its headlights beamed wild shadows across the walls of my room. Closing my eyes once again, I realized that I had to silence the nagging twist in my stomach. It wasn't something that I wanted to do but it was something that I had to do.

"Jesus, I'm so sorry," I thought. God could hear my thoughts. He could see and hear everything. "Please help me with this sin. I can't help it. I really can't. I try but the thoughts are always there. They never go away. Please, God. Please let me be normal. Amen," I prayed. But I knew, and God probably knew too, that what I really wanted from God was to make me a girl. That's all I ever wanted.

\* \* \*

Sometimes I worry I have no life and never will. Three weeks into my junior year of high school, 15 already, and I had never even kissed a girl. I imagined my peers and classmates dating with wild abandon, kissing, making out, and going to various bases every weekend. Meanwhile I was alone and probably destined to die a virgin. There were even kids in my church youth group who were cooler than me.

Joey Webster, who everyone called Web, was as punk as anyone. Though he was only 17 he already had a tattoo—Black Flag bars on his shoulder—and one eyebrow pierced. When I walked into the sanctuary, I saw that he had planted himself on the stage and was strumming on his unplugged electric guitar. It was covered in stickers for punk and hardcore bands like Dead Kennedys, The Misfits, Bad Religion, and Operation Ivy. His girlfriend Tanya was sitting next to him in torn up jeans with a flannel shirt loosely hung over a homemade and home torn Bikini Kill shirt. Both Web and Tanya had dyed black hair and wore black eyeliner and black nail polish, even to church.

"Hey, Web. Hey Tanya," I greeted them. Though I had worn my Therapy? T-shirt, I still knew I wasn't anywhere near as cool as them. Still, they gestured for me to come over. So I grabbed a seat on the edge of the stage. I pretended to join Tanya in watching Web play, but my eyes were firmly fixed on the door, the same door that Hillary had yet to come in. If Courtney was going to ignore me to go off with her motorcycle guy, then there was always Hillary.

Most of the chairs in the sanctuary had been stacked up and put into the storage room as they were when there wasn't a service. The youth pastor had made a circle of 20 or so chairs off to the far side of the space. Tall, with long blonde hair, the youth pastor Dave was in his late 20's and working his way up to actual pastor.

"Everyone put their bags over by the stage," Dave called out. "Come grab a seat in the circle." Looking around, I finally saw Hillary and my heart skipped a beat or two or possibly up to seven total beats. As she walked in with her younger sister and some other girl, her eyes eventually met mine and she gave me a friendly wave. I waved back, smiled awkwardly, and turned bright red, though not necessarily in that order.

With a begrudging manner that only teenagers could muster, we all slowly melted over and found our spots in the circle. Though I had tried to stay back so that I could snag a seat next to her just after Hillary sat down, I was too late. Her sister and friend had already beaten me to it.

Instead I had to grab a leftover spot that was at least across from her. Maybe we could at least exchange a glance or two.

Turning his chair backward, youth pastor Dave pressed his chest into the chair back and leaned his arms atop the edge. Nodding his head, he looked around at each of us. There were about 20 of us kids. With a few exceptions we all knew each other from Sunday night and Wednesday youth group as well as Fired Up, which was what they called the Sunday school class for teens.

"I just want to say thank you, Lord Jesus for bringing such a fantastic group out tonight. I know the last place you wanna be on a Saturday night is in a church, right?" Dave started out. A couple of the most dorky kids laughed at his sad excuse of a joke. But he continued on. "There's nothing you could be doing out there that's cooler than what God has planned for us tonight. You know, I think God has a reason for bringing each and every one of us here tonight. I think His spirit is gonna come down and just fill up this space. You know, Matthew 18:20? 'For where two or three gather in my name, there am I with them.' Right here, right in this room, right now. Let's take a quick minute and pray, alright? I want everyone to close their eyes and pray, just you and Jesus having a chat. Let's tell our friend Jesus why we came here tonight, what we want to get out of this fellowship tonight."

Though I knew exactly why I had come, I didn't feel particularly up for talking to God about it. Letting my eyes open, I looked around. Everyone else seemed tightly shut including both Web and Tanya. Hillary, her beautiful blonde hair hanging down in lustrous tresses, was deep in prayer herself. I closed my eyes again just as Dave started back up.

"Thank you, Jesus. Thank you for bringing these kids together tonight. Thank you for bringing your spirit here to this lock-in. Thank you, Jesus for the sacrifice you made on the cross. Thank you for the healing power of the blood you shed for us, Lord. Amen," David said as he finished up his prayer. Then he forced a goofy smile onto his face. "But hey, this isn't all serious you know. We're gonna have fun tonight too. Tons of fun, guys. Yeah. You know, I think Jesus had fun. I think he was a fun guy. I'll tell ya, like some of them times when he stuck it to those Pharisees? He had some good jabs, right? He was witty. Christ was a cool man. He was the coolest."

Hillary caught me looking at her and she shot me a little smile. In response I half rolled my eyes as if to say 'what a dork pastor Dave was.'

Her smile widened a little and just at the edge of perception, she nodded. Pastor Dave was continuing on through and had branched into the topic of why Jesus was the ultimate grunge rocker.

"I'll tell ya, I like some of Nirvana's jams. They rock. But I look at Kurt Cobain and I see a sad person who needed the healing power of Jesus. If someone had thought to share the gospel with that hurting man, he'd be alive today and probably be cranking out some pretty great Christian grunge rock." At that I couldn't help but let out a slight laugh. Trying to disguise it with a cough only made Hillary laugh too.

"All right," Pastor Dave said. "You're right. Enough preaching. Let's have some fun here. We've got all night."

\* \* \*

After we'd devoured all the pizza, Web jumped up on stage and hooked his guitar up to church's amps. Running up after him, Tanya grabbed the church's bass and slung it over her shoulder. In between popping a few power chords, Web moved carefully around the stage flipping switches and adjusting dials.

"Matt!" he called out. "C'mon, we're jammin'."

"Yeah?" I asked, looking up from the game of Trivial Pursuit that a few of my fellow youth groupers had set up on the carpet.

"We need a drummer, Matt," Tanya said as she tapped out a few deep bass notes.

"I only did band for two years," I said not so much to excuse myself from playing but rather to excuse what would no doubt be rather poor drumming on my part. "And that was back in junior high." Instead of replying, Web motioned me up with a bob of his head as he started grinding out the opening chords to "I Wanna Be Sedated." Or possibly it was another Ramones song. They were all fairly interchangeable.

Doing my best to be cool, I bit my cheek to avoid letting a huge smile erupt. Running up, I did my best to navigate the jungle of wires, pedals, mic stands, and guitar stands that filled up most of the stage. I hopped behind the drums, didn't bother to adjust the stool, found a couple of sticks on the floor, and gave the bass a good pounding. Then as Web and Tanya led into what did in fact turn out to be "I Wanna be Sedated," I gave the drum kit my best marching band throttling and tried to keep up. In my head I was David Grohl or Keith Moon, though I probably sounded more like a 15-year-old band kid who hadn't picked up in a drumstick since junior high. It didn't matter. I felt impossibly cool.

Looking out over the sanctuary, I saw that most of the girls had huddled around the back wall where they were industriously engaged in braiding friendship bracelets. Then I saw it. Hillary had stopped and turned around. She was watching us play. I beamed a huge, hopefully cool smile her way and she gave me an ironic thumbs up and smiled right back at me. Bob and Tanya then shifted right into Green Day's "Basket Case" which thankfully wasn't that crazy on the drums. I gave it my all and tried not to think about it too much. Punk wasn't supposed to be played well. It didn't matter. All that mattered was that Hillary was still watching us play, her head bopping slightly along to the music.

\* \* \*

"I heard about what you did at American Christian," Web said as he loaded his guitar into the trunk of his beat up little bright red 70s Toyota. Outside the air was still uncomfortably hot and heavy with humidity, though a cool breeze rustled through the pines that lined the big, mostly empty gravel parking lot. His gear properly stowed, Web looked over to me, his suddenly serious face bathed in yellow flood light. He made a point of looking me right in the eye. "You know who else would have done that? I'll tell you, that's like something Jesus would have said to the Pharisees, Matt. I'm not kidding."

"Thanks, man" I said even though it took me a second to realize that Web wasn't being sarcastic.

"Pastor Dave sucks," Tanya said as she walked up. After our fourth song, he had officially banned live music from the lock-in and told Web to go take his guitar out to his car.

"So much for being locked in, though," I laughed.

"Hey Matt, you want a beer?" Web asked, holding out a can of cheap lager for me.

"You brought beer to a lock in?" I laughed.

"Left over from fishing," Web explained. He gave one to Tanya who cracked it open and took a sip.

"Um," was all I could get out. I had never had a beer before and quite frankly I would have never predicted having my first at a church youth group function. A part of me was scared because alcohol was one of the many, many sins that we were warned about on a near daily basis at school, at church, and at home. I had never even set foot in a bar. Bikers and drug dealers hung out at bars. Still, I didn't want Web and Tanya to think I was a dork.

"It's cool if you don't, Matt," Tanya assured me. "But don't worry. I just came from inside and Pastor Dave's already asleep in the office, snoring his heart out. Passed out before 11."

"Oh, no, no," I said as I took the can of beer. "I was just thinking 'I could go for a beer,' you know?" Popping it open, I took a drink of mostly yeasty foam that tasted bad but not quite as bad as I thought it would.

"So you're going to Davidson, right?" Web asked. Both he and Tanya went to Lakeside.

"Yeah," I said. "It's my first time in public school. It's pretty good."

"You know Tall Preston's friend Michael Adams?" Web asked.

"No," I answered and tried to look casual as I choked down a few more sips of beer.

"He graduated last year," Tanya said dismissively. "Oh I know who goes to Davidson. You know that girl Courtney? The redhead who goes out with Mary's C's cousin Jordan?"

"Courtney Wilkerson," I answered. Yes, I knew Courtney. I knew her red hair, her green eyes, her endless hotness, her grown up worldliness. "Yeah, she's cool."

"She's like below us, right?" Web asked. He and Tanya were both starting their senior year.

"Yeah," I said. "She's a sophomore. She hangs out at Orwell's sometimes."

"Where we should be," Tanya laughed sadly. "Uh. My dumbass mom made me come to this thing. Thankfully, Web agreed to come too or else I'da gone crazy."

"Parents made you come too?" Web asked as he chugged down the rest of his beer.

"Yeah," I lied in hopes of sounding cooler. Not that there was anything wrong with admitting that I had come solely for the purpose of talking to Hillary. But I didn't quite feel like dealing with the encouragement that Tanya and Web would no doubt heap upon me if they knew. With a few more gulps, I downed my beer. One drink wouldn't be enough to get you drunk right? I half remembered something from DARE about blood alcohol content. "Y'all wanna go back in?"

"Not yet," Web said as he passed out a second round of beers. "It's nice out here."

"Yeah," Tanya said with a wicked smile. "And I wanna hear about you and Hillary Barton. Cause I saw y'all being flirty in there. She's cute, you know, for a wholesome chick."

"Okay," I said, my face bright red from both embarrassment and alcohol. "Okay, fine. My mom didn't make me come. I'll tell you the real reason I'm here at a lock-in."

\* \* \*

It was a little past one in the morning when I ventured outside again, this time by myself. Inside I could hear the muffled conversation and laughter. A little dizzy from the two beers Web gave me, I sat down on a bench not far from the church's main entrance. At this hour there were almost no cars driving past, though beyond the pine trees you could hear the hum of the traffic out on nearby Washington Road. For a little bit I just sat and listened to the ever present crickets, the whooshing of faraway cars, and the chatter from inside the church. Then I looked up and saw her.

"Hey Matt," Hillary greeted me as she sat down next to me on the bench. "Watcha doin? Needed to get away from it all?" Though it wasn't moonlight, just the sodium yellow glow of the church parking lot lights, she still looked amazing. Her eyeliner had gotten a bit smeared over the past few hours but her shining pink lip gloss had been freshly re-applied. She was wearing short jean shorts and Vigilantes of Love T-shirt. Even in her casual clothes she looked amazingly beautiful.

"A little bit," I said nervously, though I tried my best to appear stoic and thoughtful. "It's quieter out here, I guess."

"Yeah, says the guy in the band," she teased me. "Rocking out on the drums. Y'all were good. You should start a band."

"Maybe," I let myself smile, though I felt the butterflies in my stomach swarming.

"What would you call it? What's your band's name?" Turned toward me, she rested her elbow on her bare knee and put her chin in her hand. There was a small cut on her leg, like she had cut it shaving earlier but it had started to heal.

"I don't know," I answered after thinking about it for a second. Then

I lied because I felt like all the many, many band names I had ever come up with, or drawn logos or fake album covers for were stupid sounding. "I never thought about it."

"Really?" she said sarcastically. "You of all people never thought of a band name?"

"What does that mean?" I laughed.

"You're always the one making up stories and stuff. You never once thought about if you were in a band what it would be called? Never once? Really?"

"Okay," I smiled embarrassed. "I would call my band Ganymede. After Jupiter's moon." At home I had not only drawn a fake album cover for the made up band, I had actually taken apart a CD case and put the artwork in it so it looked more real.

"Ganymede," she said, rolling the name over in her mind. "I like it. It's very… it's a very smart name. Astronomy and Greek literature too."

"I guess. So how's school going? How's junior year going?"

"School's school. Same old. You know how it is. Except now everyone misses you," she said thoughtfully.

"No they don't," I replied. "But thank you for trying to cheer me up."

"I'm not trying to cheer you up," she said defensively. "It's true. Why would you think that? So negative?"

"Jason Evans does not miss me, for one," I pointed out. Being away from ACA's bullies was just one of the nice things about Davidson. Not going to gym class was another. Courtney was a big one, but I didn't want to think about her when Hillary Barton was sitting here alone with me at night being nice to me.

"No, I suppose not. But there's a lot of people other than Jason Evans at school."

"That's true. I guess I just always felt kinda unpopular at American Christian, like I never played football or anything. And never had the right shoes."

"Yeah, but you always had entertaining stuff to say in class. And in chapel, which by the way I think you were right to say. You have courage and stand up for what you believe in. How many other people can you say that about? Plus I liked your little comic books. I'm just saying, school is less interesting, less fun with you not around. And maybe it's something you don't notice until it's gone."

"I miss you," I said. "I do. I miss seeing you every day. You always put me in a good mood. You're like the nicest person. And kind. And fun. And cool. I only came to the lock-in 'cause you were gonna be here."

"Really?" she asked, her eyes locked on mine. I saw her bite her lip a little.

"Yeah," I said, shaking my head. I looked right back at her, right into her big brown eyes. "I know it's stupid. I just wanted to…"

"It's not stupid," she said. "It's nice." I think I leaned in but it might have been her. But suddenly we were kissing. I was kissing a girl. I had always thought it would be hard or awkward but it felt so natural and simple. I reached out and stroked her hair and put my other hand right on her leg, feeling the cold, smooth skin of her freshly shaved thigh. Her arms wrapped around me and for what might have been a minute we were there together, intertwined.

Then she broke it off. Wiping her mouth, she half smiled nervously. I could still taste the fake strawberry stickiness of her lip gloss and feel the chilly night air where her saliva still sat on my skin. My whole body was suddenly alive and I felt a dull ache in my boxers. She stood up and looked at me with an expression that seemed to be equal parts joy and sadness.

"I should go back in, Matt," she said softly. As I watched her walk away, my mind reeled. I had actually kissed a girl. I had kissed Hillary Barton. Were we going together now? Did she like me? Had she always liked me and just never told me? Nothing I had experienced in my 15 years had prepared me for this in the slightest.

* * *

The smell of electrically griddled pancakes woke me up. Dragging myself off the hard, carpeted sanctuary floor, I stiffly climbed my way out of my sleeping bag and stood up onto wobbly legs. Craning my neck back and forth, I cracked my spine back into something resembling its normal state. Early morning sunlight was streaming into the sanctuary from the large front windows and I could sense a general commotion coming from the sanctuary-adjacent church kitchen. My dry mouth screamed for coffee.

Walking into the kitchen, I saw youth pastor Dave standing over the counter making pancakes while a small crowd watched or readied plates.

Stumbling over to the coffee urn, I poured myself a cup and loaded it up with sugar. Looking around, I didn't see Web or Tanya or Hillary. I hadn't actually talked to Hillary since we kissed. By the time I had gone back the previous night, she was already fast asleep in her own sleeping bag. Glancing at the microwave clock I could see that it was only 8:13 a.m. Chances were she was still asleep.

Leaving the kitchen, I bumped right into her and nearly spilled my coffee all over her. Hillary was wearing light pink pajama pants, last night's T-shirt, a messy ponytail, and a serious-looking expression. My mumbled apologies were met only with a frown.

"What's up?" I asked in the manner of one who has their make-out partner greet them not with joy but with severe sternness.

"Matt," she said sadly. "Can we talk? Out in the lobby." Agreeing, I followed her out to the lobby all while hoping this was an act. Perhaps she wanted to keep our new love a secret. She was simply waiting for a private moment to happily embrace and potentially make out again.

"So what's up?" I asked again once we were safely in the lobby. Hillary looked up at me like she had failed a math test and that, somehow, failing that math test had killed my kitten.

"Matt," she started. "Last night, after we, well, talked. I came back in and prayed to God to forgive me. And I hope we can both be forgiven for our sin that we committed. But that means repenting."

"Okay?" I said. Quite frankly, I was starting to feel my anger boil up. I had not only kissed a girl for the first time. It had actually been Hillary Barton. It had been cheerleader and popular girl Hillary Barton. It had happened. And now, instead of it happening again, God and the Bible and church were starting to stick their faces into this to ruin it for me.

"I like you as a friend, Matt. You know, I think that's what God wants for us," Hillary said. She looked up at me and smiled sadly. I was probably making an expression but it wasn't sadness or smiling.

"Hillary," I started, hoping I could maybe reason with her. "I don't think the Bible says kissing is a sin. Not specifically."

"Matt," Hillary said. "Lust is a sin. And a temptation. Would it help you if we prayed together about this?"

"No," I muttered. Then I turned around and left her there in the lobby. My church clothes were in my bag. I had to get changed. The last thing I wanted to do was sit through another stupid Fired Up lecture with youth pastor Dave, but I didn't have a choice. The worst thing was that I knew Hillary was probably right.

The Bible was full of rather specific statements about lust being really bad. I didn't want to go to hell. I didn't want to backslide into sin. I wanted to be a good Christian. Sin, I was taught, never brings real happiness. True happiness can only be found in Jesus. And here I was running away from Jesus.

As I gathered up my sleeping bag and walked over to where all our backpacks were piled up against the far wall, I prayed and asked God to forgive me for kissing Hillary and for drinking beers. Then I said amen and regretted it. I wasn't sorry, not really.

Maybe I hadn't actually repented. But maybe it was because I kept thinking about what Hillary had said. Not what she had said about Jesus though. She had said "our" sin, as though it were a sin we shared. It was a shared moment. And then she used the word "lust" in reference to me, as though she had lusted after me or currently still lusted after me. Then she said that she was "tempted," that she wanted to keep doing this with me or do more with me. That gave me some hope. It wasn't much hope, but it was a little bit. Maybe she would change her mind and be open to sinning again after Sunday night youth group or maybe at another lock-in.

Walking over to the bags, I looked through them until I found mine. I set my sleeping bag down and pulled out my hopefully not too wrinkled church clothes. Then I saw it. Her bag was next to mine. I knew it because it had her initials—HAB—embroidered on it. Next to it was her gym bag. It was sitting slightly open. Inside I could see the thick red and white fabric. It was her cheerleading uniform. I knew it well. It had been the cause of another one of my many, many sins.

# Chapter Five

## "You're Just Like an Angel"
## December 2nd, 1994

When December of my sophomore year finally rolled around, I was determined that I would ask Hillary Barton to the winter formal. At the time it seemed like a shoo-in. That week, she had called me not only a "really great guy" but also a "great friend." Okay, granted, we weren't the sort of friends who ate lunch at the same table or hung out on the weekends or had the same social group, but in her estimation we were great friends and I was willing to work with that.

My friends, and by 'friends' I mean the other losers with whom I shared a lunch table, actually made fun of me when I declared my intentions. But I dismissed them as naysayers because they weren't even trying to ask anyone out. After all, glory belongs to those who dare to dream and they were content to sit on the sidelines. So screw them. Yes, I was going to disturb the universe, I was going to ask her out and let the footmen snicker if they wanted to.

So on an ever so slightly chilly, Georgia winter afternoon, just after a particularly nasty biology test with one hell of a multiple choice section, we were walking over to the parking lot and for the first time in my life I approached a woman romantically. Hordes of butterflies were flying around in my stomach having the mother of all dogfights. My palms went sweaty. My first instinct was to forget about it and ask her tomorrow. I would have done that had I not come to the same conclusion the day before. No, the time for hesitation had passed and nothing was going to stop me.

Biology was our last class of the day, so all I had to do was manage to get into a conversation with her just after the bell rang, then I could hopefully, through witty banter, keep the conversation going all the way

44

out to the parking lot. Then I could save my question popping until the utter last second before her mom pulled into the parking lot.

All through class, I rehearsed our conversation in my head. In my internal mental version of our conversation, Hillary would present a series of objections that I would in turn defeat with my unassailable logic. I wasn't on the football team, well yes, but my academic skills were top notch. I didn't have a car, yes, but that reduced the possibility of our dying in a fiery wreck since I would have a more experienced driver chauffeuring us. I wasn't cool, sure, but that just meant that my future income was going to be higher than average. No matter what objection, I was sure I could counter it.

Of course, using skilled debate rhetoric would only work if I could get a good conversation started. This couldn't just be a simple question like "What are you up to this weekend?" or "What do you think of Planned Parenthood? Horrible, right?" No, it would need to be a real conversation starter, something that could keep us talking and keep her occupied so that other people couldn't interrupt us. Sure, I had thought about the obvious thing of just asking her right out instead of delaying it, but delaying it seemed to be much more within my comfort zone.

I finished my test first, and then while I was sitting at my desk I figured out my conversation starter. I'd make Hillary a little comic book. I'd made them for her before. Mostly they involved versions of our teachers as grotesque supervillains. Mrs. Perkins, the biology teacher and a rather rotund woman, was reimaged as a monstrously corpulent monster with a gaping Sarlacc-esque maw in her stomach, devouring everything in her path. Today I had the brilliant idea of doing something a little different and so I created a new hero; The Cheer Beater.

Cheer Beater was a caricature of Hillary Barton and I gave her the secret identity of Ellery Bantam. Subtle, I was not. Cheer Beater had a baseball bat covered in spikes and her superhero outfit consisted of a cheerleader uniform with a skull on it, a cape and some boots with spikes on them, because why not have more spikes if you can? Plus spikes are easy to draw. They're just little triangles.

Cheer Beater's first adventure began with mild-mannered high school student Ellery Bantam in biology class. Suddenly a meteor crashed into the school, right into the biology classroom, killing Mrs. Perkins and leaving only a smoking crater. Everyone is shaken, but luckily the teacher was the only fatality.

But then, suddenly, Perkins rises from the smoking crater, now hideously mutated. Her tentacles violently rip students from their seats and stuff them into her giant mouth. No one, not even the police or the army can stop Perkins, despite a good page of college-lined loose-leaf paper covered in violent explosions, jet fighters and tanks fighting the horrifying mutant high school teacher. Finally Ellery Bantam is able to duck out, change clothes, and then proceed to fight Perkins with graphic, blood-drenched cartoon violence.

It was perfect, right? What teenage girl wouldn't like a hand-drawn, amateur comic book in which she is depicted graphically killing her biology teacher? It was definitely going to be a conversation starter. That's all I needed. Hillary had seen my comics before. Not only had she laughed out loud at them, on at least one occasion, she liked one so much that she asked to keep it. But she had never actually starred in an adventure. I felt like this would definitely score me some winter formal points.

So as the last bell of the day finally rang, I gathered up my stuff as quickly as I could so that I could be ready to leave before her. That way I could react to her direction-wise and not risk having her beat me to the door. Carefully I watched out of the corner of my eye as she gathered up her stuff. As soon as she had her backpack, purse, and jacket in hand and was headed to the door, I pounced. Thankfully none of her friends had managed to get her into a conversation yet, so I had my in.

"Hey, Hillary!" I greeted her, practically tripping over every desk and my own feet in order to get over to her. Today she had worn her slightly baggy denim overalls with a DC Talk T-shirt underneath. One strap of the overalls just hung down and if you looked carefully—stared carefully really—you could see a little patch of skin in the gap between her shirt and overalls.

"Hey, Matt" she smiled. Smiles were good. Smiles were positive. Smiles were indicative of people saying yes to going to the winter formal with me. Because dancing was sinful, we couldn't have dances at American Christian Academy. Instead of dancing, people got dressed up and had dinner. Actually, I had never been to one of the formals or to the banquet we had in lieu of a prom. Dancing was a one-way ticket to hell. "I made a comic for you."

"Oh cool, thank you," Hillary beamed. Taking the pieces of paper, she flipped through it. "Oh, is this supposed to be me?"

"Yeah, I figured you deserved a starring role."

"Cool," she smiled, her pink lips dabbed with strawberry gloss. "I like it." As we walked through the crowded hall and out to the front entrance, out into the sun lit parking lot, she kept glancing at it, smiling or chuckling slightly from time to time. After school, the parking lot was the place to be, where everyone hung out as the parents' cars cued up to pick up the kids. For a moment, she scanned the parking lot, then casually handed the comic back to me. Sheepishly I took it back, folded it up and put it in my pocket. It had done its job after all.

"Cool," I muttered back while scanning the parking lot for my mom's white Ford Escort. This was it. This was my moment. All I had to do was utter the words "Hillary, will you go to the winter formal with me?" Ten little words. Heck, all I really needed was "Wanna go to the winter formal with me?" Seven words. Sure, I could drop with me to get it down to five, but that might make a little too ambiguous. "What is it, like, December?" I asked, for no reason at all, other than just to say something.

"Yeah, it is. December second," she said as though I had asked her if the sky were blue. It was pretty obvious. In fact, it was on all the calendars. Plus I had a little spot on my watch that told the date. All day in school, we had to write the date on all the assignments we turned in, which is weird, because the teacher would have given the quiz to everyone in the class on the same day, so the date couldn't be that important. Your name, I get why you put your name, but the date seemed irrelevant.

"December is such a big month." I said as though months were categorized. Though to be fair December is kind of a big deal. January, I feel, we all just try and rush through, but December is a pretty big deal, especially in the retail and tinsel industries. "There's a lot going on in December, it feels like."

"Yeah, totally, with Christmas and everything," Hillary agreed. Even I wasn't quite sure why she was still standing next to me. I was losing it. I was losing her. I needed to bust out my seven to ten words and get this over with. Either she would say yes, in which case I'd also have to refrain from ever again saying "Life's not fair." Angels would sing rapturous songs around me and life would be, for once, amazing and fantastic and joyous.

And if she said no, well, then I'd basically still be at square one right? That wouldn't be terrible. It would just be a continuation of the status quo right? Or it would possibly destroy what fragile husk of me that remained after being the least popular kid in a terrible, jock friendly, totally lame, hellhole of a Christian high school. So it'd either be awesome or it would end my life. No reason to drag it out, right?

So, I managed to drag it out until her mom's minivan pulled up into the parking lot. Through the window I could see Hillary's well-dressed, jewelry-covered, Southern belle matron of a mom. My mom was a college professor whose fashion sense and social standing were non-existent. Hillary's mom probably belonged to a country club or a book club or ate club sandwiches or something.

Then Hillary opened the passenger door and with her mom in earshot I knew I had to do it then and there. This was it. This was really it. This was most definitely and really it. My stomach went cold, my hands tingled and I may have even blacked out for a moment. But, in one quick, awkward falsetto syllable I blurted it out.

"Hillary, do you want to go to winter formal with me?" I asked.

Her head tilted a little to the side, like a curious dog. She smiled and her eyes lit up. Unlike most of the girls who put their hair up in hair-sprayed bouffants, hers was naturally straight and just hung down beautifully. Her lashes were thick and clumpy from too much mascara and her lip-gloss went a little beyond her lips, but she was beautiful. Standing there at the door of that giant powder blue American automobile, in front of Hillary Barton, I never felt so small or frightened in my entire life.

"Aww," she said it like I was cute, like a puppy. Then she smiled and added "That's so sweet." Nothing that starts with a compliment like that will ever end well. This was to be no exception. "You know Daniel already asked me, but maybe if that gets cancelled or whatever, then sure."

And she gave me a hug, pressed her breasts right into me. Sadly, I knew that that was as close to second base as I was going to get with her. I just mumbled a weak agreement as she gave me a little wave, hopped in the car and pulled the door closed.

All I could do was just stand there in the parking lot, looking down at my feet. But then I noticed that there was a bag by my feet. It was a black and red Georgia Bulldogs canvas tote bag. In all the awkwardness of my invitation, she had set it down and forgotten it. I was about to tap on the door and let her know, when I realized what was in the bag. It was her cheerleader uniform. Her red and white cheerleader uniform. Her top, her skirt, and even the little colored twirls of ribbon they'd put in their hair when they cheered at games were sitting right there.

I didn't even have a chance to hesitate. Something took over my brain and locked me in. I stood there motionless, my heart pounding in my chest, my stomach chilling me to my core. I stood there and let the car pull away. As they left the parking lot and pulled out onto the main road, I slowly and deliberately took the tote bag, picked it up, squished it hard down into my backpack, and zipped it right up. As far as I could tell no one had seen me. Not the elementary kids milling about, nor the alternative kids playing hacky-sack, nor the various parents in their cars, nor the little crowds of girls gossiping. No one saw me. It certainly wasn't a particularly Christ-like thing to do. It was wrong. It was a sin. It was weird. But it was also a million-in-one chance when I saw it. God forgives anything, right?

* * *

For the whole time I spent there waiting for my mom as well as for the whole ride home, I was a bundle of pure nerves, a ball of crazed energy. My mind was awash with plans, logistics for how I would spend my weekend, how I would manage to try on an actual, honest-to-God cheerleader outfit. I couldn't wait. I could feel myself shaking in heady anticipation, the feeling of that tight top, the movement of the skirt. I longed to twirl or kick up my leg or jump. Maybe I could even go outside in it.

Tonight, a Friday night, I'd be home, like usual. Of course my parents would be home too. Most likely they'd keep themselves busy all evening, my dad probably watching TV, my mom probably reading or working on the computer. Most likely my sister would be out with friends. As an athlete, she was much higher on the social scale than I was. People would actually invite her to things.

That would leave me mostly alone for the evening, though not quite as alone as I would have liked. Some serious privacy was what I really wanted. Sadly, I wasn't going to get that, at least in my house. My parents were firm believers in the idea that my bedroom door shouldn't be able to lock. I was lucky to have a door. I had classmates who didn't.

So while my parents were unlikely to come check on me, I still couldn't risk something crazy like trying on Hillary Barton's cheerleader outfit in my room. Honestly, I'm not even sure what my parents would do if they walked in on me. Military school was a possibility. My dad was always threatening that.

Saturday and Sunday might afford some time alone in the house, but you could never quite be sure. Sometimes they'd all go off to the store or something and actually give me the option of not coming along. Other times, I would be dragged along regardless of my wishes. It was all too unknown. There was no real way to plan out a time. Already I had thought of just keeping the uniform. Maybe no one saw me take it. Even if anyone did accuse me, I could always deny it.

Then again, I'm sure it would cause Hillary some trouble if she lost it. So I rationalized that I would just keep it over the weekend. Then on Monday morning I would just leave it somewhere at school for someone else to find. Of course, keeping it for just a weekend meant that I would really have to try and make the weekend count. I wouldn't be spending this weekend playing *X-Wing* or *SimCity*. No, this weekend I was going to be a cheerleader.

* * *

As soon as I got home, I ran to the bathroom with my backpack. It was all good. I probably had about four or five minutes in the bathroom before it would arouse any suspicion. Of course, my mom was probably busy with her own things and most likely wasn't paying any attention to me. But it's better not to risk it. Locking the door behind me—in the one room in the house where I was actually allowed to lock the door—I zipped open my backpack, pushed aside my notebook, and pulled out the tote bag.

My heart pounded as I pulled out the different pieces of the uniform. The explorers who first unearthed Tut's tomb weren't nearly as awed as I was with an actual cheerleader outfit in my hands. The synthetic fabric was thick, thicker than I would have expected, but still soft. It smelled sweetly of sweat, of girl sweat, of Hillary Barton's sweat.

Sure, I had the whole weekend, but I couldn't wait. Carefully, I laid out the items from the bag on the bathroom counter; the skirt with its thick red and white pleats, the white top with its giant red A, the red cheerleader underpants that they wore over their regular underpants, the thick red leggings for chilly autumn nights, and lastly the long dangly, hair tassels that clipped in. It would be far too risky to try and head into Ellen's room to grab a bra. No, I'd have to try it on with what I had.

"I'm gonna take a shower," I yelled, just in case my mom heard me.

A 3:30 p.m. shower was a little odd—not crossdressing in a stolen cheerleader uniform odd—but definitely a little out of the ordinary. No one would notice me though. So I turned the shower on cold so the bathroom wouldn't steam up. I didn't want the mirror to fog up on a rare and incredible moment like this. I definitely wanted to see myself in the mirror.

What was amazing was that the outfit actually fit. First I had pulled on the over-underpants, followed by the skirt, which actually had three buttons on each side. It took a little bit of a breath in, I had to ride it a little high, but I got the skirt on. Next, I pulled on the top. I figured I could forego the leggings or the hair clips. Then I was wearing an honest-to-God American Christian Academy cheerleading uniform.

For a moment there I just checked myself out in the mirror. Sadly, I was just a skinny 15-year-old boy with short greasy hair, eyebrows that were starting to get unruly, and arms that were starting to get a little hairy. But I could see her staring back out at me. I could see the perfect, beautiful girl there. It was like how Michelangelo could look at a block of marble and see the statue of David underneath. I could look at the sad, pathetic, ugly, un-athletic, loser boy there and see the girl underneath. Maybe it was just imagination, but it worked for me. I felt beautiful. I felt oh so beautiful.

In my head I was there, out on the football field with my squad, out in front of the school, out in front of the students, my classmates, their parents, and the public. I was someone special, someone who was wanted, who was desired, who fit in and had friends and a life.

I'd kick up my smooth legs, shake my pompoms and yell, "Be aggressive! Be be aggressive!" They'd all cheer for me. When I told them to shout "dee" they'd shout "dee" and when I asked them to shout "fence" they'd shout "fence" too. I'd be friends with the other girls on the squad. After the thrill of a football game on a chilly autumn night, we'd do our make-up and our hair, put on cute dresses and go party together. It'd be perfect and I'd be one of them.

In the bathroom, I tried a couple kicks just to see how high I could get my leg, but there wasn't much room between the tub and the sinks. I could have done it sideways, but then I wouldn't be able to see myself in the mirror. I spun around in circles, letting my skirt twirl up, but that also wasn't great for the mirror either. There were a few dances, a few moves, but then I realized that my time as a cheerleader would have to be short.

Too long and my mom might suspect something. Good things never last forever.

As quickly as I could, I took off Hillary's cheerleader outfit, stuffed it back into the Georgia Bulldogs canvas bag and stuck the bag behind the guest towels on the top shelf of the bathroom closet. After all, I had a whole weekend. Maybe my dad, mom and sister would decide to go shopping without me and I could put on the outfit and actually venture out into the yard, just for a few minutes. I could run and spin and flip and cheer out in the real world and not just in my bathroom. Maybe I could even try some of my sister's make-up too and really feel beautiful. But for now, it was best to hide it. There would be other chances.

Quickly, I ducked my head under the still-running shower so I could get my hair nice and wet. It was necessary to sell the illusion that I had actually showered and not just gone into the bathroom to try on a stolen cheerleader uniform so I could pretend for a moment that I was a pretty, feminine, beautiful girl. Wrapping a towel around my waist, I let my hair drip down onto my shoulders. I grabbed my backpack and headed into my room. No one saw me. No one asked. No one noticed. But I still worried.

* * *

"Is there a lost and found?" I sheepishly asked Mrs. Cox, who worked behind the desk in the main office.

While lying awake in bed Sunday night, I had thought about several options related to the future of Hillary's cheerleading uniform. I could leave it randomly— dead drop it—somewhere at school and hope it got back to her okay. That would be the most anonymous method. It would allay any suspicion that I had stolen it because I was a crossdressing deviant, but that would be the riskiest option as far as making sure it got back to Hillary. I imagined she would get in trouble if she lost it. What if some hateful, jealous cheerleading colleague found it and destroyed it out of spite? What if there happened to be another crossdressing weirdo at school and they found it and kept it for good?

Should I keep it for good? This was a question that weighed heavily on me all weekend. Had anyone seen me take it? I didn't think so. The odds of getting caught were minimal. Hillary might have suspected something, but would likely never have proof. Keeping it forever would definitely have some benefits. Instead of just having a rushed weekend to be a cheerleader, I could be one any time I had an hour to myself. Instead of just having it in the bathroom while I pretended to shower, I could go outside, feel the sun on my legs, the breeze, feel alive. But I suspected that might get Hillary in trouble. It would be even more trouble for me if my parents ever found the uniform during one of their periodic ransackings of my room.

No, this was the best way. Turn it into lost and found. If they asked questions I would simply deny everything, play dumb, and plead ignorance. The office staff would figure out it belonged to Hillary, summon her via PA, and she'd be back with her possessions. Then my only sin would be crossdressing rather than theft. Any sin was bad of course. But it would be better to commit one sin rather than two.

"What is it?" asked Mrs. Cox, who I always thought looked a little bit like a cross between Barbara Bush and a rather plain nun.

"Just some clothes," I shrugged. Yes, clothes. Glorious clothes. "I found them in the parking lot this morning."

"Okay. Thanks," she said as she put them under her desk and got back to typing on her electric typewriter.

"Okay," I muttered as I left the office to head over to homeroom. A part of me felt bad about giving up the cheerleader uniform. But it was at that moment that I realized that for the entire weekend, I hadn't felt the least bit bad about Hillary rejecting me. I was just so hung up on clothes, her clothes to be specific. So that was sort of good.

# Chapter Six

## "Maybelline Eyes"
## Saturday, October 12, 1995

It was on the Saturday of Columbus Day weekend of junior year that Michelle invited me over to take part in her grand scheme. The three-day weekend, she said, would give us lots of time. Our first stop was the grocery store, which was luckily in easy walking distance. Michelle had been saving up her money for some time and now spent it all on aluminum foil. Some basic geometry had determined that no fewer than 30 rolls would be enough to cover the floor, ceiling and walls of her bedroom. Taking into account overlap and loss from tearing, led her to 35 rolls. With my help, we bought all they had at the store and I helped her carry it back. That was how the new Factory was born.

"There were actually three different Factories," Michelle explained. "You know, over the years, so it only makes sense that there would be a fourth. Then when we have money there will be a huge space. Maybe Downtown. That will be the fifth Factory. That will be the one with the real parties." On Michelle's desk were dog-eared and bookmarked copies of Andy Warhol books; his diaries, big picture books of his art, another just a second-hand paperback biography with half the back cover torn off. I had to admit there was a certain glamor to the whole Warhol world. Though drugs still scared me and sex was still quite unexplored for me, and though the art didn't interest me too much, Michelle had told me about Candy Darling and shown me her pictures.

Growing up in the 80s and 90s, in a Republican evangelical house, I really hadn't been exposed too much in the way of gender nonconformity. Sure, there was that episode of *Happy Days* when Richie had to dress in drag for a fraternity initiation and fend off advances from Fonzie. But dressing as a girl was presented as embarrassing, shameful and silly. It was something a guy would only do if forced into it against his will. There were never portrayals of guys who wanted to dress up as girls, who enjoyed it and had fun with it and looked forward to it. There was only shame.

Candy Darling was many things, but she was not ashamed. And I was amazed. One of Michelle's books had a couple of photos of her and I was mesmerized. Who even knew it was possible for a guy to not just dress up, but actually become a beautiful woman? Michelle told me all about Candy Darling; she was the quintessential Warhol Superstar; model, a movie star, a muse who had started life as a boy from the suburbs only to become a glamorous woman in New York City and who had sadly died far too young. The idea that someone like her could even exist had opened my world. If she could exist then maybe I could too. Maybe I wasn't as much of a freak as I thought because at least there were other freaks like me. Maybe dressing up wasn't something shameful I had to hide, but something I could one day share with the world.

"My parents never use their camcorder, so we could totally do a movie. Get people to star in it," I offered, unsure of what exactly we would film. The idea of anything too vivacious seemed unwise and I certainly wanted something more exciting than eight hours of watching a building sitting there. "We're out of tape."

"Damn," Michelle bunched her face up into a frown and surveyed her bedroom. Two walls had gone up pretty easily, but the others would require moving the bed, the dresser and the desk. Empty boxes and cardboard rolls littered the floor along with a large assemblage of Michelle's clothes and other personal effects. "Two walls are still pretty good. For now." She flopped onto the bed, either exhausted or dramatically feigning over the top exhaustion. Sometimes with Michelle it was hard to tell.

"I'm sure Andy Warhol didn't silver up the Factory in one day," I offered hopefully. "And if you sit in the right spot, it totally looks all silver." Holding up my hands so my fingers formed a couple of L's (something I had seen film directors do) I viewed the corner of the room and imagined my shot. For a few seconds I tried to think of the films we could make, perhaps an Andy Warhol biography if we could find a suitable blonde wig. Then I would have an absolutely perfect excuse to dress up because we'd need someone to play Candy Darling.

"It's a good beginning. It looks like the Factory."

"Now you totally have to do a Factory shoot for your next photography assignment," I gushed. "It would be perfect."

"Spot on." Michelle, agreed, grabbing a three-ring binder jammed full of school papers, Michelle pulled out one that had seemingly been shoved in randomly. For a moment she scanned the paper before reading "'Breaking the Rules. In this assignment, students will demonstrate basic knowledge of portrait photography with artificial light. The portrait should illustrate the theme of breaking rules, crossing boundaries or stepping outside the ordinary.'"

"Simple enough," I said. "Who's more out of the ordinary than Warhol?" And then I thought about it a little more. Sure, Andy was a unique guy, but Candy Darling was way more out of the ordinary. She crossed boundaries and broke the rules through her very being. A thought was wheedling its way into my mind, taking root, daring me to say it out loud, to actually say it to another person. But I had just had a fresh start at another school, I actually had real friends for the first time.

Did I want to come out and fly the freak flag? Did I want to potentially ruin everything, lose all my new friends, or be rejected by every girl in the world? Did I want to be a dejected sad lonely person my entire life? Or did I want to bottle all my feelings and my gender confusion up and be normal and happy like everyone else?

"Yeah, but who would be Warhol?" Michelle asked, staring into the foil, past it, through it as though it were a portal to the real Factory and the ghosts of all the superstars were hovering in a world just beyond the wall.

"Well, you would," I said. "And then I'd be Candy Darling." For some reason I said that and it came out of my mouth. In the back of my head a thought kept rattling around. Michelle was weird. She was into weird. Heck, she was into the idea of gay people and gender benders and sexual deviants.

"That's perfect!" Michelle's eyes went wider than I had ever seen them. "Would you really do that?" I could see the gears beginning to turn inside her head and different types of gears turning in the pit of my stomach. It would still be possible to back out of being Candy Darling at this point, but I felt empowered as Michelle got up and began darting about the room, grabbing little items here and there and beginning to set them into specific piles.

"Sure," I offered as coolly as possible. Maybe I could dress up as a girl while maintaining a sort of ironic detachment, like all those jocks who dressed up as cheerleaders for the powderpuff football game. As long as I didn't actively admit enjoying the whole process, it would be fine.

"Then let's make you famous," Michelle smiled and handed me a pile of carefully selected clothes. "Go change while I get my camera ready."

Smiling, in what I hoped was a self-depreciating way, I took the pile of clothes, already noting that texture that was so different from ordinary guy's clothes; stretchy, silken, cool to the touch. With its black and red floral pattern the empire-waist baby doll dress that Michelle had grabbed for me didn't quite seem glamorous enough for the real factory. But it would work, even with the lace edging on the sleeves and the tiny satin bow that sat on the waist, just between my toilet paper breasts. Still, it worked.

With a slight twirl, I looked at myself in the mirror, trying to take in all the angles if I could. Ignoring the fact that I still looked rather like a boy in a dress, I took a few steps back and forth, imagining myself as a regular girl getting ready for school, imagining what it felt like to just wear a dress on a normal day, out and about, just as any regular girl would. Then I took a soft, tentative step out into the hallway, hoping none of Michelle's family would see me.

"Look at your hairy legs!" Michelle guffawed as I came back into her room. "Tights'll look better." She reached into a drawer and fished out a balled up opaque black pair. Dutifully, I put them on and awkwardly pulled them up as Michelle turned her attention to her dresser top where she had put out a bunch of make-up palettes, pots, compacts, brushes and pencils.

Sitting back down on the bed, I tucked my feet up under me and ran my fingers along the lace edging of the dress. It fit so well that, for a moment, I silently hoped Michelle would offer to let me keep it. Looking down at my forearm, I think I noticed my arm hair for the first time. I suddenly wished I could shave it and really complete the look. It would be nice to have the full look with every preparation done.

Michelle came over and sat down on the bed. The make-up started with a cool, wet foundation that she smeared all over with her fingers. She then moved on to eye shadow, eye liner, mascara, and blush, pausing only to direct me to move my head one way, look another, look up, look down, turn my head, puff my cheeks or blink. I dutifully obliged with each step, following her each direction as carefully as I could, feeling all the sensations of sharp pencils or dry brushes moving about my face. In the past, I had tried to use my sister's make-up but her collection was limited and my skills nonexistent. I never did much more than to make a mess of my face. This was different. Michelle, while not quite at artist level, was still much more advanced than I was and I eagerly awaited the final product.

Michelle finalized the make-up by smearing on some slick and sticky, strawberry flavored gloss. Then she fooled around with my hair, flipping it, brushing it, putting barrettes in it until she was at last satisfied. Finally, she jumped out of the room and quickly returned, brandishing a pair of shining black, two-inch heels which she tossed onto the bed. Gleefully, I slipped them on, finding that they fit almost right, close enough for a photoshoot at least.

Walking in the heels wasn't too difficult. Honestly, I had never found walking in heels that complicated (I had had plenty of practice with the shoes in my mom's closet). Eagerly, I trotted over to the full-length mirror and smiled. It was the most girled-up I'd ever been. My make-up was a tad overdone, but I loved the dress. I thought I looked amazing. Though, if I studied myself too much, I could still see the boy in the dress, looking ridiculous. So I tried to ignore it and push that feeling deep, deep down, as far as it could go.

I was all girled-up and with another person and I felt a giant smile creep across my face. I could be a cute girl. I could totally be a cute girl. I was a cute girl here with a friend. I wanted to go out in the world and explore and meet people and see if they treated me any differently. I wanted to shop at the mall, or go to the park, or just take a walk in the sun and feel my dress move around my legs. But first—pictures.

"What do you think?" Michelle asked as she started kicking away all the clothes and clutter away from the silver foil-lined cover.

"I love it!" I felt myself say before I realized the full implications of how that might come across.

"Me too!" Michelle gave me a wide smile. "You're the perfect model. Now help me clear all the crap away from the silver so it'll just look like a big silver room." We quickly scooted all the clutter out of the way and threw a bunch of stuff on top of the un-made bed. Michelle pulled her desk chair over to the silver area, set it right in the middle and bid me to have a seat. "Are you ready to be a superstar?"

* * *

"You know, you can tell me if you're gay," Michelle said after a long, thoughtful pause. As far as questions go, it pretty much made sense. While I hadn't exactly volunteered to dress up like a girl, I had readily gone along with it without protest or hesitation. I'd put on Michelle's clothes, her mom's shoes, put on make-up, styled my hair and hadn't made a single silly comment or joke about it.

Maybe I should have. Maybe I shouldn't have just sat on her stool, posing for portraits, letting her photograph me, coming up with my own little poses that I thought looked cute or sexy. Maybe, after we spent two rolls of film, I shouldn't have suggested going for a walk to get some fresh air. Maybe I shouldn't have smiled and bounced along, laughed and twirled my dress or seemed quite so happy. Maybe I shouldn't have seemed incredibly happy to be walking down the street in broad daylight while dressed up as a girl. Well, it was too late for that.

In the Book of Deuteronomy, right after laying out the rules for lost and found and before espousing the proper etiquette for stealing eggs from fallen birds' nests, God made it rather clear that I, in putting on a woman's garment—in this case a baby doll dress—were an abomination unto him. It wasn't the first time I had abominated myself unto the Lord my God and it wouldn't be the last time either.

"Oh no. I'm not gay," I protested, probably a little too quickly and a little too loudly. While I knew that I liked girls, I still wasn't quite clear on what it meant exactly to be gay. Did gay just mean you had sex with the same sex, or were bi people gay too? Did enjoying dressing up as a girl and wanting to be a girl make me gay? Did it fall under that broad category of behaviors that made one gay? The thought of being gay, actually being gay, still terrified me.

After about half an hour strolling through the old, tree-canopied streets of The Hill, we'd found ourselves sitting on a small grassy hill just on the edge of the college. The sun was still shining brightly, but a slight breeze had come in, chilling me just a little bit. Michelle, in her torn jeans, boots and flannel shirt didn't seem to notice the weather as much. This part of the campus was mostly deserted, just a patch of grass and trees near the maintenance buildings and a parking lot. All of the real school buildings were on the other side of a low brick wall and row of trees. A few people came and went from the parking lot but otherwise it was all quiet and still.

"It's okay if you are. I think it's cool," Michelle offered, glancing over. She pulled a pack of cigarettes and a red plastic disposable lighter out of her front pocket. "You want a smoke?" she asked as she stuck one in her mouth and let it hang there.

"Sure," I said, though I didn't actually smoke. Michelle handed me the pack and I pulled one out of the foil and put it in my mouth. Even before it was lit, it was a new and different taste, slightly nutty and only a little plasticky. With a flick, she held out the lighter and used her hand to cup around it, blocking the wind. As I inhaled I sputtered a little with a tiny cough, but didn't really have any issues breathing in the smoke. It certainly wasn't like those cartoons where you people cough up a fit and turn red and half die on their first puff of tobacco. "Thanks."

"You should always light a girl's cigarette for her," Michelle explained. "It makes you look more attractive to her."

"Oh yeah?" I said before realizing that I should have said something like 'I'll remember that next time I'm trying to make out with a chick' or something else fiercely heterosexual.

"So you're not gay?" Michelle asked skeptically, her eyes fixed forward, something I had noticed she did when she was thinking about what to say. Michelle gave the impression that every word of every sentence that she ever spoke was planned out well in advance.

"No," I protested again and then realized that Michelle wasn't going to let me deny my way out of this. "But…" I found myself trying to formulate the words in a way that wasn't embarrassing or didn't make me sound gay or like a sexual deviant or a weirdo. There weren't any really, so I instead just said, "I like girls. I do. I'm totally into chicks. It's just, you know, I like to… express my feminine side too."

"I can see that," Michelle flashed me a smile. "You're like skipping along in your little dress. It's cute." My face turned red as I realized I had been enjoying being a girl a little too much.

"I guess I just like to explore the idea of being more like a girl. You know, I just like the idea of like, being a girl or dressing up as one. That's all." I said. Yes. That's all. Just wanting to be a girl. "But not so much like, the being with guys part of it, obviously." There you go. That certainly hetero'd it up.

"Girls can be with girls too," Michelle put out there and then laughed. "Maybe you're double gay, like a guy who's a girl who's into girls."

"Yeah," I laughed too, happy that even if I were a freak, at least Michelle was still my friend. Hopefully she wouldn't tell anyone though.

I definitely didn't want Courtney to know anything since I doubt her older, job-having, motorcycle driving boyfriend wore dresses and skipped down streets picking flowers and putting them in his hair. Then it suddenly dawned on me that Michelle was going to take this afternoon's photos and develop them and turn them into her teacher to be graded. Other people would definitely see them. What if they were so good they won the principal's monthly art award and were displayed outside the school office for four entire weeks? The photos I could laugh off, but not if Michelle told them anything. Panic suddenly gripped me and I turned to Michelle with a serious look and said "Please don't tell anyone, alright. Just between us."

"Totally," Michelle said, just as seriously. For a moment we just sat there looking seriously at each other before she cracked a half smile and said "You know, I never wear that dress anymore since I stopped going to church. Trade it to you for your Garbage CD."

"What about a tape of it?" I offered and then decided to sweeten the deal. "And a tape of all the Garbage B-sides?"

"Angelfish?"

"Yeah, I'll put Angelfish on there too," I conceded. There weren't enough Garbage B-sides to fill a 60-minute blank tape anyway. One half could be Angelfish, Shirley Manson's first band before Garbage and the other I could fill up with songs like "Subhuman" and "#1 Crush." For months I had been searching the different music stores in town for Garbage maxi-singles but had only found two different versions of the "Vow" single.

"Deal," Michelle reached out and we shook on it. "Enjoy your new dress."

"I will, thank you," A big, bright smile exploded onto my face and I was utterly powerless to stop it.

"When are you gonna wear it?"

"You know, just... around," I said, trying to think of times I could wear it other than those moments when I was home alone, and my parents weren't around.

"At home when you're alone and your parents aren't around?"

"Yeah. That's pretty much it," I sighed, running my hands along the length of my new dress, feeling the smoothness of the fabric and the delicate lace edging. Maybe I could put on my dress and wear it out into the backyard, feel the sun on my legs, and hope none of the neighbors saw me. That was probably about it. When I got dressed up by myself inside I mostly just looked at myself in the mirror, though sometimes I would get brave and try and do something normal like sit and watch TV while wearing pantyhose and a skirt. Mostly I just tried things on and enjoyed the experience of wearing them. The world outside was something else entirely.

"No, we need to get you a good excuse to wear it out."

\* \* \*

After lunch, Courtney had history on the second floor of the main building, followed by sculpture in the art building, then she'd head back to the main building for English, her final class of the day. That meant that I would run into her when I came back from art, but not between her sculpture and English class because my last class of the day was in the Annex. That meant trying to rush over the main building to bump into her, hopefully chat for a second or at least say hi, then head back over the Annex. The only problem was that running back to the main building so I could run into Courtney meant that I didn't have any time to stop at my locker and pick up my biology textbook. But good luck trying to explain that to Mrs. Rolston who was more than happy to give me an hour's detention for coming to class unprepared.

Detention consisted of staying after school to help the custodians for an hour. Usually kids were tasked with some basic, fairly easy, non-disgusting labor such as sweeping floors or dusting classrooms. Mr. Jefferson, the head custodian, had handed me a rake and told me to go out and rake leaves in front of the school. It was late October, so there were barely any leaves on the lawn. Autumn usually didn't get to Georgia until mid-December at the earliest. Sometimes it just got skipped all together.

Luckily, out front, I didn't have any supervision, so at least I didn't have to rake well. Instead I just stood there, moving the rake slightly, watching the bums sleeping at the bus station and the cars going by. From inside the school, I could hear the jazz band and the orchestra in their separate rooms, practicing all at once, a cacophony of mismatched instruments and styles.

Looking inside the windows, I could see the classrooms were empty. Schools are weird ghost towns after hours. Then I could hear the big doors of the main entrance open up. For a second I tried to look busy, but then I realized it wasn't Mr. Jefferson, but just a student with a broom. Then I realized it wasn't just a student. It was a girl. It was Courtney. Courtney, resplendent in baggy jeans and a tight white T-shirt and Docs, her red hair pulled back into a ponytail. Lazily, she was sweeping the steps, doing about as good a job as I was on the leaves. I decided I had to go up and say hi.

"Hey, what are you in for?" I slid up, trying to be as cool and casual as possible.

"Bullshit," she looked up and I think I almost saw her smile. "Get this. Mr. Grady gave me detention for smoking. Yeah right? Did he see me smoke? No. He said I smelled like smoke. That's crap."

"That's total crap."

"Like, if you don't see me smoking, then you can't give me detention. That's in the First Amendment."

"Oh, this school is totally fascist."

"They are literally worse than Hitler."

"Totally," I agreed, though to be fair, being forced to rake leaves for an hour isn't quite as bad as the Holocaust, but I didn't want to be disagreeable. Instead, I just set down my rake and sat on the steps. It was nice when she set her broom down and sat down next to me.

"The world is so much bigger than this stupid school and this bum town," she said, her eyes fixed right ahead. "We could just hop on a bus right now and go… anywhere." My heart sped up at the thought of getting on a bus with Courtney, having an adventure, sharing our time. Our legs were touching. She had sat down so closely that our legs were touching.

"You're right. There is so much we're missing out on."

"Our parents had to pick here. Of all the places in the world you could live. They pick Disgusta, Georgia." She looked over at me and laughed. She had a sad little laugh but her eyes were such light green that they were almost clear.

"We can do better than a bus," I smiled. "We won't be like our parents, stuck here."

"That's what I fear the most in this world," Courtney sighed, her eyes fixed on mine. "Being like my parents. Just the same stupid job day in and day out and nothing to look forward to but the same stupid vacation to the lake every year. Just a crap life. I don't want that, Matt. I don't want a crap life."

Faith DaBrooke

"Me too," I said and gazed into her eyes. "That's what I'm afraid of too." Her skin was so pale, I could see little tiny blue veins under her eyes. Her light pink lips formed into a brief smile. And all I wanted in the world was to live in this moment with her forever.

# Chapter Seven

## "I Know You Called"
## Friday, October 20, 1995

We were supposed to be studying. At least that's what Michelle told her parents. But as far as we were concerned we were supposed to be adding more tin foil to the wall. At least that had been the plan. But since it turned out that Michelle hadn't actually bought any new tinfoil, we were just hanging out in her room being unproductive. On her dresser a pink boombox—now covered in stickers—filled the room with music.

"Hey, it's Michelle, is Jim there?" she was laying back on her bed talking on the phone while I flipped through the titles on her bookshelf. Mostly they were classic novels that didn't interest me though she had a few on dangerously interesting topics like witchcraft. She even had a copy of The Satanic Bible. "Can you tell him I called? I'm looking for stuff. Paper stuff. No plants. Just paper. Okay, thanks."

As dramatically as one possibly can, Michelle sighed as she hung up the phone. It hit the receiver with a heavy clang and a bit of bell sound. Sitting back up, she swung her feet over the edge of the bed and looked over at me.

"Nuttin?" I asked even though I knew the answer. Michelle wanted acid bad and had been making her way through every contact in her little black book.

"This town sucks," she said with a heady dramatic flourish. Collapsing back into the bed, she laid there for a second, mingled amongst dirty clothes, and stared up at the ceiling. Above her a black and white poster of a thoughtful and poetic looking Kurt Cobain stared back at her. She held the phone tightly to her chest. Then she looked up at me. "Wanna see if we can get on the radio?"

"Cool," I said. After returning a *Sandman* comic back to her shelf, I went over and turned the radio up. When not playing a CD or a tape we always had the local alternative station Channel Z on. Maybe we would switch to the hard rock station if there were commercials, but otherwise Channel Z was the one to listen to. "Gimme the phone."

Thanks to my many attempts to be the 95th caller—who would win concert tickets, T-shirts, or early release CDs—I had the station phone number memorized. Sadly though, I had never won anything. Even after waiting all night for the announcement and then hitting redial over and over and over again.

"No," Michelle protested as she sat up and swung her legs over the edge of the bed. "Not yet. What are we even gonna ask them to play?"

"I dunno," I unhelpfully offered.

"Wait, watch this," Michelle smiled like a striking snake. She dialed the number—which she must have had memorized—and put the receiver up to her ear. After a second her eyes lit up. "Hi, Channel Z?"

"Are you on the air?" I excitedly whispered. There was a 10-second delay if you got on the air. Most of the time when you called the DJ would answer during a song. Michelle shook her head to signal that it was just the DJ.

"Hi," Michelle piped up. "My name is Barbara Bernstein. My friends and I were hoping you could play that Hole song. You know the one. The one about dinosaurs." Michelle almost lost it but a quick suck in of breath enabled her to hold in the laughter. Barbara Bernstein was our school principal. As far as I knew there was no Hole song about dinosaurs. Although to be fair I wasn't too familiar with their first album. No one had their first album.

"No, it's definitely a real song," Michelle continued. "It starts out with that guitar bit where it's like 'der der der' really hard. Then Courtney Love comes on and she's singing. You don't know that one?" Then she quickly mumbled a thank you, slammed down the receiving, and busted out laughing. I was also doubled over on the floor, my face turning red. This was a class.

"My turn," I said. She handed me the phone and I dialed in. "Hey, Channel Z. You're the best. I was hoping you would play a song for me and my friends! Yeah. It's off the *Jurassic Park* soundtrack. It's called T Rex Rocks. It's by Hole. No it's 100% real. It just came out. It's the German only version of the soundtrack. It's big in Germany." After a second I hung up the phone.

"We gotta wait a while," Michelle advised. "Otherwise they'll get annoyed."

"Who should we call next?" I asked.

"Hmmm," Michelle said as her eyes narrowed to a slit. It was something she always did when deep in thought. And she was often deep in thought. It was sort of her thing. Michelle gave off the impression that she was about to say something profound. Maybe that's why everyone listened to her.

"We could call the bowling alley and ask if they have 10-pound balls," I suggested.

"Okay, that's lame," Michelle replied. "That's like a fourth grader's prank call."

"Let's call Courtney," I suggested. "See what she's up to. I think she's grounded."

"She's always grounded," Michelle said absent-mindedly. Then something clicked for her and she looked up at me with laser bore eyes. Her mouth went into a wide, open smile. It was evil like all Michelle's smiles. She rubbed her hands together. "You like Courtney. You totally do. Oh my God, you're turning bright red." It was true. All of it was true. Of course I liked Courtney and I could feel my ears getting hot with embarrassment.

"I don't know," I looked down.

"Dude," Michelle said. "That's cool. Matt and Courtney. Courtney Wilkerson. Courtney Bailey. Maybe. You guys would maybe be cute. She's dating Jordan though, Matt."

"Jordan," I spat out. I couldn't compete with Jordan. He was older, probably old enough to buy alcohol. Plus he had a motorcycle while I didn't even have my license yet. Who would Courtney rather hang out with? Guy on a motorcycle who can drive her around? Or me being dropped off by my mom?

"Well," Michelle said as she plopped down to the floor. "I don't really like Jordan either. I don't think anyone but Courtney does. Her parents sure as hell don't."

"She's just so," I searched my mind for the words to describe how wonderful she was. Vast volumes of poetry could only begin to describe all the praises I wanted to heap upon her. "...perfect. She's just so perfect in every way."

"Call her," Michelle said matter-of-factly. "I'll go get the directory."

With that Michelle popped up and ran downstairs, her Doc Martens pounding on the creaking old hardwood floors of her family's 19th Century house. Setting down the phone, I stood up and went over to Michelle's tall dresser where there was a mirror.

Looking at myself all I could see was a skinny, scraggly haired boy who lacked any of the manly cool that someone like Jordan. With my wispy blonde beard starting to come in and my slightly crooked nose and heavy eyebrows that were threatening to grow into a unibrow, I would never look delicate and pretty like Courtney either. My dad believed that when we were tempted it was because demons were literally swimming ethereally around us, putting ideas into our heads. Sometimes our guardian angels could fight them off using the power of Christ. But if we weren't being godly enough the angels would be underpowered and the demons would win. They would continue putting ideas in our heads, driving us to sin. I wondered why, of all the demons out there, I had been picked by the demon that made me want to be a girl.

I should have prayed to God. I should have banished the demons by thinking the words 'in the name of Jesus Christ, my lord and savior, I command you to depart from me.' I should have asked God for forgiveness for allowing myself to be tempted. I should have been reading the Bible and praying so I could power up my angels.

Instead, I thought about how wonderful it would be to be Courtney, to look like her, to have her body, to see that face in the mirror, to feel my long hair on my slender shoulders, to wear a skirt on a hot and muggy summer day. I imagined my angels withering away to nothing and fleeing back to heaven as horribly disfigured demons reached right into my brain and twisted my thoughts to sin and sexual perversion.

Michelle had her make-up scattered all over the top of her dresser. It sat in an almost invisibly fine layer of pale beige powder. There were compacts, black-stained tubes of mascara, eyeliner pencils and their ragged shavings, and a couple bottles of half-empty nail polish. But it was the lipstick that caught my eye.

Grabbing it, I looked at the bottom where a plum red sticker declared its name as Vamp. Unscrewing it, I rotated it up and carefully applied a bit to my lips. Looking in the mirror, I saw a boy with lipstick on. It was way too dark for me anyway and wouldn't have looked good without some eyeliner to match.

"Nice lipstick," Michelle said casually as she tossed the school directory to me. It fluttered over and landed at my feet like a wounded bird. She went over and plopped herself back on the bed. Picking up the directory, I started flipping through it. It had the numbers of all the students in school. Courtney was a Wilkerson so I made my way to the back of the book and found her. Michelle handed me the phone and my stomach went cold.

"What should I say?" I asked nervously.

"I don't know, Romeo," Michelle answered. With shaking fingers, I dialed six numbers of her phone number and paused before the seventh. I looked up at Michelle like someone who was about to climb the gallows. She just stuck her tongue out at me, reached over, and hit the last number. It started to ring. Then it rang again. Then someone answered.

"Hello," came the greeting from an older sounding man with a slow as sawmill gravy Southern accent.

"Is Courtney there?" I asked.

"Who's calling?" He sighed as he said it.

"It's Matt. She knows me from school," I sputtered out, fumbling over each word. "It's about a World History project we're working on. Pyramids." On the other end of the line I heard him shout her name. Then there was a click.

"Hey, Matt," Courtney said in a slightly sleepy voice. I wondered if she were stoned. Either way her tone indicated that my call was not an unwelcome one. "What's up?"

"Me and Michelle are hanging out," I said in what I hoped was a cool rock star voice. "Thought we'd see what you were up to."

"Watching *X-Files*," she said. "It's cool though. It's like a re-run. It's the one where, like, the cave robot finds the alien-like viruses in a volcano."

"Sure," I said. I had no idea what she was talking about. I was not an avid *X-Files* viewer. Also that sentence made zero sense. "You wanna come meet us up at Daniel Village?" It was a strip mall within walking distance of all our houses. There wasn't much of anything to do there other than shop for groceries. But at least it was hanging out.

Suddenly, Michelle snapped the phone receiver out of my hand. "Hey, Courtney," she said. "Me and Matt gotta get more tinfoil. You can come over and help us decorate my room."

"Sounds cool," Courtney said. "But I'm grounded." The way she said it made it sound like a question.

"Okay," Michelle said. "See you in school. Also Matt totally thinks you're…" Before she could finish I wrestled the receiver from her hand and slammed it down hard.

"What the hell, Michelle!" I yelled. She laughed a little bit.

"Oh come on," she said with sly intention. "That's what you wanted anyway. You want to tell her about your crush so she'll break up with Jordan and run into your arms."

"Yes," I said, my voice heavy with exasperation. "But still. Don't just tell people that other people like them. That's not cool." Michelle rolled her eyes and started dialing.

"Are you calling Courtney?" I asked, my voice going high pitched in frustration. She replied only with a knowing look and did a good job fending off my attempts to grab the phone back.

"Hello?" she said when the other side answered. "Channel Z? My friend has a crush on a girl and is hoping you could play something special to melt her heart. Yeah. It's that Hole song about dinosaurs." This time she utterly failed to keep her laughter contained.

"You suck," I said, still sulking. I came up on the bed and plopped down next to her, my body language hopefully displaying every ounce of abject dejection I felt. She just kept laughing. Then she slowly caught her breath and looked up at me with a glare that told me to calm down, that her blabbing to Courtney was not a soul-destroying betrayal but rather a funny joke. I was not buying it. Then she quieted down and seemed to go into deep thought mode.

"Halloween is but a week away, my dear Matthew," Michelle finally said after apparently stewing it over in her brain for a while. Clearly she had something in mind. "My dear, Candy."

"Yeah," I asked disinterestedly.

"Our mutual friend Lindsay is having a party next Saturday in celebration of this most macabre holiday. And we have to prepare our costumes."

"Costumes?" I scoffed. "What are we five? That's lame." Everyone knew that Halloween was best celebrated by waiting 'til the last minute then ironically making up a costume from whatever was nearby at hand.

"It's not lame," Michelle corrected me. "It's awesome. I'll be the pop art genius Andy Warhol and you shall be my muse Candy Darling."

"Okay," I agreed, probably too readily. But it was Michelle. My head swam—drowned more like it—in images of shopping for dresses, for a beautiful blonde wig, of shaving legs, of being a real girl or failing to look as much like one as I could.

"It's Halloween," Michelle pointed out. "No one'll care."

"I already said 'okay.'"

"Candy, my muse." Michelle's usual, thoughtful but extravagantly mischievous smile appeared on her face. The song on the radio faded and the DJ came on.

"To all you ya-hoos out there! There's no such thing as a Hole song about dinosaurs. So stop requesting it. And to shut ya up, here's an actual Hole song for ya. This is Hole's 'Doll Parts.'"

* * *

Although my dad retired from the army, his internal clock hadn't. Every Saturday morning, he would be up at 6:00 a.m. or earlier. As far as he was concerned, it was a virtue. That meant that anyone who wanted to sleep in on their day off was slothful and probably a degenerate. It didn't matter that I had only gone to bed at 2:00 a.m.

A crack followed by a jet engine roar woke me up. Groggily I looked up and saw my dad had shoved my door open and was busily vacuuming my carpet. This was entirely intentional and it certainly wasn't about cleaning floors. No, this was his favorite way to drag me out of bed. His other method—no doubt an army favorite—was to come in singing the revelry trumpet song at the top of his lungs. Then he would unceremoniously tilt my mattress over until I fell out into a heap of sheets, pillows, and angry befuddlement.

"What in the ever-loving fuck are you doing?" is what I wanted to say. Instead I mumbled out a few sluggish words of tired protest.

"While you've been lying in bed all morning," he reported in his usual holier-than-thou baritone. "I've been up since 6:00 a.m. getting many things accomplished. Now get up and get dressed. We have an important church function." They were all important church functions. Wednesday night Bible study, Monday night prayer group, vacation Bible school. They were all important to him and that meant I had to be there.

Today was Saturday morning evangelism. And of course it started early. I had no choice. I never did. But as I threw on some jeans and a T-shirt, I vowed then and there to grow up and start my own church where nothing was ever scheduled earlier than noon.

Ten minutes later I was sitting in the passenger seat of our minivan sipping a can of generic store brand cola and listening to Christian talk radio while my dad droned on. The general theme was how, as a follower of Christ, I was supposed to live my life in a way that presented an example of God's love to the heathen unbelievers. That meant neat hair, good posture, patriotism, no band T-shirts, putting the cap back on the toothpaste when I was done with it, and respecting my elders even when I disagreed with them on matters of theology.

Forty minutes after that I was standing outside Augusta's only Planned Parenthood with 15 or so other people from church. None of them were kids from youth group. One of them was the assistant pastor. In his mid-30s, he was wearing pleated jeans with a bright purple church T-shirt tucked into them. He gave us a good Christian smile and herded us all over to one area of the wide sidewalk away from the building entrance.

The only real concession Georgia had made to autumn was to let a cool, damp breeze blow in from off the river. Otherwise it was a sunny and pleasant morning downtown. The Planned Parenthood was located on a mostly empty area of Broad Street. Actually the entire downtown was mostly empty but this area felt somehow emptier than normal. It was in a three story brick office building that looked nearly identical to the ones on either side.

"Remember," the assistant pastor started up his speech. "We aren't here to harass anyone. We're not here to yell at anyone or judge anyone. The women who come here to this place think they need an abortion but what they really need is God's love. We're gonna pray for them and that's it. Each person you see just offers a silent prayer to God. Ask Him to bring His healing power to their lives, to change their hearts, to let Christ into their lives. But first, there is a strong demonic presence that surrounds this building. The Adversary has this place in his grip. Before we start, let us all lay hands on this building and pray to banish the darkness here."

With that we all walked up to the building. Each of us put the palm of our right hand on the brick. Looking over at my dad I could see the earnestness with which he did this. His eyes were clenched tightly closed. His mouth moved slightly as he silently prayed. A few others had already started their own silent prayers when the assistant preacher started praying out loud for everyone.

Instead of praying, I simply held my hand against the rough brick wall and waited for it to be over. I believed in God. I really did. I believed that Jesus came to earth and died for our sins. I believed that he rose on the third day and will come back in glory to judge the world for its sin. But being a Christian—being my dad's type of Christian—seemed way too hard. Of course I knew the stock answer to that. If it all seemed too hard, you were supposed to pray and think about how hard it was for Christ to bear the cross up to Golgotha. But this wasn't how I wanted to live my life.

\* \* \*

Later in the car ride home I sat silently sipping from my big foam cup of sweet tea. Stopping for lunch out was the best part—really the only good part—of Saturday morning mission work. Usually that meant going to my dad's favorite barbecue joint or all you can eat Chinese food buffet.

"Dad," I asked. "You have to accept Jesus to go to heaven. But what about people in China who never even hear about Christ. Right?"

"That's right. That's why it's so important for Christians to evangelize. To bring the gospel to everyone in every part of the world," he explained, parroting what we were taught in church. That never seemed right to me.

"But let's say you're a good person. But all you ever knew was Hinduism. But you still did your best to be a moral and upright person, and to help other people. Wouldn't Jesus be able to look into that person's heart and know they did their best? Doesn't he say 'No one will come to the Father except through me?' So that sounds like it's ultimately up to Him right? Like Jesus is the only one…"

"No," my dad said way too forcefully. "That exactly *is* the type of thinking that the Bible warns against. Christ doesn't want lukewarm, wishy-washy Christians. Christ says in Revelation that if you're a lukewarm Christian He will spit you out of his mouth. You're worthless to him. No person in my house is going to be worthless to Christ."

"That's not what I was saying…" I tried to interject. It was too late. He had started a rant and was going to finish.

"The problem with America right now is that it's full of nothing but lukewarm, wishy-washy Christians who want nothing more than a feel-good gospel. They don't want to hear about judgment or hell. They think

73

Christ was nothing more than a lovey-dovey hippy. They think it's okay to allow abortions, the murder of millions of babies. They think it's okay to teach witchcraft and Satanism in schools that I pay for with my tax dollars. Meanwhile kids are getting expelled for even bringing a Bible to school. They think it's okay to let faggots run around spreading AIDS. They think they're being compassionate but they are dooming all these souls straight to hell. That's what your wishy-washy Christianity leads to. So no, Matt. My house is not going to be compassionate. Maybe that's not PC. But no one in my house will be a lukewarm Christian. We will be God-fearing warriors for Christ. And when I stand before Christ on the Day of Judgment, I will be able to say that I raised up my son according to the Bible, that my son is not a wishy washy Christian, or deceived by Satan, or a faggot."

My blood ran cold. I was gay, or at least sort of gay. I would have to keep that secret. I could never tell him how I felt. While I could imagine a beating, military school, or being kicked out of the family, I had no idea how he would react if he knew I liked dresses and spent my days wishing I were a girl. No matter his reaction, I was certain it wouldn't be good.

* * *

The mirror was starting to steam up, so I adjusted the shower a little. After a second it started running colder. Taking a towel, I wiped away the steam and looked at myself. In Michelle's dress—my dress—I still looked like a boy but I could imagine how I would look as a girl. I smiled sadly then quickly took it off. Folding it up, I quickly tucked it into a draw under some washcloths and went back to the shower. I turned up the heat again, waited for it to get right, and hopped in.

After my shower, I wrapped my dirty T-shirt around the dress and bundled all my clothes up together. Holding them tightly to my chest, I ran into my room and closed the door behind me. Not wanting to ruin my dad's perfect Judgment Day, I needed to make completely certain that no one in my family ever found this dress.

There were a few options but the whole thing was rendered much trickier by the fact that my parents liked to periodically "clean" my room. Like my dad's early morning vacuuming that had nothing to do with cleaning. Instead, it was an excuse to root through all my stuff to look for contraband or anything else that they could yell at me for. A flowery dress definitely fell into the latter category.

My first thought had been to hide it in Ellen's closet. If they found it in there, they would simply assume it was hers and pay it no mind. But if Ellen came home unexpectedly, the surprise new dress in her closet might raise some unwanted questions. Another option was to stick it in a bag and hide in the crawlspace under the house. But then again my dad might find it while he was doing whatever it was that he did with the sump pump. Plus I didn't want to risk getting my only dress moldy. The vent in my closet was out because my dad might try and change the filters one day. I had also considered sealing it in a freezer bag and duct taping it up to the inside of the chimney. That seemed far too risky, though.

So instead I went over to my desk. It was a tilting art desk that my parents had gotten me during junior high. The idea was to encourage my art. While I did draw, I almost never used the desk. It was modular and made of bright red metal tubes. Each was capped by a small piece of plastic. First I rolled the dress up tightly, hoping that it wouldn't get too wrinkled. Getting down on the floor, I lifted up one leg of the desk. With my spare hand, I pulled off the bottom cap and shoved the dress up inside the thin metal tube. Then the plastic cap went back on and I set the desk back into place.

For a second I thought about my immortal soul. Was I risking an eternity of endless suffering in hell? Sure, I had gotten saved in kindergarten. And while some preachers said 'once saved always saved,' others said that backsliders would end up in hell. Plus there was the one unforgivable sin: blaspheming the Holy Spirit. I was pretty sure I wasn't doing that but I was definitely sinning. And what's more, I wasn't repenting. I wasn't even interested in repenting. I wanted to sin more.

But what really worried me, more than bullying, more than my parents finding out, more than God or hell, was that I didn't care about any of it. All I had ever wanted was to be a girl. That could never happen. Magic wasn't real. Everyone told me miracles were real but I've never seen a single actual miracle. But wearing that dress I felt just a little bit, only a little bit, like a girl. I needed that. I really needed that. And no bully, or threat of military school, or eternity in a lake of fire was going to stop me needing that.

# Chapter Eight

### "I'm Invented Too"
### Saturday, October 28, 1995

While there seemed to be miles of dresses, most of them were no good whatsoever. Everything was too small or too large. The few that were my size were anything but pretty. There were ugly brown dresses that looked like something my mom would wear to church. There were also big poofy-sleeved 80s dresses, or ones with hideous patterns. Looking up, I could see Michelle six racks over looking through the men's suits. There were a couple things in her hands but she didn't seem to be having any better luck. Giving up my search, I walked over to her.

"Salvation Army clothes always make me want to wash my hands," I said. She was trying on a black blazer that was clearly too large for her.

"I think with jeans and a turtleneck…" she pondered. "Then I just need a blonde wig.

"Maybe I should just go as a can of soup?" I dejectedly offered. Uncomfortable thoughts swirled around in my head. While it was unlikely for Courtney to show up to Lindsay's party, it was still a possibility. And as much as I wanted to be Candy Darling for Halloween, I also didn't want Courtney to see me in a dress.

"Dude, c'mon," Michelle said with a touch of condescension. "One. It's Halloween. No one cares. And two. David Bowie switched back and forth on genders all the time. And who's cooler than David Bowie? No one. Not now. Not ever." Hanging my head a little, I had to admit that her logic was unassailable. David Bowie was, without a doubt, the coolest person of all time. And he did wear make-up and dresses. Then he married a model. "Trust me, girls will still want to mack on you even if you're all done up as Candy Darling."

"Courtney?" I asked, slightly flabbergasted.

"Oh yeah," Michelle said as though it were the least important thing in the universe. "Courtney. Courtney Wilkerson." Without a bit of a shrug and forced absentmindedness, she went back to browsing.

"What?"

"I'm just saying," she said as she put back a far too large but well faded Styx T-shirt. "Let's go look at all the rest of the dresses."

"What are you saying?" I asked as I followed her over. Though I had only known her for a couple months, I already knew that this was classic Michelle. Knowing something or figuring something out made her button up tightly. Personally I think she liked the power. Or maybe I was reading too much into it. That was classic me.

"I'm just saying," she said thoughtfully as she flipped through the rack of donated dresses. "Do you really know Courtney? I mean really know-know her? Other than cute punky girl with the big green doe eyes?"

"Okay, not much," I admitted, grabbing a lovely red satin dress off the rack and folding it over my left arm. It was a medium which would probably fit me. "I mean I know she's dating that asshole, and that she likes raves, and punk music too, and drugs of various types."

"I'll give you half credit for that, Matt," Michelle said with a bit of an eye roll. She held up a leopard print dress which prompted me to make a little bit of a disgusted face and shake my head. "Just maybe get to know her a little better before you fall head over heels for her."

"Yeah, 'cause that's how attraction works," I snapped sarcastically. Pulling another dress off the rack—a tight light blue one—I draped it over the other. These were the ones worthy of the fitting room.

"Get to know her a little better," Michelle replied as she pulled another off the rack and held it up. It was black and A-line. I shrugged and added to my growing pile.

"That's what I want to do," I defended myself. "I'm gonna go try these on."

"Okay," Michelle said. "I'm gonna check out the records."

"Fine," I said, stewing as she walked off to the other side of the store where the media and housewares were displayed on jumbled, chaotic shelves.

As I went into the fitting room, I overheard one of my fellow thrift shop patrons—one who had watched me go into the fitting room with a bunch of dresses—mutter under his breath. "Must be another one of them city fags," he spat out not quite under his breath. Maybe it was for my benefit.

Taking off my clothes behind the safety of a flimsy curtain, I tried not to think about all the ways that actually crossdressing out in the world could go. The red dress was first. I pulled it over my head and then struggled to zip it up. Once I had it on, I looked in a flimsy, dirty mirror. It fit wonderfully and I couldn't help but smile. I imagined how it would look with heels, a blonde wig, and some make-up. It would be perfect. I would be perfect. Maybe I was a city fag after all.

\* \* \*

Growing up, we never celebrated Easter with anything other than church. When friends at school mentioned Easter baskets full of candy and presents or the fun of Easter egg hunts, all I could do was shrug. My dad considered the eggs, rabbits, and chocolate as pagan in origin and thus Satanic. In his worldview, Satan was trying to secularize Christian holidays by muddying them with pagan imagery. Thus chocolate rabbits—innocent though they may seem—were Satanic.

In fact, anything that wasn't explicitly Evangelical was Satanic. The children's cartoon *The Smurfs* apparently featured authentic spells and witchcraft and was thus a nefarious and diabolical instrument to lure children into Satanism. It was the same with *Bewitched* and most of Disney's animated canon.

When I was six, and Dad was on one of his holy kicks, he decided that our family would not engage in the satanic secularization of Christmas. That meant no tree, no carols, and no presents. My mom, no doubt anticipating a revolt, put her foot down on that one.

But when it came to holidays, there was one that was steeped in the vilest and depraved Satanism: Halloween. That meant no pumpkins, no black cats, nothing going bump in the night, and especially no trick-or-treating. Some years there would be a church 'harvest festival' so the kids could get some candy. But the only costumes allowed were Biblical characters. That meant throwing together robes from towels and sheets so you could be David, Moses, Mahalaleel, or Eliphaz. So Lindsay's party was to be, in fact, my first time actually celebrating the holiday of Halloween.

As Michelle's mom drove us to the party, I sat alone in the back seat and thought about how much I had backslid. Preachers were always warning about the dangers of being a backslider. It had been a frequent topic at American Christian's weekly chapel services. I was absolutely a backslider. Listening to rock music? Smoking cigarettes? Drinking beers? Crossdressing on my way to a Halloween party? I was definitely a backslider.

But none of it felt wrong. I mean, sure there was the guilt. There was always guilt. Church and school and my parents made sure of that. But beyond the guilt, none of it felt wrong. Sure my music had swear words in it. But who did that really hurt? And sure I was wearing a beautiful, satiny dress, and a blonde wig, and Michelle's mom's heels (this time with permission), and make-up. But did that hurt anyone?

My parents would be angry and disappointed if they knew. But Michelle's mom wasn't. In fact, she thought I looked amazing and even insisted on taking a few photos of Michelle and me. So if she wasn't upset, then maybe it was really just on my parents. Maybe they were choosing to get upset and no one was really hurt.

* * *

Nine Inch Nails was blasting from a boombox, orange and black streamers hung down from the ceiling, and a slasher movie was playing on the TV. Dressed in vampire black, Lindsay tried to greet us at the door but fumbled over her words. Then she took out her plastic fang teeth and held them in her hand, letting saliva drip, as she gushed over our costumes.

"Y'all look great!" she exclaimed as she led us into the living room. "Matt, I didn't even recognize you! I thought you were a girl." Hearing that felt good. Looking around the room I saw a few people from school sitting on the couch or chairs, nibbling chips and drinking red cups full of soda. My nervousness faded down another notch when I caught myself in a mirror. My make-up was messy, my wig was shiny plastic, but I felt pretty. And I was actually wearing a dress and heels and make-up to a party.

"I'm gonna go look around," Michelle said distractedly. "For stuff." Rumors had it that Mary's brother Tall Preston's friends from Richmond were coming. Michelle assumed that anyone who went to Richmond would probably have drugs of some sort. She wandered off to find them.

"Matt," Lindsay said with a wide, giggly smile. "Did Michelle do your make-up?"

"Yeah," I replied, a little annoyed with Michelle for leaving me alone and vulnerable. Then I saw Mary come up. Small, thin, and naturally blonde, Mary didn't appear to be wearing a costume. Though it was possible that it was simply too subtle a costume for me to get.

"Ooohh," Mary gushed when she saw me. "Matt, you look fantastic. Just like your photo!" I suddenly found myself dragged along and sat down on a couch in the den. Through the back windows I could see Michelle out on the deck, talking with Tall Preston and an equally tall guy with long dyed black hair who looked to be wearing a Jim Morrison costume.

"I think I'm gonna go get a coke," I said.

"I'll get you one," Lindsay said as she popped up and headed off to the kitchen. Looking over to my right, I saw Mary sitting there on the couch staring at me with big cartoon eyes. I smiled back nervously, crossed my legs, put my hands in my lap, and did my best to look small and inconspicuous. It didn't seem to be working.

"So you're like Michelle's muse, huh?" Mary asked. "That's like a good place to be in, right? I don't actually have a muse, I mean, other than the world. I really like plants, like, you know." Mary had won pretty much all the art awards at school. Not only did she take all the most advanced art classes, the art teachers had pretty much excused her to do her own thing in those classes so that she could work on her portfolio for getting into college. Her own thing was extreme close up photos of plant structures. They were so close up in fact that they were almost geometric and abstract. I had no doubt that she would be getting into the art school of her choice.

"I guess," I replied half-heartedly. A part of me was beginning to regret coming to a costume party dressed as Candy Darling. I was neither as brave nor as beautiful as the tragic Ms. Darling. My skin crawled as it hit me that I was actually out with no clothes to change into. I didn't even have regular boy's underwear. What if there was underage drinking and the cops raided the party like in movies? My parents would find out that their only son was out crossdressing. I swallowed hard.

"It's hard to draw people," Mary said. "At least I have trouble. I think most people who can draw are either really good at drawing people or really good at drawing buildings and structures. I think I'm one of those structure people. In elementary school, when all the girls in my class were going through this horse phase, I couldn't draw horses to save my life."

"Yeah," I said as Lindsay handed me a plastic red cup and plopped down on my left side. "Me neither."

"I thought you could do people," Mary corrected me. "Because you always draw comic books."

"Yeah," I said. "I meant horses. I can't draw horses."

"Matt," Lindsay interrupted. "Where'd you get your dress?"

"Salvation Army," I answered, my mind occupied by an elaborate nightmare where my parents had to pick Candy Darling me up from the Sheriff's Department. I imagined it would be an awkward trip home, assuming they deigned to pick me up in the first place.

"I have like, this really pretty yellow floral baby doll that I think would look good on you," Lindsay offered. "I mean with your regular hair color and not a blonde wig."

"I'm not sure the blonde works for you," Mary interjected. "I mean, I get it's a costume and you're going as Marilyn Monroe, but you would look better natural."

"I'm not Marilyn Monroe," I replied. Then I saw what she was saying in the mirror and my heart leaped up into my throat, my palms went sweaty and my mouth went dry.

\* \* \*

"Courtney's here," I said to Michelle with the urgency one usually reserves for nuclear attack warnings. I had seen her come in with Jordan. His arms were wrapped tightly around her. Instead of a costume he was dressed as his regular self, but Courtney had at least drawn eyeliner whiskers on her face. Before they could see me, I had ducked away from the foyer and run as fast as my heels could carry me, through the living room and den, over to the back porch where I found Michelle. She was talking to a tall lanky guy with long dyed black hair and a safety pin and patched covered leather jacket. "I need you to change clothes with me."

"What?" Michelle asked with an expression that perfectly conveyed that she thought I was completely crazy.

"Change clothes with me," I repeated, more of a demand than a request. Then I added a bit of whining to it. "Please? C'mon. I can't let

Courtney see me like this." Michelle rolled her eyes so hard I thought they might fall out.

"Ms. Darling," she said snarkily. "It's Halloween. No one gives a crap. It's a costume." Instead of responding, I simply scrunched up my face and telepathically sent her an even more frenzied demand to change clothes with me. Sighing, Michelle turned to the guy she was talking to and offered a brief apology which included the words "my crazy friend."

Grabbing me by the bare arm, she dragged me over to the bathroom, shoved me inside, and slammed the door behind us. Then she locked it and looked up at me like I was the most contemptible child in special school for especially contemptible children.

"Oh my God, Matt," she exclaimed. "What the hell is wrong with you? For weeks we've been planning this. At no point did it occur to you that your crush would be here? Like when we were shopping, or trying out wigs, or when you were shaving your legs, or doing your damn make-up? Did it not occur to you?"

"Yes, but..."

"Then you should have picked a different costume!"

"Just do me this one favor," I begged.

"Dude," Michelle said. "I can't even remember the last time I wore a dress. You wear dresses way more often than I do."

"Please, Michelle," I pleaded like a child. "I made a mistake, okay?" Instead of saying something, Michelle glowered at me and shook her head slowly. With a sigh, she pulled off her coat and started unbuttoning her shirt.

"Thank you, thank you, thank you!" I beamed as I pulled off my wig and set it on the counter next to what was presumably Lindsay's toothbrush. Reaching around, I started undoing the zipper. "I totally owe you."

"Yeah," Michelle said. "You do. This dude Aaron from Richmond was chatting me up. And he's actually a dealer. You think he's gonna like me if I'm wearing a bright girly-girly red dress?" Stripped down to my bra and panties, I looked at her quizzically. She shook her head again in disbelief, took off her shirt and handed it to me. Once her pants were off, she started putting on the dress. After zipping her up, I quickly washed my face as best I could. Thankfully Lindsay had make-up remover on hand, though I was going to have to apologize later for getting mascara all over one of her towels.

"Thank you," I said again as I looked at us in the mirror. The suit was too small for me but it worked. Michelle was swimming in the red dress and looked miserable.

"My shoes'll never fit you," Michelle said.

"I'll go barefoot and tell people I'm Paul McCartney," I suggested with a shrug.

"Yeah," Michelle said sarcastically. "And I'll tell people I'm going as a cowardly transvestite."

\* \* \*

"Hey Courtney," I said as I slid up to her. She was by herself out on the patio leaning against the railing. A cigarette dangled from her hand. It was a slightly chilly night there under the yellow floodlights. Conversation floated all around us from the various groups of smokers. Beyond the deck there was only lawn, pine trees, and the sound of distant cars off beyond the darkness. Michelle's pants were cutting into my skin like razor wire. Still, I felt good as I smiled and lit a cigarette. Courtney was here. I was in boy mode.

"Hey," she said dreamily as though speaking through a bit of a chemical fog.

"I like your costume," I said, my voice full of hope.

"Thanks, man," she said slowly. "Are you wearing a costume? I can't tell."

"What the fuck, dude?" came a brash voice form behind me. I felt a meaty hand on my shoulder. Suddenly, I was whipped around and shoved across the deck. My feet caught on a wooden deckchair and I fell back hard. My cigarette bounced across the deck. Looking up, I saw Jordan standing over me.

"What the fuck, Jordan," Courtney yelled as she punched Jordan on the shoulder. He turned to her and yelled for her to shut up. Then he turned me as I clumsily found my way back up.

"Don't fucking talk to her, you little shit," Jordan ordered, with fire in his eyes. I realized I was trembling. Was he going to fight me? Did I have to fight? I didn't want to fight Jordan. Not only was he bigger than me, I had no doubt that he was more violent than me and fought dirty. I stared with my mouth open.

"Jordan!" Courtney yelled. At this point all eyes were on the three of us. More people had come out onto the deck, including Lindsay's parents.

"We're leaving," Jordan announced angrily. He grabbed Courtney and practically dragged her out past everyone. Not knowing what else to do, I stood there with my mouth agape and waited for the shaking to subside.

"You okay, Matt?" I heard someone finally say. It was Tall Preston. He patted me on the back and handed me a can of beer. Next to him, Michelle and the Richmond guy stood there looking concerned.

"Yeah," I mumbled. "Thanks for the beer."

* * *

Over time, the deck cleared out a bit. I thought about going back in, but was kind of enjoying sitting by myself. Tall Preston had gifted me a six pack of beer, which he said Jordan had brought. He figured I deserved to have it. Though I had serious doubts about my ability to consume that many, I happily took the pack and found myself a spot on a deck chair. All I wanted to do was stew in my thoughts. Courtney seemed forever out of reach. But I tried to remind myself that Hillary had too. Maybe my loneliness was punishment from God for crossdressing and for jerking off to my sister's fashion magazines and clothing catalogues.

Looking up, I saw Emma Krasinki walking over to me. One grade below me, Emma played violin and took all the AP classes and the most advanced math and science courses too. With her curly brown hair and glasses, she had always reminded me a bit of Kennedy the MTV VJ or maybe Lisa Loeb. We had debate together. I had always thought that while she was pretty cute, she was also sort of boring and nerdy. And she wasn't wearing a costume.

"You okay, Matt?" she asked. It was a question that I was starting to get sick off. Then she sat down next to me. "I heard you got in a fight with Courtney Wilkerson's boyfriend."

"Sort of," I said. "It wasn't really a fight. Not much of one."

"Isn't he, like, 30?" she laughed.

"I think he is," I laughed too. "The hair on his temples is greying." Finishing my beer, I set the can down on the deck. Grabbing the six pack by the plastic rings, I pulled myself another can off and offered one to Emma.

84

"Thanks," she said as she popped it open and took a sip.

"Out drinking on a Saturday night. I always thought you were a bit of a goodie two shoes," I said and regretted it. I was two drinks in and my tongue had gotten itself quite loose.

"I am," she sighed. "I mean, not all the time. I'm not like ballerina bad, but I can drink a beer at a party. I'm more like goody one shoe." The ballerinas were the crazy ones at Davidson. Apparently they were known to sip off water bottles full of vodka during school. Most of them smoked cigarettes and pot. I had even heard that some did cocaine on the weekends.

"I try to be good," I sighed thinking about all the times I prayed earnestly for forgiveness and really meant it when I said I would repent. "But I'm starting to think that all those people who tell me to be moral and upright are full of crap."

"Well, Matt," she said. "Don't be that guy level of bad. At least be more moral and upstanding than him, than Courtney Wilkerson's boyfriend."

"Jordan," I spat out, loading those two syllables with as much disgust as I could.

"Seriously," Emma asked. "Why is a 30-year-old hanging out with a bunch of high school kids? I mean, I get he's dating Courtney Wilkerson. But like, I won't be 30 until the year 2010. That's a long way off."

"Seriously," I agreed. "He needs to get a life."

"I don't even have a life," she lamented. "And I'm cooler than that guy."

"Oh, c'mon," I protested with a bit of a smile. "You're at a party. You're being bad. That's a life right there." Emma smiled back. There was a shine in her eyes. Her smile seemed to convey deep thought. There was an intelligence behind it, a bit of bitterness, a wicked sense of humor. Or maybe I was just a little drunk.

"I guess so," she said as she kept smiling. She reached over and gave me a pat on the arm. "Here we are at a party. Hanging out with friends. Partying. Us and all the bugs around the lights."

"Where are you gonna be when you're 30?"

"Not at a party with a bunch of high schoolers," Emma laughed and took a long sip off her beer. Subtly as I could, I shifted my weight into hers a bit. Our legs were touching, her boot kept bumping into my bare foot. "I don't know. Maybe in Congress. Maybe hiking the Andes. Maybe I'll be playing in the symphony in New York. I don't know."

"I want to be in New York too," I said thoughtfully. "At the premier of my new movie."

"Can I come to the premier?" she asked with a little bit of a wry laugh.

"I mean," I said playing along. "You're gonna be in New York anyway, you know. If you're not busy playing in the symphony. Or if you're free after that. I think my premier is at nine."

"Yeah," she said happily. "I can come. I'll come. Can we get dinner after? I know a place that does good Chinese."

"In New York?" I laughed and turned my body more to face her. Reaching over her, I grabbed the last two beers and handed her one.

"Yeah," she smiled as she cracked open her new beer. "In Chinatown."

"Okay," I agreed. My hand was on her leg. She didn't flinch or do anything. She didn't react in any way. That was good. That was very good. "Fifteen years from today. We'll meet up and get Chinese food. In New York." Her hand was suddenly on top of mine. I could feel it through my whole body.

"It's a date," she said. Then I leaned over and kissed her. And she kissed me back. And our arms danced all over one another. And for a moment Jordan didn't matter. And Courtney didn't matter. And all that mattered was that this was happening and it was real.

# Chapter Nine

## "A Simple Prop"
## Monday, October 30, 1995

Sunday was tricky. Throughout all of church, including both Fired Up and a particularly long sermon about Jesus washing the apostles' feet, all I could think about was Emma Krasinsky. As I dug into my Officers' Club Belgian waffle, I thought about how odd it was that I had spent much of Lindsay's party making out with her. That had come out of nowhere.

"Do you think Emma Kransinsky and me are going together?" I asked Michelle as soon as I could get home and have semi-private access to a telephone.

"I don't know," came Michelle's answer. She was chewing on something and I could hear the TV in the background. "I feel like that's a question that you should be asking Emma Krasinksy."

"I mean, I'll see her sixth period for debate," I said.

"You guys were like going crazy," Michelle said. "When my mom came, I practically had to pry you two apart with a crowbar. So, I think you should find her before school and be like 'hey, Emma Krasinksy, let's go together.' And then stop pining over Courtney, dude."

"Yeah," I agreed. "That's probably what I'll do. I guess that means I have a girlfriend."

"I mean, maybe. If she says yes," Michelle pointed. "I wouldn't have put the two of you together."

"Me neither," I said.

"You like her?"

"I guess," I said. While I had never actually crushed on her, knowing that someone is willing to make out with you can have a surprising influence on your attraction to them. I had never actually had a girlfriend before. I wasn't actually sure what that entailed. Would we hold hands in the hallway? Would I have to hang out with her every weekend? Were flowers involved? What about dancing?

"You're such a hopeful romantic, Matt," Michelle said sarcastically.

"What's up with you and that Richmond guy?" I asked, a little bit of teasing in my voice as though I might burst into a song about arboreal kissing at any moment.

"Aaron," Michelle replied. "I don't know. He seems okay. He wants to hang out sometime, so I gave him my number."

"Wow," I said sarcastically. "It sounds like we are both just head over heels for the new people in our lives." Michelle laughed.

"Ask Emma to go with you," Michelle said. "I gotta go. My dad wants to use the World Wide Web." With that she bid me farewell and hung up. Heading back to my room, I thought about how best to ask her. I would have to go up before class. What was her first class? I had Courtney's schedule memorized but I wasn't sure about Emma's. I would find her by the flagpole first thing. And I would say something about how I had fun, and I thought she was cute, and would she like to go with me. It would be simple.

* * *

None of the times I had rehearsed it in my head were there friends involved. But Monday morning, with 15 minutes to go before class, I saw Emma at the flagpole. She was wearing a dark green sweater and jeans. In her hair she had a couple little plastic hair barrettes like a kid might wear. Instead of being alone like she was supposed to, she was standing in a small group with three other girls whose faces I knew but whose names I didn't.

Cautiously, I approached the group earning myself a few cold and curious looks from whoever Emma's friends were. They were fairly nerdy looking and two of them were carrying heavy black instrument cases. Then I realized they were all orchestra people. I wasn't any type. I took art classes but the art kids never stuck together like the band, drama, or dance kids did.

Emma looked up at me with an expression that I couldn't quite read. Once we had made eye contact, I knew that there could be no backing out. I was going to have to go up and talk to her. With a couple of brief words of apology, she peeled herself off from the group and walked over to me. I smiled weakly.

"Hey, Matt," she said coyly. Her curly chestnut hair hung down in her face and her glasses slightly magnified her already large brown eyes. I still couldn't read her expression. In school, they had spent weeks teaching us the stages of mitosis and meiosis both. We had learned to multiply fractions. We had learned to diagram sentences. We never learned anything useful though, such as how to ask a girl out.

"Hey, Emma," I sputtered out. Now she smiled and brushed some hair out of her eyes. Nervously, she swung her black, hard plastic violin case in a tight, slow arc. For some reason I had always been attracted to girls with glasses. Personally I blame a too early exposure to the Chipettes. Glasses were supposed to make a girl look nerdy but I liked it. I thought it made them look smart. Besides, it was the 90s and nerdy and smart were finally cool. Our rock stars wore cardigans, corduroys, and Buddy Holly glasses. "I had fun Saturday, at Lindsay's party."

"Me too," she beamed. Then for good measure she repeated it absentmindedly. "Me too."

"So, you wanna go together?" I mumbled. Turning my head I started intently at a nearby bush. It was the kind with prickly leaves that would stab you when you walked by it.

"Sure," Emma said casually as though I had asked her if she liked sandwiches.

"Cool," I replied. "So we'll be going together." I had no idea what this involved or what the next steps were. Yeah, I could probably rattle off the causes of the US Civil War, but how going with a girl worked they never bothered to teach us.

"So I guess I'll see you at lunch," Emma said. Now her expression was easy to read. She was into this idea, this new thing of ours. That meant she was into me.

"Cool," I said, and felt myself smile. Apparently we were going to eat lunch together. Would she come to my table or would I go to hers? Honestly I didn't fancy the idea of sitting with the orchestra people. I liked my—really Michelle's—band of merry misfits.

As the first bell rang, another thought entered my mind. Were we supposed to kiss now? Would we hold hands in the hallway? I was going to have to consult an expert on this one.

"I gotta go," she said and gave me a little wave. I gave her one right back and nodded awkwardly.

\* \* \*

"What are you supposed to do when you go with a girl?" I asked Michelle during art class. Instead of actually teaching us technique, the teachers would give us acrylics, watercolors, or charcoal and sit us down in groups of four in front of various still life setups. The fake flowers, colorful glass bottles, and plastic grapes had been trotted out for years and rearranged hundreds of times for students to paint. "I mean like, in school."

"You go together," Michelle said sarcastically, as though she were frustrated by my ignorance. "You just go together. It's not that hard, Matt. You're overthinking it."

"What does that mean though? Going together? Boyfriend-girlfriend? Holding hands between classes? Kissing at school? Making out in the library?" I asked.

"Dude," Maria Rodriguez interjected. A year below us, she did her best to dress like Gwen Stafani despite the limitations of the school dress code. "You have to sort that out with her. You gotta figure that out, like, as a couple."

"Who are you going with?" asked Anthony Marquette, another junior in our group. He liked to add political messages to his artworks, mostly about Malcolm X and Civil Rights. I tended to hide penises and vaginas in my artwork, mostly for the amusement of Michelle.

"Emma Krasinsky," Michelle answered for me. "Sophomore."

"She's cute," Maria said, apparently giving the union her blessing.

"Just be sure and wear protection," Anthony said. It was a popular message and one we got from school, our TV sitcoms, and on MTV too. "Like you learned in health class."

"Got it," I replied sarcastically. This was clearly not helpful. And in that sense, it reminded me of the sex education I did get. All they had taught us about condoms was that they didn't work to stop either pregnancy or AIDs.

\* \* \*

Back at American Christian Academy, sex education was just one section of a Bible class. Yes, along with history, algebra and science, we had Bible class. And six long, awkward weeks of ninth grade were spent learning what the Bible had to say about sex. Actually, it was less what the Bible actually said about sex (which actually included a lot of things like incest, rape, sex slavery and breasts that are like baby deer) and more what our Southern evangelical preachers thought we should believe about sex. In fact, the class was actually taught by a woman who I think had no qualifications other than being married to a Baptist preacher.

It was best, we were told, if we refrained from sex, until marriage. Heck, it would probably be best if we didn't even date. Or think about sex. Or masturbate. Or view secular media that might contain sex. Mrs. Coverdale even had horrific slides of various diseased genitals as helpful illustrations of the dangers of premarital sexual intercourse.

"Imagine," she had said in one Friday afternoon class. "Imagine if someone gave you a beautiful present, all wrapped up with beautiful wrapping paper and bows. And you're so excited to get it! But when you open it, inside you just find a used toaster. Ugh. Who would want that?"

Of course, as someone who had, continuing on with this bride-as-toaster metaphor, never even eaten bread, much less toasted it, I felt I would have been fine with getting a used toaster on my wedding night. I conceded that I would probably end up saving my own virginity until marriage. This was mostly because I just assumed that I'd never lose it anyway, so I might as well at least make it about being a good Christian, instead of about just being a loser who couldn't get girls.

"Your purity is the greatest gift that you can give your future spouse," Mrs. Coverdale continued in her syrupy Southern accent. "That is what God wants for your life. For you to be able to have a pure gift to give your spouse, and not a dirty old toaster." She snorted, amused at her own attempted joke.

Though I'd never been to Mrs. Coverdale's husband's church, it was pretty much like every other one in town; hellfire, brimstone, liberal bashing, followed up with pleas for money and the obligatory altar call at the end. Then after that you could go out to lunch and gossip about who wore what best or was sinning a little more than usual.

Needless to say, our sex education class didn't have anything to say on the subject of whether or not it's okay for a guy who's attracted to women to also want to wear their clothes. Seriously, it didn't come up. I even checked the index in the back of the textbook and it didn't even get a mention.

Nor did it tell you how to actually go with a girl. I mean it had said to not have sex and not to give in to temptation. But it hadn't mentioned whether I was supposed to talk to her between every single class or who was supposed to migrate to whose lunch table. Once again, school had failed me.

* * *

In the end, she joined my lunch table and even informed me that it was one of the cool tables. I hadn't actually known that but I had to admit that it was nice to hear. We also found a natural groove of waiting for each other after second period when our classes were across the hall. We would walk together, hand in hand, over to the Annex where she had third period advanced calculus and where I had third period chemistry. In debate we would pass notes. We would meet up after school left out and wait for our rides together. And if we felt like it was safe and none of our parents could see, we would kiss each other goodbye.

Some nights I called her or she called me. We talked for an hour or more about music and movies and TV. She liked PJ Harvey, Tori Amos, and Radiohead. Her favorite shows were *A&E's Biography*, *Law & Order*, and *ER*. *ER* was one of my favorites too, so on Thursday we both watched it while talking on the phone, gagging at the gory parts and dissecting the human drama that went along with it. Sometimes I'd listen to her make fun of all our classmates. She could be brutal. But in a fun way.

After our first week, it was only natural that we spend time together on the weekend. We decided on dinner and a movie, the classic date. We would go to Dizzy Chicken and then watch the Ace Ventura sequel. My dad said he would give us a ride and that made me more nervous than a date did.

As we drove over toward the mall end of Wrightsboro where Emma's lived, I silently dreaded all the ways that my dad could embarrass me. My dad's minivan smelled like a combination of farts and pine tree air freshener. Plus he only ever listened to talk radio of either the Christian or right wing varieties.

Silently, I hoped that he would stay as quiet as possible and I counted the days 'til I would be able to drive. One hundred and fifteen more days until I turned 16 and get my license. Unless 1996 was going to be a leap year. Maybe it was 116. Either way, it couldn't come fast enough. Thankfully the drive to the theater was short. Still he managed to embarrass me.

"Emily," he asked. "What church do you go to?" Seated next to her in the middle back seat, I shot her a quick look of apology. This was always how my dad started conversations. What church did people go to? I think he used it to judge them a little bit, like how maybe their church wasn't quite as holy as Agape Christian Fellowship or something.

"Emma," I corrected him. "It's Emma."

"Yeah," Emma replied nervously. "We're Jewish, so there's, um, Congregation of Israel. It's a reform temple. We don't really go that often, though." This surprised me and not in a bad way. It had never occurred to me that Emma was Jewish. Suddenly she felt exotic and vaguely foreign.

"You know what the Bible says about the nation of Israel and the end times?" my dad asked because of course he did. "Those Jews who come to Christ…"

"We're here!" I interrupted. We weren't actually at the movie theater. But I could see it. And to me that counted. It especially counted if I could stop my dad from talking about the Book of Revelations.

"Well," my dad conceded. He drove us up to the theater, pulled up to the curb, and looked back at me. "Call me when you need a lift home. And Matt?"

"Yes?" I asked, rolling my eyes.

"Remember our talk, okay," he said sternly. It was about how I took the name of Christ and how people who did that weren't supposed to give in to the sin of lust. I nodded in agreement and he slipped me some cash.

"Thanks, dad!" I said.

"Nice to meet you, Emma," my dad called out as we hopped out of the minivan and made our way to the box office.

\* \* \*

After the movie, we grabbed a booth at Dizzy Chicken, a casual dining spot that was next door to the theater and happened to have the best chicken finger baskets in town.

"Sorry about my dad," I said as the waitress came and brought our sweet teas.

"It's okay," Emma laughed. "You know how many times a week I get asked about what church I go to? Way too many. Disgusta, Georgia. Right smack dab in the center of Jesus Christ's own Bible belt."

"Yeah," I said, avoiding her gaze. "My parents make me go to church. My dad's really religious."

"What about you?" she asked. "You're not that religious, right? I mean, we did just spend half the movie making out." She shot me a sly smile.

"I mean, I guess so?" I answered. "I'm Christian, but I'd like to think that Jesus was maybe a little more chill than what people like my dad would have me believe. You know, like, is beating someone over the head with a Bible really the best way to show God's love?"

"Yeah," Michelle said. "That's why I like Reform Judaism. Nice and chill."

"So what's it like, being Jewish?" I asked and then felt a slight regret. "Was that, like, a racist question?"

"No," Emma laughed. "I mean, you've yet to accuse me of killing your Lord, so I think you're fine." Then she looked out the window at the people who were still wandering in for the 9:00 p.m. shows. "It's like, people are different in all these different ways. And being Jewish in the South is my way, I guess. Thankfully most Christians see us as, like, sort of okay. Like, you know, Jesus was Jewish and all that. I don't know. I haven't really ever had anyone be anti-Semitic to me. But my grandpa tells me stories about when he was growing up in Poland. He was in one of the camps. He doesn't tell me stories about that part of it, though. Just the bits from before age 13. That's when he got sent off. I don't have any family on that side other than him."

"Oh my God," I said. "That's horrible."

"So I guess you carry that with you a little," she explained. "Inside. It's just the way I'm different. You know, we're all different." She looked back at me and smiled sadly. The waitress came by and set down two baskets of chicken strips and curly fries for us.

"Yeah," I agreed because I was unsure of what else to say.

"Sorry, I got you bummed out," she said. "'Good job Emma, bring up the Holocaust on your date night.'"

"It's okay," I said. Standing up over the table, I gave her a kiss on top of her head. Her hair smelled like apple candy. "It's really interesting. I don't ever get to hear about anything other than Jesus. You know, my dad had this book called *The World's Most Dangerous Cults*. And the first chapter was Hinduism." Emma and I laughed at that.

"Take it from a Jewish girl, Matt," Emma said. "Jesus was definitely more chill than your dad thinks."

* * *

"Dear God," I thought as I looked up at the pale green stars above my bed. "Please forgive me for having lustful thoughts about my girlfriend. And for making out with her during a movie. Also for watching a secular movie that didn't glorify God. Didn't glorify you. It's just hard, God. And I know what they say, that what you endured on the cross was far harder than anything I have to put up with, so I shouldn't complain. But it's hard, God. It really is. I'm sorry, God. I'll do better."

Then I realized I was lying to God and God knew that. I remember once asking the pastor how to deal with temptation. His answer was to read your Bible and pray. That was their answer to everything. I did that but it never helped. And when I explained that, they said to read your Bible more and pray more too. When I had asked my dad, he questioned why I would be dating any way.

"You should wait until you're more mature. I mean, look at Christy Jones in your youth group. In prayer group this week, she said that she had decided not to date at all in high school since it wasn't worth the hassle." Of course, I knew Christy Jones. She was a giant dork, overweight and with pimples. It was easy to stay pure when no one wanted to date you.

"Dear God," I started my prayer again. "Is it a sin to date a Jewish person? She's not Christian but the Jews are your chosen people after all. Everyone in the Bible was Jewish including Jesus and the Apostles too." Then I thought that maybe I should read my Bible and figured that thought might have been God speaking directly to me.

Reaching over, I flipped on my bedside lamp. My Bible was sitting on my nightstand. It wasn't a commandment or in the Bible or anything but everyone I knew always kept their Bibles right on top of their nightstands. My own Bible was called *The Word for Teens*. It had been translated into what some Bible publisher thought was cool, hip slang for teens.

Flipping to the concordance, I looked for references to dating. They were all in Paul's letters; Romans, Corinthians, and whatnot. I didn't even bother to read them. I knew precisely what Paul's opinion of dating was. He was dead set against it.

Turning off my light again, I pulled the sheet up over myself, and flipped over on my side. Maybe that thought about the Bible wasn't God speaking to me after all. People in church talked about having angels appear to them at night to give them messages from God. Other people would get special messages when the Spirit moved upon them. God never seemed to do that for me. So failing any angelic messages, I decided that God was probably okay with Emma being Jewish. He wouldn't be okay with the lust thing, but at least the Jewish thing was okay. That was good for tonight at least.

* * *

Emma had never been to Orwell's or to the Catalina Club. So on our second weekend of officially dating, she talked her mom into driving us to downtown on a Saturday night. Inside we grabbed seats at a big beat up couch in the back that Michelle and Aaron had scored. I bought Emma a cappuccino and grabbed a red eye for myself.

"All the people down here are so weird," Emma said disparagingly as a guy walked by sporting a green Mohawk and spike studded leather jacket. "Like, I get it. You want attention." Then out of the corner of my eye I spotted something. It was Courtney. She was out on the sidewalk, standing by the building as though she were waiting for someone. My heart dropped. And I realized what I was feeling was something that I never felt with Emma. I didn't just see Courtney. My entire body felt her presence. My mouth went dry, my palms went sweaty, and my insides squirmed.

"I'll be right back," I said to Emma with a fake smile. "Gonna go grab a smoke real quick. Be right back." After practically running outside, I was careful to slow down when I got outside. I wanted to sidle up to Courtney all casual like.

"Hey, Matt," she greeted me. She was wearing a little black waitress dress, fishnets, and her Docs. Then she held a cigarette up to her blood red lips and took a long drag.

"Hey Courtney," I said as I fumbled with my own pack of cigarettes.

"Sorry about Jordan the other night," she said sheepishly. "He just gets pissed off sometimes. He doesn't mean anything by it."

"It's fine," I said in a way that I hoped came across as nonchalant.

"Cool," Courtney said. "What are you up to?"

"Michelle and her boyfriend and I were hanging out inside. And, um, Emma too."

"How is your girlfriend, Matt?" Courtney asked me. "Good?"

"She's good," I said as I lit up my cigarette.

"You know, I never would have seen y'all together," she said.

"Wait, why?" I asked. I didn't dare ask, but did she not see Emma and me together because she wanted to be with me instead?

"You know," Courtney said, her bloodshot eyes half closed. "Just like, you seem cooler than her I guess. Like y'all aren't on equal cool levels, you know?" Wait, there are cool levels? Who was I on equal cool levels with? Was I out of Emma's league? Was I too cool to be going out with her? Was I wasting my time?

"Who's on my same coolness level then?" I asked as casually as I possibly could. I knew exactly what answer I wanted.

"You know," Courtney said in her usual way, somewhere between thoughtfulness and sleepiness. "Like, cool people. Like Michelle or me."

"So you and me are on the same coolness level?" I asked.

"Yeah," she said with a shrug. "We're like the cool ones, you know. Like, we don't buy into like what The Man's selling us. Like rebels without a cause and all that, you know?" Yes, I knew. I knew clearly. My heart was racing.

"Totally," I said swallowing hard. I could feel drops of cold sweat dripping down my back. Suddenly I felt like I was outside my own body, watching the scene from far away. Had Courtney really just said what I thought she said? That I shouldn't be dating Emma and I should be dating her instead? I was pretty sure that's what she was hinting at. Of course she couldn't just come out and say it. We were both with other people after all. She had to be coy. "I hear ya."

Courtney smiled hazily. And I swear to God, I swear to all that's holy that she winked at me. She shot me a wink and a finger gun to go along with it. That was a secret sign. It had to be. I smiled back and looked into those light green eyes. There was a constellation of freckles across her nose just below those big green eyes. I knew what I had to do. I knew exactly what I had to do.

\* \* \*

*Animaniacs* was on but it was one I had seen. Plus it was a hippo heavy episode. So I muted it then grabbed the phone and pulled it over to the couch. I dialed Michelle's number. She picked it up on the third ring. I recognized her lazy, after-school 'hello.'

"Michelle," I said triumphantly. "Big news. I broke up with Emma today after school."

"Dude," Michelle said, her voice heavy with frustration. "You are so stupid. Why would you break up with her? You could have lost your virginity if you had stuck that through to prom."

"Because Courtney said I was cool, okay," I tried to explain. "Courtney said that she and I were quote 'on the same cool level.'"

"Oh gee, Matt," Michelle said sarcastically. "Sounds like she clearly wants to jump your bones. Oh my God, I thought that Emma was gonna be the end of this Courtney stupidity, Matt."

"No, you don't get it, Michelle. She said that people of the same coolness level should date. And she said that Emma and I weren't on the same coolness level, but Courtney and I are on the same level. She basically said that we should be dating. I think this was like her clearly saying I should go for it."

"Yeah, she said this clearly via a complex code that only you can understand?" Michelle responded. "But she has a boyfriend, Matt. And he's already tried to kick your ass once. You have zero chance with this girl. C'mon, dude, you don't break up with someone to go out with someone else when that someone else has a boyfriend. You need to stop this Courtney thing. You're letting the fact that you have the hots for that girl mess up all these great opportunities."

"Oh come on," I said exasperatedly. "What great opportunities?"

"One," she started and I could hear her counting out on her black nail polished fingers. "Losing your virginity. Two. Actually having a girlfriend. Three. You chickened out of being Candy Darling on Halloween. You missed out on your one good chance to be a girl somewhere other than my room or your room."

"Okay, I will go out as a girl again. Totally. Just name the night and I'm there. All dolled up, okay. And as for Emma. I so totally made the right decision," I said defensively. "I really feel like this is gonna happen with Courtney." Inside I was starting to doubt if I had made the right decision. I didn't love Emma, but it was nice to have someone to make out with. She had even let me touch her boobs over her shirt and bra. But did that make me nothing more than a selfish person? Was I using her? Breaking up with her probably was the right thing to do.

"How'd Emma take it by the way?" she asked. I could hear her chewing on something.

"I don't know yet," I said, sort of wondering myself. I figured not well, but as to specifics I couldn't be sure.

"You don't know?" Michelle asked incredulously. "How do you not know?"

"I gave her a note after school," I explained. "I told her not to read it until she got home."

"Oh my God," Michelle moaned, her voice skittering into anger. "You are the most cowardly person in the entire friggin world, Matt. You couldn't even be Candy Darling at one party. And you couldn't even dump your girlfriend to her face." Michelle was right, of course. I was a coward and always had been.

# Chapter Ten

## "They Don't Know, They Don't Care"
## Friday, November 5th, 1994

I knew it would be easy to snag something from my sister's closet this afternoon, especially as she had basketball practice after school until 5:30 p.m., giving me a good two hours. While my mom was home, she was busy in the computer room. My dad was out at the store, leaving me nearly alone. All I had to do was walk in my sister's room, open her closet, grab a dress, then head back into my room and find a suitable place to hide it for the evening.

Secretly I lamented that my sister was such a tomboy. Ellen was mostly interested in things like sports, camping, and ROTC. Sadly, she had only the bare minimum of dresses, skirts or other fun clothes. If it weren't for weekly chapel day and church on Sunday she probably would have just worn jeans and T-shirts for her entire life. So it was slim pickings for me when I wanted to raid her closet for clothes to try on.

Sure, one should never take things without asking. But my options were limited. It's not like I could just go to the store and pick things out. Heck, my mom wouldn't even let me do that for my own boy clothes. She still insisted on picking those out for me, despite my numerous and unending protests. So, at least until I could drive in two years' time, there was no way I was going to get my hands on my own dresses. As unethical as it was, I had no other choice but to raid my sister's closet.

My favorite dress from my sister's closet was her dark yellow floral babydoll dress. It had cap sleeves, an empire waist, and a scoop neck which still worked for me as my chest was still smooth and hairless. It had a pattern of delicate red and green flowers and was a little heavier than cotton, maybe a cotton and Lycra mix. I'd worn it so many times, probably more than my annoyingly tomboyish sister actually had.

100

No one was nearby at all, so I figured I didn't even need to be stealthy. Flinging on the light, I headed into her room and took in the slightly powdery feminine scent that I think was just talcum powder. My ears at alert for the creaking sound of my mom moving about, I ventured over to her closet and carefully opened the double doors. They folded up as they slid aside, a slight clatter of shutter-like slats rattling the otherwise quiet house. For a second I took it all in, what there was of it at least.

Ellen had a sparse handful of dresses. The yellow floral I liked quite a bit, and there was a similar black floral babydoll dress that was suitably stylish. Beyond that there was a plain and serious dark blue church dress with squarish lines and thick starchy fabric. I may have tried it on once or twice just because but it was rather ugly and plain. Lastly there was a plaid cotton dress with a similar lack of shape. There was no way you could put that one on and twirl or bounce or feel happy or free.

There were a handful of skirts too. An ankle length khaki and an ankle length denim skirt were both styles popular with the modesty-seeking Baptists who ran the school. There was also an A-line black skirt with a light lace fabric. It was knee length but I liked it okay as it did have a bit of movement to it. And that was about the extent of Ellen's feminine clothes. These were basically there for church or chapel days at school. The rest of the time she wore jeans. Stupid tomboys. They didn't know what they were missing.

For just a moment, I thought about grabbing some underwear too, thinking that wearing boxers under a dress really wouldn't be appropriate. Also, if I wanted to look truly feminine, I'd have to have a bra to stuff too. On those rare occasions when I had truly unfettered time to dress up, I'd sneak a bra and underwear from my sister, borrow a dress and sometimes borrow shoes from my sister or my mom. Mom actually had a couple pairs of high heels, whereas my sister had some more basic, less exciting shoe options like brown Mary Janes or flats. If I were feeling particularly daring, I'd try some of my sister's make-up.

As hopeless as she was with clothes, she was even more hopeless when it came to make-up. All she had was one eye shadow pallet with about 100 colors. It was one of those generic drug store Christmas gift impulse items. There was maybe some lip gloss and that was about it. My sister rarely wore dresses. She never wore make-up.

Suddenly I heard a creak and my heart not only stopped, it actually dropped down into my stomach and then rebounded right up into my throat before settling back down and beating a thousand times a second. My mom. Crap. Instantly, I forgot about underwear and just grabbed the yellow dress before quickly and carefully moving the empty hanger to the end of the closet. Not only was my sister a hopeless tomboy, she was also anal retentive and would notice an empty hanger. She always moved her empties to the far left.

My sister's room was right across from the bathroom, with just four feet of hallway separating the two doors. As fast as my fingers could move, I balled up the yellow dress and stuffed it into my pants, right between my stomach and the buttons on my jeans. With my T-shirt over top, it would take a Gestapo level search to notice anything amiss.

I could hear my mom's footsteps coming closer. Chances are she was headed to my parents' room, down at the end of the hallway, past my sister's. My plan was to shut off the light then duck straight into the bathroom before my mom could see me. Then I could stash the dress in the bathroom, behind the guest towels on the top shelf. No one would disturb that spot.

With my mom nearing, I planned to execute my daring maneuver, but as soon as I turned off the lights, I realized that I had been spotted. With a curious, and not altogether accusatory look mom asked "What are you doing in your sister's room?" Just act natural. No big deal. Try not to sweat. Try not to shake. Don't panic. Come up with a convincing lie.

"Looking for the cat. She likes to hide out under Ellen's bed." Okay. That worked.

"The cat'll come out. Don't go poking around in your sister's room."

"Okay," I shrugged, stepping toward my own room, down at the opposite end of the hall.

"Did you do your algebra homework?" she asked.

"Yes."

"So I can check it then?" she asked, this time stepping into full accusatory mode.

"I'm almost done."

"I want to see it before dinner."

"Fine." I conceded, slinking back into my room. Honestly I didn't care about my algebra homework. Solving for x was the least of my concerns. Safely in my room, I hid the dress down into the bottom of one of my pillowcases. Later I would take a shower, then I could try it on in the privacy of the bathroom. Then, depending on what options I had, I would either throw it in the laundry or sneak it back into the exact same spot in Ellen's closet.

* * *

"C'mon, Matty!" my dad said as he burst into my room. I was lying in bed, happily listening to Garbage and reading the library's paperback copy of Carl Sagan's *Cosmos*. While my dad considered Sagan to be something of a Satanist due to his espousal of evolution, my mom was happy to let me read any book I wanted so long as I was reading. I wasn't allowed to rent *A Clockwork Orange* but my mom had no problem letting me check out the book from the library. Sex, violence, evolution? None of the content mattered provided that I was reading printed material from the library.

Science books had always fascinated me. But the ones from the library were always way more interesting than the creationist books my dad owned and encouraged us to read. All the creationists ever did was quote the Bible and try to attack evolution. The science books in the library were full of black holes, dark matter, collapsing universes, pulsars, and the ever present possibility of finding extraterrestrial life. Plus the secular scientists seemed to be way more knowledgeable about everything compared to their creationist counterparts.

"What?" I said, doing my best to load the single word with annoyance and contempt.

"Are you ready for some football?" my dad said, doing an impression of the guy from TV who sang the football song.

"I'm good," I mumbled.

"No," my dad said. "We're not gonna sit inside all night being weenies. We are getting out and getting some fresh air. We are going to the football game."

"I don't want to go to the football game," I said, though I knew it was pointless. My dad had grown up playing high school football. He loved sports; baseball, basketball, football, and even soccer. When Christian talk radio wasn't being blasted through the house, sports were being played loudly on the TV.

When I was growing up he had forced me to play little league baseball, and basketball, and football, and soccer. I hated every moment of it. Mostly I just warmed benches, but other times I got yelled at for sitting down in the outfield or having no idea what was supposed to happen when a ball got thrown my way. My least favorite part was getting picked on, pushed around, and made fun of by all my teammates. No complaint of mine ever got me out of a single practice or game. My protests tonight were going to fall on deaf ears, too.

"C'mon, you little weenie," my dad said in a childish mocking tone. He loved to mock me like this. "I don't want to go out and have fun. I want to sit inside being a little wiener girl all night. Now, let's go." With a sigh and eye roll, I dog-eared the book page. Then I slowly got up and grabbed my jacket.

"Fine," I sighed as theatrically as I could.

"You need to get out and socialize more," my dad scolded me. "All this time spent by yourself isn't healthy."

* * *

Uncomfortable bleacher wood dug into my rear while above me, thousands of bugs danced around the floodlight towers. Conversations, shouts, and applause simmered from the crowded Home section. Along the fence that marked the boundary of the field and audience, drums and horns rattled from band members bedazzled in ridiculous quasi-military uniforms. Drenched in sweat, some players ran about while others sat unarmored on the bench, their cheers mixing with the general roar. Between the spectators and the spectacle, the cheerleaders danced, shouted, and kicked up their legs. With every cry, their breath wisped away in tiny clouds.

I let out a sigh. The second quarter had started, but the game seemed to be dragging on forever. That's how I tended to feel about pretty much every sporting event or game. Not only could I not follow the action of the game due to my ignorance of the rules or usual strategies, I didn't care who won or lost. Okay maybe I secretly hoped that American Christian would lose. Then everyone would be upset, sad, frustrated, and angry. I longed to infect everyone around with my own misery.

Then a smack to the back of the head brought me back to the abject sadness of my own reality. Turning around, I saw the greasy thin frame of Tim Wheeler and the messy looking goofiness that was Chad Nichols. If we were friends, it was only because we happened to be the three least popular kids in our grade.

"What's up, chicken butt?" Tim spat out. His teeth seemed to be too large for his mouth and his head too large for his skinny body. Pimples covered his shining face.

"Stop it," I swatted toward them. Glancing over, I saw that my dad was fully engrossed in the football game. Though he had been out of the Army for a while, he still had that regulation haircut. It was the same cut he always had the barber on the Army base give me. 'Short on the sides and back.' I never liked it but my opinion had never been seriously considered. His stomach was starting to get paunchy and his gut pushed out his golf shirt over his khaki shorts. For a short sharp moment, I was embarrassed to be seen with him. Then I remembered that I really didn't care what Tim or Chad thought about anything.

"Whatcha doin' dorkus?" Chad asked as he hunkered down on the row behind me. Tim plopped down next to him.

"Watching the game," I lied. I wasn't watching it. I was waiting until I could go home.

"Too small to play, huh?" Tim laughed and jabbed me in the ribs. It made my skin crawl.

"Or maybe you'd rather be out there with the cheerleaders!" Chad guffawed. "I bet you'd look cute in your little skirt, you fag." That was always the go-to insult. You were acting like a girl, or you were a girl. Or you were gay, which was also, in a sense, acting like a girl. We were in 10th grade now, but it still felt like junior high. Shaking my head slightly, I seethed. These were my best friends and I didn't like them at all.

"Why don't you guys shut up?" I said, turning back around. There was a flick and I felt a sharp pain in my ear. Turning around again I shoved at Tim. "Don't flick my ear, butthole." They both laughed.

"You know, I tried to play football," Tim said. "But Duke didn't want me to get injured."

"Oh yeah," Chad said with practiced skepticism. "Tell us all about your Duke scholarship."

"Which one," Tim said with all seriousness. "I've already got a full ride. Duke just doesn't know whether to give it for basketball or for academics."

"Yeah, right," I rolled my eyes. Tim responded with a hard shove that nearly knocked me over.

"Shut up, faggot," Tim said, his voice full of hurt and anger. "You don't know a damn thing."

"I'm going for a coke," I announced, standing up. Before they could agree to go with me, I hurried away and jumped down from the bleachers. Behind the long stack of bleachers was a quiet yet chaotic space. The drums and horns of the band, the cheers and applause, and whistles were all a little muted. A large swarm of elementary kids were running around and shouting as they played some variation of tag or hide and seek. A few little pods of older people stood around talking. Two suitably mustachioed Columbia County sheriff's deputies milled about. Beyond them, hundreds of cars and trucks filled a dirty gravel lot that stretched all the way back to the high school building.

The concession stand was in a dusty cinder block bunker on the far side of the stands. At the counter two little old ladies—I recognized them as early elementary school teachers—were busy filling up paper cups of soda and popcorn. Rows of fizzing cups sat on their counter, their fizz slowly fading. Handing over my fifty cents, I grabbed a coke and took a sip.

Slowly, I started making my way around the area behind the bleachers. My mind drifted back to the dress that I had stuffed down into one of my pillowcases. Visions of my horrified mother discovering it during routine laundry filled my head. Maybe she would be discrete about it and not say anything. Or maybe I would be sent off to military school.

"Faggot!" someone shouted at me. I looked up startled but it was too late. Jason Evans had run up from behind me. In one quick motion he snatched the coke out of my hand and threw it right into my face. I stood there while cold, soon to be sticky, cola ran all down my face, my shirt, and my pants.

With a sadistic smile, Jason pushed me back. I landed hard onto the dirt so hard that my breath was knocked right out. Before I could catch it, before I could recover, Jason jumped down on top of me. Sitting on my chest, he landed punch after punch on my shoulders while a couple of his friends kicked my legs. As I did my best to cover my face, I thought about what my dad had said about socializing. He was so utterly wrong and at that moment I hated him even more than I hated Jason.

\* \* \*

Dark paneled wood lined the principal's office. Behind his large desk and high leather chair was a floor to ceiling to bookshelf. Sitting in there reminded me of all those lawyer commercials on late night TV.

"What's up, Matthew?" Principal Barron asked. He was in his early 40's and wore suits with the Christian themed neckties. Today's was greyish silver and decorated with tiny black crosses. His beard was reddish and he sported a little bit of a mullet that fell down past his collar in a clear dress code violation no student would be allowed to get away with.

"I just had a problem," I fumbled over my words. I wanted to express how unfair it was that bullies could get away with beating up other kids every day. I wanted to express how utterly humiliating it was. There had been days when I had cried and begged my parents to not make me go to school because of how endless the bullying was. I wanted him to fix it. "Because like, Jason Evans won't leave me alone. Like at the football game Friday night he threw a coke in my face and then shoved me down and hit me. And in gym class he's even worse. And that's not very Christ-like."

"So why are you bringing this to me?" the principal.

"'Cause you're, um, the principal," I replied, though I felt my voice go up as though I were asking a question. It seemed the most obvious thing in the world to me. He was in charge of the whole school. He could make this stop.

"You know, Matthew," he started. "Maybe if you participated in school life a little more, expressed some real school pride, your fellow students would respect you more. You're not involved in any sports or extracurricular activities. You're always dressed up all grunge-ified. And you're definitely not going to be making friends if you're ratting on your classmates for a little rough-housing. Now, I want you to take that lesson to heart. And I want you to pray on this. Jesus has a plan for your school career and I bet that plan doesn't involve you being a burn-out."

"Okay," I mumbled as I stood up and turned to walk out. This was also my dad's solution. Dress nicer, play sports, and pray to Jesus. I was already praying and reading my Bible every day. I didn't want to play sports. And I was not about to trade my jeans and flannel for the Southern male uniform of khaki pants and golf shirts.

"And Matthew," he called out as I reached the door. I turned around. "Tuck in that shirt." My head hung low, I walked over to my locker. Nothing was ever going to stop.

\* \* \*

Every Tuesday morning after homeroom, we would shuffle into the gym for chapel. The basketball court would be covered with metal folding chairs, though usually I would hang back and sit on the bleachers. Usually it would start with the school chorus singing a few hymns. Sometimes they would get a preacher from a local church to come and deliver a sermon, usually about drugs, sex, or the dangers of listening to secular music. Other times there would be a Christian improv troupe who would do sketches about drugs, sex, and the dangers of listening to secular music. One time it was a Christian weightlifting group who tore phone books in half and broke bricks in order to demonstration God's infinite power. Also they warned us about drugs, sex, and the dangers of listening to secular music.

That morning I was a little tired from staying up late to watch *Alternative Nation* on MTV and I was still seething a little from my meeting with Principal Ward. In first period, right after meeting with him, I fantasized about bringing a Gatling gun to school. I'd set it up at the end of the hallway and then when everyone crowded in after class got out I'd unleash a hail of lead on them. I'd cut down every stupid preppie and jock in the place. I would make them pay for every time they excluded me, or made fun of me, or beat me up, or forced my hand onto their dick in gym class. The school would run red with blood.

Of course, where would I even get a Gatling gun? Instead I tried to push it all out of my head. So I sat up on my bleacher perch and looked around to see where Hillary was sitting. She was upfront with the cheerleaders who weren't also in chorus. All I could see of her was a ponytail bobbing gently as she talked and laughed with her friends.

Then I noticed a slightly unusual commotion at the front of the gym. Principal Ward was there with a few adults I didn't know, as well as preppy princess Christina Holmes and baseball jock Tyler Williams. Even from my far-off perch, I could see that Christina was crying but trying to hide it. Then I realized that I recognized the adults. They were Christina's parents. Her dad was the pastor of Holy Trinity Baptist Church and had done a few chapel services at school.

Stepping up to the microphone, Principal Ward started in on the opening prayer. Though they were always a little different, the opening prayers usually ran through the same basic themes; success on the sports field, that we would do everything to glorify God and not ourselves, that none of the student athletes would be injured, and that God would send His spirit to us. Then he ended it with the classic amen. Only instead of yielding to the chorus, his expression turned sterner and he looked out over the audience of gathered high school and junior high students.

"Even as students," he began. "God has expectations for us. And those expectations extend to your family, your school, your city, your country. As Christians, you have a responsibility to uphold God's commandments and to live your life as an example of Christ. In Matthew chapter five, verse 14, God commands us to be a light unto the world." The gym was suddenly filled with a loud rustling sound. A thousand students, give or take, had pulled out their Bibles and flipped to the gospel of Matthew so they could read along.

"A light unto the world," Principal Ward continued, his eyes narrowed angrily. "What does that mean? Well, we all know that when Adam and Eve sinned, they ceded control of this world to Satan. And to this day, Satan rules this world. And the Adversary has filled this world with poison, with sin. Drugs. Secular music and movies. Abortion. Pre-marital sex. Homosexuality. AIDS. It's a rotten, sin-riddled world. But the Lord wants us to be a light in that darkness. He commands us to be a light in that darkness. And when we fail to be that light, we don't only hurt ourselves, we hurt our country, our community, our school. Now, on that note, there are two students here, who have failed to be that light. They have failed to resist Satan's temptations. They have failed to maintain the Biblical purity that God commands. They have failed themselves and failed you. And now I'm going to call them up as their impurity needs to be addressed, here, in the open, amongst the school, amongst this gathering of Christians."

With that, he took a couple steps to the side and held out his hand toward the microphone. Slowly and with trepidation, Tyler and Christina walked up to the microphone. Christina was still doing her best to hold back her tears but her smeared eye make-up betrayed her. They both maneuvered themselves awkwardly around the microphone as though they didn't want to be too close to each other. I saw that each one was clutching a folded piece of paper.

"I wanted to apologize," Tyler kept his head down and began to read slowly and purposefully from his own paper. "For failing the school by giving into the temptation of pre-marital sex. That is a sin. And it disrespected y'all, and the commandments of God. I have asked my savior Jesus Christ for forgiveness and I hope that you can forgive me too. Thank you." Then he stepped aside and Christina stepped up.

"My fellow students and brothers and sisters in Christ," was as far as Christina got before she broke out into heavy, ugly tears. She looked up at Principal Ward and then hung her head and he gestured for him to continue. "I apologize for my lust and for my impurity…" The rest of it was hurried, mumbled, only barely audible through Christina's sobs. Standing there in front of the entire school, she looked utterly defeated.

They had sex. I wasn't privy to the details of their personal lives, and no one ever let me in on the school's gossip anyway. But as I sat there watching Christina tearfully apologize to the student body, to me, I couldn't help but feel that she had done nothing wrong. Even if she had sinned, she had done it in private and it was none of my business. Principal Ward didn't need to drag it out into the open and put it on display for the entire school.

Making them come up and apologize when they had done nothing to hurt any of us didn't feel Christian. It felt like something a bully would do. Maybe that's why Principal Ward and our PE coach never cared to do anything about bullies. It's because they were bullies.

All through chapel, through the songs, through the sermon, I couldn't pay any attention. Instead a dull feeling stewed in me. It wasn't anger or confusion, but it seemed to borrow from both. Something had always bothered me about school and church but I had always had trouble putting my finger on it. It was an idea that seemed slippery and ethereal, but I had finally gotten a grasp on it.

All the people, all the leaders who lectured me about how to live up to Christ's example, were just as lost as I was. I couldn't resist the temptation to dress in girl's clothes, and Principal Ward and my dad couldn't resist the temptation to be bullies. Where was the transformative power of God's love? Where was the Holy Spirit working in us? Where was any of it?

As he wrapped up his sermon, the guest preacher—Christina's dad of all people—started talking about the movie *Dead Poets' Society*. With his carefully honed Southern preacher voice, he boomed about the scene where the students stand up on their desks to protest their teacher getting fired. His hands pulled tightly into fists and his face began to redden, he told us that we all had to show that kind of courage when it came to standing up for Christ.

"Every person in this room," he implored us. "Every head bowed. Every eye closed. If you're willing to stand up for Christ. If you're willing to stand up for Christ in this secular world, I want you to stand up on your chairs right now! Stand up for God!" One by one, my fellow students stood up. Those at the front stood up on their metal folding chairs. Around me in the back, kids stood up on the bleachers. But I didn't stand up. Instead I sat there with my eyes wide open watching it all. It was all wrong. Everything was so wrong but there was nothing I could do about any of it.

# Chapter Eleven

## "Line My Eyes and Call Me Pretty"
## Saturday, December 9, 1995

"Queens never get carded," Randy threw out there, rather flippantly, in the way that only a dying Southern gay man can. "You'll be fine gettin' into The Forum." He had that perfectly noble Southern gay gentleman voice. His mannerisms were effeminate but genteel and laid back. And he viewed me with something that wasn't quite disdain, wasn't quite indifference, and definitely wasn't comradery.

Randy was in his early 50's, rail thin, with short blond hair and a little mustache. As he spoke, he smoked endless Marlboro Ultralights and he carried himself with the demeanor that nothing really mattered. In a way it didn't. For me, Randy was probably the first out gay adult I'd met and definitely the first HIV positive person.

When I was little, everyone was worried about catching HIV off toilet seats and from syringes hidden in the McDonald's playground ball pit. Gay people I had met. I mean, I knew kids in school who were probably gay. They just weren't out yet. But actually meeting an HIV positive person on the other hand? That was something else.

But Michelle's friend Aaron—the guy who went to Richmond and who Michelle insisted wasn't actually her boyfriend—was our chauffeur for tonight. He had insisted we make a brief stop to see Randy. Actually, we weren't there to meet Randy, but rather his roommate or boyfriend. I wasn't sure. All I knew was that there was drug dealing involved.

As soon as we had arrived, Jim had run into a backroom with another guy and hadn't come out, leaving Michelle and I to chat with Randy. Michelle seemed familiar enough with him at least. Michelle knew everyone. I don't quite know how since she was 16, but Michelle knew everyone. Michelle was sitting next to me on a beat up floral couch

112

absentmindedly flipping through a gay porn magazine, leaving me to sit there, hands in my lap, under Randy's gaze.

"How old are you even?" Randy asked, carefully blowing out a steady stream of smoke from the side of his mouth. His voice had either been deep fried or slow boiled for eight hours with ham hock added for flavor. Either way it came with sweet tea—free refills included.

I just sat there, wearing my new dress and fishnets and felt a slight drip of sweat slide slowly down my back as Randy looked me over. It was an early December evening but honestly it could have been any time of year. Georgia only has two seasons; too hot and way too hot. Thus far I had felt really pretty, but the way he looked at me suddenly made me think about every little flaw in my outfit and my appearance. Should I have gone for different shoes? I probably should have gone for better shoes.

"Sixteen," I sputtered out. It was hot and it was stuffy, even though Randy lived on the sixth floor of an apartment building. This was also something new for me because everyone I knew lived in one-story ranch houses. Apartments were a little seedy, a little scary. It was only years later that I'd learn that seedy and scary people really do have the most fun.

"Sixteen?" Randy scoffed. "Honey, take that dress off and go home." But, of course, I would ignore him. It had taken me a long time, a damn long time, to put this dress on and go out.

* * *

"Seriously? We're going to Pueblo?" I asked as Aaron's car pulled into the parking lot of the local family-friendly casual dining Mexican restaurant. I was starting to regret coming out tonight. The plan was for me to dress up and then Michelle and I would go out together, maybe to Orwell's or for coffee or something. We would take loads of pictures. But now it felt like she was letting her not-boyfriend make all the decisions.

"I want to get food," Aaron said, his mind apparently made up. He was wearing torn up jeans, a Who T-shirt, and an old army jacket. His long, unwashed brown hair was tucked behind his ears. While I was certainly grateful to have the ride, I wasn't quite sure what Michelle saw in the guy. Secretly, I suspected drugs were involved somehow in the equation, though I felt it best not to ask. It was easier to just go along with him, since the alternative would be to be dumped out in the parking lot and have to call my parents to come pick me up. That would be out of the question.

"Hey," Michelle said as she turned around in the front seat and patted my leg. "Even Candy Darling had to eat. Besides, I don't think Courtney will be there." I rolled my eyes.

As we parked, Michelle hopped out and Jim slowly stepped out, leaving me sitting in the back with a thousand terrible thoughts running through my head. Really, I had never even considered the possibility of ever going out while dressed as a girl. Sure, I had hoped, I had dreamed, I had fantasized, but I had never really thought that it was real or that it would ever be an actual experience. Going out in public as a girl? But here I was. I was actually doing it. I was actually about to go out in public. Of course, in my fantasies it was always somewhere glamorous. Not a casual dining restaurant full of kids and families and people. Instead of unbuckling my seatbelt and getting out of the car, I was glued to the seat.

What would people think? What would the good Christian families who went to church and owned guns and paid their taxes and voted Republican think of me? Would they even let me in the restaurant? Would they spit in my food? Would they come over and throw drinks in my face and call me a faggot and sneer and laugh and then punch me? What if my preacher was in there or a teacher or one of my family friends or a neighbor? What if they recognized me and then told my parents? It was an old fear I knew well, though now I faced it for the first true time in reality, here at this Mexican restaurant.

"After you, darling," Michelle opened the door and reached in, offering me her hand with its black nail polish and silver rings. Slowly and carefully I stepped out of the car while every instinct in my body screamed to run away. Shutting off my brain, watching it all from far away, I got up out of the car and stood up. With Michelle at my side, I walked across the parking lot on a bright December evening, with my leopard print dress, fishnets, blue eye shadow, painted nails and my torn up, gigantic, black, men's army combat boots. We walked right up to the door and right into the restaurant.

As we walked in, the hostess either didn't notice or didn't care how I was dressed. Either one worked for me. But as we walked through the restaurant, I could see people look up at me. As I felt the eyes bore into me, I knew for sure that I damn well wasn't going to let them see me turn or run away or get upset. Instead, I just kept my head up and did what I could to block them all out and pretend they weren't there. I wanted to hide in the dark and cry my eyes out, but there would be plenty of time for that later.

"Let's just like, have tea and then go," I quickly suggested as we sat down. "I'm really not hungry."

"Really?" Michelle gave me a raised eyebrow because she had seen it all too. Across the booth from us, Aaron didn't seem to be too interested in me either way. He just dug into the chips and salsa and started perusing the menu. At least on the bright side, no one from church was at Pueblo's tonight, so hey, accentuate the positive. "C'mon."

"I don't know," I said, trying to give the saddest most pathetic face I could. It must have worked, because Michelle stood up and gestured to me to follow her.

"Aaron, we have to hit the restroom. If she comes, will you get us two sweet teas?"

"Sure," he said. Then he looked up at us and asked "You think they'll card me if I try and get a beer?" I just shrugged. Were we now going to add drunk driving on top of the drug dealing?

"C'mon," Michelle bade me to follow her over to the bathrooms. I followed, slightly unsure of what her plan was. Were we really just going to the bathroom or was this something else? What was it that girls did together in the bathroom? Was it just talking or were tampons involved? They didn't need two people to install a tampon did they?

"Wait," I whispered as Michelle went to push open the door to the lady's room. "Are you sure that's okay?" Based on the reception I'd gotten in the dining room, I was imagining the sheriff's department being called and then having to have my parents bail me out of jail for sexual deviancy. That was definitely not a conversation I wanted to have with them and it would definitely get me kicked out on the streets. Hopefully Michelle's parents would let me stay with them. Really it would be her fault.

"Seriously," Michelle rolled her eyes and dragged me inside. Honestly, I have to admit I wasn't that impressed by my first ladies room. I'd imagined flowers, delicate potpourri in little dishes, a few candles and maybe some violin music. Instead it was just like the men's room only minus the urinals. A strange and different smell hung about the place and it wasn't altogether pleasant. Thankfully, we were alone.

"We're gonna get in trouble," I continued to whisper. "I'm gonna get in trouble. I'm going to get my ass kicked by a bunch of rednecks."

"Don't let those people get you down. They suck," Michelle said.

"They do suck," I agreed.

"We can't let the worst people be the ones to decide what we're gonna do."

"I know," I said, though I knew that that was what I always did. Since fifth grade, I'd spent all my time trying to fit in, trying to blend in with people I didn't like, trying to win the acceptance of people who I hated, tried to copy people whose fashions I didn't like, whose opinions I didn't like. I tried to bury who I was and do everything they wanted of me and it never worked. They made fun of me for not having the right clothes and then no matter how many of the right shirts or right sneakers I got, it meant nothing. They didn't like me. They looked down on me even more for trying to fit in. They laughed. They always laughed. At least tonight they were mocking me for something I wanted to be, instead of something I was trying to fake.

"You're like the bravest person I know," Michelle said, as she unspooled some paper and flushed. "Just for coming out here tonight."

"Thanks."

"I mean it," she said, making eye contact with my reflection in the mirror. "This is big. You're awesome tonight. You really are." I didn't feel too brave. Mostly I just felt sick to my stomach and wanted to go home. But I also felt that way every day at school for all of junior high and most of high school, so I figured I could manage. In pants or a dress, I'd never been popular so I might as well wear a dress.

* * *

"You okay walking back from my house?" Michelle asked as she leaned over and lit my cigarette. "You can get cleaned up there. And changed."

"Cool," I said as I leaned back on the hood of Aaron's car and watched the endless stream of car headlights make their way down Washington Road. Evening's darkness brought a cool wind that made the night seem slow. The smoke calmed my nerves and made me forget about dinner. It hadn't been too bad after all, if you just ignored our fellow diners. The staff had been nice at least and if there was spit in our food, I couldn't tell, so it didn't really matter. Jim was standing next to a randomly parked car, talking to the driver through the window, though I couldn't see what was going on.

For a moment we just stood there in the chilly parking lot, smoking our cigarettes. This was our last stop and then it was back to Michelle's where I'd change back into my boy clothes, wash off my make-up, and then walk home. I'd keep my nail polish. It was suitably neutral enough, even for my dad, mostly because he knew that I was dating a bona fide girl. That had gotten me pretty far with him thus far. I think he was happy for definite confirmation that I wasn't gay. Besides, with a son dating, he had far less to worry about than with a daughter. If it made life easier, I was happy to get the long end of the stick this time.

"Okay," I said, though I still had my misgivings. Aaron was almost certainly a drug dealer and had definitely had two beers with dinner and then drove.

"Remember what Jesse said?" Michelle asked, staring off into the distance the way she always did when she was formulating one of her grand plans.

"No," I replied. Jesse had said plenty of things, but I had no idea what Michelle was referencing.

"Queens never get carded," She turned to me. "We can go to the gay bar, to The Forum and you won't get carded."

"What about you?"

"Girls don't get carded either. It's perfect."

"Wait, why would we go to the gay bar? We're not gay."

"You don't have to be gay to go the gay bar," Michelle explained. "We're going there because we can get in without ID and then we can drink and have fun. We just make sure we get a ride there and back and we're set."

"That's like a whole other level," I said, trying to imagine what a gay bar would be like. Bars were scary. They were dark, dirty places full of sad, lonely alcoholics. I assumed a gay bar would be that, but with people having butt sex in the bathrooms.

"It'll be fun," Michelle insisted.

"Yeah," I sort of said skeptically, as though it were a question.

"Hey, Matt," Michelle smiled as we headed off into the night, back to her house, back to The Hill, back home "Candy, I mean. You went out in the real world all girled up to the nines and you survived. Not bad for your first time." I just smiled and wasn't even sure what to say. Indeed, I had gone out as a girl and survived. And, honestly, despite the rednecks and the jerks and the comments and the looks, it wasn't that bad for my first time. It wasn't that bad at all.

# Chapter Twelve

## "And If You Want to Talk for Hours"
## Thursday, January 4, 1996

The entire world seemed grey. Above the grey sky was full of grey clouds and at the edges of the horizon, a thin wall of fog had settled. Cars and trucks zoomed by as I walked down the litter-dotted edge of barely living grass that lined the side of Wrightsboro Road. All around me, strip malls and fast food joints lined both sides of the road until they receded into the distance, lost in grey winter mist and endless pine trees. While I had told my mom that my destination was the library, I walked right past it, toward my real destination.

Reaching the gas station, I crossed the parking lot, passed the people filling up at the pumps, and headed up toward the store. Bright neon beer signs and other signs and advertisements helped to disguise the fact that the mini-mart was nothing more than a cinder block box with a couple of large windows in front. The lack of fanciness didn't bother me. I knew this store well. It was an important resource for me. They never carded.

"Pack of Camel Lights," I said as casually as I could. If the elderly, overweight, Black cashier had been fooled by my aloofness, she didn't say so. Instead she blindly pulled a pack from an overhead rack and set it on the counter.

"One seventy five," she said like a bored and disinterested gas station employee. From behind the counter talk radio rattled out from a small boom box. I smiled and handed her a dollar and three quarters. Then I put the cigarettes in the front right pocket of my torn up jeans and left.

I had never bought my own cigarettes before. Michelle had always bought them here though and she always shared with me. Courtney used to steal hers from her stepdad who bought whole cartons and kept them in the freezer. As I walked away from the gas station I carefully pulled off the plastic outer wrapper and then opened the box. Once I pulled off the foil, I was met with the familiar wet forest scent of an unsmoked pack.

Buying them doesn't make me addicted, I thought as I pulled one out and put it in my mouth. Earlier in my smoking habit, when I was only smoking one a day or so, I made a deal with myself. I wasn't addicted unless I bought my own. Somehow I figured that the act of only bumming them off others protected me. But now I had bought my own. Still, it's not an addiction until you have to do it. I enjoyed it. And everyone did it anyway.

Flicking my cheap clear red plastic lighter, I lit the smoke and breathed in. It was January. A brand new year. A leap year. Walking back along the edge of the road, back towards my neighborhood, I let the traffic roar past me and thought about all the possibilities that a year could hold.

* * *

The entire window at the front of Orwell's was fogged up. Outside of it you could only barely see 8th Street in all its abandoned and dilapidated glory. Downtown was always deserted. On a chilly day in early January it somehow felt emptier than usual. Maybe it was because it was a Thursday and weekends were the usual time for hanging out at the coffee shop. Maybe half the city was travelling for Christmas.

Michelle had only gotten back from her extended Christmas trip to her grandparents that morning. When I walked in, she was sitting at a second, or possibly third-hand, table by the side wall under a framed magazine page with a photo of Johnny Rotten. She was sipping from a coffee mug that was only slightly smaller than her head. A Delia's catalog on the table was open to the T-shirt page.

"I got you a present," I said sitting down. From my jacket pocket I pulled out a small CD shaped package wrapped in red and gold paper and decorated with a stick-on bow.

"A puppy," she said dryly as she put a hand out and slid the present across the table as though it were a secret spy document. "No, wait. There's no air holes. A dead puppy. You got me a dead puppy!" She smiled in a fake way and clapped like a little kid.

"How'd you know?" I joked. Carefully, Michelle found the seam and sliced into the paper with a long black polished fingernail. Pulling the paper aside she turned over the double CD and let herself smile a little.

"*Mellon Collie and the Infinite Sadness*," she said looking over the tracks. "Did you like *Gish*?"

"I only have *Siamese Dream* and the new one," I said.

"Hmmm. Thank you for the record," Michelle said as she put the CD away in her bag. "I also got you something for Christmas." She looked up and smiled in her usual way. It was a subtle look that didn't indicate amusement so much as a minor joy in the fact that she knew something that other people didn't.

"What?" I asked, suddenly desperate to know. Michelle's expression meant it would either be an amazing present or it would be some farcical joke that perhaps only she got. Or it would be something else entirely. She liked to look like the kind of person who plays her cards close to her heart, but I had gotten to know her.

"Stacy Gill," Michelle said confidently. She took another sip of coffee and narrowed her eyes.

"What's Stacy Gill?" I asked, confused. "Is that a person? Or is it like an adjective and a noun? Like that's one stacy gill you've got on you, fish."

"Stacy Gill is a human. A human girl," Michelle explained. "She goes to Richmond, where she is friends with Aaron. Her favorite bands are Hole and Bikini Kill, though she also expressed a favorability towards Garbage. Plus, she said she's bisexual and that should indicate a possible acceptance of all your fun little gender bending."

"You're trying to set me up with this girl?" I said with frustration rising in my voice. "You're supposed to be helping me get with Courtney, not with random Richmond girls." Michelle rolled her eyes theatrically. The idea of being set up dug a knife right into my self-esteem's heart. Memories of being the dorkiest, least cool kid at American Christian gripped me. Was the charity of friends the only way I was ever going to get a real girlfriend?

"Courtney is never going to date you, Matt," Michelle said as though she were explaining it to a kindergartener. "And if you keep pining over her, you are gonna die a virgin. What's worse? You're gonna go to college a virgin!"

"You don't know her," I protested. "She says things to me, like, I mean the way she says things. She's very clearly hinting at things."

"Clearly," Michelle said flatly with a heavy thud of sarcasm. "Dude, I'm sick of hearing about it. And I do know Courtney. I've known her a lot longer than you. So stop being stupid."

"It's not stupid!" I defended myself. "Feelings aren't stupid."

"Some feelings are totally stupid, okay?" Michelle replied. "Just, c'mon. Do this for me. One date. A double date with Aaron and me so it's not super awkward or weird. And I'll stop bugging you."

"You'll stop bugging me?"

"For like a month," Michelle said. "I reserve the right to call out a friend on their crap."

"What's she look like?"

* * *

It turned out that Stacy Gill was really tall with a slender frame that made her height seem even more towering. Her black hair was thin and pulled back into a tight ponytail, though a few whips had managed to escape her hair tie and fell down to frame her face. Dark red, almost purple, lipstick contrasted sharply with her pale skin and her greyish blue eyes closed up tightly when she laughed. She wore a black tank top, baggy jeans, and an unbuttoned vintage mechanic's shirt with a Pennzoil patch on the shoulder and a name patch that said "Anthony."

The plan that Michelle had devised involved us all meeting up at Orwell's on Saturday night. She and Aaron would come early to have a better chance of snagging a four top table or one of the booths in the back. Then Stacy Gill and I would saunter in one at a time, join Michelle and Aaron, talk, make googly eyes, fall in love, get married, and never think about Courtney Wilkerson ever again.

Walking in, I had seen them in the back and realized that I had been the last to arrive. After a quick wave of acknowledgement, I grabbed my red eye and found the seat that had been reserved for me next to Stacy. For a brief moment, we had made eye contact as I sat down. Awkward, polite smiles were exchanged.

I looked over at Michelle who was clearly studying us. Aaron tucked one strand of his long dyed black hair behind his ear and reached out a hand to introduce himself. At some point, I had realized that he hadn't actually been wearing a Jim Morrison costume at the Halloween party. That was just how he dressed every day.

"Stacy was just telling us about spells," Michelle announced. I noticed that she seemed to barely pay attention to Aaron when they were together. They were sitting a good foot apart and her attention seemed focused entirely on Stacy and me.

"Just some simple things really," Stacy blushed. "Protection spells, really."

"So you're a witch?" I asked, my curiosity piqued. Witchcraft was absolutely forbidden by God. It was basically Satan worship. Still, like anything dark, shadowy, and sinful, it held a certain fascination for me. I felt myself backsliding and imagined the Lake of Fire, but pushed the thoughts away.

"Wicca," Stacy corrected me with a practiced tone of one who had corrected a number of people on the same vocabulary. "It's an ancient religion that goes back millennia but the Christians, when they came to Europe, didn't understand it so they called it witchcraft and condemned it."

"Huh," I said soaking it in. Having spent my entire life hearing other religions condemned as cults or Satan worship it suddenly occurred to me that I had never even heard what the other side had to say. "So it's not Satanism?"

"No, not at all," Stacy said. "Satan is something that's part of Christianity. Only Christians care about Satan. There's a Goddess, connected to nature and the Moon. Old. Worshiped by the Celtic tribes way back before the pyramids were built."

"So you can do spells? Like magic?" I asked, my head full of images of death curses, voodoo dolls, and blighted crops. I saw Aaron and Michelle exchange a subtle signal of some sort. It was a quick, almost imperceptible shared look.

"Spells are a rite," Stacy explained, her eyes wide. "Something sacred. Think of it like a prayer, but more of a ritual. Like, I was just telling them about protection spells. You can do a mirror spell so any hex done against you bounces back to the person who did it. Or you can bless an object like an iron ingot or a bundle of twigs and use that as an amulet. That puts a protective aura around you. Spells are a way to use spiritual power to affect change in the real world and should always be positive."

"So how do you learn how to do a spell?" I asked.

"There are books," Stacy explained. "I could teach you sometime."

"That'd be cool," I said with my mind more firmly on the possibility of hellfire and more on the possibilities of what could happen alone with Stacy doing magic. Witches—Wicca— they did spells in the nude, right?

"We gotta go meet a guy," Michelle announced as she stood up with Aaron dutifully following her.

"What guy?" I asked skeptically.

"A guy," Aaron said casually.

"Drugs. A drug dealer," Michelle said with a smile. "We are meeting a guy to buy drugs. LSD specifically. So we'll be right back." Once again, I exchanged an awkward smile with Stacy as Michelle and Aaron walked away. Stacy let out a quiet nervous laugh.

"I'm gonna switch," I said quietly as I moved over to the other side of the table. I took a sip off my coffee and looked up at Stacy. Was she taller than me? "That Wicca thing is really interesting. You know my family is so churchy-churchy, that I never get to learn about anything really."

"Are you churchy-churchy?" she asked with a hint of worry in her voice. Taking a sip of my coffee, I let the sweet and bitter flavors roll around on my tongue while I thought about her question. My parents' relationship with church—my dad's especially—was an easy answer. Devoted. Central to their life. My stomach went a little cold as I tried to think about where I really stood. Maybe I was churchy-churchy. But I didn't want to be right now. Not here in front of Stacy. I wanted to make a good impression. She wasn't Courtney, but still I wanted her to like me or at least not dislike me. Would I go all Peter and deny Christ in front of her? Would I hear the cock crow? Were Christ and the church really the same thing? Making out with girls and drinking beer were definitely way more fun than church.

"I don't know," I answered.

"You don't know if you're like a hardcore Christian?" Stacy asked skeptically.

"I'm a Christian," I said timidly. "I got saved when I was five. But I'm starting to think that's just my parents' thing. I don't know. Jesus says good things in the Gospels. 'Judge not lest ye be judged. Do unto others. Turn the other cheek. Whatever you do to the least of my brothers you did unto me.' It's all good stuff. I like Jesus. But I don't really like church."

"What is there to like about church?" Stacy joked. "I stopped going when I was 12. I told my mom that I didn't believe in it and she let me stop going. She still goes."

"Yeah, I don't think my dad would let me do that," I said. "Honestly, I don't know if I've ever believed in it. Not really. Not with the kind of faith that can throw mountains into the sea. Even when I was little, there was always this tiny part of me that doubted things. Like, every single adult in my life said whatever about God and Jesus. So I accepted it. I went along with it. But parts of it always bothered me."

"Like what bothered you?"

"So this one time," I said, letting my mind go back to that Baptist church in Anniston, Alabama. I could see the big boardroom style table in the preacher's office. All his books lined the wall. Cheap, fake wood paneling was everywhere. For whatever reason my dad had gone there to talk to him and brought me along. And I remember that preacher—a big round man with a big round head and bushy mustache—greeted me and said that I was going to heaven unlike all those sinners who had rejected Christ. "I must have been five years old. I asked our preacher at our church a question. I said unsaved people go to hell. Even if they never heard about Jesus during their life they'd still go to hell because they weren't saved. But in the Book of Acts—I probably wasn't this articulate as a kid—Saul is persecuting the Christians and God appears to him as a bright light and tells him what's up. So here's the thing. Why does God let one person go to hell when they haven't even heard of the Gospel, and meanwhile here's this other unsaved sinner who gets a whole celestial light show and booming voice from heaven? That's not fair."

"No, it's not," Stacy agreed. "So what was his answer?"

"I don't even remember," I shrugged. "The preacher went on this long-winded, winding, discussion of all sorts of random topics. Then after a few minutes of off-topic rambling that didn't even address my question, he looked down at me and said 'does that answer your question?' And I said yes. And I thanked him. But it didn't answer my question remotely! I was as confused, more confused actually, than when I started. But I said yes. And that one moment I think sums up my entire spiritual life from age five to now." Stacy laughed.

"I was in Sunday school," Stacy said thoughtfully as her eyes looked over to the left, to the past. "Lutheran. And I asked some innocent question of a theological nature. I can't even remember what it was. Did Cain and Able bang their sisters? I don't remember. But the teacher looked at me and said in this totally Stepford Southern Sunday school voice 'Asking questions isn't ladylike.' And then I asked my mom about it and my mom said to mind the teacher. So there you go."

"Pharisees, the lot of them," I said. "That's what I don't like about church. All the mean things that the religious people say. I've seen some serious cruelty from church leaders. It's like the religious leaders today forget that Jesus spent like half his time going off on the religious leaders of his own time. They're the exact same."

"It sounds to me," Stacy said, "that maybe you're not done with God. Maybe you're done with Christians."

"Totally," I agreed.

"Think about how big and amazing the universe is," Stacy said, using a sweep of her arms to demonstrate the size of the cosmos. "Think of how cool, like, an owl is. The God they tell us about is this mean, petty, jealous, angry dude. That dude is unhappy. An unhappy God like that can't create something as cool as owls. Much less the whole entirety of the universe from protons to galaxies. Sorry, I just think owls are cool." She smiled bashfully.

"They are pretty cool," I agreed. "You know they can turn their heads all the way around?"

"I know, right? And eat a mouse whole!" she beamed.

"This one time, I was out smoking a cigarette on my street late, like two in the morning," I said. "And this huge white owl was perched on top of a stop sign. Fifteen feet from me. It was spooky as hell but also insanely cool. It was big. It was as big as the stop sign. For a second we just looked at each other. We had a moment, that owl and I. And then it took off. It flew away without a sound. Like 100 percent perfectly silent. Like a ghost."

"White barn owl," Stacy said confidently. "You know owls, especially late at night like that, are messengers from Hecate. The goddess of magic and the Moon."

"Why would she send me a messenger?" I asked. For ages I had waited for a message from Jesus that didn't feel like it was from my own brain. Sometimes I would ask a question and open my Bible to a random verse, but that never really worked well. Seeing a messenger from a pagan goddess was my first real spiritual experience. At the moment I saw that owl, I felt something. I had just never known what it was. "That felt like it was a real thing with that owl. What was the message?"

"I don't know," Stacy said with her brow bunched up in thought. "But it was spiritual in nature. Hecate can guide people who are lost. She can grant power and protection. She has a strong connection to women and women's power. And she can grant wishes." My mind reeled. Was this all real? Had Hecate, the goddess of women and women's power come to me? Was she watching over me? I sure as hell felt lost. Did the goddess know that I wanted to be a girl? Was she coming to me that night so that I could make a wish and become a girl? Was she guiding me? Or was Hecate a demon? Was I being tempted by Satan?

"You know a lot about this," I said.

"Because the exact same thing happened to me," Stacy said. She took a drink of her coffee and leaned in a tiny bit closer. "When I was little. My mom left my dad and took my brothers and me. We moved into this apartment. And one day my dad picked us up from school. A surprise. And he took us up to Clarke Hill where there was this cabin, like a campsite, by the lake. That night I woke up and saw the same thing you did. An owl. And I had the same moment. And the next day my mom was there with cops. And I found that my dad had actually kidnapped us. And many years later I found out that he had hit my mom. And that's why she left. And he picked us up from school and left an answering machine message for her saying he was gonna kill us and then kill himself. I don't know if he was full of shit. I think he was always full of shit. But that owl was there. Hecate had sent me a protector."

"Oh my God," I said.

"Oh my goddess," she shivered a little as though she were trying to shake off a bad feeling, and smiled nostalgically. "Sorry, I don't want to bum you out."

"No," I said quietly. "It's fine. You're not bumming me out at all." For a second, Stacy looked around and then took another sip of coffee.

"They're not coming back, are they?" she laughed. "I think they were planning on giving us alone time all along." I forced a little laugh and looked up nervously, unsure what to say. The last thing I wanted to talk about was the fact that Stacy and I had been set up, which meant that this was a date of sorts.

More specifically it was a tryout, an audition. That whole notion that our friends expected us to be interested in each other romantically made me too self-conscious to even think about what I thought about Stacy Gill. Whenever I let my mind go there, all I could think about was Michelle studying us from afar to see if she had indeed been correct in thinking that Stacy and I would be a good match.

"Weird, huh?" I said nervously.

"I'm sorry," Stacy stammered. "I bummed you out. TMI right? That's... I'm sorry. I talk a lot."

"Yeah, but it's interesting talking a lot," I said and then regretted my butchering of the English language.

"Want to go for a walk?" Stacy asked, a hopeful look on her face.

* * *

Downtown Augusta's main thoroughfare wasn't, for whatever reason, called Main Street. Instead it was an extra-wide, multi-lane road known as Broad Street. Other than government offices and the newspaper building, there hadn't been much on the street since the era of white flight, though a few stores still desperately clung to their old locations despite the changing economic times.

On a weekend night like this it was all buttoned up tightly leaving the streets empty of traffic, be it by vehicle or foot. Stacy and I seemed to be the only ones on all of Broad Street. As we walked by a dark and locked-up taxidermist shop, she turned to me and smiled in the weak auburn light of a street lamp.

"I haven't seen him in eight, nine years," Stacy said, continuing the story about her dad. "Last I heard he was off in Florida somewhere. He sends me cards sometimes, but my mom just gives me the cash and doesn't let me read them."

"That's weird," I said. For a moment I thought about reaching out to take her hand, but it didn't quite feel right. "That she won't let you even read them. What do you think they say?"

"Nothing," Stacy said. "I've dug them out of the trash. He doesn't write like a personalized message or anything. It's just the message on the card, the printed one. And then he signs it 'Jim Gill' and that's it. I've overheard him and my mom talking on the phone sometimes. He pays her child support and she bitches at him if it's like an hour late. I think he has another family. It's like totally fucked up."

"Sounds like it," I said. "Do you ever want to see him?"

"Not really," she shrugged. "Sure, this part of me loves the idea of some proper 1950s nuclear family. But that's always been a lie, right? Every family is some sort of screwed up. What about yours? How's your family screwed up?"

"So many ways," I said, my reply punctuated by a sad laugh. "I don't think I've ever seen my parents happy."

"Really?" Stacy asked, skeptically.

"Yeah, really," I replied. "They, uh, have always fought. About money, mostly. Though my dad also loves to go off on my mom about how she's not as holy as he is."

"Sounds awful," she said thoughtfully. Then she pointed over toward the river. "Let's go to the graveyard." St. Paul's was an old church near the river. Its graveyard marked the southern edge of the Augusta's Riverwalk park.

"I know it sounds horrible," I said as we jaywalked our way across the empty Broad Street. "But I wish they would get divorced." We made our way across a cracked and broken parking lot that was half overgrown with weeds. Then we entered the stone wall-enclosed church yard through the open wrought iron gates. Though it was night time, the well-kept churchyard and the freshly mown grass around the graves dispelled whatever spookiness there might have been.

"No, I don't think it sounds horrible," Stacy said as she sat down on a stone bench. I took my place next to her, though I was careful to leave a little space between us. "All the worst people in the world are the worst because they're unhappy. They're miserable and they take that out on cashiers, and waitresses, and other drivers, and their kids too."

"How's your mom, though?" I asked. "Is she happy?" Turning toward her I offered a sympathetic expression as I tried to figure out her body language. Did she suggest the graveyard because she wanted to make out in a private place? Or maybe because she's a witch and they simply like graveyards? Or maybe she just wanted to go for a walk. There were no obvious signs, like her touching me. Maybe I was supposed to touch her? I was not well practiced at this. In my whole life, I had only ever kissed two girls and one of them prayed to God for forgiveness afterward.

"My mom? She's fine," Stacy said as though she weren't. "She's a nurse. Nurse practitioner actually. So she's not really around at all. Always working weird hours and stuff. I learned to cook for myself when I was, like, eight. Maybe if I ever saw her, I'd know if she was unhappy or not." Then she looked around and chuckled slightly. "I hope Aaron and Michelle didn't leave-leave. 'Cause they're my ride."

"I don't think they were intending to drop the acid tonight," I joked. Stacy looked over at me with a worried but slightly bemused look. There on that bench, in the graveyard, our eyes met for a moment. She blushed and looked down. And then I leaned in for a kiss. Our lips met, but she instantly pulled away. Looking up again, her eyes met mine again and then she quickly looked away. Stacy swallowed hard and looked up once more with a sad smile on her face.

"This is really fun, Matt," she said thoughtfully. "But let's take things slow, okay?"

# Chapter Thirteen

## "Chase the Costumes She Shall Wear"
## Saturday March 2, 1996

Dusty rows of CD, tape, and record racks sat on the marble floor 40 feet under a large ornate dome. Between once grand, now grimy multi-story windows colorful music posters hung down suspended on rods. Most of the posters were for classic artists like Led Zeppelin and the Rolling Stones, though there was a Nirvana poster too. I was busy flipping through the CDs in their long plastic anti-theft cases but hadn't found anything yet. Housed in an old bank on Broad Street, Radioactive Records was the priciest record store in town. But they made up for that by having a wide selection of more esoteric B-sides, rarities, bootlegs and other gems from the dead letter office of musical recordings.

"You can call me if you wanna hang out," Michelle was explaining excitedly. In her hands was her shiny new beeper. Small, black, and heavy, it had a screen to display a number and a little red light on top.

"I thought beepers were for doctors and drug dealers," I said disinterestedly as I finished the B section of the Rock & Pop CDs and moved on to C. "I know you're not a doctor. So I can only assume..."

"Please," Michelle rolled her eyes. Clipping the beeper to the belt-loop of her baggy jeans, she shifted over to the CDs and started absentmindedly flipping through them.

"So why do you have a beeper then?" I asked as I moved on to the D's.

"C'mon, Candy. You know how popular I am. I have many, many people vying for my attention," she looked up at me with a faux-haughty expression. "See if I ever call you when you beep me."

"I don't even see how you manage to afford that thing," I said jumping over to the G's. Any time I went to a music store I always searched

129

for Garbage singles. My collection was sorely lacking in rare Garbage CDs. "My dad says that I have to get a job. That's some serious bull. Like flipping burgers or whatever is gonna teach me responsibility and all that nonsense." Clacking my way through the G's my mouth fell open. Pay dirt.

"Jobs are lame," Michelle said. "But it's good to have money, especially your own money. Christmas and birthdays don't come quite as often as they should. What'd you find?" Craning her neck, Michelle looked over at the album I had in my hand. It was a Garbage bootleg called *Crush*. Its cover was a picture of Shirley Manson from a Rolling Stone article. A quick look at the back showed a few songs I'd never heard before.

"Cool," Michelle said as she shifted over the vinyl. Michelle liked all the Alternative bands but was also a connoisseur of Sixties bands like the Doors and the Velvet Underground. "You gonna get it?"

"Yeah, I think so," I said as I mulled the decision in my head. Tucked under my arm was another rarity that I couldn't get anywhere else. It was a Nirvana bootleg called *Outcesticide*. It also had a bunch of rare songs and B-sides I'd never heard before. The only issue with the bootlegs was that they were thirty dollars when a regular album sold for ten or eleven. Bootlegs were mysterious. No one knew where they came from, who made them, or how those people magically had access to incredibly rare songs, B-sides, and live tracks. "I only have enough for one."

"Get the Garbage then," Michelle suggested.

"Why?" I asked as I looked the two bootlegs over.

"Because everyone knows that's the one you're gonna get," Michelle said. "Oh, speaking of redheads that you have crushes on. I talked to Stacy again. Stacy Gill."

"I know who Stacy is," I said. "And she's not a redhead. Also she's not into me." After our first awkward night out, Stacy had become a semi-regular at our Orwell's Saturday nights. But though we had talked a few times and hung out as part of the group, there hadn't been much chemistry between Stacy and me.

"Uh, Matthew," Michelle said condescendingly. "She never said she didn't like you. She said that she wanted to take things slow."

"Well, things are going slow," I interjected. "Glacially. She's not into me and I'm already into Courtney. And don't roll your eyes…" It was too late. She rolled her eyes.

"Stacy told Aaron that she liked you that first night, but after that you acted like you were totally disinterested."

"I kissed her," I protested. "She was the one disinterested in me. Also why do you care about this?"

"Because someone has to mash you two people together," Michelle said as she mimed pushing two heads together. I rolled my eyes. "Scoff all you want, but she liked you and probably still likes you so long as you don't act like a jerk."

"Look, Michelle…"

"So," she interrupted me. "Aaron has to make this short film for his film class and he's gonna direct it. But he said that you and me could write it! Also you're gonna be in it. And so's Stacy. And you could play two rolls. A guy and a girl role! And Stacy's bi. She'd be fine with that."

"What's this movie gonna be about?" I asked.

"We'll write it tonight," Michelle said.

"I'm gonna get the Garbage CD," I announced. I put the Nirvana back at the front of its section on my way up to the counter.

"I know," Michelle said. "I totally called it."

\* \* \*

Monday at school, Michelle caught me in the hallway between first and second periods and handed me a carefully folded up piece of college ruled paper. Then she shot me a conspiratorial look and melted back into the crowd of students in the bustling hallway. I slid the note into my pocket and made my way toward AP American History.

As the teacher told us all about William Jennings Bryan's opinion of the gold standard, I pulled out the note and discretely unfolded it. I'd always envied girl's handwriting, though it baffled me how they had learned to write any differently than I had. We all did the same penmanship exercises in elementary school. Yet somehow girls had bubbly, feminine handwriting. Sometimes I practiced trying to write in a more feminine way but I could never quite figure it out.

Michelle's handwriting wasn't feminine, though. It was as sloppy as any boy's. But her note showed that she had clearly put a lot of thought into this movie of Aaron's.

*The Factory - Iteration #4*

*Project - A movie (Writer/Producers - Michelle Hughes and Matthew Bailey, Director Aaron Turner, Stars - Stacy Gill, Matthew Bailey. Others? Tara? Courtney? (No, Matt!), Lindsay? Tara?*

*Inspiration - Warhol. Empire (Bold, but too long). Poor Little Rich Girl (yes!). Chelsea Girls (yes!). Women in Revolt (yes!).*

*Themes - Wealthy socialites! Washed up movie starlets! Kidnapping! Lesbians and Gays! Murder!*

*Thoughts? To be discussed 7th period in ART!*

Folding the note back up, I returned it to my pocket. Michelle's knowledge of Andy Warhol's films was clearly much more advanced than mine. All I knew about was *Empire*, which was a single eight-hour shot of the Empire State Building. A version of that with the Lamar building—Augusta's tallest—had a certain appeal. It would be easy to shoot. But the idea of playing a wealthy socialite or a washed-up movie star was much more exciting.

As the teacher moved on from the gold standard to the silver standard, I sat in my uncomfortable desk and wondered about Stacy. Soon after the initial setup attempt, I learned from Michelle that she had told Stacy about my crossdressing. While Michelle assured me that Stacy was cool with it, the non-reciprocated kiss in a graveyard made me skeptical.

One night when Stacy and I had talked on the phone, she told me that she first realized she liked girls was when she was 12 and watched a Blondie video on MTV. I had told her I had never had a single epiphany. Instead my feeling of wanting to be a girl had sort of always been there. When I talked about it, Stacy listened but never really said anything that clearly showed acceptance or disgust. Instead it had been extra neutral "hmms" and then more "hmms."

\* \* \*

When art class finally rolled around, Michelle caught me on my way to the art building. Since she was normally quite stoic, it was slightly off-putting to see her so bouncy and excited. Once we were finally sitting down in front of a hastily assembled still life with big brown art boards in our laps, Michelle asked me to take out the note. Putting her colored pencils away, she pulled out a pen and a spiral notebook.

"So we're writing the script now?" I asked, looking over.

"No, there's not gonna be a script" Michelle said as though it were completely obvious. "We'll ad-lib it. Improv."

"That's not gonna be good," I pointed out.

"It'll be real," Michelle said as though that were the only thing that mattered.

"I'm pretty sure Andy Warhol used scripts." Saying that earned me an eye roll of near lethal proportions.

"Sometimes," Michelle said in her most exhaustively condescending voice. "But we are not shooting a conventional film here. This is an *avant garde* art film. What we need is an idea and some characters and a really cool title and then we throw it all in a room and roll the camera. The movie will happen. That's authenticity. That's art."

"Fine," I conceded. "Am I the washed-up movie starlet or the rich socialite?"

"You're the drug-addicted blonde movie starlet," Michelle said, as though she were pulling from the already complete movie idea in her head. "And her twin brother who is a gay porn star."

"I don't want to play a gay porn star!" I spat out.

"You're okay with playing a blonde starlet but not a gay porn star?" Anthony Marquette asked as he finally butted into our conversation.

"It's for art," Michelle said. "And no chickening out this time, Candy. Courtney ain't gonna be there."

"What are ya'll making?" Maria Rodriguez looked over skeptically.

"An *avant garde* art film," Michelle explained. "I'm thinking of calling it *Milk*. Or maybe *Leather*."

"*Slick Girls*," I threw out there.

"That's not bad," Michelle nodded as she wrote it down in her notebook. Then she looked back up at me with a completely serious expression. "Stacy will be the wealthy socialite. You're totally gonna try and seduce her when you're the starlet, but it turns out she's secretly a man and into your gay twin brother, also played by you."

"Standard movie plot," said Maria dryly as she went back to artwork.

"Exactly," Michelle agreed as she continued furiously writing ideas down in her notebook. Out of the corner of my eye, I spotted the art teacher walking around making critiques of the students' art. I poked Michelle who looked up. Quickly she put the spiral notebook and pen on the floor and went back to her drawing.

\* \* \*

During my time at American Christian, I had to wear clothes that fit within the school's strict idea of appropriateness. That meant khaki pants, golf shirts, and nothing else. Though students continually protested that shorts made sense for the Southern heat, the administration had always remained unmoved. One of the nicer things about Davidson was finally being able to wear jeans and band T-shirts to school. Still, my mom declared that I needed new church pants and insisted on dragging me through the discount store men's wear section.

"I don't need any church pants," I protested. "The ones I have are fine."

"They're falling apart," she said as she handed me another pair to try on. Though I rolled my eyes and sighed dramatically, it had little effect on her.

"You're seriously gonna make me wear pants from K-Mart?" I sighed again. This time she turned around and shot me a look that was equal parts hurt and fury.

"Money is tight right now, Matthew," she said with a voice like a miserable dagger. "Your father and I are trying to make ends meet. At least I am. He's doing God knows what. But you could at least be a little cooperative and helpful and start pulling your own weight."

"Fine," I mumbled, knowing that I wasn't going to win this fight. With Ellen off at college the family was down to three of us. My parents had invented a new game to take advantage of our new family dynamic. It involved their taking turns with me to talk shit about the other. Growing up, they had always tried to hide their fighting. They failed. But at least they tried.

"Fine, Matt," she spat out passive aggressively. "Now go try those on. And show me each one." With an even more dramatic sigh, I shot her a glare and then trudged off toward the fitting room. Maybe my dad was right. Maybe a job was what I needed. I could buy my own stuff. And more importantly, it would keep me out of the house.

* * *

After my mom dropped me off at Aaron's house, I started helping Michelle decorate his parent's living room. Like most Southerners, Aaron's family never used their front door or their living room. Instead they used the side door and spent their time in a less-formal den.

Ostensibly, living rooms were for company, but often they went unused even when visitors came over. I had told my mom that I needed a ride so I could work on a project. Technically I wasn't lying. It just wasn't my school project. It was Aaron's.

Thankfully, the living room didn't need too much. With its white couch, loveseat, and carpet, paintings of Mediterranean scenes, glass coffee table, and ornate drinks trolley complete with crystal decanters, it was already fancy enough for Michelle's liking. Michelle had found Aaron's mom's box of white wine in the fridge and was distributing plastic cups full to the cast and crew.

Aaron was our director. His metal head friend Kenny, the cameraman, had a giant professional-looking camera they had borrowed from school. Michelle was the writer, the producer, and would also act. She was also the costume department. For that role, she had raided her mom's closet and borrowed a few of the fancier gowns. I'd be one of the leads and Stacy would be the other.

"Okay," Michelle announced. "Actors, put on your costumes. Just find something you like. And then we'll do some make-up. And make sure you know your parts!" That last part was odd as there wasn't much of a script. In fact all we had was our roles and a few brief notes of motivation. None of the characters were actually named. Michelle had said that we were supposed to make everything up on the fly so it felt one hundred percent real.

Michelle then started to instruct Aaron and Kenny on camera placement and blocking. Getting up, I started rooting around through Michele's mom's evening gowns, I looked up and saw Stacy coming over. She wore a nervous smile and sighed slightly. I smiled back with an expression that somehow managed to be more nervous. Then I took a long sip of my plastic *Little Mermaid* cup full of wine.

"So what are you gonna wear?" Stacy asked as she examined a few silken, beaded, and sequined dresses. Though Stacy and I were both well aware of my predilection for girls' clothes, it still felt truly weird to be dressing up so openly around her.

"I like black," I replied as I held up a long, slinky black dress with some sort of subtle abstract design in sequins. "Maybe this."

"I like black too," she said. Then her eyes lit up and she held up a small hat with a little black net that hung down in front. It looked classic and properly vintage like it was from the 1940s. "And this. I'm definitely wearing this. Maybe with some red. Femme fatale red."

"Okay, I'm gonna go change in the downstairs bathroom," I announced as I stood up with an arm full of dress. Michelle had also promised me her mom's faux fur leopard print coat and I had brought my own thigh high fishnets.

"Cool," Stacy said, still rooting around the pile of expensive clothes. "I'll grab the bathroom upstairs."

\* \* \*

"I just can't handle New York City today!" I announced dramatically as I swooned into frame, my eyes hidden by giant black sunglasses. Collapsing onto a perfect white couch, I threw my high heel adorned feet onto the coffee table. "God, I could use some heroin or some cocaine! Mrs. Van Houten! Come to me, Mrs. Van Houten. Where are you?"

Stacy entered, a cigarette dangling from her bright red lips. Her long black gloves were already falling down her arms as she sipped wine from a martini glass and sneered at me. Behind the camera, Michelle frantically gestured for us to do something. But since we had never gone over gestural communication beforehand, it was all meaningless. Aaron stood nearby watching silently.

"Trixie Deveroux! You bedeviled whore!" Stacy spat out. "There's blood all over the bathroom. Were you having your period or did you murder the pool boy?" I stood up triumphantly but wobbled a bit on my four-inch heels.

"I did indeed murder someone, but not the pool boy," I announced with a grand sweep of my arm. Walking over carefully to the drinks trolley, I grabbed a crystal decanter and took a swig of a horrible brown liquid. Gagging, I choked it down and then looked over at Stacy.

"Who did you murder?" she asked. "That rapscallion of a senator?"

"My own twin brother," I said. That prompted Stacy to walk over and slap me for real. It stung badly.

"You bitch!" she shouted.

"It's because you were cheating on me with him, you contemptuous whore!" I sobbed. "I know you loved him!" Stacy stormed over to me and grabbed me about the waist, pulling me tight.

"I only ever loved you," she said as I pulled away. Stacy pushed me down onto the couch. As I fell back, she drank the rest of her wine in a quick gulp and threw the glass away to shatter on the floor.

"Mrs. Van Houten!"

"Call me Rebecca," Stacy said as she straddled me forcefully. "But there's something you must know about me. I'm not Mrs. Van Houten!"

"No!" I shouted desperately.

"I killed her!" Stacy said conspiratorially. "My name is Richard Stevenson and I was your brother's gay lover. I realized that killing the old bitch and taking her place was the only way I could ever work my way into high society."

"Kiss me, you murderous bastard!" I said with all the fake love in my heart.

"Cut!" Michelle said as she walked into the scene. "Do that again, but better."

\* \* \*

Although Michelle insisted on announcing take numbers, it didn't really matter. We would act out scenes that we made up in front of a camera until someone started cracking up with laughter, at which point Michelle would call "Cut!" and we would start over. After three or four of these, Stacy announced that she was going out for a cigarette. That seemed like a good idea. As Michelle worked with Aaron and Kenny to review the footage we'd shot, I followed Stacy out to Aaron's porch.

Stacy and I found a spot on a porch swing. As the seat gently rocked back and forth on its chains, Stacy and I pulled out smokes. I made sure to light hers because I had heard that lighting a girl's cigarette makes you look seventy-five percent more attractive.

"You seem comfortable," Stacy said. "I mean, with make-up and a dress and heels and stuff."

"It's hardly my first time," I pointed out and then regretted it. Even though Michelle had assured me that Stacy was cool with it, it probably wasn't a great idea to point out to a girl how bad I was at being a guy. "I just, um, you know. I'm comfortable with myself. My heterosexuality. You know, enough that I can express my feminine side."

"That's cool," Stacy said. For a long half minute she sat there nodding her head slightly and smoking her cigarette.

"Cool, thanks," I said. "I think you're really cool too." Then it was a longer moment, a minute more sitting there in silence as I struggled for things to say other than the word cool.

"I just wanted to say," Stacy finally broke the silence. "I had fun that night downtown, you know, where we went to the cemetery."

"We should hang out again," I said. "Maybe try again, or whatever."

"Yeah, I guess," Stacy replied. "We could. Totally." While I was fairly new to being 16 years old, I had already learned that women were something of an enigma. Courtney seemed to speak in a flirtatious code that only she could understand. Hillary was a walking contradiction. Okay, Emma wasn't that complicated. But Stacy made up for that. Stacy's words and body language and behaviors were all unclear.

I couldn't tell if she liked me. The first time I had kissed her on the bench in the graveyard, she had acted all uninterested. And yet we had exchanged numbers and talked on the phone. We had talked all through an entire episode of *The X-Files*. When she came down to Orwell's for a second and a third time, she chose to sit next to me. But then sometimes, like now, Stacy would show nothing at all. I couldn't figure her out.

Still, she had said that she wanted to take things slowly. It had been over two months since we first almost kissed. That was slow. Maybe I was wearing make-up and a black slinky evening gown, but I could still show Stacy that I was masculine and take-charge. I turned to her and leaned in to kiss her.

"Um," Stacy said nervously as she backed herself away from me. Her eyes showed sadness and I could feel the gears turning, sometimes grinding, in her head. "You know, I think we should just be friends."

"You don't like me?" I asked, the sting in my gut starting to turn to anger. I tried to push it down.

"I do," she said looking away. "As a friend."

"Why don't you like me? You at least owe me an explanation," I said, trying to keep my voice from going to full anger, or worse, to full crying. Stacy stood up and took a few steps back.

"I just, I'm sorry," she stumbled through her words. "I just thought I might be okay with the crossdressing. But I don't... I mean it's cool for a friend but not for, like, a boyfriend. I'm just not... it's just not what I want, okay? I mean you're a good..."

"Fine," I said bitterly, letting the word hit the pavement with an iron thud as I got up, strolled right past her, and walked back into the house. Stacy said something, likely designed to comfort me or dull the feeling of rejection, but I ignored it. Anger tightened every muscle in my body. This wasn't something that I had asked for. Michelle had put this whole stupid thing together and it left me kicked right in the face by rejection.

Heading into the den, I found Michelle packing up her stuff all the while sipping boxed white wine from a blue and red plastic Braves cup. With an extra dramatic sigh, I kicked the side of the couch. Then I slumped down and sighed again for good measure.

"What's up your butt?" Michelle said as she looked up. I walked over and found my cup. Michelle had nicely filled it for me. It didn't matter. I was still mad at her. In one long, slightly sloppy gulp I downed the sour wine and got a little involuntary shiver.

"What's up my butt?" I asked sarcastically. Plopping down on the couch, I glared at Michelle. "Uh, how about you trying to hook me up with a girl who's a total goddamned dyke?"

"Don't say that," Michelle corrected me. "C'mon, Matt. You of all people should know not to spew homophobic insults. There's nothing wrong with being gay…"

"Except, apparently, my particular flavor of gay turned Stacy off," I spat out. "I can't be normal and I can't even manage to be gay right!"

"Matt," Michelle said, her features melting into an expression of sympathy. "That sucks. I'm sorry. I thought it would be good. You know. She's bi. You're a guy and a girl in one body. Right? That should work."

"Well, it definitely sucks," I replied as I slunk back down into the couch.

\* \* \*

Though spring had come, there was a certain damp chill to the night air. The street in front of my house was as quiet as it always was late at night. Hidden behind trees and lawns, the houses were still as though the world was on pause. In other places, the world was still playing. Maybe in New York or Tokyo, it was on fast forward. But here, in a suburb in Richmond County, Georgia, life had been paused.

With a click of my white plastic gas station lighter, I fired up a cigarette. For a while I stood there watching the stop sign at the end of the road. Suck in. Clouds out. It looked as though the owl wasn't going to show up today. It wasn't Hecate guiding me, telling me that I possessed feminine energy or whatever. There were no pagan goddesses letting me know that wanting to be a girl was okay. It was nothing but an owl.

No girl wanted to date a guy who wanted to be a girl. That's not how the world worked. They wanted real guys who were masculine. They wanted guys who weren't perverted or gay. Everyone was tempted by something. We all sinned. Why was I being tempted by this particular sin? Why did this have to be mine? Why couldn't I be tempted to steal or gamble or anger? Why couldn't I have normal sins like everyone else? Why couldn't I have sins that meant girls still wanted to hook up with me?

Would anyone ever really love me? Sure, my grandma said she loved me. And my mom and dad said they loved me. But that love was always expressed with the idea that even though they didn't like what I did sometimes, they still loved me anyway. They loved me with unconditional love. That's what unconditional love was. It was loving me despite who I was. God loved me too and that was also unconditional love. God loved me despite all my sinning. All of them loved me despite who I was.

All my life I had heard those three words, I love you, from my mom and my dad. My dad had forced me to play pee wee football even after I had told him how much the other kids on the team bullied me. He drove me to practice, ignored my tears, then later tucked me in and told me that he loved me. Driving in the car he ranted about how gays deserved to die, not knowing that he wished his own kid an eternity in hell.

All those times he raged at me for not being Christ-like enough and made me feel like shit. Every hyper critical speech about how I was only getting A minuses, about how my posture wasn't perfect, how I let secular music rot my brain, how my hair was too long, how I was too bookish, how I was too introverted, too prone to daydreaming, how I was acting like a 'God damn girl.' But he loved me.

And of course all those times my mom watched him do this to me, refused to stand up to him, meekly surrendered to his bullying because it was the easier path, and then told me that she loved me. What did that love mean? What did it get me? What was it even worth?

It suddenly occurred to me that unconditional love is total crap. I didn't want someone who loved me no matter what I did or loved me in spite of myself. I wanted someone who loved me for me. I wanted someone who would love all of me, including all my flaws. Because when you really got down to us, our flaws are who we are. If we were all perfect and sinless we'd just be a big planet of Jesuses. Everyone would be the same. Fuck unconditional love. I wanted conditional love. I wanted a girl to love me, the real me: mistakes and sins and dresses and all.

# Chapter Fourteen

## "All Tomorrow's Parties"
## Friday, July 19, 1996

A heavy soup of humidity hung low around the sagging streets of downtown Augusta. In summer, not even the bombardment of the daily afternoon thunderstorm or the setting of the sun could bring relief from the heat. The collection of vintage desk fans perched around Orwell's could do little to remedy the coffee shop's lack of air conditioning.

My iced coffee—black with 10 sugars as God intended—was doing little to keep me cool. Through the walls, I could hear the thumping of some punk show at the Catalina next door. A few familiar strangers were seated around the shop, huddled in little groups. Mostly they were teenagers, although there were also a few of those old people who always hung around teenagers.

Though Michelle had come with me, she had wandered off to find other friends. Either she was looking to score drugs or looking to score more acquaintances for her endless network of people. She spun it like a web. Often I wondered if I were in the inner circle, or if she simply made everyone believe they were in her inner circle. It's possible no one was really, that we were all equal nodes in an endless network.

Unfortunately, that left me sitting at a small two-top table by the wall. Drinking my iced coffee slowly, I watched the people come and go. There were skinheads and Oi kids and only they could tell the subtle differences between their subcultures. There were a few goths including one dude who wore a top hat and a black velvet cape. Most of the punks were next door. That left people like me, who were just alternative without being too specific in our style.

I was wearing red corduroys I had picked up at Salvation Army, a big baggy Smashing Pumpkins T-shirt, the one with the Zero on it, and

141

my Army surplus store combat boots. But mostly I was excited to show off my hair. That afternoon I had dyed it green with a pack of lime Kool-Aid.

For a moment I thought about heading outside or to the show. Web and Tanya had said they were going to come down to the show tonight. But I didn't quite fancy the idea of getting slammed around in a hot, humid, extraordinarily loud punk club that smelled like a locker room. Honestly, I didn't really want to be around people that much.

"Hey, Matt," came a pretty voice that made my brain skip a beat. Maybe I did want to be around people after all. Assuming they were the right people of course.

"Courtney!" I said, unable to hold back a giant dorky smile. With a casual familiarity, she sat down at my table. Her copper red hair was pulled back into a tight ponytail and her big green eyes were lined with heavy black make-up. Even in a black T-shirt and cut-off jean shorts, she looked insanely beautiful.

"We haven't talked since school got out," she said in her usual slow, dreamy way. "What's been up, man?"

I told her all about what I had been up to since junior year ended; Michelle and I taking over Aaron's final film project, my sister coming back to UGA for summer, a trip to Savannah to check out SCAD. Then I thought I might try to make her jealous.

"Then I was sort of seeing this girl Stacy," I said. Maybe that would make me more attractive, knowing that I could be snatched up at any moment by a bevy of available women. Courtney would have to act quickly if she didn't want to lose me. "But she wasn't really what I was looking for, you know."

"Sure," Courtney said. "I think I saw y'all around a couple times."

"I'm not seeing anyone now," I blurted out stupidly and then tried my best to look casual and cool.

"The right person'll come along, man," Courtney said with a sly, knowing look. Meeting her eyes, I nodded subtly as if to tell her that I understood her coded phrasing. Obviously there was Jordan. But once he was out of the picture—any day now, really—Courtney would see that she and I were meant for each other. Then she glanced outside suddenly. "I gotta go. But give me a call, man. We'll hang out sometime."

"Do you wanna give me your number?" I asked. I had it. It was in the student directory. I had it memorized.

"Michelle's got it," Courtney said as she wandered off. Silently I watched her go. Finishing my coffee, I crunched all the ice cubes and thought about what to do. I thought I had enough for another coffee. Or should I go find Michelle? It became immaterial when I noticed Michelle gliding into Orwell's and up to my table.

"Okay," Michelle announced as though she had discovered a cure for cancer but needed to keep it a secret. "I heard about this party tomorrow. It's in my neighborhood actually. It's gonna be insane."

"Cool," I said disinterestedly. "Guess who wants me to call her so we can hang out?"

"I'm gonna guess Courtney," Michelle said sarcastically. "The girl who's standing out there on Ellis Street making out with her boyfriend."

"It's complicated," I said looking at my feet. "What time is this party tomorrow? I have to work. It's my first day at Buy-n-Save. I have to work from noon to three."

"It's a raging kegger," Michelle replied condescendingly. "It doesn't start 'til later. Until, like, seven at least. Your Kool-Aid dye is running down your head dude"

"What?"

"You've got green sweat pouring down your face," Michelle laughed. "Yeah, go look in a mirror. Your face is covered in green Kool-Aid."

"Wonderful," I spat out sarcastically.

\* \* \*

Buy-n-Save was near my house, but we never shopped there. For whatever reason my family went to other grocery stores. It was fitting as it was hardly my first choice for a job, either. I had spent a long Saturday afternoon using my newfound driving skills to go around to every music and video store in Augusta, Martinez, and North Augusta. There were countless applications filled out and countless employees who said that they would review it and let me know. My next tier below that was fast food joints since I figured free food couldn't be that bad. That went a little better and I even managed to snag an interview at Taco Bell. They never called me back. And so Buy-n-Save it was.

In my effort to be a good employee on my first day, I had arrived 30 minutes early for my shift. Thinking ahead to my three-hour shift, I lit a cigarette. I would need to build up my nicotine levels. The Buy-n-Save was, like most things in Augusta, in a strip mall. There was a drug store, a bank, a sandwich shop and a used bookstore. Not wanting to look bad, should my new manager (whoever that was) see me, I stood by the Coke machines outside the neighboring drug store.

As I filled the air with ashy clouds, I looked down at my baggy jeans and beat up boots. What if I went and threw on a dress? What if I did? What if I put on make-up too and brushed my hair real nice? What if I dug through my dad's files and used my sister's birth certificate and social security card? What if I told them I was a girl? And I could just be a girl at my job and no one would know any differently. They would treat me like a girl and I could be a girl every time I went to work. I could have one real place where I would be nothing but a girl.

But that would never be. Flicking my cigarette butt into the parking lot. Instead of running home to grab a dress, I walked right into my first real job. There were papers to sign in a small, sad office. There was a 10-minute long VHS movie about how to properly bag groceries and how to break down boxes. And then they gave me a golf-shirt with the Buy-n-Save log and my very own nametag featuring my legal, boy's name. Ah well, it turned out the uniform was jeans and golf shirts. So I wouldn't have been able to wear a dress anyway.

* * *

"So this is certainly one hell of a raging kegger," I said my voice just above a whisper. We were standing in the high-ceilinged foyer of a large Victorian mansion in one of the nicer areas of the Hill. The presence of Michelle and I must have brought the average age of attendees way down to 68. Even the waiters carrying around little trays of drinks and hors d'oeuvres were wearing nice suits. Classical music was playing at a reasonable volume and fancily dressed old people were casually chatting in rooms that looked like they belonged in museums.

"It's the address that Joey Carter gave me," Michelle said as she looked around. She shrugged her shoulders and raised her head up high as though she owned not only the place but the neighborhood around it. "C'mon."

"I don't think we're supposed to be here," I whispered desperately as I followed Michelle into the ornately decorated parlor. I suddenly felt quite self-conscious in my jeans, boots, and Nirvana T-shirt. If Michelle felt out of place in her black dress and baggy flannel shirt she didn't show it. "We're gonna get kicked out."

"Then we get kicked out," Michelle said as she grabbed a small puff of food off a passing tray. She tossed it in her mouth, gave it a chew or two, and made a slightly disgusted face that she let morph into a wicked glare. "They're not gonna arrest us."

"They might," I pointed out as I watched a tray of champagne being carried past by a serious looking woman in a black men's suit. While I thought about grabbing one I didn't want to get in trouble. For all I knew this was the Mayor's party and he would have the Sheriff's department nab me for underage drinking. While we got a few quick glances from the revelers, no one seemed to think it too odd that a pair of teenagers had crashed their party.

"Just act cool," Michelle said. "It's a big enough party that no one will even notice us. And if they do, just tell them we're looking for Joey Carter. I bet this is his grandma's house or something."

"So we're just gonna party with old people?" I asked incredulously.

"No," Michelle said as she shot me a look. "C'mon. I have an idea."

Michelle led me through room after endless room of the large mansion. Her eyes fixed like a predator, Michelle slowly worked her way through grey haired couples, trios and grouped. We wandered through a billiards room with a red felt table, a library complete with a roller ladder, and through a myriad of sitting and living rooms. Finally, she stopped at a long dining room where an enormously gaudy chandelier hung above the most gigantic table I had ever seen. The dining room was empty of party goers, although waiters were passing through it on their way to and from the adjoining kitchen.

"Here," Michelle whispered conspiratorially as she went over to the wine rack that took up most of one wall. It had to have held a thousand different wine bottles. Looking around to make sure the coast was clear, Michelle waited until the room was empty. Then she quickly slipped off her flannel shirt, pulled out a random bottle of wine and wrapped it up in her shirt. Then she grabbed a second and wrapped it up with the other. Clutching the shirt-covered bottles like a baby, she made a frantic gesture with her head.

"What?" I asked.

"Go!" Michelle mouthed as she started back out of the dining room. "Find a door. And try to look casual."

Thankfully there was a back door in the adjacent room. It led out to a magazine-ready backyard complete with a pool and Chinese lanterns hanging above. Hoping to go unnoticed, we found a gate that led out to the driveway. We practically ran up the drive, out to the street, and around the corner. There we hid behind a couple cars. For a minute we caught our breath. The street was dark and the houses all nestled among pines were quiet. A few cars passed and after another minute we were satisfied that no one had followed us.

"Nice score!" I congratulated Michelle as she unwrapped the shirt to reveal two bottles. One was a Cabernet and the other a Merlot. "How do we open them?" Michelle narrowed her eyes into a quizzical look and shook her head.

\* \* \*

A nearby drug store had a reasonably priced corkscrew. We also snagged a few extra plastic bags from an unattended register so as to better hide our bottles. Like nervous spies on a secret mission, we snuck back behind the strip mall. Under the cover of night and a few streetlights, we walked a few short blocks and then cut through the woods that bordered the college campus. Emerging from the trees, we found ourselves in a back corner of the campus. Bordering a small parking lot courtyard were the Art Department's kiln building, a maintenance building, and the back entrance to the physical plant. Michelle and I found a lone, weathered picnic table by the kiln building and made ourselves at home. As it was near her house, the area was one of Michelle's favorite spots to smoke.

"Damnation!" I muttered as I tried to open the bottle of merlot. Instead of coming out in a single piece, the cork was disintegrating. Shaking my head, I handed the bottle to Michelle. I pulled out my cigarettes and lit one. "Why can't they just put a regular cap on it?"

"'Cause then it wouldn't be fancy," Michelle explained as she examined the fragmented remains of the cork. "Wow, you really did a number on this." Grabbing a nearby stick off the ground, she proceeded to start poking the top of the bottle to push the cork down. After a few tries the cork plopped into the wine. Michelle took her well-earned first swig.

"Nice job," I said.

"Just try not to drink little cork pieces." Michelle handed me the bottle. Taking a swig, I experienced my usual reaction to alcohol. It was a small gag followed by an involuntary shiver.

"Blech. I think I got some. But I swallowed them." Sitting there on that picnic table, I breathed out a long, fine cloud of cigarette smoke and realized that we had gotten away with stealing wine from some random person's house. I let myself laugh a little.

"Hey, gimme your lighter," Michelle said as she pulled a plastic wrapped item from her bag. As she unwrapped it, I saw that it was a small joint that had been carefully packed inside a folded up Ziploc bag. I took another swig off my bottle as Michelle carefully put the joint in her dark red lips and took a long, endless drag. After a minute or so she let the peculiar smelling smoke out with a tiny cough. Then she held out the joint for me.

Tentatively, I took the joint from her. As I slowly brought it to my mouth, a thousand anti-drug commercials, PSAs, posters, and slogans filled my head. I thought about the mustachioed sheriff's deputy who came to America Christian to try and tell us about the dangers of drugs. I thought about how desperately cool he tried and failed to be. I thought about my friends and I asking him a question about made up, non-existent drugs so that we could prolong the presentation and not have to go back to class.

The voices of Nancy Reagan, youth group leaders, pastors, and my parents echoed in my mind. And I ignored it all and was surprised at how easy it was to ignore them. How dangerous could drugs even be? Michelle, Courtney, everyone was doing them and everyone was fine. Taking the joint, I held it up to my lips, inhaled, and immediately started choking.

"You never smoked before?" Michelle said with genuine surprise. "Breathe in deep. Hold it in as long as you can and then let go." Nodding through my sore throat sputter, I gave it another try. This time worked a little better and I was able to keep the smoke down. After what felt like long enough, I let the smoke out in another, thankfully smaller, coughing fit. Then I grabbed the merlot and took a long drink to soothe my torn up throat.

"First time," I said softly.

"Don't worry," she smiled proudly. "I won't tell anyone. Though you probably won't get high until like your third time. Like your body has to build up a tolerance or whatever."

"That sucks," I said, taking another pull off the purloined merlot.

"Just how it is," Michelle said thoughtfully as she took the bottle back from me and drank. Then she took a seat and methodically took a few more hits off the joint.

"Am I paranoid or is that a..." I started but didn't finish the sentence. There was indeed a police car driving down the campus road right toward the little parking lot. Instinctively, Michelle pinched out the joint and wedged the roach carefully between two slats of the picnic table's seat. As speedily as I could while still being quiet, I returned the open bottle to our shopping bag and slid them both behind my legs. As the cruiser came closer, I dropped my cigarette casually to the ground and put my foot on top of it. My heart was beating a million miles an hour. The cop car was coming right toward us.

"The people at the party must have called the cops," Michelle whispered. As it pulled up into the parking lot, I realized it wasn't actually a Richmond County Sheriff's department car. It was Augusta College campus police. Still, it pulled into the parking lot and came to a stop 30 feet from us. Its headlights were on, leaving Michelle and I in a bright glare that made us a squint. A head popped out of the driver's side window.

"Evenin'," said a uniformed, male voice with a pronounced Southern drawl. "Y'all students here at the college?"

"No, sir," Michelle said in her best impression of calm nonchalance. After a good helping of wine and half a joint, it wasn't a particularly good impression. "Just two kids from the neighborhood."

"Y'all drinking beers?" the cop asked. Visions of authority figures calling my parents to come pick me up from the college police station flashed through my mind.

"No sir," Michelle answered. Technically it wasn't a lie. We were drinking wine. It was probably fairly expensive wine, though I certainly wouldn't have been able to tell.

"Outstanding," said the cop. "But this is private property of the college. "Y'all should head on back to your own yard if you wanna hang out."

"Yes, sir," Michelle said dutifully. With a smile, I stood up and carefully grabbed the shopping bag so it wouldn't clink or spill. Michelle smiled as she subtly slid the joint out of its slot and folded it into her hand. As we walked back toward the street, Michelle gave the cop a cheerful little wave. The cruiser stood there until we had reached the street and then slowly it drove away back toward the main area of campus.

"That was close," I laughed, the real fear finally hitting me. What if we hadn't talked our way out of it? What if he had smelled our pot or administered a DUI test? What if he had found the wine? Parents definitely would have been called and there definitely would have been consequences.

"So," Michelle said with equal parts frustration and resignation. "Wanna try St. Mary's?" The church occupied several blocks and included a school, a rectory, and a few other buildings. It also had some nice trees in its mostly unattended church yard.

\* \* \*

With clumsy fingers, Michelle began to peel the foil wrapper off the top of our second bottle of wine. Slowly she fumbled with the corkscrew though she eventually got the sharp bit to land dead center in the middle of the cork. A few moments later the cork popped out of the bottle.

"Cheers!" Michelle said sloppily as she took a drink off the bottle. Then she wiped her mouth and handed me the bottle.

"To senior year, man!" I said holding the bottle aloft. "One more year in the hellhole that is Disgusta, Georgia."

"Then we'll be in New York," Michelle announced. "After college, though. First college, and then New York."

"HOPE scholarship," I pointed out. The State of Georgia had introduced the HOPE scholarship recently. It meant that any senior who graduated with an A average would get a free ride to college paid for by the state lottery. The catch was that it had to be a state school. Since it meant free college, my parents—and most of my classmates' parents— were pushing hard for us to stay in state for college.

"Yeah," Michelle agreed. "But college'll be fun. And then New York. Still, senior year, man. That's crazy. That's like three weeks from now."

"No, don't say that," I protested. Then I took another drink off the second bottle. If the pot had done anything for me, I wouldn't have been able to tell. The half bottle of wine I had already drank was making me woozy and stumbly legged. Thankfully there had been a nice bench in the St. Mary's on the Hill churchyard. But the wine had also made me warm and happy. "Summer never ends. I just declared it."

"Nah, man. Matt," Michelle said. "Senior year. Reserved parking spaces. Sitting at the outside tables at lunch. Dude, you gotta lose your virginity, man. You're gonna be a senior. You gotta get that V-card stamped. Or punched. Is it stamped or punched? Whichever. Just go out and don't break up with the girl before you banged her."

"I should call Courtney," I suggested. "Let's go find a pay phone right now. You have a quarter?"

"No, you gotta get... No. You know what? You should stop listening to me, dude. You should just chase your heart, you know," Michelle said, stumbling over her words. "I mean, Jordan is a jerk off and you're a good guy. And you should just go after Courtney and like, do it, man. Do it! Go have sex with that little redhead girl, man. Not now though. You're drunk. You'll say something stupid."

"Have you lost your virginity?" I asked. "With Aaron? You know, you and Aaron?"

"No," Michelle said sadly.

"What?" I asked with surprise. "Why? You're giving me crap about my V-card and yours is totally unpunched."

"So it is 'unpunched' then," Michelle said thoughtfully. I handed her back the bottle and she took a long pull.

"You're a virgin?" I asked. Michelle turned to me and shot me the most serious look I had ever seen on her face.

"Can I tell you something and you can never tell it to anyone else in the world ever? Like at school or nobody?" Michelle asked.

"Of course," I said.

"I like someone at school," she started to explain. Then she took another drink and looked off into the darkness. "At Davidson."

"What?" I asked. "Why don't you date him and have sex with him instead of Aaron?"

"It's Erica Kohl," Michelle said softly. Then she turned to me and smiled a sad, drunk smile. I took the bottle back and took a swig. "She's a sophomore. Or I guess a junior now. She does ballet."

"I know her," I said. Erica Kohl had been in my algebra 2 class. She was tall, thin, with long chestnut hair and big brown eyes.

"She's perfect," Michelle said forlornly. "So perfect. I've had a crush on her since eighth grade. I've only had crushes on girls."

"Why didn't you tell me you were gay?" I asked. "You know I wouldn't care." Michelle turned to me and I saw that she was crying. She reached out her hand and took mine.

"I don't want to be gay," Michelle sobbed. "It's too hard. Being gay means being alone forever. I don't want to be alone. I want to fall in love and date someone I love. I don't want to be alone forever. I don't want to be gay." I reached over and put my hand around her and pulled her in closely. I realized then that there were tears falling down my face too.

"I know," I said half-crying and half-laughing. "I understand. I know what it's like to know that about yourself. I don't want to be gay either. I don't want to be transsexual. I don't want to be a freak. I don't wanna be alone but I'm gonna be alone too and go to hell and I can't help it."

"Matt," Michelle said through snotty tears. "This sucks."

"Yeah," I agreed and then I snorted. "It does." I offered Michelle the bottle and she took a drink.

"Finish it," she said, handing it right back to me. In one quick gulp I drank the rest of the wine and then tried to wipe the tears from my eyes.

"Hey, Matt," Michelle said with tears streaming down her face. "If they ever invent the surgery, you can have my vagina. Then you can be a girl."

"That's gross," I laughed. "Would you take my dick then?"

"I guess," she laughed. "I don't know how the surgery works."

"I wish you could go make out with Erica Kohl," I said.

"And I wish you could be a girl and still bang Courtney," Michelle laughed again. "Yeah, I'll donate for you. Yeah, you can have the whole bloody mess of them."

# Chapter Fifteen

### "Don't Let Me Become a Backslider"
### Sunday, July 21, 1996

Twice on my stumble home I had to stop by the side of the road. Crouching down by the trees, my mouth and nose full of stomach acid and half-digested wine, I twice vomited and wiped my mouth on my shirt. After the second time I felt a little better while still feeling absolutely horrible. When I finally reached my house, I walked around to the back. I figured that the sliding back door was the quietest. Thankfully my parents were asleep—mom in the master bedroom and dad in the guest room—and didn't hear me crawl into bed. As the room spun around me, I closed my eyes and waited to pass out.

When my dad came into my room shouting out the tones of revelry the next morning, I opened my eyes blearily. It felt like I had only managed about five minutes of sleep. My head was pounding, my stomach was in revolt, and I felt like I had chills. Everything hurt. All I wanted to do was sleep. Either sleep or die. But my dad had other ideas.

"C'mon lazy butt," my dad said as he came over and pulled the sheet off of me. "Gotta get up for church." Church. Why did church have to start so bloody early in the morning? I was sick of church, I thought as I sat up in bed.

Looking down at my vomit stained shirt I realized how badly I had been backsliding. Drinking, smoking cigarettes, doing drugs, dating girls and lusting after them, dressing up as a girl and going out with my friends. On the one hand I was happier than I had ever been in my life. I thought back to the guys at American Christian who would torment me. They would brag about partying, smoking, drinking, and banging girls. They would tell me that I would never even get close to a girl. I had been the least cool kid at that school. And I still hadn't been a good Christian. Now I was a worse Christian but at least I was gaining cool points.

Standing up made me want to vomit again. But I steeled myself and kept it all down. A quick shower, some clean clothes, a shave, and a big cup of coffee, and a quick cigarette would make me feel better. And if I vomited again? Well, then maybe I could convince my parents that I had a stomach bug and I'd have to stay home from church.

* * *

I didn't throw up. And the shower, shave, clean clothes, cigarettes, and coffee did not make me feel any better. If anything the coffee sloshing around in my stomach made me feel worse. All through the first praise and worship, the offering, and the meet and greet, I stood or sat focusing on keeping my breakfast down. After an hour or so the preacher finally started his sermon and I was able to sit down without interruption.

"Open your Bibles to First Kings, chapter 14," the pastor called out. Then he began to read. "'He will uproot Israel from this good land which He gave to their fathers, and will scatter them beyond the Euphrates River, because they have made their wooden images, provoking the LORD to anger.' Now, I know what you're thinking. Pastor Ellis, I haven't made a single wooden idol. You can come check out my whole house. Check the shed too. Check the bed of my pick up too." That line earned a quiet chuckle from the congregation.

"Not a single wooden idol," the pastor continued. "Not a single graven image of a false god. Won't find one. But is the Lord really talking about wooden idols here? I think I can safely venture that there aren't too many Ba'al worshipers sitting here today. Maybe one or two right?" That earned him another chuckle. Pastors were always telling lame jokes. Seminaries must be full of failed standup comedians.

"But there are other idols," the preacher continued. "Because an idol need not be an icon of wood or gold. An idol can be anything that we allow to come between us and God. Maybe for you that's TV, or gossip, or fishing. We all have our personal idols. And the United States, like the Israelites, has its idols. If we as a nation turn against God, then God will turn against us. What idols does America put in front of God? Here we have a nation that murders millions of innocent children in its abortion clinics. Do you think God will protect a nation like that? Or will He scatter us and deliver His anger? What about a nation that teaches evolution in its schools? That teaches children we are nothing but monkeys? What about a nation that accepts homosexuality? That teaches in its public schools that homosexuals are 'normal,' when in fact they are degenerates living in sin. I think God looks down on a country that tolerates homosexual predators and I think He will deliver his righteous anger. Hurricanes. Economic recession. A plague of AIDS."

Every week it was the same. But something about this week pissed me off. I had always known that I was sort of gay or transsexual or something. But Michelle was my friend. According to church and the pastor and the Bible, God was going to send Michelle and me to hell to suffer for eternity. At that moment I wanted to march right into heaven so I could demand a conversation with God about this whole thing. In my heart I still loved God or at least an idea of God. But I disagreed with Him and knew for once that I was right and God was wrong. Or maybe the preachers and the Bible had gotten God wrong. Something was wrong with this whole situation and it wasn't me and it wasn't Michelle.

* * *

"So, I have a question," I announced, my mind still working to try and piece everything together in a coherent thought that could be worded in a non-blasphemous way. "What happens when you know the Bible is wrong about something, or rather that people haven't interpreted it right?"

"The Bible is the inerrant word of the living God, Matthew," my dad snapped.

"Yeah," I said. "But look at the South prior to the Civil War. All the preachers said the Bible supported slavery. And slavery was wrong. What if right now all the preachers and churches are saying that homosexuality is wrong but they're just as wrong as the old pro-slavery preachers?"

"Matthew, the Bible is absolutely clear that homosexuals are an abomination. Do you know what these degenerates do with each other?" My dad was starting to get red in the face. I could see how tightly he was gripping the dashboard. Next to him in the passenger seat, my mom looked out the window and pretended to be engrossed in the pine trees, power lines, and strip malls we drove past.

"There's nothing wrong with being gay," I said. I was starting to shake but I did my best to hide it. Adrenaline was coursing through my veins, arteries, and even my capillaries. My dad wanted me to go to hell. He didn't know it specifically with me, but that's what he believed. They all wanted me in hell and they didn't even know what it was like. They hadn't spent every night praying about this, feeling that guilt, feeling a feeling that you couldn't control, that you couldn't make go away. They didn't know a damn thing. "Gay people aren't hurting anyone."

"Oh, they're not hurting anyone," my dad said sarcastically in his 'whiny liberal voice.' It was the voice that he always used when mocking anyone who disagreed with him. "The gay people you think are just fine and dandy are out spreading AIDS right now. Did you know homosexuals give blood on purpose to spread AIDS? They kidnap little children and molest them to spread AIDS."

"That's an old wives tale," I said. "You don't have any evidence…"

"Matthew," my mom let her voice rise. Finally she was in the conversation. Finally she was going to bring her own cowardly passiveness to bear. Honestly, I didn't even know what she really believed. All she had ever done was let my dad believe for the both of them. "Be respectful. Let's just change the subject…"

"No, mom," I said angrily. "Jesus didn't say one thing about gay people…"

"In the Book of Romans…" My dad tried to quote the Bible but I interrupted him. I had angrily looked up homosexuality in my Bible's concordance during the sermon. I had read every verse. There were seven of them and none were in the actual gospels.

"That was Paul, not Jesus," I pointed out. Of the entire Bible, I hated Paul the most. He was a weird, hateful man who hated sex. He had probably been a virgin and so he wrote endlessly, lashing out at anyone who was getting laid.

"Paul was moved by the Holy Spirit when he wrote those words…"

"Paul was just a guy," I yelled. "He wasn't Jesus."

"Matthew, I have had enough of this from you today," my dad said through gritted teeth. As we reached a red light, he turned around and shot me a look that indicated he wanted to kill me right then and there, just like the Bible said you should do with insolent children. "You want to defend this sick, twisted, crap, you don't do it while you live in my house. Not in my car. Not around me. I am the head of this family and my family will worship the Lord and respect His holy word. Every last word of it. When you pay your own bills and earn your own money then you can sit there in your own house defending whatever degenerate God damn faggots…"

"John," my mom interrupted. "Language. You shouldn't be using that kind of language in front of him. What kind of message is that sending?" *In front of him.* She loved to talk like I wasn't even here. God I envied Ellen getting to be off at school, away from them. One more year and I was out of here too.

"It is my car and I speak how I want in my car," my dad said coldly and defensively.

"Yes," my mom said sarcastically. "Despite every paycheck that I put in our checking account. It's all yours. The house. The car. Everything. The stupid boat."

"Don't bring up the boat again, Linda" my dad sneered.

"You could have mentioned it to me," my mom said. "You go out and spend $25,000 on a boat without even consulting me…"

"God damn it," he muttered, then he let his voice rise again. "I spent 30 years working for this family, earning money. My money. I fought for this country. And now that I am retired I have earned the God-damn right to buy a boat so that I can go to Clark Hill and have a little peace and quiet without you harping on and me and little fag lover there in the back trying to piss me off."

"It is family money," my mom said, her face red, the familiar angry tears beginning to stream down. "For family needs. You go off to Clark Hill in your boat. And I'll be here balancing the checkbook, putting a kid through school and trying to save up to put the other kid through school, and trying to make ends meet."

Slinking down in the back seat, I did my best impression of an invisible person. It used to be easier when Ellen was here. Her leaving had fractured our fragile family dynamic. It used to be that they wouldn't argue in front of us, but now that it was just me alone they had stopped trying to hide it.

My dad, the preacher, politicians, teachers. They always railed about family values. Well, here they were on display. And somehow this was okay. Rage and swearing and bullying were okay. But Michelle liking Erica Kohl and me wanting to be a girl? That wasn't okay. None of it made any damn sense.

\* \* \*

"Dear God," I prayed that night as I lay alone in my bed staring up at those same green glowing stars. "None of this makes any sense. I don't feel like I'm a bad person. I don't think Michelle is either. And I wish I could go to heaven and have a chat with you about this. That would be really helpful. You know, a real answer would be nice. Like a real conversation. I can't trust the preacher. Or my parents. Maybe this is a sin but I don't know if I can trust the Bible either. I'm just a kid, God. Am I really gonna go to hell because I can't figure this out? That doesn't feel right. I know we're not supposed to ask for a sign or test you. But, God, I could really use some guidance here. I can't imagine that you're hurtful or a bully, because you love us. You loved us enough to die for us. Just please help me figure this out, Lord. Because none of this makes any sense."

# Chapter Sixteen

## "That Legendary Divorce is Such a Bore"
## Monday, October 14th, 1996

There was no couch. That felt wrong. It felt conspicuous as though the choice had been deliberately made to go against the cliché of a thousand cartoons and TV shows. Instead there was a desk and three chairs in front of it. It felt like the principal's office. It did not feel like a space to relax or let one's guard down.

Behind the desk sat a man who looked like he could have been a high school principal. An older, middle-aged man, he was mostly bald. He had a mustache and glasses and wore a brown suit with a tan shirt and a green tie with little pictures of golf balls. Behind him were framed posters that showed scenes of nature with Bible verses superimposed over them. Beaches and Psalms. Foggy cliffs and Proverbs. Light filtering through a forest and Isaiah.

"Matthew," the man greeted me as I sat down. "I'm Doctor Miles. Doctor Miles Johnson. But you can call me Doctor Miles." This had been my parents' idea. They had wanted me to see a shrink. And not just any shrink but a Christian shrink. My dad must have insisted on the guy being a good Christian. I wasn't here seeing a therapist because they cared about me. No, this was entirely done to assuage their guilt over potentially screwing me up psychologically. But I wasn't screwed up at all. I was happy.

After dinner on Sunday night, in a time frame that came dangerously close to interfering with *The Simpsons*, My mom and dad sat me down on the couch to have a talk. Mom sat down right next to me. The expression she wore was quite familiar. It was that one where she's just about to burst into tears but hasn't quite yet. My dad stood over us, his expression as stern as his uncomfortable-looking perfect posture and

158

military haircut. It had been four years since his retirement and he still wore the same jarhead haircut.

"Matt, your dad and I wanted to let you know that we are going to be separating," she explained as she failed completely to contain her emotions. "I want to make it clear that this is not your fault, okay? Your dad and I have our differences and have grown apart. This doesn't mean we love you any less. This doesn't change that we love you."

"Finally," I thought. "About friggin' time." But I didn't dare say that out loud. Something told me that shutting up would end this conversation quickly. There was no reason to drag the awkwardness out.

"I'll be moving into an apartment," my mom said. "And I want you to think of that as your second home, okay?"

"Do you have any questions, Matt?" my dad asked. It took him long enough to get involved in the conversation about the dissolution of his own family. No, I didn't have any questions. No, I didn't want to talk about it. And so they had taken my silence as a sign of a deep existential depression, when in fact I had been relieved. In my entire life I had never once seen my parents happy together. They hated each other and fought constantly. It was about time someone ended their broken marriage.

"So how do you feel about this, Matthew?" Doctor Miles asked. He wore a smile so fake it could have belonged to a Miss America contestant.

"I'm good," I said coldly. "I don't need to talk to a shrink."

"You don't need to think of me as a 'shrink'," he said. "I'm here just to talk. You know, anything you say is just between us. I'm not here to be a spy to tell your parents anything. We can just talk. Divorce is a big deal. It's okay to be upset."

"I'm not upset," I said even more coldly. Of course he was going to report back to my parents. They were the ones paying him after all. "I'm 100 % fine. I'm good. I'm not gonna talk to you, dude. So you can stop wasting your time." I'm sure he answered. And I'm sure his answer was something well-rehearsed about listening and sharing and Jesus. I didn't need to hear it. Instead I got up and walked right out. My parents were in the waiting room, seated on opposite sides. My dad looked up from a news magazine. My mom just looked up.

"I'm not talking to this guy," I declared. "You can't make me. Can we go?" We all trudged to the cars—three separate cars—in utter silence.

I had just used my own money to buy my very own car. Of course, it wasn't so much a car as it was a beat up, rusted 1970s Chevy pickup truck, but it was a vehicle. The parts that weren't rusted were red and so I had already dubbed it The Red Baron. It wasn't much, but it meant finally having a decent amount of freedom.

Hopping into Red Baron, I sat in the cab and waited for both to drive away. Fishing through the tapes in the glove box, I found my angry mix (Stabbing Westward, Nine Inch Nails, Korn, Filter and a few others) and shoved it in the tape player.

Lighting up a cigarette, I did the numbers in my head. Fall quarter at UGA started in August of 1997. Seventeen days left in October. Then nine more months. Two hundred and seventy three more days, give or take a week or two. I didn't know exactly when freshman orientation was. It was less than a year but it felt like an eternity.

After a few drags on the cigarette I hit eject on the tape player. I wasn't angry exactly. So I fished around until I found an old copy of R.E.M.'s *Green*. I didn't know quite what mood that fit. Maybe it was hopeful, a little nostalgic, and perhaps a little sad. But no, it wasn't really any of those. It was a new emotion. It was the feeling of knowing that something had changed forever and that things were going to keep changing forever too.

* * *

Though I hadn't mentioned anything to anyone, somehow everyone in the youth group knew that my parents were getting divorced. My dad probably put in a prayer request at his small group Bible study. No one gossips quite like church-goers. My mom's absence from church today must have also seemed all the more evident.

Through the entire Fired Up, everyone was staring at me, shooting me with invisible rays of caring and pity from their sad looking eyes. Everywhere I looked were these sad but encouraging half smiles. It was sickening but I couldn't say anything. An angry reaction would only elicit more concern, pity, and attention.

During the sermon, it was no better. I could feel eyes on me. So during the short break between the meet and greet and the start of the proper sermon, I pretended to be going for a bathroom break. Instead I went outside and made my way to the side of the church by the air conditioners.

An open field with a few trees separated the church from the road. I leaned against the aluminum siding of the side wall and lit up a cigarette.

Watching the cars drive by, I breathed sinful cigarette smoke into the temple that was my body and decided that I wasn't going to come to church any more.

It wasn't that I didn't love God. I wasn't going to give up believing in God. But I had never really liked church. God, I decided, was bigger, more powerful, more interesting, more loving, and more creative than any mere church building. Sure, God was there when two or more met in His name. But God was everywhere, too.

Christians were all hypocrites anyway. My dad was a Christian but he was the least Christ-like person I had ever met. American Christian was full of assholes; students and faculty alike. Hell, I was a Christian and I was definitely in the running for the world's biggest hypocrite. Here I was smoking a cigarette at church. The last thing any of us needed was to be in a room with a bunch of other hypocrites stewing in our hypocrisy.

Stomping out my cigarette, I lit another. And standing there outside the church I started to pray. "God, I know you know my heart. You know I've been trying. You know that I believe in what you taught here on earth. I love you and want to say thank you for dying for our sins so we could go to heaven. But it's not easy. It's not easy, God. And I know that the cross was harder. But Lord, please understand that I'm trying, okay? I'm trying."

After a long while, I started to notice that people were streaming out into the parking lot. Church was over. For the first time since I had snuck out, I wondered what if anything my dad might say to me. Maybe I could feign a stomach thing. If I doubled down on that maybe I could use it to stay home from school on Monday too. Grabbing a dryer sheet from my pocket I gave myself a quick head, torso, and hands rub down. That would mask the cigarette smoke. Then I headed over, hoping to melt naturally into the post-church crowd.

"Matt, how are you?" I heard a familiar voice. Turning around, I saw Hillary wearing an expression of general concern. She had cut her hair. It was much shorter now and only came down to her chin. Still, she was as beautiful as ever. "I was so sorry to hear about your parents getting divorced. That must be hard." I probably shouldn't have snorted in response. She looked up at me, confused and looking a little bit hurt.

"It's a good thing," I said. "My parents were miserable."

"Still," Hillary said. "I bet it's hard for you. Divorce is such a terrible thing."

"Divorce is not always a terrible thing," I corrected her. "I wish people could just get that." Hillary started to say something but then stood there with her mouth open slightly, her hands frozen mid-gesture. Something told me that neither American Christian nor Agape Christian Fellowship had ever taught anyone anything nuanced about divorce.

"So you still drum anymore?" Hillary asked.

"No," I said disinterestedly. I had never even actually played drums except in junior high band. And that didn't count for anything. But that's how people were. They get this one little idea of you, one tiny part of your personality, and latch on to that. To them you're just one quirk and that's all they need to know. "Well, it was good seeing you. I like your new hair."

"Thanks," she said sweetly. Then I turned and walked away. If I never came to church again would that be the last time I ever talked to Hillary? Probably was. And then I realized at that moment, for the first time, that if college was coming up I was probably going to be having a lot of final conversations soon.

\* \* \*

Growing up, I had been the exact wrong kid for sports. Not only was I disinterested in the game, its rules, its outcomes, but I was also completely uncoordinated and lacked even an iota of athletic talent. What was worse was that I was smart enough to know that the participation trophies we got at the end of the season were meaningless bits of cheap plastic.

Still, it never stopped my dad from forcing me to play in every last sport. I picked grass far in the outfield of little league baseball, I warmed the bench for basketball, I got slammed around by bigger, meaner kids during pee-wee football, and I was always off-sides in soccer because I tended to daydream and generally missed what was going on whenever people ran down one side of the field or the other.

And yet my dad kept signing me up every year and dutifully yelled from the sidelines every game. I think he figured that if he kept trying hard enough, then one day I would magically like sports and begin to excel at them. So I think that, at least in his own head, it made sense to drag me out to Olmstead Stadium on a Friday night to watch a minor league baseball game. I figured it was his way of trying to bond. Never mind that I would have been much happier hanging out with my friends.

The baseball game was classic Americana but because it was

Augusta it was actually kind of sad. Ten rows of bleachers lined each side of the field but they were mostly empty. There was no rousing organ music, no enthusiastic vendors walking around hawking red hots, no wave or cheers. Instead they pumped in classic rock over old speakers and you had to go up and get your own refreshments.

By the bottom of the first, I was already bored and ready to leave. An hour earlier I had called Courtney's house and left a message on her parents' answering machine. I didn't care if the Greenjackets won or lost. All I cared about was getting home to see that magical red light blinking on our machine. I sighed theatrically. Maybe in an alternate universe, mirror-me and mirror-Courtney would be spending this Friday night together. Instead I was stuck at a boring baseball game.

"Hey, Matty, grab these," my dad came up from behind me and awkwardly thrust two foil wrapped hot dogs at me. They were covered in yellow mustard and sauerkraut. As I took them, he rearranged the plastic cups in his hands and sat down on the metal bleachers.

"Now, don't tell your mom, okay," he said as he handed me one of the plastic cups of foamy beer. "I think you're old enough to enjoy a cold beer at a baseball game."

"Thanks, dad," I said. Then I took a gulp. He watched and then smiled happily.

"That's not a new flavor for you, huh?" he laughed. "You're an old pro at drinking beer, huh?" I cringed, realizing that I hadn't gagged at the flavor like a first time beer drinker would have.

"I, um," I sputtered but he stopped me.

"C'mon, Matty, you're a senior now," he beamed. "You're becoming a man." This was starting to get truly weird. This was the same dad that had once threatened to beat me black and blue if he ever caught me drinking. This was also the dad who had never once in my 16 years called me 'Matty.'

"Yeah," I said because I was unsure of what else to say.

"About time you finally figured out the secret to enjoying a good game. Beer and hot dogs. One of those dogs is yours by the way. I know you usually do ketchup but a real hot dog is with mustard and kraut. When I was in the Army we used to get really good wursts in Germany. In Rammstein. In Germany it's always with mustard and kraut. That's the way a man eats a dog, Matty."

"Okay," I said biting into the dog. Mustard wasn't bad but the sauerkraut was. So before I took another bite, I used a bit of napkin to scrape off all of it that I could.

"You know," my dad said as he chewed his own dog. "I wish I hadn't bought that damn boat. I'll tell ya. But if it hadn't been that boat, it would have been something else. You know, Matty, treasure what you have because you never know if you'll lose it." Okay, now he was getting philosophical.

"Can I grab my book?" I asked. I had brought a book to read but he had made me leave it in the car.

"No, you are not gonna bury your head in a book," he said, returning to his usual form. "We are going to enjoy a good old-fashioned nine innings and have some real father-son bonding time."

"Yes, sir," I said. At least I had beer. And how long could a baseball game really be? As I sipped on my beer, I did my best to ignore my dad's newfound emotions and instead tried to let my mind drift. I would get home and there would be a message from Courtney on my machine. Jordan would have been shipped off to a prison for the mentally psycho and Courtney and I would finally be together.

\* \* \*

There were three different music stores in the mall. Usually we would hit those first, then make our way to Body Shop to look at clothes, then maybe a couple more clothing shops before finally heading to Spencer's for a good laugh before grabbing a bite at the food court. Then if we were feeling up for it, we'd do something silly like wading in the fountains or going up and down escalators until security chased us out.

This time however, we had hit the food court right after the music stores. I had snagged a "Stupid Girl" single and the new Bush album. Michelle hadn't gotten anything. While she was a music fan, she hadn't quite picked up the same collector's bug that I had. Though collecting was certainly easier with grocery bagging money coming in.

"Divorce is good street cred," Michelle pointed out as we found a table and set down our trays. "You know, like no *Ozzie and Harriet*, *Leave It to Beaver* goodie two shoes upbringing anymore. Gives you a little bit of an edge."

"I guess," I said noncommittally as I started to unwrap my chicken sandwich.

"Your parents being weird?" Michelle asked as she pulled open a ketchup packet and started a pile on the paper lining of her tray.

"Oh my God, yes," I said, probably too loudly. "My mom keeps trying to like, force the idea that everything is normal and hunky dory. And my dad. Oh my God. He's either trying way too fucking hard to bond or just ignoring me completely. Thankfully the latter is getting to be way more frequent."

"God," Michelle said, her mouth full of fries. "I wish my parents were ignoring me. It's all SAT this and college that. And bullshit."

"Being left alone is actually great," I said. "All I have to do is tell my dad I have to work or go to the library and study and he doesn't question me at all. Heck, I've been taking every extra shift I can. I think as long as I'm going to school and paying for my own gas, then he can stay wrapped up in his own crap and not bother me."

"Dude," Michelle said in that excited way that she got when she was hatching a grand plan. "If your dad is so wrapped up in his own crap that he's barely paying attention to anything you do? You're barely supervised. This is perfect. We need to try the Forum."

"Forum is a bar," I pointed out. "They're not gonna let us in. I don't care what Aaron's drug dealer's roommate's friend said." I took a bite of my sandwich and then snagged a fry from Michelle's tray.

"Well," Michelle threw out there. "Then we go and they turn us away. No big deal. But if they let us in, Matthew, Candy. We could be drinking actual alcoholic drinks in an adult setting. In a real bar. A real bar? Can you imagine that?"

"You want to go meet other lesbians."

"You could meet other transsexuals," Michelle pointed out.

"Don't call me that," I said. Something about that word made my skin crawl. Maybe it was that it had 'sex' in it. Or maybe it was the idea that transsexuals were just freaks who got trotted out on bad TV for a sensationalist laugh.

"Fine," Michelle rolled her eyes. "Sorta gay, girly, good Christian boys who like to wear pretty dresses. Whatever you wanna call yourself."

"Do you really think they would let us in?"

"I do," Michelle said with enough gravitas for a Henry V speech on the eve of a battle. "This is our moment. High school is finally about to get awesome."

# Chapter Seventeen

## "If I Could Walk Away From Me"
## Saturday, November 16th, 1996

We were hoping to get into at least a little trouble. Now that my hair was shoulder length, I finally wanted a chance to get the perfect feminine hairdo, however, our budget meant that we would have to do it ourselves. I'd bought a deep, natural looking amber color, dark red but not too flamboyantly fire engine red, as I wanted something stunning, but that I could still get away with on Monday. Michelle had brought her curling iron, promising me that she would make me look super-hot. I'd shave everything, let Michelle do my brows and make-up and then I'd wear some choice items that Michelle had managed to borrow from her mom's closet. There was a tight black, spaghetti strap dress that came to just above my knee, a waist cincher, and a pair of patent black four inch heels. Michelle had also pilfered a few jewelry items including a silver Tiffany necklace, an intricate sterling silver cuff and some clip-on earrings since there was no way I could hide pierced ears from my parents.

When we were finally done with the make-up, seemingly endless brow plucking and the curling iron, I looked in the mirror and immediately was blown away. It felt amazing to look and see this new person staring back at me. I absolutely loved being her and my entire body went warm with wonder. Every time I had borrowed my sister Ellen's clothes or found random scraps from the yard sale pile, every time I had tried to do my make-up with what scraps were left after my sister went to college, every birthday candle, every dandelion, every time I closed my eyes every night of my life I had wished I could be this woman for real. With my designer black dress and matching heels, make-up, expensive jewelry and classic looking curls I looked about 25. And totally hot, like I was some beautiful grown up, adult woman with a job and a fancy car and apartment and credit cards.

Michelle seemed equally amazed and started a running list of things we could do if made convincing adults. Bars would only be the beginning. We could buy cigarettes anywhere instead of just the couple of places that never carded. There were liquor stores and porn shops too. The entire amazing adult world seemed almost within reach. But first, Michelle insisted on photos.

Out in her yard, I posed on the lawn as Michelle went through a couple of rolls of film. Fairly new to being a model and a muse, I did my best, running through a series of poses that I thought looked demure, coy or sexy. Smoking seemed cool, so I posed with a cigarette, making kissing faces at the camera as I blew smoke in what I hoped was a seductive fashion. These, she promised, were not for photography class submissions, but would maybe be publicly displayed in a gallery one day when we were famous. Michelle never had any doubt that we would be famous. All we had to do was get out of Augusta.

* * *

Getting into the bar proved far easier than I had ever thought. First there was a door that led from the parking lot into a little room with a guy behind a counter and a bouncer. Another door led into the actual bar itself, presumably. We just had to get past these two.

"Evening, ladies," the man behind the counter said with a Southern lisp. "This is a private club. Are you members?" Having no idea how to respond, I just stood there tight-lipped, hoping that Michelle would take the lead. Michelle was the expert on this. I was just the arm candy.

"No?" Michelle answered, letting the 'oh' fill the space in case she thought of a 'but' she could add.

"Well," the guy behind the counter said. "You can become a member, but there is a five dollar membership fee. Payable in cash only." We paid our five dollars each and the bouncer stepped aside. The whole private club thing must have been a way to skirt whatever local law might have prevented a gay bar from operating.

"Here we go," Michelle smiled, brighter than I had ever seen her and we walked into our first gay bar, actually my first bar. I might have imagined it, but I think she may have even done a happy little squeal. The Forum was a giant square cement bunker, windowless, but with silver and gold metallic foil strips lining the walls from floor to ceiling. A disco ball and colored lights flashed. One wall had a bar and the other the stage and there were a few tables scattered in between. By the door there was a stack of gay newsletters and magazines and a bowl of condoms. Though it was a Saturday night, there were only a handful of people, mostly older and mostly huddled around the bar.

"It's the Factory," I said as I took it all in.

"Oh my gosh," Michelle said. "We should get a drink."

"What do we drink?" I asked nervously. Though I was out at a bar, drinking was still entirely new to me, though I was definitely starting to notice that all the sinful things preachers warned about were way more fun than prayer, hymns and church.

"Vodka cranberry," was her answer, I think because it was one of the only cocktails she knew and because mixed drinks were infinitely more glamorous than a few stolen cans of beer or bottles of wine coolers or boxed wine could ever be.

"Great," I said and we strode up to the bar. Walking in heels wasn't too bad, though I was starting to wish my nails looked better. I'd not painted them and they were bitten down. As we approached the bar, I started to feel self-conscious over them and immediately my mind started focusing on everything that was wrong with my appearance. My hips were slim, my walk was probably mannish, my hands were big and my cuticles overgrown and my voice would definitely give me away. Suddenly I felt nervous, open and exposed. Looking over at Michelle she seemed half-drunk already, just on the endorphin rush of being in a bar for the first time. And not just any bar, but a shining, sparkling, light flashing, private club of a gay bar.

"How much cash do you have?" Michelle asked as she gave the bartender a little wave. Like any good Southern lesbian, the bartender wore a golf shirt and sported a mullet.

"Hopefully enough," I said. I had gotten paid a few days before. But, unfortunately, I wasn't entirely sure how much drinks cost.

"Cool," Michelle shot me a wicked look and then as the bartender came over ordered for us "Two vodka and cranberries, please."

"Well vodka?" she asked.

"Oh, definitely," Michelle nodded. "Well is my favorite."

"Right," said the bartender who quickly whipped us a couple. She set two dark pink glasses with ice, garnished with lemon. "Together that's $12."

"I'll get it," I said, putting down a five and a ten. "Keep the change." I had never seriously said 'keep the change' to anyone and it felt incredibly grown up. At six dollars each, I would do okay money-wise, though I wasn't quite sure how a vodka cranberry would affect me intoxication-wise.

"Cheers," Michelle smiled, holding up her glass.

"Two beautiful ladies out on the town," I said in my best girl voice. We toasted and I took a big gulp of my first drink out in a bar.

"It's good," Michelle said after her own first gulp. It was good and didn't taste much like alcohol at all.

"It's perfect."

* * *

We were already four drinks in when the lights dimmed. Despite being unaccustomed to vodka cranberry, I was surprised that I wasn't feeling particularly drunk. If Michelle wasn't drunk on the liquor she was definitely drunk on the experience. As far as I knew, neither of us had ever seen a drag queen show and I knew I had no idea what to expect. Michelle, I think, probably didn't either, but kept shooting me excited, giggly looks as we waited for the evening's event to start.

"Ladies and gentleman, homos and breeders, bisexuals and heterflexibles," sang out the announcer over the PA. I could see him with the microphone in the little booth in the corner to the right of the stage. "The Forum is proud to present the star of the Southern Belles Revue, two-time winner of the Miss Augusta Pageant. Give it up for Amanda Bonetonite!" Everyone cheered but no one came out so the announcer repeated it "Amanda Bonetonite! C'mon, I need Amanda Bonetonite!"

"Sorry, honey," came a booming flash of a gay, Southern voice. "You couldn't afford me." She was tall and built like a barrel, but wore a sparklingly black sequin dress, clear platform heels and a huge blonde wig. Her light blue eye shadow went from her fake lashes all the way up to the fake eyebrows she'd drawn on halfway up her forehead. Her lipstick extended at least an inch past her lips and her cheeks were so rosy with blush they could win horticultural awards. "Give me that," she said saucily as she snatched the microphone from the DJ's hand. "Last time I asked him to give me something, the doctor said they were gonna name a new type of chlamydia after me."

"Ya'll like pretty girls?" she asked and the audience clapped and cheered. "Well too bad, we don't have any here tonight." Stepping off stage, she started walking toward the tables. Luckily, Michelle and I were seated at one of the tables in the middle, so maybe she wouldn't make us get on stage or anything like that.

"Where you from, sugar?" she said, wrapping herself around a skinny, middle-aged man in a camouflage hat.

"Waynesboro," he said.

"Sorry?"

"Waynesboro," he said louder and a couple people in the back clapped.

"Oh, I heard you, honey. I'm just sorry." Everyone laughed and Amanda made her way to the next table. It was full of a group of young, blonde girls who had dressed up for a Saturday night out.

"Look at you girls," she said and they shouted, clapped and went woo. "You're so excited to be out here. If you were out looking for Mr. Right tonight I think you might be out of luck."

"It's Caroline's birthday!" one of them drunkenly shouted.

"Really? You don't look a day over 75. I bet you love sucking dick, don't you Caroline."

"Hell yeah!" she shouted and held up her drink. Amanda Bonetonite looked out over the crowd and made huge pointing gestures to Caroline's table while all the girls there cheered.

"Ya'll taking notes? I know she ain't half of you's type, but hey, a blowjob's a blowjob." She leaned in to the next table where a couple buff young guys were sitting. "If you close your eyes she looks just like Patrick Swayze." As the drag queen made her way around to the tables, I felt complete dread come over me. The last thing I wanted was any attention at all. What if she came by the table and noticed that we weren't 21? We'd get kicked out and banned for life and then my parents would find out that I got dressed up as a girl and then went to a gay bar. Luckily she didn't get too deep into the tables.

"All right," she said, stepping back on stage "I bet y'all are already sick of me. So, I want you to give a big, Forum welcome to the girl that *Time Magazine* called the 'sexiest piece of ass this side of Kentucky, Miss Lexie Vixen!" With that, Amanda Bonetonite, stepped off stage and went and stood in the shadows by the DJ. Then a single spotlight appeared on stage and Lexie Vixen stepped out the door and onto the stage.

Unlike the first drag queen, Lexie Vixen was young and petite. Instead of a classic dress she was just wearing a black teddy, tight black shorts and thigh high fishnet stockings with a garter belt and black stiletto heels. If she wore a wig it looked natural, like platinum blonde hair that fell in tresses long past her shoulders. Her make-up wasn't weird or too much, but just made her face prettier. As she began her routine, set to Madonna's "Erotic," I just sat there watching and couldn't have looked away if I had tried. She was, in a word, beautiful and I couldn't for the life of me imagine that she was a guy. It just wasn't possible. There was the way she moved, the sultriness of her hips swaying. I swear she even had real breasts. I had never imagined that it was even possible. I had never imagined that someone born a boy could ever be such a beautiful woman, perfect in every way. Suddenly, the world felt just a little bit bigger.

# Chapter Eighteen

### "Walking Into Spider Webs"
### December 1996

"This is unhealthy," Michelle said judgmentally. "You can't waste all your time pining over a girl that already has a boyfriend. A psycho boyfriend at that." Our favorite couch at Orwell's was taken by a group of skater kids from Lakeside, so we were stuck on the badly stained plaid couch against the back wall. There was no show at the Catalina Club tonight, but Orwell's was still pretty vibrant and busy with the usual teens and punk and other malcontents.

"I am not pining," I said as I added more sugar to my giant red eye coffee. "And I thought you were fine with this." I was doing my normal Orwell's activity of watching the door in case Courtney came by. When we met outside the art building earlier today, she had told me she was coming. And she was going to come with Jordan. I hated Jordan and I worried for Courtney. She was always riding on the back of his motorcycle and he was usually a few beers in. Courtney said that was just how he was and that he never rode while on anything crazier than beers. But if she were here, she hadn't come in and hadn't paged Michelle yet either. Even from the back, I could see it was crowded outside. Without a show tonight, everyone was just hanging out on the sidewalk. That would probably mean the Sheriff's Department would come by at some point. They were always hassling us.

"Mary told me that Lindsay likes you," Michelle pointed out as she sipped on her giant coffee.

"Maybe you're right. Maybe it is an all new era," I said.

"It's senior year," Michelle pointed out. "Have you ever had a girlfriend? I mean a real girlfriend. For longer than one day? Or longer than the duration of a church lock-in?"

"Have you?" I replied snarkily.

"I'm not gonna answer that," Michelle said.

"Then I don't need to answer your question. Sometimes I guess what you want is out of reach," I mused. Courtney was within reach, but not within my grasp. Why did she have to have that stupid boyfriend? "I'm not gonna date some random girl just so I can have a girlfriend. Love is the point of this, not just ticking off boxes on some imaginary high school list."

"Well, go hit on Courtney then."

"I don't know," I shrugged dejectedly. "It's complicated."

"Everything always is," Michelle said, her eyes darting to the front window. People were starting to gather near the big picture window and the door.

"Hmm."

"Something's going on," Michelle said as more people headed towards the exit. Beyond the general murmurs of the gathered, excited shouting could be heard.

"What's that?" I asked, craning my neck to look, but I couldn't see anything other than a few punks and rude boys gathered around the door. Some girls looked worried and some of the guys looked highly entertained and exchanged laughter and shouts.

"Not sure," said Michelle and suddenly the sound of breaking glass tore the air, followed by a terrible, bloodcurdling scream. More people ran outside and the frenzied shouting only intensified. Some people searched around for napkins or clothes while others just stumbled around unsure of what to do.

"Holy crap," was all I could get out. I set my coffee down and Michelle did too. For a second, we just stared at each other, then sat there, watching it all unfold. But I didn't know what to do, so I just sat there watching it, waiting for some sort of signal to jolt me into action, whatever that action might be.

"Let's go see what's up," Michelle set, getting up. I followed. Everyone was in panic, but Michelle swiftly led us out onto the sidewalk where people were watching the scene. Some wore looks of amusement, others horror or concern. Broken glass lay everywhere, mingled with blood. The picture window of the abandoned shop next to Orwell's was completely shattered. The owner of Orwell's and his wife had already come out and were helping a couple people who had cuts from the glass on their hands or faces. And on the sidewalk, with a crowd around them, two guys were grappled together in a fight and one of them was clearly winning. It took me a second, but then I noticed who was winning. Then I saw Courtney, standing just a few feet away.

"Jordan!" she shouted, tears streaming down her cheeks, leaving ugly black streaks. "He was just talking to me. Stop it!"

"Shut the hell up, Courtney," he screamed, moving his body threateningly toward her as she stepped back. "You goddamn bitch." Courtney quickly took a few more steps back as Jordan angrily landed a few more punches, then shoved the loser to the ground. I saw he was Mikey, a friend of Tall Preston's. His face a mess of blood and with a sickening feeling in my stomach, I realized that Jordan must have pushed him into the window, maybe accidentally, maybe deliberately. Jordan circled and then gave Mikey a few sharp kicks to the ribs. Mikey wasn't unconscious, not yet at least, but he was bleeding badly and lying in a pool of sick black blood on the asphalt street. Jordan had a few cuts on his hands and was bleeding too, a gash on his forehead was sending a steady stream of blood down the side of his face. His eyes were wild, crazed, animalistic, his breathing heavy with adrenaline.

"Jesus Christ, stop!" yelled a girl, I didn't know, but recognized as one of Mikey's friends. She was crying too and ran up, standing between Jordan and Mikey. Instantly, Jordan shoved her aside so hard that she lost her footing and fell back. Even 30 feet away I could hear the horrible sound of her head hitting the pavement. With that about 10 different guys rushed up and all launched on Jordan, shoving him to the ground and landing blow after blow. All the other Chelsea-cut oi girls ran over to help Mikey's friend up. She stood up, looking dazed.

Someone must have called 911 a while back because two Sheriff's Department cruisers came up 8th, their lights and sirens blaring. As if on cue, the guys who had jumped on Jordan melted away into the gathered crowd and Jordan just stood there, in the middle of the street, bruised and bloody and defiant, standing over Mikey who was still struggling to get up. Seeing the cops, he gave Mikey one last kick in the ribs and yelled "Goddam asshole, don't fuck with what's mine."

Hysterical people had started pointing at Jordan, begging the police to arrest him, screaming that he had jumped Mikey and shoved him through a window and then hit a girl. In an instant two of them tackled him to the ground, handcuffed him and then pulled him up, while the other cops checked out Mikey and the girl and sent out commands on their radio. Michelle and I just stood there, stunned, sharing blank looks. Courtney stood a few feet away, looking furious as tears streamed down her face. I could tell she was shaking.

"This is all your fault, bitch. As soon as I get out I'm gonna fucking kill you, you slut!" Jordan shouted as the cops pulled him up and shoved him in the back of the car. I watched him angrily kicking the seat in front and struggling with his cuffed hands.

"Courtney," I said under my breath, and started to take a step forward but she just put her hands in her face and ran off, down towards Broad Street.

"Shit," was all Michelle could get out as Courtney ran away.

"We should, um…" was all I could stammer out.

"Yeah," Michelle said quietly as more lights and sirens filled the night. Additional Sheriff's Department cruisers and an ambulance had already arrived. Walking up toward Broad Street, we found Courtney sitting in the doorway of a closed shop. She was sitting with her knees up tight to her chest, her arms locked right around. She had stopped crying. Instead she was looking straight ahead, rocking back and forth almost imperceptibly.

Michelle sat down next to her and put an arm around her and they just sat there together, doing nothing. Still not knowing what to do, I just stood a few feet away. Slowly, Courtney slumped her head over onto Michelle. I decided to sit down too, on the other side of Courtney and put my arm around her. No one said anything because in our 17 years we never had to say anything like what might have been said in a moment like this. So we just sat there for a while, listening to the sirens a couple blocks away, the sounds of commotion muffled by the distance. Finally it was Courtney who spoke.

"Matt, can you give me a ride home?" she croaked.

"Yeah," Michelle said. "Let's get out of here."

* * *

The whole ride back up John C. Calhoun Expressway was quiet. I thought about putting on a tape, but it seemed best to ride in silence. Michelle took the passenger seat which left Courtney sitting between us. Michelle had a curfew, but Courtney didn't, so I dropped off Michelle first, then drove Courtney home, mostly in silence.

"I don't want to go in yet," Courtney said softly once we had pulled up in front of her house. The street was quiet but the lights in her house were still on despite the late hour. Even on the street, in my truck, I could still hear yelling inside but couldn't hear any of the words that were being shouted. It was just shouting, angry shouting. The night had started to get chilly and the only noise to distract us from the fighting was the gentle pinging of the truck cooling, the distant trains and our own breathing. We sat there for what felt like an hour but must have been only a few minutes. I didn't know what to say or what could be said but finally she broke the silence with a loud sniff. "I'm completely fucked, Matt," she said resolutely, her head hung low.

"No, you're not," I said, in what I hoped was a comforting, uplifting way. I never really knew how to deal with upset people, so I just offered hopeful platitudes. "It'll be okay."

"No," she said softly, looking up at me. In her wide green eyes, smeared with messy black make-up I could see real fear. "You don't realize how bad it is. It's bad, okay."

"I know," I said, reaching over her and pulling out some napkins from the glove box. She took them and wiped her nose.

"He's really gonna try to kill me. I believe it. He said he was gonna kill Mikey if he ever talked to me again. I mean, me and Mikey went out for like, two days. And then he just said hi and Jordan freaked out and tried to throw him through the window and he's probably in the hospital now and Jordan's gonna get out of jail and try to kill me too. And then when my mom and dad find out that I was hanging out with Jordan again, then they're gonna freak out too and I don't even know what they're gonna do. And I'm dead either way. He's not bad, Jordan. He's just... he gets mad sometimes."

"We can run away," I said and then felt sort of stupid for saying it. I slid over a little on the seat and put my arm around her. She just buried her head in my chest and I could feel she was shaking. "Like on the bus. We just disappear for a couple days, until it all blows over."

"All I've ever wanted to do was run away." Courtney said, but not to me, maybe just to hear the words out loud. "But it never, ever works." Hundreds of times I had fantasized about being close to Courtney, holding her in my arms, but not like this. All I wanted to do was keep holding her in hopes that would somehow make it better. Sometimes though, the world just doesn't get better no matter how tightly you hold on.

# Chapter Nineteen

### "You Say 'Like' Too Much"
### Friday, December 6th, 1996

As there was air conditioning and reasonably comfortable chairs, the downtown branch of the library was a popular spot for homeless people. But, they tended to keep to themselves, so no one seemed to mind. It was also a popular after school hangout spot for Davidson kids, since our parents pretty much had to let us go to the library if we asked. Also most Davidson kids were huge nerds and many of them actually studied at the library instead of just hanging out and smoking cigarettes in the parking lot. Occasionally, I'd peruse the UFO and occult section when there was no one outside to smoke with.

It was Friday after school and it had been two weeks and I still hadn't been back to Orwell's. I didn't really want to go tonight either. My dad was expecting me home by 5:00 p.m. anyway, which gave me enough time to hang around the library, hoping that Courtney would show up. She was still grounded, but the library was allowed. You just had to pretend you were studying and hope your parents didn't realize that you were actually just hanging out.

After smoking two cigarettes in a row, my throat was good and dry so I decided to go see if there were any good videos at the library's special video annex. You'd think a library would keep things well-organized, but all the video tapes were in the order in which the library got them. So everything was mixed in a big jumble and you just had to flip through covers and take what you wanted up to the counter to get the actual video. Sure, it was a pain, but they had old movies and French New Wave films that I could watch and pretend to study for my future directorial debut. After a little bit, I found a copy of *Battleship Potemkin* and also some old sex education films which I hoped would be hilariously entertaining.

Those, along with a book about how ancient aliens actually built the pyramids, would keep me happy through the weekend.

When I came out into the parking lot, my heart skipped in my chest. Courtney was sitting there on the curb in jeans and a flannel shirt, smoking a cigarette. I hurried over to her as quickly as I could walk. The last thing I wanted was for someone else to sit down next to her and get her in conversation before I could. Luckily no one was around and so I said hi and sat down next to her there on the curb.

"Hey, Matt," she said sweetly, her eyes bright.

"I was gonna have a smoke too," I said. Scooting up next to her, I lit one up even though my mouth and throat were already raw.

"Cool," she said. "Thanks for letting me copy your history homework."

"No problem," I said. "Happy to help. I know you've... you know, had a rough couple of weeks."

"That would be one way to put it, yeah."

"Sorry," I said, wishing I hadn't brought it up at all.

"S 'okay."

"Are you safe?"

"He's like, not getting out anytime soon." Courtney said coldly enough that I couldn't tell if she were relieved or upset or maybe a combination of those and every emotion in between. "They charged him with everything. Aggravated assault, trespassing, stalking, like other kinds of assault. Like three kinds of assault I think. All of it, all together, it's like 50 years."

"Shit. Really?" I gasped. Obviously, I was no fan of Jordan's, but it seemed so surreal that that one fight would be the end of his life. He wouldn't get out of jail until he was in his seventies.

"Yeah, and he can't come within 500 feet of me or my house or Davidson."

"Wait? He's out?"

"Yeah, he has a court date. I don't know, I guess his mom bailed him out or something."

"Shit," I said, noticing my language had started to get cruder lately. And I used to be such a good Christian boy.

"Yeah. But his cousin told me he was back down in Millen at his mom's house now. She said she wasn't gonna pay for a lawyer or a bail unless he came down there. I guess she's worried he'll go off."

"So you're safe?" I asked hopefully.

"Safe enough," she said, taking a long drag on her own smoke.

"You don't need a guy like that," I said and sort of wished I hadn't. A huge part of me wanted to make a speech about how great I was and how amazing a boyfriend I'd be and how nice I was and how I'm a great kisser. But then that general cowardice that always haunted me made me realize that self-aggrandizement would make me look haughty and boastful. Now wasn't the time to try and hit on Courtney. She'd just been through a rough patch and was still going through a rough patch. Maybe once she got out of that rough patch, then things would be good.

"Guys like that are the only ones who like me," she laughed a little defeated laugh and shook her head.

"No, that's not true," I said, wondering if I could just come out and say that I liked her and I was a nice guy who wouldn't treat her like a jerk or assault-and-battery people.

"Maybe," she said. "It's just…"

"What?"

"I want it to get better. Just for once. I want it to get better. But it just always keeps getting worse." Quietly, she let a tear slide down her face.

"It can get better. It can. You are an amazing girl. C'mon, you're fun and you're adventurous and you're smart and you're pretty. You're really pretty. You're beautiful." I was taking it too far. That was definitely into the like-like category. "It'll get better."

"No, Matt."

"C'mon. You met me. So that's your social life already getting better," I joked and luckily she laughed.

"Yeah," she said, rubbing out her cigarette on the pavement. She smiled at me and I smiled back. "You're okay."

"Just okay. That's fine," I laughed, flicking my cigarette out into the pavement. Courtney was still looking up at me, her perfect pink lips a little smile, her bright green eyes looking into mine.

"You're a good guy, Matt," She bit her lip slightly and I don't remember if I leaned in or if she did. Maybe we were both leaning in together. Maybe there are just moments that are meant to be and you both know it and not leaning in isn't even an option. But I do remember that she kissed me, right on the lips and we kissed deeply and passionately and I ran my hands through her hair and she put her hand on my leg and we kissed in that library parking lot. In that one embrace we allowed ourselves to forget all of the crap of the world; tests, homework, our parents, exes, school and our shitty town. All of it. It was all a million miles away.

\* \* \*

Christmas was coming. In Augusta that meant tacky lights on houses, temperatures in the low 60's, and probably rain. It meant two weeks off school. It also meant that Courtney's parents finally started to ease up on the terms of her grounding.

Courtney must have said something to them, because only a couple weeks after our first kiss in the library parking lot, I suddenly found myself invited to dinner at the Wilkerson house. Actually, I had learned, Courtney was the only Wilkerson there. Her mom and stepdad were Harrisons. So technically it was the Harrison house.

They lived off Walton Way, not too far from me. The December air was crisp and clear and made the neighborhood houses' various decorations seem all the more vivid. Pulling up to Courtney's I saw that her house—a Victorian complete with a widow's tower and two-story wrap around porch—was unadorned with lights or plastic reindeer.

I parked my truck on the street and then nervously walked up to the house. It would be nice to spend time with Courtney that didn't consist of the five minutes between classes, the 10 minutes before school, or in the library after school. Maybe one day we could even make out without homeless people watching us.

When the door opened both her parents were standing there. Both were older, maybe in their 40's or 50's, and looked well dressed, and friendly. They introduced themselves by their first names—Bill and Beverly—and invited me in. It was a nice house with furnishings that were more expensive than mine. There was something of a lighthouse theme for the formal living room decorations. And the house smelled like woody potpourri and that powder you put on carpets before you vacuum.

I was herded over to the couch where I took a seat with Bill in an easy chair to my right and Beverly on the couch to the left of me. Being surrounded made my nervousness go into overdrive. As did the fact that Courtney was nowhere to be seen. Bill and Beverly? They knew. They knew that I wanted to have sex with their daughter. They knew and they could see right through me. I steeled myself for a contempt-driven interrogation of my morals and motivations.

"So Matt," Bill started in on me first. "You know Courtney from Davidson?"

"Yeah," I said then corrected myself. "Yes, sir." Yes, sir. I have put my tongue in your daughter's mouth. Yes, sir. I have grabbed her boobs over her shirt. Yes, sir. I have tried to finger her, though she sort of pushed my hand away. Yes, sir. I have in fact dry humped your daughter in the microfilm room of the downtown branch of the public library.

"Oh, that's great," Beverly spoke up. "Are you an artist? A musician?"

"Visual arts," I replied.

"That's great," Beverly said. "Courtney auditioned for ballet. Though I guess she's not enjoying that anymore."

"It's easy to get burned out," I said. "You know with all the AP classes and fine arts too."

"Are you taking AP classes?" Bill asked me.

"Yes, sir," I said. "I'm in AP English and European History."

"That's great," Bill said with a warm smile. "Are you on track for the HOPE scholarship? All A's?"

"Right now," I said. "We've got midterms coming up though. So a lot of studying. It's hard to balance that and work."

"Oh, you have a job?" Beverly interjected while beaming. "That's very responsible. What are you doing?"

"It's just bagging groceries." I stammered.

"That's fantastic, son," Bill said. "You gotta start somewhere. I keep telling Court that a job would teach responsibility and you get a paycheck, which isn't too shabby either."

"It's okay," I said. Then I looked up to see that Courtney was bounding down the stairs. Instead of her normal punky look she was wearing a black floral dress, ballet flats, and no make-up. She threw me a little wave, then came down and sat beside me. Courtney reached over and gave my hand a brief but affectionate and encouraging squeeze.

"Look who finally decided to grace us with her presence," Beverly said disdainfully.

"Sorry," Courtney mumbled.

"Well, kids," Bill said as he stood up. "Do you like lasagna? It's been in the oven about an hour and should have a nice crispy, bubbly cheese layer on top. My own special recipe."

"Matt, you want to help Courtney set the table?" Linda said. "And I'll start getting the food ready."

"His lasagna's actually pretty good," Courtney said to me in a reassuring way. We went into the kitchen and began to fetch heavy china plates with gold rims, dark blue cloth napkins, glasses, and cutlery from various drawers and cabinets. As Beverly busied herself with tossing ingredients in a big wooden salad bowl and Bill grabbed the giant casserole dish from the oven, I was again bombarded with questions about my life. This time it consisted of inquiries about SAT's, college letters, and potential majors.

I was two bites into the admittedly quite good lasagna, when I realized that Courtney's mom and step dad liked me. And then, as I doused my salad with ranch dressing from a plastic bottle, I realized why they liked me. It was simply because I wasn't Jordan. They would have been happy with any law-abiding, non-psycho, high school-aged warm body that Courtney had brought over. It was nice to know that I was liked, but it still felt kind of cheap.

"Sorry," Courtney said as we settled in on her front porch's swing after dinner. "They're like total dorks." It was chilly outside but in a crisp and refreshing way. Though we were only a few blocks from Walton Way, the entire area was blanketed with a quiet and calm disturbed only by the white noise of the fan keeping a giant plastic snowman inflated on a nearby yard.

"It's okay," I said. "They're like a billion times better than my parents." I was completely stuffed full of lasagna, salad, and cake. As such I didn't feel particularly amorous despite sitting super close to Courtney. The reality of it suddenly hit me though. I was sitting on a swing with Courtney Wilkerson at her house. I had just met her parents. We were going together. Courtney Wilkerson was my honest-to God-girlfriend.

"You're probably the only reason they didn't spend the entire night arguing," Courtney laughed despondently and shook her head.

"You know," I said with a smile. "It's been a while since I've heard a good parental argument. I kinda miss it."

"Really?" Courtney asked skeptically.

"No," I clarified. "I was being sarcastic. My parents split up back in October. They're still hashing out paperwork and lawyers and bills and stuff. But at least they stopped arguing in front of me."

"Parents suck," Courtney said.

"So, when'd your parents get divorced?" I asked. "I mean, unless it's like, bad."

"No," Courtney shook her head slightly. "I guess I was like five or six maybe? I was little. It was back around the time when the Challenger blew up. Remember that? On TV?"

"How was it?"

"Hmm," Courtney scrunched up her face. "It was just weird, like confusing. You know? Like I didn't know what was going on. And everyone was way too nice about it. Like, even if I was a kindergartener I still knew people were all being too nice. They dropped me off at my gramma's for a while. My dad moved out. He has a new family in Nashville and I don't ever really see him. Then my mom got with Bill a little while later. Then it just sort of settled into normal. You know, I guess it's weird. 'Cause you can never really know what it was like to live like someone else did. Like you can never know what it was like to grow up with two un-divorced parents if you didn't. Or like you grow up in New York you never know what it's like to grow up in Georgia. Or a girl can never know what it's like to be a boy or vice-versa."

"Totally," I agreed. "I always wondered what it was like to live in one place all your life. With roots. And cousins nearby and grandparents in the same town. I spent my whole life moving around from place to place, never settled, always the new kid. The only stable thing was my family. And now that's fallen apart. I don't have anything tying me down I guess."

"You got me," Courtney said. And I had to admit that it was really nice to hear.

* * *

"So, God," I started the prayer, thinking it out loud. God could read my thoughts. He could read all our thoughts. That having bad thoughts was a sin had always bothered me a little bit. Sometimes you can't control what you think or how you feel about something. How can it be a sin if you can't control it? Ah well, that wasn't what this was about. With my eyes closed I laid there in bed, under the old green army blanket that I had always used for covers, and tried to focus on my prayer.

"I know that I asked for Courtney and me to go together," I prayed.

"And you answered that prayer. And yes, I said that I would be a better Christian if you answered my prayer. But I still don't know, God. It still doesn't make sense to me. I don't want to sit in church and have the preacher tell me that I'm going to hell for things that I can't help. I can't help it, God. It's hard. And I think before I agree to anything, I have to sort all this out on my own.

That's fair right? Because all the people that tell me what the Bible says or tell me what you say, they're just people. I feel like they're bringing their own interpretation of things and maybe that's not the right interpretation. So, I gotta figure this out on my own. Of course I still believe in you, and love you, and everything. And I'm grateful that you died on the cross for our sins and for creating the whole universe and everything. I just need to know the truth. I know I should read the Bible about this. But what if the people who wrote the Bible were wrong? Or the people who translated it?

I don't know. I just wish this wasn't so hard, Lord. Because I feel terrible about my lust, and about my sin, and about wanting to be a girl too. I do feel really bad. But also, I kinda don't. I mean, maybe I'm just awash in sin. I don't know. I don't know, God. Please help me understand this all better. Thank you for everything, Amen."

As I laid there in bed, waiting to fall asleep, my eyes fixed on the bright red numbers of my digital alarm clock, I let my mind dwell on a thought that had never occurred to me before. What if the Bible wasn't the word of God? What if it was all wrong? What if we really were all alone in a cold, uncaring universe with no one watching over us? Would that be freedom? Or would that be the most terrifying thing ever? Or could it be both all at the same time? What if there was no heaven or hell? What if there was reincarnation instead? When I died, I could be reborn as a girl and for once not have to wish.

# Chapter Twenty

## "As Far from God as Angels Can Fly"
## Friday, March 7th, 1997

Like me, Web had once gotten kicked out of American Christian. It was back when I was in eighth grade and he was in 10th. The principal had announced that there would be random drug testing of students. The first and only name randomly selected was that of Joseph Webster. Web refused and was expelled.

Pretty much everyone knew the school had it out for him. Though anyone who knew him knew that Web was a serious Christian, he was also an unabashed punk. The school tended to look down on anyone who wasn't a khaki shorts, golf shirt-clad athlete. We called those types "Smilin' Joe ACS." And we hated them. But Web was cool.

"This place is awesome," I said as Web pulled open a rusted metal gate and let us into his new place. Now that Web was attending Augusta College, he had moved out of his parents' house and into a massive, dusty, empty floor of a downtown warehouse. One corner featured a mini fridge, a hot plate, and some wooden crates that had been repurposed as both a counter and a table.

In the center, dwarfed by the open space of the room, sat a couch, some chairs, and a life-sized cardboard cutout of a galactic bounty hunter. The TV was plugged in via a bright orange 100-foot extension cord that stretched across the whole space. In another corner a bed and dresser sat behind a jury-rigged system of privacy curtains. By the freight elevator, there was an assortment of guitars on stands, stacks of amps, and a drum kit. Above it all massive belt-driven ceiling fans lazily spun.

"Thanks, man," Web said as we headed in. Tanya was sitting on the couch drinking a beer, dwarfed by the immensity of the place. "It's great. Lots of space and no neighbors to complain about the band practicing."

He, Tad the drummer, and some girl from Augusta College had just started a new punk band called Pixiedeath.

"You could have a whole rave here, man," Courtney said as she looked around, her eyes wide. With a quick jog, Web ran over to the fridge where he retrieved us a couple cans of beer. He handed us the drinks and motioned for us to grab a spot in the living room area.

"How'd you find this place?" I asked as we found spots and cracked open our beers.

"His dad owns the building," Tanya answered. "Gave him cheap rent just to get his butt out of the house."

"It worked," Web shrugged. Next to the couch were several tall stacks of CDs. Web went over and, after some careful selection, grabbed one and put it in a nearby boom box. Bad Religion's *Suffer* started blasting out at a volume that seemed to be lost in so large an empty space.

"How's the band going?" I asked.

"We've written like a couple songs," Web explained. "We had Michael Vig, you know that kid? He played bass on one. Still trying to find a good bass player. We talked to this guy Benji. His band played Buttjam two years ago. Did you go to that?"

"Yeah," I said. Buttjam was an outdoor concert to save a local landmark called the Butt Bridge. Most people in town—myself included—cared less about architecture and just thought it was funny to rally behind the slogan 'Save Our Butt.' Still, it was a good show with lots of local bands and even a couple of national bands.

"Everyone went to that," Courtney pointed out. "'S'not like there's ever anything to do in Augusta."

"Wait," Tanya said excitedly. "So you two kids were at the Save Our Butt concert together before you even knew each other?"

"Yeah," I said thoughtfully, turning to Courtney. "It's like it was fated for us to meet each other. Like, it's God's will or something."

"Nah," Courtney shook her head. "Nah, all like fate, and God and stuff. That's all bullshit, man."

"What do you think, Courtney?" Tanya asked. "What's the meaning of it all if there's no God or anything?"

"It's just like the universe, you know," Courtney said. Then she squinted up her eyes and carefully thought about each word as she continued. "I thought about this a lot. You can smoke weed and drop acid and think about this. Your mind's just open. I just sit and think about this.

You know, like, Stephen Hawking right? The universe is so endlessly huge. Totally mind boggling, right? There's a billion galaxies for every grain of sand. And, like, a billion stars and planets in every galaxy. That's too big a number to even count, right? You think that out of all of that, this one planet is like the one most important thing? Nah, man. We don't even have any idea of what we don't know about anything." I sat, watched in silence, and reveled in the fact that my girlfriend was not only pretty. She was smart too. And cool. And a punk. That was awesome.

"That's a good point," Web conceded. "I'll totally admit that the universe is amazing. But that just means that it had to take something even more amazing to make it happen. The Earth is tiny right? But I have faith that we are important to God. I know that I can feel the love of Jesus Christ in my heart."

"That's cool but," Courtney shook her head. "I just, you know, different strokes for different folks, right?"

"Seriously," Tanya said. "It's a Friday night. Let's not get all theological here."

"Totally," Web agreed.

"Hey Web," I asked. "You gonna go see *Jedi* this weekend?"

"Yeah," Web said enthusiastically. "Man, I haven't seen that on the big screen since I was in kindergarten. That's gonna be awesome."

There was a thing I had noticed with all the Christian leaders around me. Pastors, Christian school faculty, my own parents. They were all about appearances. Web and Tanya were as Christ-like as anyone when it came to treating people well. But because they drank or smoked cigarettes and cussed, all those church people wouldn't have even considered them real Christians.

I was glad that Web hadn't left for college. We could sit around, smoke cigarettes, drink beers, and talk for hours. There were endless topics: movies, music, God, the universe. It was all open for discussion. Plus, after a while, Web and Tanya headed off to their curtained-off area. That would leave Courtney and me alone on the couch to make out until the night had to end.

As we went to leave, Web let Tanya pull open the big freight elevator gate. The two girls hopped in and Web pulled me aside. There was a deadly serious look on his face as he led me past the band area.

"Be careful, man," Web said just above a whisper. "Courtney's awesome. But she's not a Christian. People date non-Christians and then backslide hard."

"It's not like that, Web," I protested.

"I know, I know," he said. "I don't want to give you a hard time. I just want you to be careful, man. Don't let a girl, even a redhead, get between you and Christ, okay? You'll get pulled right down to hell with her."

"I won't," I said. "Thanks for the beers."

"No problem," Web said. "Stay cool, Matt."

\* \* \*

As always, the Riverwalk amphitheater was empty, making it a fantastic place for two teenagers to sit and make out on breezy Saturday night. Since I wasn't Jordan, Courtney's mom and stepdad had enacted a full pardon for all of Courtney's past trouble. I was practically waiting for them to start dropping hints about marriage.

My mouth was wet and my balls ached. Courtney had told me that she had had sex with two guys—Jordan and a friend's older brother—but with me she wanted to wait so it would be special. But I didn't care about special. I finally had a real girlfriend and here I was still somehow a virgin with high school graduation mere months away. With one hand up under her shirt, under her bra, grabbing her bare breast, I started sliding the other down to her waist. She stopped me as soon as my fingertips went below the edge of her jeans.

"Not here," she said with heavy breath as she pushed my hand away.

"C'mon," I begged and brought my hand right back. "No one's around."

"No, not in the fucking amphitheater, Matt," Courtney said as she pulled away. Sheepishly, I sat up straight and sighed.

"I'm sorry," I said half-heartedly. "You're just so hot. I just want us to do it." The condom in my wallet had been there for years and had worn a ring into the imitation leather.

"So do I," Courtney said. "Just not, like, in the amphitheater in the middle of public."

"Okay," I whined. "It's just, I like you so much."

"I like you, too," Courtney said and offered a slightly flirty hand. I took it and pulled her closer. "Just, you know, I wanna do it somewhere normal. Not here."

"Okay," I agreed. The last thing I wanted to do was push too hard and mess up my relationship. How often in life do you really get the thing you want? In my 17 years it had never happened before. So the last thing I wanted to do was screw it up. Courtney was the best thing that had ever happened to me. I did my best to push down my jealousy. Sure, Courtney had had sex with two other guys. But maybe she had taken things even more slowly with them.

"Dude, what is that?" Courtney said looking up. "Is that the comet?" It was a clear night and even with the light of downtown, the stars were bright. But there was a new fixture sitting still in the night sky. The Hale-Bopp comet was bright and visible above us. It was the first comet I had ever actually seen. When I was in kindergarten grownups were all excited about Haley's comet but I hadn't seen it. Hale-Bopp was big, bright, and kind of exciting.

"The universe, huh?" I said with just a hint of awe. Then I remembered Courtney's own musings on the universe. Did she really think its vastness meant we couldn't really understand anything, much less God? "So, you never went to church growing up?"

"Sure," Courtney replied. "I mean, at my gramma's sometimes. But my mom and stepdad aren't ever religious."

"So you never got saved?" I asked.

"No," Courtney said matter-of-factly. "You know, you can be a good person without being saved or going to church."

"Oh, I know," I said, barely listening. Instead I was imagining a realm of endless torment. I was imagining Courtney suffering forever, bathed in a lake of fire, an army of demons inflicting infinite torment on her for a million years and a billion after that, and forever more.

God is love. That was the phrase people liked to use. It was on coffee mugs, and T-shirts, and even billboards. But here I was, wanting the love of a God that was going to make me, Michelle, and Courtney too all suffer forever in hell. Even if I stopped backsliding and really focused on being a good Christian, Courtney was still doomed. With existential bravado I imagined somehow journeying into hell to rescue Courtney, my love, from the flames. As she couldn't enter heaven we would have to find our own place in the afterlife where we could be together forever, for once free from demons and angels alike.

"I like you a lot," Courtney said as she laid down with her head in my lap. Her pale green eyes gazed up past me to the sparkling comet far above. She wrapped an arm around my leg and let the other swing down lazily. "I know I've been with guys, but it was never special. I want us to be special. Like, how often do you see a comet in the sky? That's the biggest, baddest shooting star ever. That's as special as it gets. And me and you are sharing it together."

"I love you, Courtney," I leaned over her and we awkwardly managed a kiss. Who was I kidding? I would descend into a thousand hells for this girl. And I'd risk everything to rescue her. If that wasn't love I didn't know what was.

"I love you too, Matt."

* * *

Later that night, laying in my bed in the dark, with my imagination conjuring up pale skin and green eyes, I took care of the throbbing and pain in my crotch. It was while cleaning up with a dirty towel that the usual guilt hit me. It was a sin to masturbate. It was a sin to engage in heavy petting, it was a sin to lust after a girl. Maybe I wouldn't get a chance to rescue Courtney from hell. Maybe I'd be right there burning beside her.

But who was it that said that? The pastor said that. But what did the pastor know? What did my dad know? I was reminded of a Bible verse. Jesus said, "I am the way and the truth and the life. No one comes to the Father except through me."

Then it occurred to me. No one got into heaven except through Jesus. That meant that no mere human could say who was going to heaven or not. The preachers and people at American Christian could talk for forever and a day about various people going to hell. But who really went to hell wasn't up to them. It wasn't up to the people who wrote the Bible. It wasn't up to the Apostle Paul. It was up to Jesus and Jesus alone.

Jesus would know who was a good person. Jesus would see into their hearts. Maybe they were Muslim or Hindu or a non-believer because that was all they ever knew. Maybe hypocrites like the principal or Pastor Ellis or my parents made the Muslims and Hindus think that all Christians were bad. But Jesus would know what was in their hearts. Jesus would know that someone like Courtney had done her best with what she was given. Jesus wasn't a psychopath at all. He would reserve hell for only those people who really deserved it, people like Hitler or Jason Evans.

Or what if God were, like Courtney thought, entirely disinterested in us? I had read enough Carl Sagan to know that the universe was

190

unimaginably huge. And that was just the observable universe. Who even knew what was outside the parts we could see? Would the creator of a universe that immense be interested in one little planet? Would he be interested in one of the four billion little people on that microscopic planet? Maybe Courtney had a point.

"Dear God," I prayed in earnest. "Is this all really just beyond our understanding? Are you even listening to this? Can you even hear me? If you can, do you care at all? I don't want to go to hell, God. And I don't want Courtney to. Or Michelle either. They're good people and I care about them. I mean if 'once saved always saved' is true, which I'm not too sure about either, then I'd be going to heaven. But how can I enjoy heaven at all, knowing that people I love are suffering horribly in hell? I could use some guidance here, is all. Also I'm hoping that none of this is blasphemy against the Holy Spirit because the Bible says that's the one unforgivable sin. And I hope I haven't done that. I hope having doubts isn't that. It's not, right? I mean Jesus doubted in the Garden of Gethsemane, right? I mean that was you. So I hope you can forgive my doubting. Thank you, Lord. Amen."

As I turned onto my side, scrunched up my pillows, and got into my usual sleeping position, I felt a sudden peace. Maybe it was God who sent it to me. Or maybe it was a simple epiphany that my own brain figured out. But I knew, I really knew, that God wasn't going to send good people to hell. Even gay people, guys who wanted to be girls, and people full of doubts were safe. The real God was an unknowable power, unimaginably greater than anything a mere preacher could prattle on about, or an ancient scribe could ever hope to describe.

* * *

My mom's new apartment was in a fairly classy apartment complex, as far as apartment complexes went. I'm not sure why she chose to move out or why they chose that my dad would have custody of me for the last few months before I left for college.

All I knew was there had been a fairly contentious few months in the fall when I was drafted into becoming a messenger for them. Every visit or return home involved ferrying a big brown envelope of documents back and forth. My mom would always tape it. My dad never bothered though. Mostly they were legal papers and banking stuff.

Awkward though it was, the divorce had its clear benefits. For one, my dad had long stopped caring when I came or went. All I had to do was mutter something about work and he wouldn't even ask. My mom, on the other hand, was bending over backwards to make sure that I was happy. I think she feared the divorce would upset me and felt guilty about it.

So for our twice-weekly dinners, she would usually take me out to wherever I wanted to go. Tonight I had asked and received Dizzy Chicken. It was one of my favorites, after all. Though it was more fun with my friends before a movie, and less fun with my mom on tenterhooks, I was worried that something might upset me and screw me up for life.

"So what's new with you, Matt?" she asked as soon as there was a two second lull in the conversation.

"I've decided to become a deist," I announced looking up from the menu. I don't know why I even looked at the menu. My order was always the same: chicken finger basket with curly fries, and a sweet tea to drink.

"And what is a deist?" she asked skeptically.

"We learned about it in AP US History," I explained as I absentmindedly picked at a small hole in the plastic red and white checkerboard tablecloth. "All the Founding Fathers were deists."

"Okay," she said slowly, dragging it out intentionally so as to prompt me to continue.

"So, like, the deists believed that there's a God. But all God did was create the universe. He started it off with natural laws and then let it go. So He's not involved at all in human affairs."

"Not involved at all, huh?" she asked.

"Nope," I said. "No prophecies or miracles at all."

"So what about Jesus?" she asked. "He didn't perform any miracles, then? At least, according to your new philosophy?"

"He was just a teacher, a wise man. But just a man. No miracles. No resurrection," I explained. "And God doesn't send anyone to hell."

"Hmm," she mulled it over. "Well, don't tell your dad about this. All it'll do is start an argument."

"Okay," I said with an eye roll. Thankfully the waitress took this opportunity to stop by the table to take our orders.

"And how's it going with your girlfriend? With Courtney?" she asked. It was nice to hear other people refer to her as my girlfriend. It made it feel even more real. Like it was a part of reality and other people had to acknowledge it. Courtney and I had impacted reality together. Also it was nice that she remembered Courtney's name. My dad had a bad habit of butchering it and calling her Carla or Cathy.

"She's good," I said.

"You guys have been going out a while now, huh?" she asked in a way that indicated that she knew the answer and was building up to something. I sincerely hoped it wasn't going to be the sex talk. During puberty and adolescence I had somehow managed to avoid having to talk to either of my parents about sex.

"Since December," I said. Then I quickly did the math in my head. "Almost four months."

"Well," she said thoughtfully. "I know senior prom is coming up. While I would prefer you wait until you're older, I want to make sure you're being safe..."

"Oh my God, Mom," I practically gagged. "I know all about that..."

"I just want to make sure..." she interrupted.

"Been through it in health class," I said exasperatedly. "And, like, a bajillion after school specials, okay."

"Okay," she said in that way mothers say it when they are backing away but still want to let you know that you should feel guilty for making them back away. Prom was still pretty far away anyway. And though I knew all about safe sex, I still hadn't managed to practice it or any other kind of sex. At least I had a really hot girlfriend to not have sex with.

# Chapter Twenty-One

### "On That Big Dipper"
### Saturday, May 14th, 1997

It was still light out when I stopped in front of her house to pick her up. Though, I had still thought the entire concept as lame as anything in the history of lameness, I had acquiesced to my mom's demands that I take the normal road: renting a tux, buying Courtney a corsage, and getting our photos taken at prom so my grandparents could have copies. High school was almost over and I found my interest in rebellion fading. Better not to fight and just jump through these last hoops so you could get off to college where the real party would begin.

Fortunately, I'd have to pick up Courtney on my way to prom, so we could avoid the potentially embarrassing thing of having to stop at both of my parents' houses so we could get gawked at before also getting gawked at by her mom and stepdad. This way, there would just be one stop at Courtney's house, so her parents could gush about what a good son-in-law I would one day be. As I pulled up, I steeled myself for endless smiles and photos.

Just as I had turned off the engine, though, the front door opened and Courtney came running out as fast as she could. Her red hair was curled and pinned atop her head, bold make-up covered her pale face, and she wore a floor length slinky and sparkling light blue gown. As she ran up to the truck, I leaned over and opened the door. Hopping in, she kissed me quickly, took a deep breath and rushed out the words "Let's go!"

"Wait? What?" I sputtered. "Aren't we going in?"

"Go," she instructed, snapping on her seatbelt. Obediently, I started the truck, and as it coughed to life, I stared dumbfounded at her, wondering what was going on.

"What was that about?" I asked as I turned out of her neighborhood and onto Walton Way. "Also, you look insanely beautiful by the way."

"Thanks. You look totally handsome in your tux," she said, pulling out a cigarette and lighting it. As if on cue, I had pulled one out and lit it as well. Though there were dryer sheets and a little bottle of mouthwash in the glove compartment, I hadn't smoked all afternoon, just so I could make a good impression on Courtney's parents. It probably wouldn't have mattered. No matter what I did, they seemed to love me.

"So why the daring escape?" I asked.

"Oh my God, they have a camera and tripod," Courtney sighed. "I had to take like a hundred billion pictures."

"All that to avoid pictures?" I asked.

"And them being all crazy over you. And us," she explained. "Also I stole a fifth of whiskey. It's in my purse, so you know, for later."

"Cool," I said.

"You really do look amazingly beautiful," I said, failing to keep my eyes on the road as I looked over at her. Courtney was already naturally beautiful, even in her regular jeans and tank top, but dolled up, she was something else. Honestly, I had to admit to myself that I was a little jealous, too. All week the senior and junior girls, along with the few lucky younger ones who had been invited, had been talking about their dresses, how they were going to do their hair, what make-up to wear, what shoes would go with what. It drove me a little mad as all I had to do was go to the tux store and rent the same tux every other guy would wear, just maybe with a different color tie.

I really wanted to wear a dress, feel it move on my smooth skin, have my hair and make-up done. I longed to look glamorous, out on a beautiful night, instead of trying to look glam in borrowed clothes at the same old gay bar. At least I was headed to prom with the prettiest girl in school, though one of the stupid, preppy rich girls would win prom queen. That was just a given. But Courtney was the prettiest, plus she had attitude and was totally cool.

"Thanks, baby," she looked over with a half-grin, a cigarette dangling out of her crimson lips. "This'll be fun, you know. Lame, but, you know, fun."

"Yeah."

\* \* \*

195

"Oh, the humanity," I said as we stood there, in the back, along a crowded wall near the food tables. There were colored streamers, balloons, and lights. A DJ was playing the poppiest of R&B radio hits where the vocalist would always drag out every world so that 'baby' somehow became a 17-syllable word.

Most of our classmates were still lining the walls, decked out in dresses and tuxes but a few were already on the dance floor; some hopping around, some pretending every song were a slow dance. It all looked pretty and chaotic, like flowers in a blender.

Michelle saw us and came over with Aaron in tow. Even in a tux, he looked like he was doing a Jim Morrison impression. I wondered when he would realize that he went to prom with a lesbian. Then I wondered how many people in the room were on supposedly heterosexual dates with queers. Then I realized Courtney maybe was and did my best to stop thinking about it.

"Prom, huh?" Michelle observed in an ironically amused way.

"Totally." Courtney replied.

"You guys look great." I said, "Did you get photos?"

"No. I never bothered to pay the extra five bucks," Michelle said. "Besides, the line is super long."

"What are y'all gonna go do after?" Courtney asked.

"I don't know." Michelle said, letting the words trail off as she went deep into thought "Aaron knows a Richmond party we might go to. Supposed to be cool."

"You guys can totally come," Aaron offered. "The more the merrier." Glancing at Courtney, I tried to gauge her interest, but she shot me the tiniest of head shakes ever.

"Maybe later," I said.

"Cool," Michelle said and added, "Page me."

"We will," I promised and we said goodbye as they mingled back into the crowd.

"You know what?" Courtney said as we looked around "This place is lame. Let's get out of here." She leaned in and playfully bit my earlobe. Who was I to say no?

\* \* \*

It was as romantic as we could manage as teenagers in Georgia on an airy summer night. The stars were out above us, and all we could hear were the crickets and the rush of the river. All the lights and sounds of the city were far away. We had driven down one of the gravel roads, down a narrow winding route through the woods. Eventually, it ended at a clearing that sloped gently down to the river. I parked the truck and laid out a sleeping bag in the bed where we went and sat next to each other, enjoying the stillness of the night, a blunt that Courtney had brought, a shot or two of whiskey, and each other's company.

"I couldn't imagine a better prom," Courtney laughed as she finally extinguished her blunt. She put the cap back on the whiskey and tucked it up by her head before cuddling up to me more.

"We were only there for five minutes."

"Long enough to know it was totally lame," she said, putting her leg up on mine and intertwining our bodies. I put my arms around her and we lay there sideways, nose-to-nose.

"It's me and you against the world," I said in what I hoped was a desperately romantic way.

"Yeah," she said and I kissed her. We kept kissing, feeling like we were the only two people in the entire world. And unlike the other nights where we'd make out, this time she didn't ask me to stop, didn't push me away. We touched each other, felt each other, peeled off each other's clothes, going further and further. Courtney and I, there in the back of the pickup truck, among the pines, went all the way. My first time. They always say your first time is supposed to be memorable, and it was, but I was more focused on the fact that I was literally losing my virginity, at last losing it, and with the most awesome girl at school. I was less focused on whether I was doing a good job or lasting a long time, and more just in the moment.

For a long while, we just laid there, between the sleeping bag and the blanket, naked, our bodies still intertwined and we rested there looking up through the boughs of the Georgia pines to the stars on that breezy, clear night. After a moment, Courtney grabbed a pack of smokes and handed me one. I lit hers and then lit mine.

"You have to smoke after sex. It's, like, the rule," she joked. And so I lay there with her, feeling perhaps more relaxed and comfortable than I had ever felt in my life, and smoked my cigarette and wondered what the future might hold. All of summer stretched before us, boundless and free with promises of untold adventures and glories. School would come again, sure, senior year for Courtney and college for me, but that was still a long, long summer away.

Eventually she put out her cigarette and started to gather up her clothes. I did the same, though I watched her too, enjoying the simple fact of being able to look at her naked body, at a girl's wonderful, soft, curved, beautiful body. We slept there together, my first time ever actually sleeping with a girl. There would probably be yelling and punishment in the morning, but that was another day. I could deal with it then. I just didn't want that night to ever end.

# Chapter Twenty-Two

## "To Know That You're Mine"
## Friday, May 23rd, 1997

Washington Road stretched from the dilapidated houses of downtown to the rural wooded camping sites of Clarke's Hill Lake out past Martinez. In those 20 some miles, it passed by a thousand strip malls, parking lots, fast food joints, housing subdivisions, power lines, red lights, and pine trees. It was monotonous, bathed in yellow sodium light and covered in advertisements. Every 20 feet, signs for corporate stores and restaurants jutted out. It was asphalt, it was ugly, and it was what we had.

For hours, some nights, we would do nothing but cruise around. That's what we called it—cruising. We'd drive from one end of the strip to the other, through Augusta's chief commercial artery. Night barely offered a moment's relief from the dense and oppressive heat. We were too young for bars and too broke for movies or restaurants. There were no shows, there was nothing to do and nowhere to do it. Even though there was nothing to do, at least there were people to do it with.

As we stopped at a red light, I reached over, opened the glove box, and fumbled for a new tape. The Red Baron didn't have a CD player, so I was forced to transfer music from my CDs onto blank tapes. For a while we'd been driving along with my "Road Mix" on the stereo. It was mostly fast songs, but I was in the mood for something slightly more relaxed. As the light turned green, I grabbed one at random and put it in. Local H. It would work.

"Let's check here," Courtney said as she lit another cigarette. She was referring to a large parking lot in front of a strip mall that housed a chain bookstore, a chain restaurant, a chain fabric store, and five or six empty storefronts. Near the edge of the lot were parked two or three cars, but I didn't recognize any of them. Nor did I recognize any of the people who were hanging out by the cars, sitting on the hoods bathed in the sick yellow glow of a single light pole, smoking and laughing.

"Sure," I said and turned into the empty lot.

"That's Brad Nash," Courtney pointed out as I drove up. "He plays guitar in Tad the Drummer's band. Let's pull up." Slowly, I drove up and parked. Hopping out, Courtney waved to the group who invited us over. They were faces I knew who had names I didn't know. Brad was wearing a bomber jacket, suspenders and boots of a S.H.A.R.P., which stood for Skin-Heads Against Racial Prejudice. His girlfriend had the Chelsea cut and a plaid skirt that all the skinhead girls wore. The other guy and his girlfriend were similarly dressed. I'd seen them all hanging out Downtown a bunch of times.

"Hey, Courtney," Brad greeted her then gave me a nod.

"Sucks about Orwell's, huh?" I said. After Jordan's little show, our favorite hangout had closed and Catalina Club fell soon after. There were rumors that both were going to reopen, or that one or both would become an art gallery or maybe a skateboard shop. Instead, they just stayed closed. Some people refused to give up and kept hanging out on the street corner out front. Others migrated to local parking lots or River Walk. A few of us took to the road, spending Friday nights like this one, just driving.

"Yeah," agreed Tad's girl. I didn't know her name and didn't ask. I just wasn't in the mood for familiarity. Courtney had wanted to stop for a reason and that wasn't to socialize.

"You seen Mikey Magic P?" Courtney asked as she finished her smoke and flicked the butt away.

"Nah," piped up the other girl. "Try that Waffle House down by I-20. Him and Jamie hang out there."

"Thanks," Courtney said and I detected a little sadness in her voice. Then she looked up and asked, "You guys don't got nothing?" Brad shook his head and held up his right hand. There was a bold black X tattooed on the back—the sign of a straight edge.

"Thanks," I echoed with a little wave as I started to head back to the truck. Already the group had moved past us. I could hear one of the girls complaining about how her dad wouldn't let her wear a garter belt.

"It's not wearing nothing but a garter belt for God sakes," she complained. "You gotta keep your thigh highs up."

Courtney and I hopped back in the truck. As the engine turned over, the lights and radio fired up. I was happy to have music again. "Want to go find a spot down by River Watch and hang out?" I asked hopefully. Making out was better than driving, though it carried with it a small risk that pervy rednecks from the Sheriff's Department would grab you and take you home.

"Maybe," she said as she looked out the window. "Let's try that Waffle House."

"Okay," I shrugged. "But c'mon, we could have fun, like at the library." As Courtney was often grounded, the library was one of the few places we could spend time together outside of school. The microfilm room was a favorite spot of ours since it was dark, the door closed, and no one ever went in there. A small part of me wondered if I would develop a microfilm fetish later in life.

"Maybe," she smiled a little and tucked a strand of bright red hair behind her ears. On the pale skin of her left arm, I noticed a fresh cut, straight, two inches long just above a similar scar. I wondered what it was and feared that I knew what it was. Tonight didn't seem like a time to talk about it, though. Tonight, we'd get her the pot and X she wanted, then find a quiet spot in the woods to smoke and hang out together. In the slow flicker of the passing beams of the streetlights, she turned back toward the window and silently watched the world pass by.

\* \* \*

Courtney's mom and stepdad had eventually come to an agreement. When she was grounded, she wouldn't be allowed out of the house, but I could come over. So after school, on days when she was grounded, I'd drive us back to her house. I wasn't allowed in her room, so we'd find a spot on the couch where we hoped her parents wouldn't try and engage. Mostly they didn't. It was frustrating though, because as college professors, they kept weird hours. One of them always seemed to be home no matter what.

Today it was her stepdad Bill, but he was keeping to himself. So Courtney and I sat there on the couch, her head on my lap, me stroking her hair. On screen, cartoon mice were plotting to take over the world and we sat together simply enjoying the fact that we could sit next to each other, let our bodies touch, and share our time, even if we were just watching cartoons.

Courtney popped right up when she heard her stepdad coming in. Quickly, both of us adjusted our postures, snapping apart in an instant. We both tried to look as casual and innocent as possible. Hopefully the wine we had been spiking our Cokes with couldn't be smelled on our breath.

"I've got to run to the hardware store," Bill announced with a jingle of his keys. "I'll be right back."

"Okay," Courtney said as disinterestedly as possible. Silently, we listened as the front door closed, then the car started. Once we heard him drive away, we jumped into action. Running to the front window to confirm that the car was gone, she started pulling off her clothes. You had to remember to turn them right side out again though, so you could put them back on faster. After she had confirmed that Bill's car was out of sight, we ran up to her bedroom. There, we climbed under the covers, our clothes in a neat pile on the floor next to us, all right side out.

"Condom," she reminded me and I stopped by the dresser to grab one. Then I hopped in bed and climbed under the covers.

"This is a great way to spend a Tuesday afternoon," I smiled.

"Yeah," she agreed and kissed me. Then she looked up and said "Lights." Quick as I could, I hopped and turned them off. Then I ran right back to Courtney. We were getting pretty good at this.

\* \* \*

After the closure of Orwell's, Courtney and I, Michelle, and a few others, found a new coffee shop in a random strip mall and decided to make it home. There were a couple tables out front but mostly we'd sit in a group on the sidewalk, fill up on coffee, and hang out. It was out in Evans and, unlike downtown, it was new and clean with fresh air and trees nearby. There were no punks getting in fights and no badly played music making our ears ring for days after.

"Fuck this town," Michelle said and we all agreed. Spring was growing warmer. The azaleas were in bloom and half of Augusta was covered in a thick yellow coat of powdered pollen. Masters was over, the tourists were gone, and all that stood before us was a downhill race toward prom, graduation, one longer summer to party, and then we could officially start our lives in college, away from Augusta.

"Yeah," I said. "This town sucks." Courtney didn't say anything.

Instead she lit a cigarette. Still a junior, Courtney had another year left in purgatory. From her backpack, she pulled out a small bottle of brown whisky to Irish up her coffee. She offered it around and I poured a good amount into my own mug. It was almost impossible to get beer most weekends, but luckily most parents didn't guard their liquor too carefully.

"What should we do?" Lindsay piped up. "We should do something." It was a Saturday afternoon and evening was threatening to descend. The weekends were never long enough.

"Do what?" I asked snarkily. "Everything is lame. There's nothing to do anyway."

"The mall?" Lindsay offered. Michelle shot her down with an eye roll.

"We could go soap the fountains downtown," Mary suggested. With a good application of detergent, the fountains would spew enough foamy bubbles to cover almost a whole city block.

"That's lame," Michelle said coolly. "This whole damn town is lame as hell."

"Jesus Christ," Courtney suddenly roared. "All of you. Shut the fuck up." As we all sat there stunned, she stood up, put her hands to her head and started making her way out to the parking lot. Though I had no idea what had just happened, I followed her. In the middle of the parking lot, I stepped up to her.

"What's up, babe?" I asked. "You okay?" With wide eyes and my mouth agape, I stood there as she stepped back and forth as though she were desperately trying to get away from something but didn't know where to go.

"I'm not mad at you, Matt," she said, quickly rushing out the words. "I'm not mad, I just need a sec to chill, okay? I just don't want anyone around, okay?" I stepped forward and reached out to hug her, wanting to comfort her as best I could, but she reared back, shook her head violently. "I don't want anyone to touch me right now. Okay? I'm fine. Okay? I'm fine."

I hated to see her so upset and I didn't want to upset her further so I would just let her be and not push it. She found a spot on a curb and sat there, her head buried in her hands, rocking back and forth. For a moment I stood there by her, not knowing what to do, my stomach tied in knots, wanting to cry for want of something, anything to do.

"Courtney," I said softly. She looked up.

"I'm okay," she said. "Just gimme a minute. I'm sorry. Just gimme a minute."

"Okay," I said and turned around to walk back to our friends. Michelle found me halfway there.

"It's okay," I said, trying to reassure myself even though I was pretty sure it wasn't okay. "She gets like this sometimes. Too much pot or something, I guess."

"I guess," Michelle said. "Maybe she's worried she's about to lose all her friends."

"What? You mean like when I go to college?" I half-asked, thinking about it. Shaking my head, I shrugged. Honestly I didn't have a plan for fall. I didn't want my brain to dwell on the fact that I'd be in Athens and Courtney would still be in Augusta. "I dunno."

"Hmm," was all Michelle bothered to muster. Then after a second, she looked up and said "Be careful with her, okay? Seriously." As Michelle started to walk over to Courtney, I wondered what she meant by that.

\* \* \*

For ages, the house next door to mine had been vacant. While I'm sure the neighbors probably hated the unsightly lawn, I had found their back patio to be a perfect spot. There were wooden benches that couldn't be seen from any window in my house. Provided you cleared away the mounds of pine needles and dried leaves, it was a great spot to sit and smoke. Courtney and I often snuck over there for a cigarette break or other things that might have gotten us in trouble.

"Truth is," she paused to take a long hit off the joint she'd brought, held it, then let it out and finished. "I'm better off for this." We'd gotten our second to last report cards of the year this afternoon. Courtney had failed American History and Geometry and was barely making a D in Chemistry and English. There was no way in hell she could pull her average up in time for June. We both knew what that meant. Since Davidson was a magnet school, everyone had to keep at least a B average, or you were out. Sure, they gave you a chance to try and pass, but not that many chances.

"A lot of Davidson people go to Richmond senior year," I said as she passed me the pot. It was true. Davidson made seniors take a full load even though most of us only needed senior English to actually graduate per the State of Georgia rules. A handful of juniors would finish out senior year at Richmond where they could do a half day. Meanwhile all the Davidson kids stayed 'til three no matter what. "Richmond's like, way easier."

"Yeah," Courtney said, kicking around the pine needles absent-mindedly. "My parents are gonna freak."

"Yeah," I agreed. "But it'll be okay."

"You know what we should do, Matt?" she said, her eyes half-focused on a spot in the woods a hundred feet away.

"What?" I asked.

"Let's skip school tomorrow. Take your car, go to like, Atlanta or Athens or somewhere. Just for the weekend. I got some X I can sell and we could get a hotel room, go out to eat. Live like real people." Then she laughed, "I mean, if I'm fucked anyway for getting kicked out of Davidson, then I might as well be like, you know, really fucked, right?"

"It'll be okay," I said, already feeling the fuzziness in my face. My heart started beating faster and I laughed. Honestly, I didn't really like smoking pot. It just made me edgy. But I didn't want Courtney to think I was weird, so I smoked it with her.

"No," she said slowly, as though she were either deep in thought or halfway to a good buzz. "At some point, you know, that's gonna be it. They're either gonna like, kill me, or kick me out. I think I'm already there."

"I'll take care of you," I said lazily. "Don't worry about it." Then I scooted up next to her and gave her a kiss. She put her head down in my lap and took another hit.

# Chapter Twenty-Three

### "These Zipper Blues"
### Tuesday, June 10th, 1997

"What do you and Michelle go do on those nights where you hang out? How come you never invite me?" she asked after we finally got our coffees and found a table outside. Something told me that this question had long been stewing. Either she was just being curious, feeling left out, worried I was cheating on her with Michelle, or setting me up to trap me so I'd have to admit that I was crossdressing and going to the gay bar.

I wasn't entirely sure how she might know the last one but Michelle wasn't always as tight-lipped as she led people to believe. That left a bunch of random thoughts and potential plans rattling around in my skull.

Michelle and I had been making Forum an almost weekly thing. Should I come clean about that and risk Courtney knowing how I might be a weirdo pervert? Should I attempt to protect my masculine image by lying to the awesomest girl in the world? Change the subject? Run away screaming and claim there was a bee?

"We..." I started off slow, still trying to figure this whole thing out. "Go to Forum."

"Like, Forum the gay bar?"

"Yes."

"But you're not gay," Courtney said, her eyes squinting quizzically. "Michelle's not gay, right?"

"No," I said, wondering how far to take it. Honesty I had gotten out of the way. I'd been honest and told Courtney where we went. The real question was how far I'd be willing to take honesty. Far enough to risk Courtney thinking I was a freak? I thought back to all the girls who wouldn't have touched me in a million years.

"So, like, why on earth do you go to Forum?"

\* \* \*

We had gotten our Forum night logistics expertly worked out just in time for the end of senior year. I would head over to Michelle's late in the afternoon and bring my gym bag full of girl stuff. Normally I kept it in my truck, shoved into the small area between the seats and back wall. My parents would never think to look there. I'd get changed at Michelle's. She'd do my make-up, then we'd climb out her window, out onto the roof of the garage, then jump down to the grass in the far corner of her backyard. There was a small slope there so it was only a five or six foot jump and easily doable, even in a dress. Then it was a quick dash through the neighbor's yard and over to the side street where I'd have parked my truck. That way, we could get in without anyone seeing us.

Then we'd drive to the Forum, and we'd get past the doors and the bouncer easily because they knew us as regulars. From health class, we learned that the body processed alcoholic beverages at the rate of about one drink an hour. That meant that I could have two drinks over the course of four hours and still be fully sober to drive the couple of miles home. In my purse, I'd carry a pair of flip-flops, sweatpants and a T-shirt, all of which were easily compactable. Once we were ready to leave, I'd head into the ladies room, find a stall and change, then wash off my make-up in the sink. Being seen coming out of the ladies room as a guy wasn't a big deal because no one seemed to pay all that much attention to the gender restrictions on the bathrooms at Forum anyway.

Leaving the club as a guy wasn't a big deal, either. Sure, I only got in because I was a girl, but they really didn't care who left, and a guy carrying a purse was by far not the weirdest thing the bouncers had ever seen at Forum. Our route home was even more carefully planned. We'd take residential roads and avoid the major thoroughfares so we wouldn't run into any Sheriff's Department cars. I'd drive exactly two miles above the speed limit, because going too fast might draw attention, but then again so would going too slow. If you went the exact speed limit, cops would probably assume you're drunk, because no sober drivers were ever that careful.

Though with my carefully monitored alcohol intake and the fact that we were pretty sure Forum watered down their drinks considerably, we were almost certainly above the BAC limit. If I was ever in doubt, we would head to the back of the parking lot, away from busy, well-lit Walton Way and I would self-administer a field sobriety test: saying the alphabet backwards, walking in a straight line, and standing on one foot while touching my nose. I was always okay, again, because I'm still pretty sure we were drinking mostly cranberry juice and ice with no more than a drop or two of vodka. Michelle didn't need to drive to Forum or figure out a way to get home. She only lived about four blocks away.

Michelle and I had gotten ready and were waiting in the parking lot smoking cigarettes when Courtney arrived. I was wearing a new tight, black mini dress with spaghetti straps. I'd picked it up at Body Shop and paired it with some fishnet stockings and black four-inch heels I'd borrowed from Michelle's mom's closet. Michelle was dressed similarly, but in a tight crimson top and a super short black skirt. She'd skipped the heels and was wearing her Docs, though I kind of wished she'd done heels so I didn't look so tall. Michelle had told me not to worry. No one would notice and it was okay to be tall because there were plenty of tall girls in the world.

Courtney had also worn black. It was one of my favorite dresses of hers and it really showed off her amazing body. Along with that she'd done fishnets too but also Docs, and had done her eyes in great gobs of black eyeliner. Her lips were deep blood red, contrasted with her insanely pale skin complimented by her light red hair. She walked right up, gave me an odd look and in all seriousness said "Okay, like, I did just drop two tabs, so I could be crazy."

"You're not crazy," Michelle said.

"What do you think?" I asked sheepishly. It slowly dawned on me I hadn't kissed her or anything yet. Instead we just stood there in the parking lot, Michelle and I smoking while Courtney stood there mouth agape.

"Wow. I mean. Wow. You look amazing, Matt," Courtney said, then turned to Michelle "Doesn't she look amazing?" I wondered if she used the female pronoun intentionally or by accident.

"I did her make-up," Michelle said proudly. "You want to have a smoke or do you want go in?"

"Let's go in," Courtney said. Finally, she grabbed me around the waist and pulled me close. We kissed briefly, just a little peck, because Courtney said she didn't want to mess up my make-up. Her hand came down below my waist and gave my butt a squeeze. Michelle rolled her eyes.

"Okay, you two, leave enough room for Jesus."

* * *

Courtney had been looking over at me all night. One might even call it staring. She wore the biggest goofy grin as though this was all the wildest thing ever. She might have also been stoned. She probably was stoned, actually. Courtney was always stoned. It was a habit of hers that left me oddly turned on by the smell of marijuana. She was definitely drunk. Instead of vodka cranberries, she'd been doing straight Jack Daniels all night, on top of whatever she'd had before she showed up.

"Oh, my gosh," said Courtney. "This is so weird. Like, good weird, I guess. You know, just weird."

"It's cool, babe," I said. "You're being really awesome."

"Thanks," she said sweetly.

"I'm gonna get another drink," Michelle announced, probably just to shut us up.

"Me too," I said, because I definitely need one.

"Me too!" Courtney almost shouted, holding up an empty rocks glass.

"I'll get this round," I said and stood up, grabbing my purse. I needed a break anyway. Slinging the purse onto my shoulder, I walked up toward the bar, past all the tables and patrons. It wasn't too crowded tonight because there wasn't a show, but there were still plenty of people. Most of them didn't pay me any attention but a few stared, curiously, lustfully, jealously, as I walked past them in my little dress and heels. I could feel the roughness of the fishnets as my legs touched with each step, feel the movement of my dress and the bounce of my hair, the swing of my earrings. It was wonderful to be in the Forum because I felt like an adult woman in a grown up's world. People were polite, greeted me with smiles. It didn't matter if I passed or not, because they at least accepted me.

Stepping up to the bar, I found a spot next to a mulleted middle-aged lesbian couple and stood there for a moment while I waited for the bartender. There was a mirror behind the bar and in the strange light of the gay bar I could see myself looking back. Instead of a naive young boy who had never seen the world, I saw a beautiful, dashing diva, a strong and confident woman who moved through the world like she owned it, or was at least friends with the person who did.

I let myself smile slightly, watching the shift in expression. Then I made a slightly pouty face and watched how I looked. Finally, I put on my most alluring expression; coy yet sly, seductive but still a bit of a fresh ingénue, not yet made bitter by all the hell of this world. She looked back at me from that mirror and I realized that she was probably out of Matt's league.

Somewhat randomly, I decided her name was Robin. It was my middle name and I had always hated it. Maybe it was because my parents had only ever used it when I was in trouble. Or maybe it was its association with a certain caped crusader. But, I figured, since my parents had inadvertently gifted me a girl's name I might as well use it. Plus I needed a better name than the one that Michelle had given me: Candy.

Robin wouldn't give Matt her number if he hit on her. She'd smile, be polite but firm in her rejection and then go back to do whatever it was beautiful and sophisticated people really did. I'd thought about switching to beer because it was impossible for them to water down a beer, but then I thought I should stick with something more sophisticated.

\* \* \*

As I stood over her, holding her hair back, Courtney finished the last of her retching. The shrubs along the back of the bar parking lot were coated in a fine mist of alcohol and stomach acid. It didn't even smell like vomit, just whiskey. Somehow Michelle had found some paper towels and we helped Courtney wipe herself off and have a seat on the parking lot curb.

"I'll run over to the gas station," Michelle offered. "Get a water."

"Thanks," I half-mouthed and turned back to Courtney, who sat next to me holding her head.

"Sorry, Matt," she said softly and slowly.

"It's okay. Do you feel better?"

"Yeah."

"We'll get you home soon."

"I don't want to go home," she started to cry. "Home is not fun. Home sucks."

"Sorry, baby," I held her tight and thought about kissing her and then thought better of it. Instead I just tried to think of a solution. Taking her home would have been the simplest thing but I seriously doubted my parents would be cool with that. "You can stay with Michelle."

"Cool," she slurred then looked up at me with half-closed eyes. "You're cool, Matt. And you're pretty. My boyfriend is a girl. That's so weird." She laughed slightly.

"Sorry. I know it's weird. You've been cool about it though. Way cooler than I ever could have expected."

"It is weird though," she slurred. I found it hard to disagree.

"Yeah," I admitted.

"Igottathrowupagain." With that she puked again, this time all over Michelle's mom's shoes. Lord knows what they cost. All I knew was that the brands in her closet were fancier than anything my mom had. I held back Courtney's hair again and tried to stay out of the spray and hold back my own gag reflex as best I could. Finally, she was done and wiped her mouth with the clean bits of the paper towel. Looking up at me, tears in her eyes she asked, "What would you do if I died tomorrow? You wouldn't let me die would you? You wouldn't want that would you?"

"No, I'll never let you die," I said, holding her tight again and helping her clean off as best I could.

"You're nice," Courtney said. "Nice. But like, really weird. Are you gay?"

"We'll get you somewhere safe soon," I said as I tried to ignore the painful and obvious things my girlfriend was telling me. Telling her about my gay stuff, my girl stuff, had been a mistake. It was too late now. It was out. "Michelle's getting water, then we'll get you somewhere safe, Courtney."

"I'd like that."

# Chapter Twenty-Four

### "Say it Ain't So"
### Tuesday, June 17th, 1997

Courtney was there waiting for me, like she always was, sitting on the curb out in front of the public library. She was wearing cutoff shorts and a tank top, smoking a cigarette and taking swigs out of a plastic Coke bottle. I pulled up, parked and came over to sit with her. We kissed, then I lit my own smoke. Courtney offered me the bottle.

"S'Coke and vodka," she said. "Not the best, but it's what I could get." I took a brief sip and it made me gag and shake like liquor always did. It was late morning, but it was also summer, so it didn't matter if we started partying early.

"It's too hot out here," I said. On particularly hot days, you could barely tell the difference between breathing in the hot humid air and breathing in a breath of cigarette smoke. "Wanna go to the coffee shop?"

"I've been thinking I'm gonna leave," Courtney said in a dead serious way, her eyes fixed on a point somewhere far in the distance. "You know, fuck my parents anyway. You know, just grab some shit and get going."

"You can't do that," I said firmly "Where would you even go?"

"I know people. Maybe I could come to Athens. Then we'd be set," she replied. I thought about the future; me hanging out with college friends introducing them to my high school dropout girlfriend who crashes on some drug dealer's couch.

"You can't do that," I said dismissively. "You can't drop out of school. Leave your house. What are you gonna be, homeless?"

"I'm not gonna be homeless," Courtney snapped. "I just said that. I know a guy."

"Who?" I asked.

"A guy," she said as though she were explaining it to the dumbest person on earth.

"Courtney," I tried to explain in a rational way. "You can't just go off with some random 'guy' who you barely know. Who does that?"

"Don't fucking tell me what I can and can't do. I can do whatever I want." She stood up awkwardly. I stood up as well, unsure if this were just one of her constant musings about leaving or whether this was finally a serious plan.

"It's not a smart…"

"What the hell is here for me, Matt? What's in Augusta? What's in this fucking shitty town keeping me here? My life sucks. Okay? My life sucks. I'm fucking expelled, my parents are gonna call the cops on me if they find any more shit in my room. I'm in a fucking prison here, Matt. The only time I get to hang out is when I sneak out, or with you, and maybe I don't always want to hang out with you. Michelle's gonna be gone. Everyone's gone. You're gonna fucking leave too."

"No I won't," I said, hoping it would sound comforting. I reached out to take her in my arms but she pushed me off.

"Then what's the plan for fall? 'Cause fall is next week, Matt," she said, crossing her arms. Her normally pale skin was starting to turn beet red.

"We can figure that out," I tossed out there, hoping to table the entire conversation.

"Let's just go ahead and do that right now," she said coldly, planting her foot on the sidewalk.

"No," I said. "I don't want to have this conversation. Okay?" I was starting to feel dizzy and far away, as though my body was trying to warn me.

"Are you and me," she asked slowly and deliberately. "Gonna be boyfriend and girlfriend when you're in Athens and I'm stuck here all by myself?"

"Courtney," I pleaded. "I don't want to break up. I like you. A lot. Of course I do. You're awesome. You're hot and you're… awesome. I don't want to fight. I just, I don't know what to do. Okay? Seriously. This is hard for me, okay? This is a big change. This is college, this is like, the new thing, a new town, new people. I don't know the answer. I don't know what to do, okay?"

"What do you mean, you don't know?" Her words were flat, her head tilted down, her eyes focused, narrowed to slits.

"I don't know. People don't know everything, okay."

"You don't know if you want to be with me?" she asked, all the anger and hurt welling up. With the skill of someone well practiced, she stopped herself from crying. "Because you have a fancy ass college where you're gonna go try and fuck all the little UGA girls."

"I never said that."

"You don't know what to do," She shook her head and forced a laugh. "Well I do, Matt. I do. Why don't you go and bang every one of those skanky ass UGA sluts and I'll do whatever the fuck I want. How about that? What do you think of that?"

"Damn it, Courtney, don't do this," I begged her. Ice flowed through my veins and sweat fell down my back. Courtney was the love of my life. Was this really happening? Could we talk it out or was this it? Was this really it? This sucked. I wasn't ready for it. Not the big capital "I" IT.

"Go off to your sluts, faggot," she said. "Oh better yet, why don't you go put on your dress and your pretty little make-up and see how many of them UGA sluts wanna go out with a goddamn queer-ass faggot?"

"Jesus, Courtney. What the hell?" I yelled and realized that was a stupid thing to say. Part of me didn't care. I could feel myself shaking.

"Have fun in college, faggot," she said as she turned and started walking away, back toward the library. Should I follow her? Try to talk this out? Were we really breaking up or was this something we could talk through another day? Was this really happening? I didn't even know.

So I just watched her walk away, thinking that maybe we could talk again when she wasn't mad. Maybe then she'd be more reasonable and realize that we should get back together. Turning around, I slouched back to my truck and drove away in the opposite direction. Maybe this wasn't really it. Maybe she just needed some time to process things and then she'd calm down. Some words, I guess, can't ever be taken back.

\* \* \*

There was no drag show tonight. Instead the Forum was nothing more than what it was; a place for gay people to get drunk. And I needed to drink. Dutifully, Michelle had come with me. Earlier she had promised we would party hard and forget all our problems. But I was only in the mood to drink and not to party. Still, she had insisted that I put on make-up and wear a dress.

"It had to happen," Michelle said. She looked at me like I were a puppy dog and patted my shoulder. We were seated at a table in the back of the dark bar. There were no bright, colorful lights tonight. The silver strips that lined the wall sat still in the shadow, not sparkling. "It was inevitable."

"Was it?" I asked desperately. For the past few pitiful hours, I had retraced every moment, every word of every conversation, the nuance of every single time our skin touched. "I think I fucked it up coming out to her."

"You probably did," Michelle said. "But I still think it was brave of you, little Robin. You don't realize how brave you are."

"Bravery's just a nice way of saying 'stupidity.'" I sighed. I downed the rest of my rum and Coke.

"I would have said stupidity if I had meant stupidity," Michelle said.

"You told me Courtney was bad news," I pointed out. "I was too stupid to listen. And then I came out of the closet to her and look where it got me."

"C'mon," Michelle gave me a friendly punch on the arm. "You broke up with your high school girlfriend right before college starts. You know how many seniors are going through the same thing all over the country right now? This is summer. It's like Armageddon for high school sweethearts. College is, what? Six weeks away. That's six weeks to party our asses off. No Courtney or Aaron to hold us back! C'mon."

"Wait," I asked. "When did you break up with Aaron?"

"I haven't yet," Michelle said.

"Were you guys even actually dating?" I asked.

"Sort of," Michelle said, a little defensively. "But now I have a good reason to end things with him definitively. We are looking at the best summer of our lives here. This is gonna be awesome!"

"It doesn't feel awesome," I said. "It feels pretty shitty." Michelle smiled wildly, grabbed our empty glasses, and stood up.

"I'm gonna get us new drinks," Michelle announced. "You don't realize it yet, but you're like, two more drinks away from forgetting all about that girl and having fun." But I didn't want to have fun. All I wanted to do was wallow in my own misery.

* * *

The skin around my eyes burned from where I'd rubbed it raw. I had to be sure that all my make-up would be gone. Sure I probably smelled like perfume. But that would be mixed with enough sweat and cigarette smoke that it was probably not a big deal. My clothes and make-up were stuffed into my backpack, buried under a layer of guy clothes. My shaved legs felt smooth against my jeans.

I walked home slowly from Michelle's house, with cars zooming past me on the winding residential streets, and with Eels' *Beautiful Freak* playing on my Discman. My mouth was dry from too many cigarettes and not enough water. Whatever alcohol might have been in the Forum drinks had long since left my system and full sobriety was soon to be upon me.

It was just past one in the morning when I got to my house. I noticed that the living room light was on. That was odd. It would be rare for my dad to be up this late. He had probably forgotten to turn the light off. After stashing my bag in the truck cab—in the space behind the seats—I headed up to the house where my dad was sitting on the couch waiting for me.

"Hey, dad," I half mumbled as I came in. Though I tried to simply walk by to head back to my room he stopped me with his commanding army voice.

"Matthew Robin Bailey," he put his book—a thick biography of Douglas MacArthur—rather forcefully onto the coffee table. It was then that I saw it sitting on the table out in the open. My dad had gone in my room and found a box of condoms. It was a 12 pack, torn open, over half of them gone. There was no denying it, no claiming that it had been bought just in case or that it was a gag gift from friends.

"Sit down," he ordered. Begrudgingly I sat down in one of the arm chairs, avoiding eye contact all the while. Instead of saying anything all I did was sigh.

"You want to explain this?" he said angrily. Then for dramatic flourish he picked up the box of condoms and threw it at me. It landed in my lap but I barely looked up.

"No," I said flatly. I thought about those six missing condoms. That was six times having sex with Courtney, a girl who would never sleep with me again. What were those times? Over at Web's place one time. In the woods behind her house while her parents were home. In her bed one day when her parents weren't home. I couldn't remember the others.

"Well, you're gonna," he snapped. Instead of answering, all I did

216

was sneer. With a look of deep disgust on his face, he shook his head at me. "You call yourself a Christian. You declare to the world that you are a disciple of the one living God. And then you go and live your life like a disgusting heathen sinner. You fail in your duty to God, to your family, and to me."

This was his usual posture whenever he got mad. He always tried to heap on tons of God, the Bible, and religion. He would shout and threaten, but all you really had to do was sit there and take it. Sit there in silence, let him yell, and eventually he would tire and dismiss you with some statement of abject disgust like 'Get out of my sight. I can't even stand to look at you right now.'

Tonight though, I was tired and still a little drunk. This was the last thing I wanted to deal with before I went to bed. Of all the things I had done—smoking cigarettes, doing drugs, drinking, crossdressing, going to gay bars, giving up on church, backsliding as hard as any one had ever backslid in the history of backsliding—it was this that finally got me caught. The most normal, heterosexual thing in the world.

"I'm the same as anyone," I said. "For all have sinned and fallen short of the glory of God." There. You can always quote the Bible. Even that weirdo Paul and his epistle to the Romans. If I really wanted to set him off I'd have quoted Jesus's classic line about who should and shouldn't throw the first stone.

"No, Matthew," my dad said in his commanding, angry, Army voice. He stood up and waved his arms as he yelled. "This is a Christian household. We are commanded by the Living God to be Christ-like. We are in this world but not of it. But you have been letting that secular music and your non-Christian friends steer you toward hell. That's stopping right now. If you start to act like those secular people who do drugs, abortions, homosexuality…"

"There's nothing wrong with gay people, Dad," I angrily pointed out. I was so sick of this speech. I had grown up hearing endless variations of it, all delivered with anger and loud volume.

"Oh really?" he started to mock me. "'Nothing wrong with gay people?' Matt, gay people spread AIDS. They recruit children into the homosexual lifestyle. Their goal is to undermine…"

"You don't know what the hell you're talking about," I shouted as I stood up. "Gay people."

"Gay people are a plague…"

"I'm gay!" I shouted. Why did I say that? A rush of freezing cold surged through my body. Suddenly I felt like I was watching the entire scene from far away. Why did I say that? What the fuck was I doing? I felt myself starting to shake and worried I would fall over. My face burned hot. I wasn't even gay. Was I? Why would I say that to him when I wasn't even sure? "Sort of."

"Don't say stupid shit, Matthew." He thrust his finger right in my face. "No son of mine is a homosexual faggot."

"I already said it. You want me to say it again?" I said, trying to fight back my tears. Half of my brain wanted to run away and the other half wanted to throttle this man. For my entire life, he shoved the Bible and his own ideas of Christianity down my throat until I choked. Not just me. Ellen and my mom, too.

"No, you take the name of Christ…"

"Well, not anymore," I shouted and then realized that wasn't a particularly wise thing to say either. The stupid part of my brain was winning. I didn't care. All I wanted to do was hurt him, hurt him for all the bullying I had silently endured. "I'm done with all that."

"If you deny God," my dad said, his face now red. "In Second Timothy it says that on Judgment Day, God will deny you. The Bible says you will go right to hell…"

"I don't give a shit what the Bible says," I shouted and backed away from him. I was burying myself tonight. Fuck it. Fuck him. I was done with him. I did my best to fight back tears.

"How dare you speak that way in my house," he frothed at the mouth.

"Dad," I started, the anger coursing through my every vein, the adrenaline making me shake. "You can stop. Because I don't believe in it. I refuse to believe any God who could create this universe who would be so evil as to create hell along with it…"

"Matthew," my dad tried to interrupt but I shouted over him. For my entire life all there had ever been was my family. That's how it always was for military families. You move around so much. Friends, neighbors, they all rotate in and out. But family stays. But now even that was gone. Ellen was gone. My mom was gone. It was my turn now. I wanted to burn our family to the ground and walk away from the ashes. Finally ending it, taking away the family that he had created, that he had ruled, would be the greatest dagger in my dad's stupid heart.

"No, you don't get to decide what I believe. Not anymore. You don't even know what's out there. There are gay people who are awesome people. There are sinners out there who are some of the best people. And some of the worst people out there are Christians. Fucking hypocrite Christians who just wanna use Jesus to bully people. You don't even know what it's like for me, what I have to deal with. I never asked to have to deal with this gay thing. It was always there. I never chose it. But I'm not..."

"Listen here," he got right up on top of me and tried to grab my arm but I backed way. "You little ingrate. This is my house and you live under my roof. 'As for me and my house we will worship the Lord.' So as long as you are under my roof..."

"Fine," I interrupted. "Then I'm not gonna be under your stupid roof anymore." Still shaking, I walked right out the door. He was yelling after me but I refused to listen. With each hurried step, I feared he would grab me, tackle me, beat me down. But he didn't move beyond the threshold. He stood there shouting Bible verses and condemnations at me as I walked away. Fighting back tears of anger, I got in my truck, started it up and drove off into the night.

My wobbly hand dug through the glove box until I found a suitable tape. Korn. That would work. As deep bass, grinding guitars, and pounding drums filled the cab, I lit up a cigarette and tried to calm my nerves. A part of me worried that I had made an enormous mistake but another, larger, part of me knew I hadn't. I hated him. I always had. And someone had to stand up to him.

# Chapter Twenty-Five

### The Fake Behind the Fear"
### Friday, June 20th, 1997

Michelle had never finished the silver in her bedroom and only the first two walls ever got completed, but she kept them up; a monument to what we might have accomplished if we'd had a little more follow through. It didn't seem like a project that either of us wanted to finish over our last summer. It was something we started when real life seemed so far away.

Augusta had seemed like a prison we'd never escape. Now escape was real. It was happening. Recreating Andy Warhol's factory just didn't seem too important any more. The real Factory was out there in the magical world that we were about to go exploring. All I had to do to get there was live through the wreckage I'd managed to make of my life.

The boiling heat of August left everyone feeling melted. The air seemed to have a heavy yellow glow and the only relief could be found inside. Michelle and I were spending the afternoon inside her house. Ostensibly I was helping her pack up her stuff for college but mostly we were hanging out, looking through her records, photos, books and other stuff.

"I don't think you've 'ruined your life,'" Michelle said after I had told her about the fight with my dad. My girlfriend had dumped me. My family was irreparably fractured. I was technically homeless. It was my opinion that my life had been pretty thoroughly ruined. "I mean, it's not ideal, right? But I mean, if you're gonna go and do that, then this is a good time for it at least."

"That's not much comfort," I said snarkily. After my argument with my dad, I had driven downtown to Web's warehouse apartment. He had agreed to let me crash with him until I left for college. I was thankful that my Dad hadn't reported my truck stolen. The title was in his name so it was technically his truck. My stuff was all still at my house, or I guess, my dad's house.

"You talk to him at all?" Michelle asked me. It had been a few days since the fight.

"No," I said, looking over her copy of *In Utero*. It was on clear vinyl. She had picked it upon a family vacation to Germany along with an original of *Hormoaning* and some cheap Pearl Jam bootlegs. "But, I've talked to my mom and sister. I think word's gotten back to him that I'm not lying in a ditch somewhere. I'll have to talk to him at some point, I guess. I don't know." Talking to him was the last thing I wanted to do. From my conversations with my mom and Ellen, I had surmised that he had only told them about an argument. I didn't think he had told them the content of the argument or about any of my particular, ill-advised outbursts. I mean, even if he had my mom would probably ignore the gay thing. Ellen would have mentioned it to me, though.

"Don't," Michelle recommended. "He's an asshole. If I came out of the closet to my parents, they wouldn't yell at me or scream about the Bible."

"Are you gonna come out to them?" I asked.

"Um," Michelle said nervously with a little bit of guilt. She laughed a tiny bit and threw another couple shirts in a cardboard box marked 'charity.' I'd already seen a couple of the mix tapes I'd made for her in the charity box, but I didn't feel like saying anything. "No."

"Yeah," I laughed at the insanity of my own predicament. "I don't recommend it."

"I don't think with them it would be angry or violent," Michelle said as though she had imagined this potential conversation before. "It would be awkward. Uncomfortable. Embarrassing."

"I long for embarrassing," I said over-dramatically. "That would be luxury compared to ripping apart my entire life and tossing it on the fire."

"C'mon," Michelle tried to encourage me. "College starts in a couple months. Six weeks."

"Yeah," I said with a sigh.

"Think about this," Michelle said seriously. "You got the HOPE scholarship. So college is paid for. Your parents have already paid for a year of dorm and meal plan. Insurance on your truck is paid for probably a few more months. You can get a job at UGA. You are in a place where right now you literally don't need anything from your dad. So, fuck him."

"I guess," I said quietly.

"College," she said in a heavy way. "We are about to finally get out of here, Robin. Think about that, man? We're not children anymore. We are adults now. We can do what we want. We don't need our parents' permission for anything. College is the ultimate chance to reinvent yourself. No one there knows you or anything about you. You could be you, without your parents having any say at all." Michelle was going to SCAD in Savannah hoping to further her dreams of becoming an artist and photographer. I had chosen UGA, mostly because Athens meant music and was the closest thing Georgia had to a cool town. SCAD had been on my radar, but Savannah was old and stuffy. Athens had R.E.M., Magnapop, Pylon, and the 40 Watt.

"I don't know," I said noncommittally. Maybe Michelle was right. Fall was almost here. There were a few more short weeks until orientation. I'd move into my dorm room, get my student ID, grab a copy of the campus map, and hopefully find some friends to party with for the whole week we were going to have before class started. Maybe there'd be girls, too, I guess. Maybe there'd be girls who'd just been dumped by their high school boyfriends. Maybe we could commiserate together.

"C'mon," Michelle said. "You could reinvent yourself as a girl. No one knows you."

"Uh. No," I protested. "I've already ruined my life in Augusta and got my ass dumped by the one girl I ever loved. I don't want to ruin my life in Athens too."

"I'm just saying," Michelle said, offering me her yearbook. "You want this?"

"That's this year's. You just got that like two weeks ago."

"Yeah." She tossed it into the charity box. "Why look back, you know? Never look back." I stepped over and fished it out of the box. I flipped through it to the back where I found the page-long inscription I'd written to her. It was a long retelling of all the inside jokes we had shared over our two years together. I tore it out, handed it to her, and tossed the book back in the charity box.

"At least keep this," I said.

"Fine." Michelle gave me a frustrated smile and placed the torn page on top of a pile of papers. Then she picked it up again and grabbed the paper that was under it. Flipping it over, she handed it to me. It was the black and white photograph of me taken the day that she had first dressed me up for an art project. Looking at it, I could see that girl who I saw in the mirror at the Forum. This photo, in a way, was her first appearance in the world. "You should keep this, Robin, my dear."

Holding the photo in my hands, I looked it over. I studied it. This was the moment that started it all. This was the moment when I finally let another human being know who I really was. And here I was two years later, dealing with the aftermath.

* * *

It was after 10:00 and I hoped her parents were asleep. The last thing I wanted was to deal with them on top of all of this. All the houses around hers were mostly dark. A few people were up late with their lights on, but Courtney's house was dark and still. Before I rounded the corner, I cut my engine and rolled to a stop.

For a moment, I watched her house. It was a house like all the others, with a nice lawn, and cars out front. The sound of cricket chirps filled the air broken only by the whistle of a far off train headed somewhere in the night. The light in Courtney's room—the last window on the top right—was off. I lit a cigarette and tried to think of how best to do this.

All I had to do was go up, throw a pebble at her window, and get her to come out. Then we could have a sensible conversation about everything. She would listen, be calm and understand. This was complicated and it was normal to be confused by major changes like this. Of course I still liked her but I was worried about how we could manage to be together when we were apart next year. It was all so simple.

As I sat there in my truck smoking, I saw a pair of bright headlights round the corner behind me. A car I didn't recognize pulled up right in front of Courtney's house. Suddenly, I saw her bolt out from the front door. She was in a tank top and shorts that hugged her body tightly. Her long pale legs glowed in the light and her long red hair flowed out behind her as she sprinted toward the car. Before I could even react, she pulled the door open and climbed into the car. In a quick second, the car was off.

I watched as the red taillights got smaller until they rounded the corner. A part of me wanted to follow after them, to see who that was, where they were going. But in the end, my frustration managed to overcome my jealousy. I sat there in my truck and finished my cigarette. It had all been my fault and I wouldn't have had the right words anyway.

* * *

With everything that had happened, ordinary stuff seemed so unimportant. But I had worn the same clothes for five days and they were starting to get ripe. I couldn't really go to college with nothing but the incredibly filthy clothes on my back. I needed my stuff but it was in my dad's house.

My plan was to drive by the house. I would cruise by casually to see if my dad's car was there. If it was sitting in the driveway, I would keep driving. But when I approached the house, I saw the car wasn't there. He was out. For how long, I couldn't be sure. Maybe he had only just left and would be gone for hours. Or maybe he had run out on a five minute errand and would come back to find me. Hopefully I could do this without running into him.

So I parked my truck in the driveway. Getting out, I grabbed my bundle of folded up boxes and tape out of the truck bed. Carefully, as though a noise might summon danger, I crept up to the house. My key stilled worked. A part of me had wondered if he would change the locks. Inside it was quiet. Knowing he could drive up any moment, I quickly made my way back to my room. It was as I had left it. As far as I could tell, he hadn't even come into my room.

Moving quickly but carefully, I taped up the first box and filled it with my CDs along with some books. It was heavy as hell, but I didn't have time to repack anything. Drawer by drawer, I looked through all my clothes and threw them in another box. A few more items from the closet went in there too. Clothes and music were the important things. With a pounding heart, I brought those out to the truck one by one. But no one drove up.

In my 17 years I had accumulated so much junk I didn't really need. Knowing I didn't have much time, I looked around and tried to figure out what I would need at college. In my closet were boxes of once-treasured stuffed animals and toys. Those could stay. What about the cards, the notes, and the letters from friends full of inside jokes and shared miseries? Those would stay too.

The mini-fridge and TV would be coming with me. Both had been graduation gifts from parents. They went in the truck next. After them I ran out to the truck and put my boombox in there too. Another box got filled up with some random sheets, pillow cases, and a couple towels from the linen closet. Hopefully the linens would be the right size for the dorm bed. Was that it?

Out of breath, I looked around my room one more time. My room felt oddly bare and empty. There was nothing in it but a sheetless bed, an empty dresser, and some furniture. Everything else was in my truck or in the closet. Or still stuck on my walls.

For ages I'd cut out pictures of all my favorite bands to decorate my wall. There were *Rolling Stone*, *Spin*, *Alternative Press*, and *Raygun* covers, shots of the Smashing Pumpkins, Nirvana, Stabbing Westward, and a lot of Garbage. For years I had listened to my bands, letting them write the soundtracks to my so-called life. There was no time to carefully peel them off or to put them in an album. They would have to stay. One day, my dad would probably toss them all.

I looked over at my alarm clock, still sitting on my bed stand. I had been almost two hours already. That was too much time. But I would need to keep my alarm clock. So I grabbed it. Rushing through the house, I grabbed a couple of things I had missed—my Discman, my Social Security card and passport, my college acceptance packet—and headed back out.

My heart racing, I hurried to my truck, got in, and started it up. As I drove away, back toward downtown, I started to wonder how it might have gone if he had come home and caught me. Would there be another argument? A tearful reconciliation? Or would we both ignore it and pretend like nothing had happened? Maybe he had driven by, saw my truck, and decided to give me a couple hours to get my stuff.

Multiple narratives played out in my head as I drove down Washington Road toward downtown. As I passed by fast food joints and strip malls, the different scenarios unfolded in my mind. Maybe my dad would have tried to apologize and reconcile. I imagined how powerful it would feel to brush him off and let him stew there in his misery. Or maybe he would make good on his idea that gays deserve death and try and attack me. I pictured him in the back of a police car being hauled off to jail while nearby a pretty EMT tended to my wounds. Maybe spending the rest of his life alone in prison would teach him a good lesson about not being a bully.

But a hundred sermons about forgiveness also rattled around my head. Turn the other cheek. Forgive 70 times and seven more. Blessed are the peacemakers. A gentle answer turneth away wrath. Love your enemies, do good to those who hate you. My whole life I had been taught to forgive.

Stopped at a red light, I lit a cigarette and turned up the radio. For a moment I felt guilty about being the one to finally destroy my family. But then I shoved it down and pushed it away. I wasn't the one who needed to feel guilty. My dad was the one who did. He destroyed the family. The only reason I felt guilty was because of a lifetime of conditioning from him and his twisted version of religion. I had plenty of real things to feel guilty about—like Courtney—without needing to be bullied into new ones because my dad was a homophobic asshole.

Back at Web's, I parked my truck at the building's loading dock and closed the big garage door. It took me a while, but I managed to load up all my stuff in the freight elevator to get it upstairs. Then I went to lock up the truck cab and saw it sitting on the floor on the passenger side. It was my gym bag.

I reached down, grabbed a gym bag, and zipped it open. Inside I looked through the stuff that was inside. It was the stuff I used to dress up, to go out, to feel grown up and have adventures. It was the stuff that let me be a different person, at least for a little while. But it was also the reason my girlfriend dumped me. It was the reason that I didn't have a home anymore. It ruined my life. I had let it ruin my life. I zipped the bag back up.

* * *

After midnight is the only time that driving is really pleasurable in the suburban Georgia summer. With no traffic on the roads, you can enjoy the movement and the changing scenery that rolls by. Usually, I had my driving mixtapes: fast paced, high energy songs that would get your adrenaline going. But I also had a special mix of slow, sad songs for late night driving. R.E.M. had a lot of slow songs like "Nightswimming" or "You Are the Everything." Eels were good for slow songs too, like "Beautiful Freak". The tape also had the Violent Femmes "Good Feeling" and "The End" by Angelfish and "Glycerin" by Bush. They were all terribly sad songs that made you feel terrible. Somehow though, they were also necessary for when you felt like the most lonely and dejected person on Earth.

Often on these trips, I'd just drive around randomly, wherever the road took me. I'd just listen to music, smoke endless cigarettes, and take some solace in the fact that I was alone out in the world. Late at night, every place was empty, like the ruins of an ancient castle in the snow. Only the freaks ever come out at night, and despite the years I'd spent fighting it, I couldn't help but feel like I'd forever be one of the freaks. Tonight though, I had a destination, maybe a chance to shrug off a little of that freak stuff before I headed off to college.

I didn't want anyone to see me. And I didn't want anyone I knew knowing what I was doing. So I drove over to work. There were a bunch of dumpsters behind the strip mall. Late at night no one would be around. Pulling up to the first dumpster I found, I got out, and grabbed my big gym bag.

It had everything in it; the black and white photograph of me that had once hung on the wall at school, all the make-up I'd bought, my underwear, my pantyhose, a pair of heels and a pair of wedges, and all my dresses: the leopard, the black lace, even the first floral dress that Michelle had given me, the first dress I'd ever owned. It was all shoved into a big gym bag that I never used anyway. Chances were that my lack of interest in sports would probably continue on into college. I grabbed it and walked over to the dumpster.

"Dear God," I prayed silently out there by that dumpster. "Are you even there? You're not, are you? That's a dumb question. I don't know who or what you are. But I have to believe that you're not a cruel bully. Was I wrong? Was I wrong to be Robin? Was that really wrong?"

"This feeling of wanting to be a girl. I never asked for it. It's just always been here. It can't be wrong to get so tired of fighting that you give in to temptation. I can't spend my whole life fighting it. How miserable a life would that be? So it can't be wrong. Right? I mean, no one got hurt. I mean, sure, I got hurt. And Courtney got hurt too. And my family got hurt. Is that why it's a sin?"

"Is it even a sin, though? I think everything the Christians in my life told me was what they wanted to tell me. It was their words. Not yours. Not what you would have ever wanted. I don't think any of us can really know what you want. We can't. Can we?

But I really fucked up everything. I don't think that's what you would have ever wanted for me. Is this like one of those Job things where you fuck up someone's life to see if they keep their faith? Or was this something that I had to go through because eventually I'll be stronger for it and it'll all work out in the end?

I can't get rid of it. I want to be a girl. It's not going away, is it? It's not. It's never going away. But if I stop fighting and embrace it, is it just gonna keep wrecking everything? It can't always be bad, right?

It wasn't bad with Michelle. So I guess something good came out of it. Maybe other good things can too, right? I don't know. Do you even know? If you did, there's no way to know, is there? Are you even there?

"Well, if you are then here I am. This is me. I didn't get to pick who I am. This is just who I am. This is me. And, like I said, I'm tired of fighting and feeling guilty about everything. So, I'm gonna call this, you know, me signing off. I think there's a lot more about the universe and the world that I need to know before I can really know if anyone's even listening. So…"

There wasn't anything else to say, so I let my prayer, or whatever it was, trail off. I turned around and threw the bag in the truck bed. I hopped back in my truck, lit a cigarette, and started her up. Sad music greeted me when I started up. But I didn't want sad music. Rooting around in the glove box, I found what I wanted. It was R.E.M.'s *Green*.

It started up somewhere in the middle of "I Remember California." It wasn't sad. It wasn't happy. But it was something to listen to so that you could sit and think about how something had changed forever.

It had taken me an awful long time to come out to another human being and trust they would still like me when they knew about it. I'd learned to accept who I was enough to go out in public. I'd reveled in the light of day and partied at night and been a model and posed for photographs. I felt special and beautiful for the first time in my life. And it had all been real. Putting the truck in gear, I started to drive away back toward the main road. The rest of my life was waiting.

# Chapter Twenty-Six

### "Tomorrow I Go Forever"
### Friday, August 22nd, 1997

It was far too sunny and far too hot. Even the breeze coming off the river was heavy and sweltering. Michelle and I sat on the steps of the amphitheater and watched the coal barges slowly slide down the brown, muddy Savannah River. A hundred yards down the river stood a rusted railroad trestle. It had long been a Davidson Fine Arts tradition for graduating seniors to get drunk and jump off the bridge into the river. At least it had been until a few years ago when some senior died trying to pull off the stunt.

Michelle and I had met up, ostensibly for lunch, at downtown's greasy spoon diner. But after lunch we'd decided to take a stroll past school, past the boarded up spot that had once been Orwell's, past the closed up Catalina Club, and finally on to the river where we found a spot to sit at the amphitheater. Neither of us said much and I think neither of us wanted to admit that we still felt a slight inkling of nostalgia for Augusta.

"It's better to have a clean break, you know," Michelle said thoughtfully. "I think Courtney wanted that, too, but sometimes it's hard to say it."

"Sucks," I said because it did. "I worry about her, too. Sometimes it's like she wants to run full speed to the edge."

"She does," Michelle said.

"I worry that she's gonna end up back with a guy like Jordan or that she's gonna get arrested or OD or something, you know, if I'm not here."

"You're her boyfriend, not her salvation," Michelle offered.

"Was her boyfriend," I said sadly.

"Matt. I've known her for ages. Courtney's always been pushing the

229

envelope. She was sneaking vodka in a water bottle in eighth grade. Her ninth grade boyfriend was like 25, okay? You're the most normal thing that's ever happened in her life. That's good but, but you can't fix her. You're a good guy, but it takes more than that to fix real problems."

"Oh my God," I let out a relieved sigh. "Can you believe all the problems we ever had? We're leaving them all behind? Fights with our parents. Being homeless. Having to hide who we are, who we like, getting expelled…"

"Wait," Michelle interrupted. "You never actually told me how you got expelled from American Christian."

"Oh, that," I said with a little eye roll. "It was stupid."

"'Was,'" she quoted me. "Past tense. Like you said."

"So, expulsion," I thought back to that day as I started the story. It was the week after that chapel service when Christina Holmes and Tyler Williams had been dragged in front of everyone to be humiliated about all the details of their private lives. Even a week later, I was still angry about the entire situation. I was angry with the principal for such a horrible display and angry at all the teachers and the entire student body—myself included—for not standing up and pointing out how wrong the whole thing was.

There was a guest speaker that morning. Like many of our guest speakers, he was an old white man with a nice suit and a heavy Southern accent. That morning he got up in front of the entire school and started telling us the story of Numbers, Chapter 25. It was one of those classic Old Testament stories where the Israelites end up in some country full of heathens. Then they immediately start worshiping idols and such until God or His prophet fix the problem with loads of violence and bloodshed.

In this particular case, the Israelite men were having sex with the local heathen women. And God, being the Old Testament God, wasn't happy about it. Then the priest Eleazar sees an Israelite man and a heathen woman having sex. So he grabs a spear and he stabs them both right through. Two people are impaled by one spear and killed. That was the Bible lesson that day. It seemed an obvious lesson about not having sex.

Only that morning the old guest preacher decided that it would make a better lesson about abortion. In Numbers, God commanded his faithful to use violence to stop sin. And here we were, the faithful in America today, surrounded by the sin of abortion. And those anti-abortion activists who went out murdering abortion doctors were doing God's holy will.

By murdering abortion doctors, they were saving lives, stopping sin, and making God happy.

Maybe it was residual anger about the previous week. Maybe it was the fact that I had been running late that morning and had to grab the only open seat; in the front row. Maybe God was speaking through me. I couldn't say exactly why but I stood up and interrupted him.

"Are you saying murdering abortion doctors is morally right?" I asked, my voice sick with incredulity and disgust.

"Sit down, young man," the principal commanded as he stood up and stomped over to me.

"No, I asked a question," I said firmly. In my heart I knew this was stupid. I knew there would be consequences down the line. But in the moment I didn't care.

"It's the will of God, young man," the preacher said. "That we protect the innocent babies by whatever means…"

"That is disgusting," I said. "You're disgusting. Jesus told us to turn the other cheek…" At that point the principal and the gym coach each grabbed one of my arms. As they started pulling me away toward the door, I kept shouting. "You can't be pro-life and call for murder. That is not Christ-like. Would Jesus murder abortion doctors?"

I felt the hands dig painfully into my arms. Both the principal and the gym coach were yelling at me to shut up. Pushing and shoving, they got me out of the doors. Behind me, I could hear the murmur of a thousand of my classmates. As I was marched to the principal's office, I wondered if the student body agreed or if I would be a pariah.

I also wondered what my punishment would be. I knew my parents would be called and that wouldn't be good. The principal sat me down on the bench outside his office and left me there until my livid-looking dad showed up. Then they dragged me in the office where they both proceeded to yell at me. After 20 minutes of that, I was told I was expelled. And my first thought was 'if I was expelled why did you need to yell at me for a while about how bad of a kid I was and how I had embarrassed the school? Couldn't you just expel me and save the yelling?'

"So you were a political dissident?" Michelle smiled.

"I still got into college," I pointed out. "And my first choice, too."

"Well, your first choice was a state school," Michelle laughed. "So, you know, don't go bragging about that too much. Still, I'm glad you got expelled. If you hadn't, I wouldn't have ever met you."

"Me too," I said. "We had a good two years."

"Yeah," Michelle said wistfully. "We really did."

"Yeah," I sighed, then decided to change the subject for fear of getting too depressed. "So Savannah, huh? You gonna go bang some girls?"

"So, Athens, huh?" she smiled. "You gonna get pretty as heck?"

"Yeah, I think so," I said. "See you in New York some day?"

"Yeah," Michelle said. There was a lot more to say but no time left to say it. Fall was already here.

# Chapter Twenty-Seven

## "Don't Go Back To Rockville"
## September 1997

It was nine floors of chaos. Thousands of students and their parents were crowding every last narrow hallway. Mini-fridges, boxes, TVs, pillows, blankets, and suitcases were being piled inside tiny cinder block rooms. There were name tags, colorful flyers, plus kids and RA's with boundless energy.

My own room was on the second floor of Creswell, one of three large dorm towers for freshmen. There were two small beds on either side of the white cinderblock walls. Along with them were dual dressers, closets, and shelves all made of metal and built into the walls. Two windows looked out onto a small area full of picnic tables. Fluorescent lights hummed above.

I piled my stuff onto one bed—the left—that I picked at random. My roommate had yet to arrive which was nice. It meant I got to take a bit of ownership of the room before they had even showed up. Not that there was much to take ownership of. It was a fairly tiny space that seemed reminiscent of a prison cell. Unlike a prison cell though, it would mean freedom.

"It's not too bad," my mom said. "About what I expected for freshmen housing. It's about what your sister had at Brumby." Earlier, we had eaten lunch with Ellen. Though she and I went to the same school now, I wondered if we would ever hang out. She had seemed reluctant to introduce me to her friends.

"Hopefully my roommate's cool," I said. Though there were tons of students around, I had yet to actually meet a single one, much less forge a bond with anyone. I was worried I wouldn't have any friends.

"I hope so, too," my mom said. Then I walked out to her car, which was two parking lots over. She hugged me tightly. Along with advice about not drinking, studying hard, and being safe, she gave me a small envelope with some cash in it. Then we hugged some more.

"Can't believe my little boy's turning into a man," she said through the tears as she let go. For some reason that hit me right in the gut.

"Thanks, Mom," I said bashfully.

"And call your dad, okay?" she pleaded with me. "I know it's awkward, but he loves you. And he paid for half your dorm and your meal plan so…"

"I'll call him," I said, though I wasn't sure what I would say when I did.

"And don't drink," she said sternly, repeating her earlier advice.

"Okay, I won't," I lied. She hugged me tightly again. Then it really was time for her to go. I waved as she drove off. As I walked back toward the dorm, I thought about how she said I was turning to a man, and about what it meant to be a man. And I thought about all that it cost, too.

* * *

With a helpful campus map that reminded me a bit of the ones at Six Flags, I made my way to the Student Center. Along the way, I smoked a cigarette, and took it all in. There were armies of frat guys in khaki and baseball hats, groups of college athletes who towered over me, a handful of geeky kids, black clad goths, punks with spiky bracelets, and girls. There were so many girls of every type and description.

Like the dorm, the Student Center was a scene of chaos. After asking a couple people who were wearing brightly colored shirts and looked to be in charge, I found the ID line. It snaked out of the student center and along the sidewalk, past a hundred different tables representing every student organization, cause, political or religious ideology, or diet. Finally locating the end, I took my place in line. It wasn't long before others filled in behind me.

"Where you from?" asked the guy ahead of me. He had short, dyed green hair, a Misfits T-shirt, and the tiniest hint of a gay lisp. I myself had chosen to wear a Garbage shirt as a way of advertising my tastes to my fellow students. My hope was that I would find a few like-minded people in similar T-shirts. Then I would have an opening to start a conversation with them. Lasting friendships would then result.

"Augusta," I answered. "Where you from?"

"Just outside Atlanta," my new friend—or at least my new line-mate—answered.

"I'm Kyle," he said as he held out a hand to shake. As I shook his hand I found myself torn. College was a time to leave the past behind, to take control of your identity, to be who you had always wanted to be. Did I want to say Robin? Did I want to be Robin? Or had that brought me nothing but pain? I thought about Courtney standing there calling me a faggot.

"Hey, I'm Matt," I said. "Good to meet you. What dorm are you?"

"Creswell," Kyle said.

"Cool," I said. "Me too. Maybe I'll see you around."

\* \* \*

With my new Arches ID card in hand, I wasn't sure what to do. I could put my dorm room together, maybe go meet my new roommate. The dining hall didn't open for dinner for another two hours. Instead, I decided to wander around to check out the various booths that had sprung up all around the student center.

Walking through the lane between the booths, I was met by hundreds of outthrust arms offering me flyers. There was an anti-rape group, table tennis tryouts, as well as both secular and religious vegetarian potlucks. I thought about looking for a debate club. I had done debate in high school and I was pre-law, though I was thinking of changing it to film, or maybe fine art.

"Hey, are you gay?" someone asked and thrust a flyer in my face. Instead of answering, I just looked at the girl with my mouth agape. Her hands were full of fluorescent colored flyers. She looked at me quizzically. Her hair was in dreads and she was sporting two different eyebrow piercings.

"Um, I don't know," I stammered. Then I felt stupid. She had been asking everyone and hadn't been expecting any answers.

"Do you want a flyer at least?" she asked, slowly pronouncing each word as though I were either stupid or a foreign student.

"Sure," I said and I took one. They were for the Campus Gay and Lesbian Alliance. "But the thing is, I don't know I'm gay or what I am really. It's like definitely something gay-ish at least. Probably gay. I

235

prayed about it a lot, but I don't know if I'm a guy or I should be a girl. It's complicated. But kinda gay, right? You know, everyone says just be yourself. But what if you haven't figured out who you are?"

"Freshman, huh. Yeah," she smiled. "It sounds like you should definitely take a flyer. We meet every Tuesday at seven, right here at Tate."

"Okay," I said. As I walked away. I had just gotten to UGA and already I'd managed to embarrass myself in front of people.

"Campus Christians," another girl offered me a flyer. I took it and she continued. "Are you a freshman? We do a Sunday morning service in Creswell's TV room. Stop by. We're just all about having fun with fellow believers."

"Thanks," I said. As I headed out, away from the flyer people and booths, I took a moment to look down at the two flyers in my hand. I stopped along the edge of a busy path near some benches and studied both. College, I thought, is a time to reinvent yourself. I wished that Michelle were there with me and not off in Savannah. She would know what to do. Or maybe I had known all along. Crumbling up one of the flyers, I tossed it into a nearby trashcan. Then I carefully folded up the Campus Lesbian and Gay Alliance flyer and put it in my pocket.

* * *

At about midnight, I decided to take a break. The dorm room was set up. My posters had been put up on the wall with great gobs of sticky tack. My roommate had moved in. After dinner we had talked for a bit and quickly discovered that we had virtually nothing in common apart from a dorm assignment. He was pledging a frat and thinking of doing a long shot, walk-on tryout for the football team. I didn't know quite what I was doing, but it wasn't going to involve fraternities or football.

So I went outside the dorm, into the hot and muggy air of an early September evening. There were other students sitting on benches and picnic tables, hanging out, talking, and laughing. But I had always enjoyed quiet and solitude for my late night smokes. Instead of hanging out by the door, I walked around to the far side of the dorm. There a small wooded hill led down to another road and other, nicer dorms for upperclassmen.

For a minute or two, I sat there smoking by myself. I missed Michelle. And I really missed Courtney. For a while there in high school,

I felt like I had really figured things out. There was fun. There were long nights. There was safe sex, a little bit of drugs, and lots of alternative music. But now it was gone. The one person I had really trusted to know the real me was off in Savannah.

Then movement in the trees above caught my attention. I saw it sitting there silent, ghostly white. It was a barn owl perched high above me in the trees.

"You again," I said at the bare edge of audibility. I smiled. "Did Hecate send you?" Maybe I could do this. In college, you could reinvent yourself. You could be whoever you wanted to be and no one would know any different. Maybe I could find friends who would accept Robin. Maybe they could accept that I was a girl. Maybe it was God or Hecate, or just the universe itself who had sent me that owl. But whoever it was, I had gotten the message. Everything was gonna be alright. Without a sound, the owl flew away and disappeared.

Stubbing out my cigarette, I started back toward the door. For a second, I looked back to the trees to see if I could see the owl. But it was gone. For now.

"Hey, Matt," I heard a voice calling from one of the picnic tables. On the large patio that stood between the dorm and the dining hall, there were five or six picnic tables arranged in an L-shape. A group of ten or so students were seated around a couple of them, talking.

"Hey, Kyle," I said as I walked over to the group. There were guys and girls, lots of dyed hair, heavy eyeliner, combat boots, and piercings. Maybe they were goths or punks or just alternative kids.

"This is Matt," Kyle said as I found a seat at the table next to a girl in a black velvet dress. I lit up another cigarette as Kyle started making introductions. "This is Violet. They call her Vie. And Drew. That's Evelyn. This is Other Jason. That's Melissa P. She's from Augusta too. And I think you already met Red Haired Genessa 'cause she was right ahead of me in line for IDs. And that's Lydia and Casey and Dave."

# About the Author

Author Faith DaBrooke is co-creator of the weekly podcast The Gender Rebels. Her writing has appeared in *Trans Love: An Anthology of Transgender and Non-Binary Voices* from Jessica Kingsley Publishers and *Trans Bodies, Trans Selves: A Resource for the Transgender Community* from Oxford University Press. She resides in Brooklyn with her partner, cat, and two dogs.

# Other Riverdale Avenue Books You Might Enjoy

*Playing by the Book*
By Chris Shirley

*Magic University: The Complete Series*
By Cecilia Tan

*Hiding in Plain Sight*
By Zane Thimmesch-Gill

*Read My Lips: Sexual Subversion and the End of Gender*
By Riki Wilchins

www.ingramcontent.com/pod-product-compliance
Lightning Source LLC
Chambersburg PA
CBHW031220260626
47169CB00007B/2122